REDBACK

Howard Jacobson was born in Manchester in 1942. He acquired English Literature at Cambridge and returned it, over a period of fifteen years, to institutions as various as Sydney University, Selwyn College, Cambridge, and Wolverhampton Polytechnic. He co-wrote *Shakespeare's Magnanimity* (1978) and is the author of the two other acclaimed novels *Coming From Behind* (1983) and *Peeping Tom* (1984), both of which are available in Black Swan paperbacks.

Author photograph by Tara Heinemann

Also by Howard Jacobson

COMING FROM BEHIND
PEEPING TOM

and published by Black Swan

REDBACK

Howard Jacobson

BLACK SWAN

REDBACK

A BLACK SWAN BOOK 0 552 99252 6

Originally published in Great Britain by Bantam Press, a division of Transworld Publishers Ltd.

PRINTING HISTORY
Bantam Press edition published 1986
Black Swan edition published 1987
Black Swan edition reprinted 1988
Black Swan edition reprinted 1989

This book is set in Linotron Palatino

Black Swan Books are published by Transworld Publishers Ltd., 61-63 Uxbridge Road, Ealing, London W5 5SA, in Australia by Transworld Publishers (Aust.) Pty. Ltd., 15-23 Helles Avenue, Moorebank, NSW 2170, and in New Zealand by Transworld Publishers (N.Z.) Ltd., Cnr. Moselle and Waipareira Avenues, Henderson, Auckland.

Made and printed in Great Britain by
The Guernsey Press Co. Ltd., Guernsey, Channel Islands.

For
Joy and Allan Sadler, over there
& for
Marilyn and Mike Goldberg
and
Janet Haigh & Stephen Jacobson
over here.

1

A STORY I HEARD years ago, when stories still had power to charm me:

A young and well-connected Australian woman with powerful mandibles, an MA in Fine Arts, and special interests in Lorenzo di Credi, Bramante, and Berthe Morisot, stops off at Oxford as part of her first comprehensive tour of the European restaurants and galleries. (Let's give her an ordinary Australian name, say . . . Desley.) Somewhere between the Elizabeth and the Ashmolean, Desley is half accosted by, and half herself accosts, a gaunt undergraduate of the University who takes her for afternoon tea at the Randolph, a walk in Christ Church Meadows, a look at the gargoyles in New College, and an early but heavy supper of pasta and fish. A wind ensemble turns out to be playing in Oriel chapel, so they go there. Then, since it is getting late, since they have so much more to say to each other still, and since his rooms are only round the corner, above a shop that displays just one book in its window from which it is to be inferred that here at least the ancient arts of monastic binding and lettering still flourish, they go there. Despite such excellent preliminaries things now begin to take an unaccountably nasty turn. Who can explain the whys and wherefores of attraction between the sexes? As I remember, the word we used in those days to acknowledge the inexplicability of it all was *chemistry*. The chemistry was right or the chemistry was wrong. Well, from the moment these two young enthusiasts of the beautiful find themselves

7

alone and divested in the darkness the chemistry decides to play up; in the hissing alembic of their desire unpleasing discolorations and ferments occur, until at last the glass shatters and bad odours fill the room. The boy (he doesn't need a name) is overly attentive and respectful. The girl explains that she is a woman not an altar, and accuses him of lacking joy, competence, and animality. The boy, since competence at least is a male province – he isn't sure about joy – rages in silence and refuses either to walk her to her hotel or grant her fair share in his narrow bed. His ceremoniousness rebuffed, he resorts to indecorum. He will show her animality! With his hands gripping the bedposts behind him he falls asleep on his back with a fart and sweats and snores. When he awakes a few hours later, prematurely, in the black dawn of an Oxford winter, he is relieved to discover that the girl has gone; but an odd feeling, an unaccustomed tingling of the skin, a sensation of discomfort and unease around the heart, causes him, still on his back, to cast an eye over his person, whereupon he finds that she has left a little memento of herself – a Freudian gift, hard, compact, warm, in its own way perfectly formed, a faecal offering smelling of fish and pasta (of tagliatelle marinara) – nestling amongst the soft hairs of his chest, only inches from his gaping mouth.

Disgusted? Me too. My friends and I ran around clutching our stomachs when this was first related to us. We stood in corners and heaved. We rammed handkerchiefs down our throats. We rolled on the floor and beat the carpet with our fists. It was a full fortnight before any one of us was able to keep a meal down.

But there's no point in my pretending that I wasn't also intrigued. I must have been no more than eighteen at the time and an undergraduate myself. (At Cambridge though, not Oxford. We liked to think we were more careful in whose company we fell asleep in

Cambridge – though in reality it was the company who was careful about us.) Apart from the odd school holiday to the nearest and scruffiest port that could reasonably be called The Continent, and coach trips, in the company of my Aunt Hester, to the site of every ruined abbey and priory in the country, I wasn't what you could call well-travelled. Of course I had *heard* of Australia – I even heard *from* Australia, as I will shortly explain – but I had never imagined that it contained girls like Desley, capable of such erudition, athleticism, and aplomb.

Something stirred in me, even as my stomach revolted, akin I can only suppose to what stirred in Magellan, Torres, Abel Tasman, and Captain James Cook.

On August 11, 1949 – I can be certain of the date because it was my ninth birthday – my father ran off with another woman. I don't mean that he'd run off with women before – Trilby was another woman only in the sense that she wasn't my mother – but I do mean it when I say he ran. Clear your mind of all the paraphernalia of late twentieth-century elopement: phone calls to the bank and the credit card companies, removal vans for the video-cassettes, a couple of seats on Concorde. Armchair abduction. My father, and the woman who wasn't my mother, belonged to the old school. Two minutes before my party was due to start they grabbed each other by the wrist, took off down the path, turned left into the street, and really sprinted for it.

And I, defying the injunctions of my aunties to stay inside, stood at the front door and watched them go.

Ours was not, by Partington standards, an evil street. We weren't middle-class or even lower-middle-class, but we weren't riff-raff either. I'd say we were upper-lower-working with aspirations to lower-upper-lower-middling-white-collar. We were clean, in other words, largely non-incestuous, aggressively neigh-bourly (which is to say un-neighbourly), and we all lived in neat narrow two-storey Victorian slightly-better-than-workers' houses with damp cellars, brick gardens at the front, brick yards at the back, and wash-ing everywhere. We gave away our class, of course, with all that washing. We thought we could scrub and bleach our way into gentility, whereas the genteel, I have since discovered, are altogether above caring about the colour of the sheets they sleep between. Noise was another area where we got it wrong. We thought it was bad form to make any. And even worse form for our neighbours to. We expressed our outraged propriety by thumping on the walls. Remember, we weren't detached. Except for where a German pilot had been lucky with his aim we weren't even semi-detached. We shared a wall with the people on the left and a wall with the people on the right. Since we often banged on the one for no better reason than that there'd been banging on the other, and since we were also a cul-de-sac, rounded at the top like a tuning fork, there were times when the whole street was in simultaneous tom-tom communication, the reverberant message travelling all the way back to us at last so that we might just as well have been hammering at ourselves.

Considering how respectable our street was, it attracted a surprising amount of violent incident. Cars crashed outside our front doors that would have missed one another by a margin the size of the *Titanic* anywhere else. Molesters hung around our yards. Arsonists with free afternoons strolled up and down examining our structures. Already this year – and it was still only August – at least a half a dozen domestic differences had spilled on to the road, bringing us all out to our gates (I say 'us', but I don't mean my mother and my aunties who resolutely stayed inside) from where we cheered on the combatants until the policemen, the firemen, the ambulancemen and the laundrymen, all of whom we knew by name, arrived to break them up. Only a week before my ninth birthday – a mere seven days before my father and Trilby made their sprint for freedom – the military had sealed off the street for a whole morning and addressed us through loud-hailers, prior to bringing out a Second World War deserter, a starving, trembling, tubercular wreck of a man with bloodshot eyes who had been living in our midst behind closed curtains, unknown to any of us, although we must have thumped his wall innumerable times, since 1940.

I have a theory to explain the accident-proneness of our street. I believe it can all be put down to our being a cul-de-sac. There was only one way in and one way out. Hence our allure for fugitives. And hence the exasperation of normally cautious drivers who were suddenly forced to brake and negotiate a tricky three-point turn around an inadequate and congested turning circle, just as they thought they were sailing out of Partington at last. As for those of us who lived there, it should be clear why we were in an excitable state. A cul-de-sac is like a person in a condition of primary repression; it is blocked, dammed, stoppered at one end, it possesses no adequate outlet for frustrations. Short of doing what my father did.

But he ought to have remembered which was the way out and which was the dead end, that you turned right for a quick getaway, not left.

From my position at the front door I watched them tear up the street, lost sight of them, then watched them tear back down again. I made a wet, disgusted sound with my lips. I had a child's impatience with adult bungling. Which might be why the thing I most remember about their departure was the part I didn't actually see: their negotiation at top speed of that inadequate turning circle (I imagine them going the whole way round, at forty-five degrees to the horizontal, like daredevils on motorbikes), the ends of my father's white silk opera-scarf (itself a symbol of his new life: he'd never been an opera-goer as a husband) streaming out behind him, his tiny feet (those he'd always had) scarcely touching the paving stones, and only the resolutely non-airborne figure of Trilby at his side – worth running away with for her name alone, and not a whit less majestic than usual, despite the heat and the haste, in phosphorescent silk stockings and bristling fox-fur stole – preventing him from soaring off into the empyrean.

Don't worry. There's not going to be much more of this 'empyrean' stuff. I'm not a flowery man. You'll be lucky even to get any sky out of me after this. But I wish to make a gift of poetry – a gift of the possibility of his own poetry – to my father. Some people miss out on metaphor. When beauty smites them you can see the marks; their blood really does boil; their reason really does desert them; their hearts really do break. My father was one of those. I say *was* because that's how my father exists now, as a past tense. He was literal-minded to the end, literally dying of love at last in the soft arms of the woman he'd literally run away with. Which is why I feel that I owe it to his memory to get him round the dead end of the cul-de-sac allegorically, to give him the opportunity at least to soar figuratively, even though I know in my soul that if he were living still and offered the option he would choose to do it on a hang-glider. He'd conceived of hang-gliders even before there were such things. Like all unimaginative men he was in thrall to science and its gewgaws. 'One day,' I remember him saying to my mother – he was a bit of a Wellsian future-looker, wildly trusting and optimistic like all eroticists – 'one day, all I will have to do is strap some power-pack to my shoulders and I will become a bird or a fish.'

'And what will you have to strap to your shoulders to become a husband or a father?' I remember my mother replying.

You can see why he had to take off.

And why empyrean is the word I want for where he seemed headed, even if the reality was just that depressed huddle of charcoal cloud which gathered low over the town of Partington each morning and never once shifted from it, during daylight hours, in the whole time I lived there.

The town of Partington, for those who don't know it, hides itself in shame – pretending to be a village or a hamlet – a little way off the East Lancashire Road, exactly equidistant from Manchester and Liverpool, between whom, in my day, it acted as a kind of industrial mediator, receiving the waste from one and passing it on sweetened and palatable to the other. Nothing noxious issued from Manchester or Liverpool without its turning up for treatment in Partington. The rivalry between these two great cities is legendary, but it would have been far worse without Partington. Think of Henry Kissinger keeping Egypt and Israel from each other's throat and you'll get the picture. Except that no one has paid Partington a small fortune for its memoirs. A little yellow guidebook, printed on shiny paper and outlining the history of the place, its distinctive features and possessions, including a very small and very early Lowry in the Art Gallery, is available from the Town Clerk, price fifty pence. But that has never been a bestseller. What Partington does for a living today, now that Manchester and Liverpool are productive of nothing but pop singers, folk singers, dramatists and poets, I don't know. And my mother doesn't write to tell me. It would be a good place, I suppose, for a literary festival. Or, given its long history of dealing with impurities, it would do very nicely as a site for storing undesirables. I can't believe there isn't a top-secret document hidden somewhere in Whitehall containing contingency plans for fencing off pacifists and protesters and victims of virulent sexual diseases. And I can't believe that Partington doesn't get a favourable

13

mention. In the meantime my guess is that it's been chosen as a nuclear dump. In a way I hope it has. I have no fond memories of my home town – I haven't been near the place for a quarter of a century – but as an ex-citizen I would like to think that when one half of Britain finally does get around to poisoning the other half, Partington will once more have its part to play.

I say that from a secure distance of some thirteen thousand miles.

There are one or two other interesting statistics pertaining to Partington. (Pertaining, by the way, being a very Partingtonian word; *ap*pertaining even more so.) It enjoys the distinction, for example, of being the wettest town in Europe. When I was a boy I read that every day since records had been compiled some rain had fallen somewhere in Partington. The only time it hadn't rained was when it snowed. In fact, if my memory serves me correctly, what came down was almost always a hope-destroying combination of both. I have only recently learned the proper usage for slurry: it is a builder's term for loose, sloppy cement. We in Partington used it to describe what landed on our heads.

I kept records myself as soon as I could write, running out into the downpour each afternoon after school in order to check the level of the water in the jam-jar I kept on an old bird-table (no bird fancied stopping off at Partington) in the backyard. Invariably, one or other of the local molesters was waiting for me.

'Sweet?'

I'd shake my head.

'Ice-cream?'

I'd shake my head.

'Ride?'

'Where?'

This time he'd shake his. 'Where?' always got them. Where indeed. There was nowhere worth taking a ride to in Partington except out, and any self-respecting

14

pervert one might have considered accepting a sweet from who knew where out was would long since have gone there.

So I never got to find out what molesters do to little boys and whether it's a fair exchange for a gobstopper and an ice-lolly and a ride around someone else's cul-de-sac. What you don't know doesn't harm you, seasoned Partingtonians were especially fond of saying. But I can't see that it's of any particular benefit to you either.

The other thing I never got to find out was how much water fell in our backyard, since by the time I reached it, at half-past three in the afternoon, my jam-jar was invariably flooded. 'Four inches TIKO,' I used to write, opposite the date, which meant 'Four inches That I Know Of'. But it didn't really matter that I was approximate. The incessant dripping of the gutters, the sound of cars ploughing through puddles in order to plough into one another, kept us informed as to how things were going outside. I went through the whole of my childhood – that's to say from the time my mother and her sisters expelled me screaming from their breasts to the day my father and Trilby hoofed it out of our lives – without ever knowing what it was like to look through a dry window. Not that I would have seen much anyway. Partington is also the darkest place in Europe, only excepting parts of Scandinavia.

But for me the most extraordinary fact about Partington was that everybody who lived in it was called Partington. No one who has spent any time in the North of England (I'm not asking them to own up) will have failed to notice a certain tendency towards this sort of uniformity. There are more Chorleys in Chorley than you can shake a stick at, and far more Clitheroe Clitheroes than can be explained by coincidence. The Formbys of Formby are infamous. The Ramsbottoms of Ramsbottom legion. Partington, though, was not just densely populated with Partingtons, it was plethoric with them, it was swollen with a Partington pleurisy of plague proportions. We came into the world with the help of Nurse Partington, said 'Ah' for Doctor Partington, and signed our last wills and testaments in the offices of Partington, Partington & Partington. We voted Partington C. when we wanted a Conservative government and Partington L. when we wanted a Labour one. It was even possible for us to vote Communist, putting our cross against the name of Patsy 'The Red' O'Partington' who, when he wasn't on the hustings, ran the Partington Pie Shop and baked the best Partington Patties in Partington. Even the town's gentry could do no better than Forbes-Partington or Partington-ppPartington-Smythe. Which left us – our name was Forelock – fairly out on a limb. It didn't come as much of a surprise to our neighbours when my father ran off with a woman from the Wirral twice his size and six years his senior. What else could you expect from people who weren't called Partington?

In all honesty I can't say that my father's hasty departure came as much of a surprise to me either, although I did think, seeing as he'd got this far, that he might have hung on until after my party. In the whole eight years three hundred and sixty-four days twenty-three hours and fifty-eight minutes that I'd known him he had never once struck me as anything but unreliable as a guardian and ephemeral as a man. I won't dwell on his unreliability. I don't want it to sound as though I am still carrying a psychological scar. Suffice to say that until my mother and her sisters expressly forbade him to wheel me anywhere, it had been his custom to take me out in my pram, park me under a lamp-post (lamps were lit all day in Partington), and return home empty-handed three or four hours later, by and large contented but dimly aware that there was something he'd forgotten. He was always at his most forgetful in those sad squares of stunted greenery known as Municipal Gardens, where the likelihood of his falling into absorbing conversation with women who weren't my mother was greatest. He left me in a rowing boat on the Municipal Duck Pond once, so occupied was he by the talk. And another time in a wastepaper-basket from which I was retrieved, just before the gates closed, by Arthur Sydney Partington, Partington's Chief Parks Officer.

'By heck,' said Arthur, shining his torch into the basket and implanting me, on the spot, with a reverence for men in navy uniforms which is going strong to this day.

'Well I'll be buggered,' he said, lifting me out and finding the 'If lost please return to' identification-tag my mother had providentially tied about my podgy wrist. 'Well I'll go to the foot of our stairs,' he said.

I'd never heard so much swearing.

My father was fortunate that my mother's nature was reserved, else he would have found himself out on the road that night, a victim of one of those hit-and-run domestic accidents our street specialised in. But even with all the doors and windows fastened tight, the letter-box itself gagged with a tea-towel, and my mother shouting 'Shush!' although she was the one doing the shouting, the whole of Partington must have heard her.

'What sort of start to life is this you're giving the boy?' she yelled at him, while he cowered in a corner, protecting his looks. 'Well? Shush! Well? What sort of start is it?'

'Thump,' said the wall on our right.

'Thump, thump,' answered the wall on our left.

My father knew better (1) than to argue that starts in life were by and large incalculable, there being many examples of inauspicious beginnings leading to happy ends; and (2) than to explain that although he could follow the reasoning against his having forgotten which wastepaper-basket he had popped me into, he had only popped me into it in the first place in order to

17

raise innocent mirth in the choice company he'd been keeping. And I didn't chip in with my fourpenn'orth either, (i) because I hadn't yet learned to talk, and (ii) because I considered that my own enjoyment of the role of mirth-maker (you should have seen the choice company) imposed severe limits on my rights to indignation. I draw your attention, for future reference, to this early example of my scrupulousness in the matter of rights and entitlements. I was to become famous for it by and by.

So, as is often the case with people who remain silent, it was not because my father had too little to say, but because he had too much, that he chose not to defend himself verbally, but only bent his head and covered his face and wished that he were strapped into one of those power-packs he'd talked about – the kind that could transform a man into an eagle and zoom him up and away into the empyrean. I felt similarly compromised and impatient myself as I lay in the tin bath on the kitchen table, spluttering and blowing bubbles, while my aunts Hester and Nesta washed bits of old orange peel and sweet-papers out of my golden hair, and my pink little Partington penis (mere litter itself an hour earlier) rose like a rare breed of sea serpent above the scummy surface of the water.

It's unlikely (though I'm only guessing) that there was much to choose between the size of my hydrozoon, aged fourteen months, and my father's, aged twenty-seven years. That ephemerality I've mentioned – that quality of impermanence he possessed, much as if he were one of those tragically frail insects that has only a single afternoon to pack a whole lifetime of sensation into – was partly a consequence of his extreme physical delicacy. It wasn't so much that he was short – with the exception of me (and it was supposed that I'd eaten something while I was in the wastepaper-basket) everyone in Partington was short – as that he was wan. There was some emotional insubstantiality about him

18

that communicated itself to his bone structure. If he bent down suddenly, or stretched, his joints would give off a soft soughing sound, as if the last breath of life itself were seeping out through threadbare cartilage. His extremities were always cold too, and he used to boast that he could cut himself without bleeding. Where every other man in Partington was a plucky cross between Clement Attlee and George Formby – unembellished but indomitable – my father had the lost-generation look of Leslie Howard, only he also wore a melancholy musketeer's moustache, soft and yellow like a canary's eyelash, to suggest a vestige of adventurism.

He was the wrong size to be a father. I'm sure he knew that. In my early post-pram days when he carried me around on his little back and shoulders (though not as far as the Municipal Gardens), it was silently acknowledged between us that for all the difference it would have made as far as speed, comfort or elevation was concerned, I might just as well have carried him.

But the real reason I knew he was never going to make it through anything like the usual term of domestic obligation was the expression he used whenever he left the house. 'I'll be off now,' he used to say. Never 'Cheerio' or 'Toodle-pip' or 'See you later'. Always 'I'll be off now'. I realised this was just a casual expression to which he gave no conscious thought and attached no particular meaning, but I didn't believe that a man who looked forward, in his heart, to coming home each day and surrounding himself with his family, would have used it. He wasn't rehearsing for his final exit – I won't go so far as to suggest that – nonetheless, when the big day finally arrived there wasn't one of us that couldn't have said his lines for him.

'Right then,' he said, after my mother had refused, positively and flatly refused to have Trilby at my party, positively and flatly refused to believe that she was a new teacher at my primary school to whom I had

19

formed a sudden and inexplicable attachment, and positively and flatly refused to serve us our meat and mushroom patties and dinky sausage rolls and lime jellies in the shape of little bunnies looking vacant, until Trilby was removed. 'Right then,' he said – quite dispassionately, the way he did whenever he went out – 'Then I'll be off.'

The only difference was that today the I was We, and his sparrow legs were working like pistons.

What my father actually did when he went out – that's before he went out for ever – I never knew. He had no trade or profession that I was ever able to discover and I suspected that he brought home no money. What supported us was the hairdressing *salon* which my mother ran from our front parlour. My mother's *salon*, with its rows of washbasins and high-hooded hairdriers and strange women at odd angles, was a wondrous place to me. It was also a wondrous place to my father who was banned from it for life after a couple of weeks' working there as a toweller and drier. A shocking row took place, of the kind my mother had become expert in, full of 'Wells?' and 'Shushes!' and the more terrible for having to be kept from the neighbours – then he was back out again doing odd jobs. I still don't know how odd the jobs were that he did. I have trouble picturing him lifting up bricks or pushing a wheelbar-row. I do recall, though, that he was a great advocate for electricity and ingenious electrical gadgets (this was his Wellsian, mechanistic side) and that he never went anywhere without a card of fuse wire and his pocket set of finely graduated screwdrivers. I can only suppose then, since I now understand that he was a compulsive genuflector, that he wanted nothing so much as to bend his knees in the houses of the refined and the affluent, and that for him even sexuality was an act of social enslavement (his own) – I can only suppose that he spent his afternoons and early evenings fixing plugs low down in their walls for wealthy war-widows from the Wirral, women such as Trilby, to whose emotional life fate and the squabbling of nations had dealt a mortal blow, that is until my father turned up with his set of silver screwdrivers and his little card of fuse wire. And his deferential air.

I'm not electrical myself. I never knew my father long enough to have acquired any of his feeling for the force, or any of his ardour for the sort of trivial gadgetry electricity gets wasted on. But he bequeathed me his deferential air all right. If he'd stayed around we would have made an impressive team: between us we could have generated sufficient deference to light up the self-esteem of a dozen middle-class suburbs the size of Partington. Even on my own – thirty-odd years later, far from home, and a social malcontent – I can send a couple of hundred volts of homage through any household with the right connections.

(Why did my father not last longer than a fortnight in my mother's *salon*? Because my mother grew weary of catching him blowing in her customers' ears.

'Well?' she demanded to know. 'Shush! Well?'

My father was very upset. I think he thought this was the best job he'd ever had. 'I'm doing what I'm here to do,' he expostulated. 'I'm drying their hair.'

'What, with your breath?'

But her sarcasm was lost on him. Of course with his breath! Minuscule his lungs might have been, but for ladies who could afford to have their hair done once a week he exhaled fire.)

So, there were no surprises all round when Trilby and the empyrean finally claimed my father. Except, that is, for what my mother did. I knew for a fact that she'd been having secret conferences with her sisters Hester and Nesta – the Vestal custodians of our house – on the subject of the serious deterioration of her marriage, and I was pretty certain that a joint decision had been taken that my father had to go. Even I could see that he hadn't been behaving very well. He'd been shouting 'I'll be off now' at impossibly early hours of the morning and not showing up again for days. He had taken to wearing that style of shoe referred to in those days as 'pumps', in whose patent shine were reflected the sorts of good times that could only be offensive to his immediate family. And on those rare evenings when he was at home to dine with us he insisted on not removing his opera-scarf, he who had never until now shown the slightest inclination towards music or the theatre in his life. Of course he had to go. It was no mystery to me that the phrase in most frequent use between my mother and her sisters was, 'and the sooner the better'. So although the sight of my father taking off down the path with Trilby was one I felt I'd been more or less anticipating all my life, you can see why the sight of my mother taking off after them was wholly unexpected. What did I think she'd do? Stand at the front door and clap? Something like that.

I was only nine. Counting my actual birthday as the moment my party got under way I was still only ten minutes to nine. I had a pretty rough notion of what constituted marital etiquette; and I didn't know much either about the tricks loyalty and affection can play upon resolve. But there was one department in which I could boast a much older boy's expertise. Shame. Whatever else should or should not have been happening, I felt sure that my mother should not have been running the wrong way up the cul-de-sac in pursuit of my father and his mistress, rounding the turning circle, and following them back down again; and I felt equally sure that neither I nor the cheering Partingtons who were our neighbours should have been at our gates watching her. This last was a wholly aesthetic consideration. I didn't think it suited the Partingtons to look so gratified, and I didn't think it suited my mother to look so distressed and out of breath. It didn't seem to me that she was built for commotion or for speed.

There is this to be said for my father: he was wholly consistent in his taste for women twice his size. I often try to think of him, fondly, as a gallant little mountaineer of a man, conquering one peak only to give himself the courage to attempt the next. Trilby, on whose smooth vertiginous slopes I would have loved to graze myself, was Kilimanjaro to my mother's Kosciusko, and would surely have defeated her in any competition demanding the simple deposition of dead weight. So why then, if I was ashamed of my mother's fraught locomotion (what a prim little bastard I was), why then wasn't I equally unimpressed by Trilby's, since she wasn't built for speed or turbulence or corner-ing, either? Was it only because she wasn't my mother that I actually *liked* the way everything rose and shook inside *her* clothes? I don't think so. Much as one should never underestimate the attraction for the son of a genuflector of anyone who isn't related to him by blood (or marriage), I doubt if that was the beginning and the end of my preference. What I fear is that I was able to forgive Trilby any lapse because she was an aristocrat.

I had met Trilby a few times in the company of my father, secretly of course, on trams or in a rowing boat on the Duck Pond in the Municipal Gardens, and I had been able to tell from her clothes and her bold stare and her flaring nostrils and the time it took her to finish a sentence that she was an aristocrat. She didn't call me Karl the way they did at home, boiling the one syllable I had down to something like Kl; instead she filled my name with *a*'s and *r*'s and *h*'s, prolonging me in her mouth and making me rhyme with the first half of words that were never used in our house, words such as 'daahrling' and 'chaahrming' and 'maaaahvellous'. After my father took her away I abandoned Karl for my middle name – Leon – so addicted had I become to the experience of my name not being over quickly.

Naturally my family – what was left of my family – took to calling me Ln within a fortnight.

It hardly matters whether Trilby really did have blue aristocratic blood pumping away below the surface of her panting flesh. The important thing is that my father thought she was aristocratic and I agreed with him. Class is all relative anyway. Compared to us she *was* aristocratic.

And that was what made my father's capture of her so remaahkable and so maaaahvellous. Later, when the fuss subsided, my father's elopement with an aristocrat from north Cheshire came to be seen as a cause for family pride; it cast a retrospective dignity on all of us, raising our status considerably, not in the neighbour-hood – the Partington Partingtons were unimpressible – but amongst remote relatives in Manchester and Liverpool. It wasn't nothing to be a Forelock, in those parts, after what my father did for us. And it's very likely that my mother already had a premonition of this, even felt some prestige attach itself to her at the time, because why else, unless she wanted my father to get clean away with his prize, did she chase them the wrong way up the cul-de-sac when it would have been so much more effective to stay where she was and catch them coming down again? Who knows? It's possible that she wanted nothing more than to shake my father's hand, congratulate him on his social elev-ation, and be allowed one stroke of the silver fox which rose and fell on Trilby's back as if resuscitated by all the agitation.

Anyway, whatever her motives, she stopped ab-ruptly – just as she was gaining on them, it seemed to me – and watched them disappear through the open end of the street. Then, when they were quite out of sight, she did an extraordinary thing. She waved. Not aggressively. Not exactly sentimentally either. It was hardly even personal. She simply raised her arm and fluttered her fingers in the air. She might have been playing a simple old tune on an invisible and silent instrument. Though whether she was playing for their benefit, or for mine, or merely for her own, I couldn't say.

She returned, a minute or two later, with her shoulders erect and her head high, accepting the brute stares and jeers of the loathed Partingtons as if they were grovelling salutations.

'Make some tea,' she ordered Hester and Nesta in what sounded to me already like a cleaned-up accent. 'And cut the boy his cake.'

But it turned out to be a pretty subdued party.

As for my father and Trilby, they might for all any of us knew have kept on running until nightfall, and there was nothing to say they didn't keep going after that. Certainly in my imagination they never stopped until they reached Vaucluse, that exclusive eastern suburb of Sydney from which, months later, they sent me a postcard. It showed the usual view of the famous Meccano bridge, making its rainbow arch from one side of Toy Town to the other, and it contained on the back a quickly scrawled message from my father and a pyramid of aristocratic kisses from Trilby. My father didn't say he was deliriously happy now, presumably in order not to upset my mother, but he did mention that he had just set about rewiring their new house and that they owned an electric refrigerator the size of my bedroom, which I took to mean the same thing.

It was another ten years before I came to hear the story of Desley – the squatting *cognoscente* from Dromana – and the poor unfortunate she'd left wretched and retching in his Oxford lodgings. By that time I was an undergraduate myself, well into my third term reading Moral Decencies at Cambridge. The story made a tremendous impression on me. How could it not? My father and Trilby had planted Australian longings in me. From them I had learned that it was an enchanted place with dry windows to which lovers absconded – and don't forget that love and deference had early on become indistinguishable in my mind. As far as I had been concerned, the streets of Vaucluse – from which one could see both the seething harbour and the shimmering sea – were thronged with women as well bred and as ladylike as Trilby. And therefore as worthy of my devotion. Now here I was in possession of an anecdote which told, and in disturbing detail, of a very different kind of far-away femaleness, of hitherto unimagined courtship customs, of inconceivable maidenly audacity, and agility which took the breath away. (It couldn't have been easy, could it, for the girl to have mounted the boy, positioned herself precisely, and deposited her little memorandum – all in the dark and while he slept?)

Somewhere between the lover of my father and the lover of Bramante is to be found the cause of my coming to Australia. One of them brought me here. Perhaps they both did.

Thanks, girls.

2

WHAT ACTUALLY brought me to Australia (since obscure compulsions might lead you to the water but are no good for getting you across it) was a P & O liner, and what paid my passage was a CIA scholarship.

Will anyone believe me when I state that I didn't know at the time who it was that bought me my ticket? It's the truth, anyway. Not that it would have made the slightest difference had I been told. I didn't have the first idea who or what the CIA was. Moral Decencies was my subject at Cambridge, which meant that I kept my nose out of politics. I knew that there had been a couple of big wars, involving lots of countries, twice this century, but that was about the limit of my interest in unsubtleties. As for future employers, it was pretty clear that once one left Cambridge one was going to render up one's liberty to organisations invariably referred to by their initials. Those of my friends whom the BBC didn't snap up, for example, went into personnel at IBM or management at ICI. If someone had mentioned the CIA to me then, I would almost certainly have confused it with C & A, the Dutch-owned department store which had a branch in almost every English town but Partington.

So wasn't I curious as to where the money came from? Wasn't I suspicious when something calling itself Freedom Academy International suddenly began to take an intense and yet at the same time strangely absent-minded interest in me, as it were on behalf of someone else? No. Not in the slightest. In those days the idea of a secret benefactor – a rich uncle we'd never met and never knew we had – was both plausible and necessary. Don't forget that many of us were orphaned, having lost our fathers in the second of those big wars I'd heard about, or in the kind of peacetime sex and class skirmish that took away mine. In deprived swatty women-reared old-fashioned boys like myself – I'm describing a whole generation now – the Agency, with its mysterious backhanders, answered an imaginative as well as a material need; you couldn't be brought up on novels or radio serials by Charles Dickens and Wilkie Collins and not cherish the hope that there was some-one out there keeping an eye open for your welfare.

And it could have been worse. I could have gone the way of several of my contemporaries and accepted sweeties from the KGB.

But it mustn't be supposed that I came out here as a spy or a *provocateur* or anything like that. My mission was more what you might call cultural. Think of me as a sort of unofficial Ambassador of the Decencies and you won't be too wide of the mark. That will give you some idea, also, of how little I was actually required to do. Mostly – this is in the first year or two – I expressed disgust in letters to newspapers, defended the family in articles for magazines of contemporary ideas, and hung around university campuses and cafés in a crypto-pastoral capacity, offering advice where it wasn't asked. The thinking behind this operation was that I would act as some kind of biological agent in the dirty wash of Australian society; as long as I managed to slip into the spin, things would somehow turn out cleaner.

And did they?

I don't think it's for me to say.

Anyway, whatever the rights or wrongs of the way I got here, I've now settled it with my conscience. I've paid back what I was loaned. Morally speaking at least – and unless we would be beasts or bankers what other manner of speaking is there? – I've squared my debt. The spider of cynicism bit me – I'm not being fanciful: a fearsome Australian arachnid really did rear up and snap her jaws around me – as a consequence of which I am no longer a nice person. I'm the one who needs laundering now. That's why, every evening at about seven, a funereal Mercedes with shaded windows and seating for twelve draws up and directs its highly sophisticated eavesdropping equipment my way. ASIO, without a doubt. The Australian Security and Intelligence Organisation. Not the *whole* organization, just three of them. Parked outside my Vaucluse apartment five nights a week (Saturday and Sunday are beach days), listening in to thoughts I didn't know I had, tuned in to frequencies on which I had no idea I ideated.

The absurd thing is that if they took the lift to the tenth floor and buzzed my buzzer I would let them in without a qualm, pour them each a beer, and tell them everything. But then that wouldn't be so much fun for them. Nor is that what they've been expensively trained for. I should know. I helped to expensively train them. I doubt if there's a single security man in Australia, over the age of thirty, who hasn't passed through my hands. Should that sound like an idle boast, you are at liberty to check the records – if you can find them. In the meantime take it as gospel that I've fingered the psyches of the entire secret service. Needless to say, that wasn't quite how my official duties were described in the handbooks. Officially, I was their Moral Tutor.

I ran courses in Human Values – this was a natural progression from crypto-pastoralism – which were compulsory for all would-be spies, single-agents, informers, interlopers, hit-men, sneaks, squealers, stoolies, and whoever else had his heart set on working obliquely for the sound health of his country. I like to think that my lectures would have been well attended even if they hadn't been compulsory. I believe I knew how to spice up Human Values. How to put a bit of zap into them. I understood early that there was no point hanging back when you had Unarmed Belligerence II and The Four-Star Hotel Shoot-Out Diploma as rival attractions. So I scampered my charges through Basic Ethics, whipped them in and out of the Dilemma and Nicety component, and got them to cut their teeth on Ultimate Decisions. *What would you do if you found a communist/Aborigine/Pom raping your mother/sister/daughter?* never failed to stimulate a lively debate. *Do you give the order to press the button even though you know your best friend and fellow-agent is still involved in covert operations in the target area?* was also a humdinger. Human Values for daily living was what I prided myself on teaching, and in order to escape the artificial confinements of the schoolroom I placed great emphasis on fieldwork. Embryo agents, I have always found, like to get out and about. I made certain that there was never any shortage of elective modules on offer, of the kind that enabled students to visit experimental fringe theatre productions and unusual films from small Eastern European countries, with a view to having them closed down. Sometimes I would even arrange weekend-long excursions to the Blue Mountains or Bateman's Bay for the purpose of open-air group readings of avant-garde Black American homosexual novels. Back in the classroom, students would be taught how to articulate and objectify their abhorrence before moving on to basic techniques of influencing public opinion, forming pressure groups, discrediting liberals and so on. I won't easily forget the expressions of unclouded happiness on some of those faces – the Irish Australian Catholic ones especially – when they saw their first book removed from a railway-station magazine-stall. Who said teaching doesn't have its rewards?

And life certainly has its ironies. Now I'm the one they want removed from circulation.

And all because of some spider? Well no, or rather yes, but yes indirectly. The spider itself – the spider *her*self more likely – I'll come to later. Suffice it to say now that she was malignant, malevolent, and venomous, and that she bit me where no man can be indifferent to a bite. I'll leave aside, for the time being, the three ensuing weeks of priapic delirium, and the months and months after that of mortal desolation. Pride in one's humanity is a flimsy show at best, hard enough to sustain even if one never ventures outside the pack, but one quick chomp from some frothing member of a lesser species and it's gone for ever. Ask anyone who's been nibbled by a shark or sawn in two by an alligator the state of his metaphysical certainties. Whatever the poison of the Redback – the *Latrodectus mactans* – got up to in my bloodstream, it was the idea of the attack itself that affected me most powerfully. I lost respect for my own humanity and I lost respect for everyone else's while I was at it. Which is where ASIO comes in. They haven't said anything; they just park outside where I live, underneath the screeching gums, for five evenings a week – no one works weekends in Australia, not even ASIO – and listen in. But it's obvious they don't approve of what I've been doing. Or saying.

Or at least thinking.

3

'Shush,' said Aunty Hester, the moment I made my first appearance downstairs, on the day after my father's defection.

'Shush,' said my Aunty Nesta, which might have been to me or to Hester.

I could tell it was going to be an unusually horrible day.

My mother was in her room. Walled in. I could feel her suffocation. I am pretty certain that I invented the word 'immured' that day, and I was surprised, years later, to discover that it already existed.

Hester and Nesta went in and out of doors on tip-toes, conferring in exaggerated whispers, shushing each other's shushes and throwing me tragic glances. There was an atmosphere of stifled sorrow, silent accusation, and migraine about the house. And although I was too young to understand the theory of universal (that's to say male) guilt, I was old enough to know which sex suffered migraine and which sex caused it.

'Just because you didn't,' Hester's glances seemed to be accusing me.

'That doesn't mean you wouldn't,' Nesta's seemed to be concurring.

And throughout what was left to me of my childhood they would greet me each day with little suppressed gasps, as if they were astonished that I had not fulfilled the destiny of my blood and hopped it in the night.

'I'll be off now,' I said one morning – I don't know why (that's to say I do know why) – as I left the house for school.

'Don't you ever say that again,' Hester called after me.

I was all innocence. 'What?'

By now Nesta had come to the door. 'You know,' she shouted.

It's not difficult to discharge a prophecy. By the time I *was* old enough to betray Hester and Nesta and make a realistic run for it – I never saw it as a betrayal of my mother incidentally, perhaps because she'd been done already – my aunts had made certain that no other option should be open to me. Their work began the minute the empyrean claimed my father. The spinsters' web which they had been spinning in remote corners of our house even while he was living with us, grew to cover everything once he left, like gossamer over a meadow. Soon there wasn't a curtain or a carpet, not a bedknob nor a banister, which didn't feel moist and sticky to the touch. When I opened my bedroom door in the morning I had to claw my way through soft clinging filaments which would stay in my hair and my nostrils all day. Eventually a fine dank fur, which I took to be the exudation of female misery, settled itself on my books, on my linen, and on me.

Hester's and Nesta's spinsterdom was not a consequence of some cruel social mischance. They weren't, in their souls, wives to whom husbands simply hadn't come along. They embraced their single state with a brutal fanaticism. I can see how, today, they would be looked upon as heroines, but to me, then, they were objects of horror. And they tormented me wilfully. They ripped and wrinkled their stockings. They stuffed things under their cardigans to disfigure their breasts – left to their own devices, surely no breasts would have drooped and bulged as Hester's and Nesta's did. And they sat in front of mirrors by the hour, gluing moles to their cheeks and pushing barbarous black hairs into their chins with tweezers.

Could it be that they had early on spotted my father's

33

other weakness in me – seen me to be a kneeler and deferrer to women, a servile priest of the feminine mysteries – and were therefore doing me the greatest of all favours by turning my stomach? I suppose that's possible. But it didn't work. I simply ended up revering all women who weren't Hester and Nesta. And I developed an exaggerated regard – amounting almost to awe – for precise and unapparent underwear. Hence Venie Redfern and Maroochi Ravesh, the Australian synchronised swimming champions, with whom I lived and between whom I slept in a state bordering on beatitude some time before the spider bit me. But I'll come to Venie and Maroochi, *and* the spider, later.

For the purpose of my domestic education, and because my mother and Hester and Nesta didn't have much else to do in the evenings and at weekends, I was subjected to a tripartite division. Here is how I was governed and despoiled:

My mother attended to whatever bore directly upon my moral nature. It's hard for me to remember precisely now the things she used to say to me before I was nine, but I believe we discussed such matters as freedom and responsibility, tolerance and censorship, punishment and forgiveness – the very issues in fact which would later comprise a major part of my Human Values course for neophyte Australian spies. Ours wasn't a religious family, so sin didn't crop up all that often; neither did prayer, absolution, or any other of the folderols of worship; gratitude did, though, and kindness, and generosity, and the necessity never to answer back to a policeman. What I am trying to suggest is the broad and easy scope of my mother's first conversations with me – what I like to think of as their bold ethical explorativeness – because the moment my father went her mind contracted and seized, and she was left with only one theme – 'behaviour'. This might have been all right. Behaviour could have been a topic we explored together. After all, there was plenty which came under that heading I was curious about.

'Mummy, why does Daddy prefer to put his penis between Trilby's—?' for example, was a behavioural nicety I was eager to get to the bottom of. So, probably, was my mother.

But since there were no traditions of frankness between us – this was 1949, remember; men hadn't had penises all that long – since my mother wasn't bawdy and I wasn't brave, all talk between us effectively stopped. From the age of nine until I got the hell out eight years later my mother and I communicated almost entirely through grunts, stares, and the dictionary. When I came home from school and requested help with some word or idea I'd picked up in the playground, she would not wait to hear me pronounce it but would pass me over the *Concise Oxford*, open as always at 'intercourse'. This gave me an altogether false idea, as you might imagine, of the importance and recurrence of congress between the sexes.

There was one advantage, though, of my mother's descent into unhelpful silence: she felt that she ought to make it up to me by allowing me to work in her *salon* during school holidays and at weekends. I was even given pocket money for what I did although I would gladly have done it for nothing. It was my job to keep the washbasins clear of hair and to sweep curls up from the floor. If we weren't busy I would sit dreamily in a corner on an adjustable chair, cleaning out the teeth of combs with a needle. I liked it when the doorbell rang and some woman I'd never seen before arrived for an appointment. I liked it even more if there were two of them. I loved the proximity of women. I didn't even mind seeing them tilted backwards with soap in their eyes and their knees not quite together. (I still don't – ask ASIO.) It would be some years before my mother was to turf me out for blowing in her customers' ears like my father, but already – at nine or ten – I believe I had his respectful demeanour, his air of ministering to a superior species.

(Had fate dealt with me differently – had Cambridge and the CIA and Australia and the arachnid not got me, for example – I might well have ended up running a *salon* of my own. I think I would have made an excellent titivator of ladies' bangs and ringlets. As it is I have spent the better portion of my life bending over them in chairs. The question is only whether I should have turned professional.)

Hester's domain was the visual arts, and her brief was to sensitise me to them. Like her sister Nesta, Hester taught and tyrannized small Partingtons at Partington Primary School. But whereas it was Nesta's responsibility to lead them in community singing and to acquaint them with the intricacies of the triangle and the tambourine, Hester harangued them about the use of paints and pastels. The paints and pastels themselves never materialised. Neither did any paper. The art lesson *was* the harangue. Even in those days, when there was not much talk of free creative expression around, Hester was considered unusually anachronistic in her attitudes.

'I can see absolutely no sane argument for giving children expensive materials to daub with,' I can just about remember Hester declaiming one afternoon after she'd had some altercation with a parent, 'until they have fully mastered the fundamental theories of line, harmony, and perspective.'

I can remember my mother looking straight through her, and Nesta saying, 'Quite,' and me forgetting to hide my Plasticine in time.

Hester was forever confiscating my Plasticine when I was small, together with my crayons and my water paints, and replacing them with books about the lives of famous painters which I had to wash my hands and sit up straight to read. At nine I was incapable of the primitive draughtsmanship required to put a chimney on a cottage or to send the sun down below the sea, but I knew more about Van Gogh's ear and Michelangelo's lumbago than boys twice my age.

Only once did Hester reverse this process, and that was when she caught me reading the life of Paul Gauguin. I had no sooner got to the part where the painter announces, 'I'll be off now,' to his wife and children, than Hester snatched it from me and gave me back my Plasticine.

Hypercritical, theoretical, biographical, and gothical – that sums up Hester's aesthetic. But it was the gothical that got to me.

I cannot possibly enumerate all the trips Hester and I took together, on trams and trains and coaches, to inspect mouldering piles of ancient masonry – sacked abbeys, ruined monasteries, pitted priories, remains sometimes no more visible than a blister under the grass, castles and fortresses with cracked keeps and turrets crumbling quaintly into moss-grown moats. I loved those excursions. I loved the whole paraphernalia of preparation: the packed lunches, the spools of black and white film, the austere-looking pamphlets, cata-loguing every stone and bump in the country, which we unfailingly sent for in advance from the Ministry of Works. (This was before the Department of the Environment was invented, and before the National Trust had reconquered the nation's monuments and reoccupied the land they stood on.) And I loved the gentle undulations of the fields and meadows which the abbots and warriors chose, with an invariable sense of the picturesque, to build their ruins on. I loved the intrusive sheep. I loved the ivied cloisters. I loved the marauding rooks and the rabbit droppings and the dilapidated tea-rooms where you could never be certain you could even get a biscuit. And all because, I now understand, I loved Hester.

When I was nine Hester was in her middle twenties. It's possible that the signs of her spinsterishness were already visible to everybody but me. I don't know. But I am certain that the campaign which she and her sister were soon to mount, to make themselves as unpresentable as possible, had not yet begun in earnest. Perhaps I need this certainty in order that my boyish passion for her – made all the more thrilling for being illegal – should not now appear to me as unworthy. I will maintain my conviction, anyway, that had we rolled together down the ramparts of Pontefract Castle I wouldn't have been disappointed.

By the time I was sixteen though, and Hester was in her thirties, I had lost the courage to be seen with her. I made the most pathetic excuses when she proposed an outing; I feigned sickness, I invented other engagements, I lied about outbreaks of foot-and-mouth disease in the vicinity of Fountains Abbey and throughout the entirety of the Wye Valley. And then, of course, I absented myself altogether. I live now where there are no tumbling ruins, and Hester – still in Partington – lives where there is nothing else.

But in a way the last laugh is hers. Thanks to her the countryside has become forever associated for me with female company and illegal longings. To this day I cannot see the point of being out of doors on my own. I simply cannot sit under a tree, or by a stream (they're called creeks out here anyway), I cannot pat a goat or hear a bird – above all, of course, I cannot take a turn around what passes in Australia for a cloister – without great yearnings assailing me, yes, precisely of the kind my mother mutely alerted me to every time she handed me the open dictionary. Intercourse – that's what nature means to me.

And conversely (for that's not all), thanks to Hester I have never been able to embrace a woman, in nature or out of it, and not feel that I am repaying some longstanding debt of fealty to England's gothic past. Even in Australia? *Especially* in Australia!

*　　*　　*

38

The one who really influenced me however – I mean *really* influenced me now – was Nesta. And that was because Nesta had music on her side. Hester's productions were big and costly, featuring God, Nature, and the fundamental principles of line, harmony, and perspective; but they were always silent. They were pre Al Jolson. Whereas with Nesta I entered a world of waltzes and tuneful romance, where heartbreak was the throb of a tenor aria and hope hung on the echo of a horn. It was Nesta, in other words, who orchestrated my adolescence, enslaving me, in my most sensitive years, to the thrilling mutualities of light love duets, engaging my soul for ever to the *ancien régime* nostalgia – oh, why weren't we all swirling counts and duchesses – of operetta.

Operetta, note. Not musicals. For musicals – for *mere* musicals – Nesta had neither time nor feeling. She hated the post-*Oklahoma!* raucous musical boom of the late forties and fifties, and spoke out against it with the white-hot fervour of a purist. 'The rot has set in with Rodgers and Hammerstein,' she was forever telling me. 'American egalitarianism has done for operetta.'

I was used to hearing the expression of anti-American sentiment in Partington – as a town we felt that the Americans had let us down and then exploited us unscrupulously – but I understood that Nesta's ire was aesthetic not regional. It was their boisterous musical confidence she couldn't take. Their crass assumption that poignancy was a passing affliction their system could make better.

She exempted Nelson Eddy and Jeannette MacDonald from this charge, and took me along to see all their reruns and revivals. But her enthusiasm even for them paled by the side of her passion for Richard Tauber. In our very early days, before my father sang Goodbye, Nesta took all of us to see one of Richard Tauber's farewell concerts. The occasion stays in my mind because it was the only time I ever saw Nesta hysterical in public. 'Girls Were Made to Love and Kiss' must have been too much for her, because she stood on her seat – we were in the front row of the balcony of the Partington Palladium – and rent her hair. If Richard Tauber had been touring with a group, I'm sure Nesta would have agreed to be their groupie.

Some time after Tauber's death Nesta switched her allegiance to Mario Lanza. This struck me as an unexpected compromise with Hollywood, and I made that point to her; but she remained doggedly devoted to her new hero – I suppose because she knew in her bones that he was shortly going to leave her for the land of smiles also. It was part of being a lover of operetta that one should be immersed in the personal tragedies of the performers, and to be a fan of a singer in robust good health was to miss out rather. I happened to be in the audience in Melbourne on the night Nelson Eddy died, and I thought of Nesta and knew how much she would have liked to be there with me.

Mario Lanza's death occurred while I was at Cambridge. The first I heard that anything was wrong was when I received a telegram from Hester, urging me to come home as there'd been a bereavement. My initial fear was for my mother, and I headed immediately for the first of the seventeen trains that were necessary if one were to get from Cambridge to Partington in under a fortnight.

I found everyone alive at home, but Nesta under sedation and in her bed. Her lights were out, but a couple of candles burned beneath a framed picture of Mario standing on a ladder in a striped vest pretending to be a grape-picker. On the record-player 'I'll Walk with God' was going round and round.

Nesta herself looked terrible. She seemed to have poked more than the usual number of black hairs into her chin, and to have stuck three or four cushions under her nightdress. I stayed for a couple of days and tried to be of some use. I was distressed about Mario Lanza myself – I still take very seriously the conflict between duty and sentiment in *The Student Prince* – but I did what I could to get Nesta to look on the bright side.

'I've been reading what killed him,' I said to her, but not callously. 'It was the size of his breakfasts. Do you know what he ate on the morning before he died? Twenty-five eggs, forty sausages, a hundred rashers of bacon, and thirty slices of fried bread.'

Nesta waved away my words. 'Toast,' she corrected me. 'He never liked fried bread. He ate thirty slices of buttered toast. But that isn't what killed him. He was too good for this world. His voice was too beautiful. They wouldn't let him alone.'

I didn't know who 'they' were. It's possible that Nesta was in on some specific act of harassment against Mario by the little people, but I suspected that that wasn't really the point. What she was doing was gathering him into the stuff of operetta, where the great are always an endangered species having their final *fin de siècle* fling, their last Viennese waltz – aristocrats that they are – before the great demotic musical, the song and dance show, engulfs them at last. I knew how Nesta felt. I too was nostalgic for what I'd never had. We were as one on that, my poor unused Aunt Nesta and myself; we both wanted life to swirl us around beneath glittering chandeliers, within earshot of the tinkling Danube, and the merry shouts of the students of the University of Heidelberg.

(I know you can't simultaneously hear both. But you can in operetta.)

Recalling Nesta's influence over me makes me wonder just how far the spider has in fact counteracted it. I was a mock-gothic sentimental reactionary when the CIA recruited me, a musical-comedy conservative, an operetta chorus-line para-Nazi, waiting to hear that I was no

41

other than the long-lost son of the Count of Luxemburg, and therefore able to marry without ado the Duchess of Danzig. And now? If ASIO had half a brain in its head it would turn off all that bugging equipment and play me 'Vienna, City of My Dreams' or 'We'll Gather Lilacs in the Spring Again' at maximum amplification. That would tell us all just who they think they're dealing with.

4

'G'DAY.'

'Oh, hello. Good morning to you.'

''Ow are *you*?'

'I'm well, thank you. And yourself?'

'Fit as a flea on a dingo's dick. And the better for seeing you, you old bastard. Jeez, though, it's a ripper of a morning?'

'I'm sorry, I'm not able to deduce from your inflexion whether that's a statement or a question.'

'It's a bloody statement. *This* is a bloody question: D'you wanna drink?'

'Isn't it a bit early?'

'Early? Christ, you piker, it's nearly nine.'

'I see, as late as that, is it? I suppose that might account for why the old throat's tickling.'

'You're lucky to get a tickle, you old turd. Mine's as dry as a nun's nasty. Come on, no point you standing there like a shag on a rock. Let's go.'

(He embraces his old mate, whom he has met once before, sheds a tear or two into his neck, and carts him over to the sly grog shop on King's Parade, just opposite Queens' College. They grog on until they are as full as ticks, whereupon an altercation breaks out as to whose shout it is. They kick shit out of each other for a time, then they embrace tearfully, like brothers.)

'Right, mate, down to business. I'm not going to say a word about Poms – except that you're all up yourselves – but where I come from—'

'Would that be Australia?'

'Too fucking right. Astute cunt. Australia. God's

43

own. Or it would be if it hadn't been fucked by wine and cheese club propaganda cadres of sexually an-drogynous midget messiahs praying to the Hegelian-Marxist snake god of history. You know the kind of arseholes I'm talking about?'

'I believe I do, yes.'

'Well, smart bastards with your education could help us boot the bludgers up the blot. There's a boat leaving tomorrow, at sparrow-fart. Will you be on it?'

'No worries, Craig.'

This wasn't quite the way the CIA, acting in close conjunction with Australian Security, came to recruit me on the streets of Cambridge in 1962. Nor is it a censored description of how you get to work for an Australian newspaper proprietor. All I've done is tran-scribe from memory a scene that Blind Freddie himself would recognise as coming from one of the best-loved examples of the Melbourne school of vernacular-veracity drama. If I remember rightly it was called *Colin and Craig* and won the Premier's award a few years back. It's almost certain that I would have reviewed it at the time. Unfavourably. I never reviewed anything that was Australian favourably in those days. I couldn't even find a good word to say for the dramatized history of the Victorian Gold Rush, performed on roller skates, which was so popular at one time that it was on at every theatre in Melbourne. I didn't hold with all the nudity. I stood firm against what was being hailed as a Renaissance in the Australian Arts. It wasn't personal. I am by nature what you might call an anti-Renaissance man. I wouldn't have had a bar of Corneille or Calderón if I'd been reviewing at the time.

The Australians have a word for a person like me – they call him a knocker.

They also had a word for what was ailing them in the early sixties, when upright young men such as myself with double-starred firsts in the Moral Decencies were brought over on faith-healing missions: the word was Tristanism. *Tristanism?* That was precisely what I thought too, when I first heard it on the lips of a toweringly handsome Irish-American-Australian Jesuit priest, who combined the build of Chips Rafferty with the looks of the young Henry James, and called himself Dinmont Manifest. We were standing in the middle of Parker's Piece – the great flat square of open ground behind Cambridge's University Arms Hotel – in the early-evening fog, discussing the despondency and confusion of modern Liberalism, or how one was to go about allaying the itch of egalitarian envy, or some such topic. Manifest had been accidentally running into me on Parker's Piece for weeks, that is after I had accidentally run into him on my bicycle and had helped him out of the mud – I hadn't been brought up to fuss over priests, but I hadn't been brought up to knock them down either – with my usual exaggerated courtesy. It hadn't escaped my notice that since he had been riding a motorbike (albeit slowly) I was the one who ought to have ended up on the ground. Nor had it escaped my notice subsequently that he always seemed to know at what time I would be crossing the Piece, and never failed, during one of our fortuitous meetings, to leave me with the impression that I had been obscurely tempted. Was I imagining it, or was he trying to give me something? By the time of our evening conversation in the fog – a real pea-souper it was, too – during which he just incidentally and by-the-by offered it as his opinion that one of the major spiritual ailments of our time was Tristanism, I had become totally confused. His Jamesian obliquity – have I said that he didn't just look like Henry James but talked like him as well? – didn't help much either. Which 'superlative sanctities' were in mortal danger? Whose 'great greedy unsparing grasp at happiness' was it necessary for us to overcome 'the credulity of a generation' and resist?

The only guess I could hazard as to the meaning of

Tristanism was that it referred to the habitual sadness which afflicts Germans during coitus. But Dinmont Manifest seemed to be looking further afield than northern Europe. If I wasn't mistaken – and God knows I might have been – 'that remote uncultivated land, where the tone of things is somehow lighter than with us in our grey immensity and where the people have a happy instinct for what the French call *experience*', was none other than the country my father and Trilby had fled to when *they* grasped greedily at happiness.

Why didn't I come straight out and ask Dinmont Manifest what he was talking about? Because that sort of thing isn't done in Cambridge, or at least it wasn't when I was there. In Cambridge when you came upon a word you didn't know, or a concept with which you weren't familiar, you put your head on one side and let your eyes dance with keen intelligence, as much as to say, 'I believe I see more into this, old boy, than I suspect you do'. Which was precisely what my eyes said on the subject of Tristanism. But out there in the fog, all but invisible to each other at a distance of a foot, it was a pretty wasted gesture.

Of course I got to the bottom of it in the end, else I could not have come out here to cure it. It was made totally clear to me in a shower, oddly enough. (I mean the kind you have over a bath, not a downpour.) But since I had to wait and even get wet before elucidation came to me, I don't see why anyone following the story of my conversion shouldn't suffer some suspense likewise.

And did Father Dinmont Manifest get under the shower with me? Did we sing 'You are my heart's delight – Dein ist mein ganzes Herz' as we loofah'd each other's back and shoulders? Did we lose the soap?

Suffer.

*   *   *

There were four principal reasons why the CIA, posing as Freedom Academy International, found me a suitable candidate for recruitment and sent Dinmont Manifest out to haul me in.

(1) My double-starred first in Moral Decencies. I'm not going to blow my own trumpet, but degrees like that didn't grow on trees. The mixed metaphor is deliberate and alludes ironically to the paper I wrote which clinched me that double-star. It was in answer to a question on the debasement of language under socialism, and I entitled it, 'Marx and the Miscegenation of Metaphor'. I was reminded of it only the other day when I tried to join the Rose Bay and Vaucluse Branch of the Australian Trotskyite Party. I told my story to the Membership Screening Secretary who shook her close-cropped head disbelievingly before during and after everything I said. 'It takes more than one spider bite to make a leopard change his spots,' she gave as her reason for turning me down.

(2) My name. Secret organizations, irrespective of the cause they serve, are always on the lookout for people whose names reflect ambiguous or warring backgrounds. And this makes perfect sense when you consider that all political acts – whether of loyalty or of betrayal – are in fact declarations of love or hate against the family. Karl Leon Forelock – I dropped the Karl as I have already explained – must have struck them as full of promise. They weren't to know that I'd been named Karl not after Marx but Millöcker, the composer of lavish Viennese operettas; nor that Leon was in honour of Leon Jessel, who wrote 'The Parade of the Tin Soldiers', and not Trotsky, whose own name had been Bronstein anyway. They weren't to know, but their ignorance didn't serve them too badly; as a walking humming cenotaph to the waltz and the polka I suited their purposes even better than they realised.

The tarantella would come later.

(3) Rivalry with the KGB. It's not really surprising

that the Russians have always found Cambridge a handy place to recruit from. The climates are similar for one thing. And the high intake of public-school boys works entirely in their favour, since treachery smells sweet to boys whose fathers loved them so little as to send them to Eton. As the first person ever to get to Cambridge from Partington Grammar I would have caught the eye of desperate CIA scouts early. But I had something else going for me too, and after its recent humiliations at the hands of the Russians the CIA would have snatched at this as at a straw: I was the only undergraduate in Cambridge who wasn't a homosexual.

In those days homosexuals were always referred to as practising. You could tell just by looking at me that I'd had no practice whatsoever. In Partington there simply weren't the facilities.

(4) – and by far the most important – my role in the famous protracted dining strike, referred to by historians still as Black Michaelmas, at Cambridge's oldest, smallest, most gothic and most light-operatic college, Malapert Hall.

Here is what happened:

On November 18, 1958 an angry and murmuring crowd of matriculants met in the main and only quadrangle of Malapert Hall in order to press for the implementation of further and yet more dramatic measures against the college kitchens. Bun throwing, sconce refusal, gown abuse, and even random regurgitation had all been tried. In vain. The food was still poor, scant, expensive, and worst of all compulsory.

A Sinhalese prince, by the name of Chanmugan (Malapert Hall reserved a whole staircase for the Sinhalese Chanmugans), spoke for us all when he described the previous night's *bœuf à la Turque* as 'an abomination, a putrefaction, a malignancy, and a bloody fucking insult to a visiting Commonwealth dignitary'.

48

A bloody fucking insult to a plebeian from Partington also, I thought. But I didn't say it aloud. I had only just arrived at Malapert and didn't know many people. I didn't think it was my place to go putting an oar in.

'Olly, olly!' shouted the Home Counties lawyers. (Olly, olly! was Malapertese and denoted encouragement.)

'Olly, olly, olly!' echoed the engineers.

The Cambridge University Rugby Team was made up entirely of Malapert engineers, each of whom was indistinguishable from the other and each of whom was here today. I was very much taken by the vast squareness of their heads, and by the fact that all their eyes were small and set far back, as if Nature had known what they would be about and provided protection. There'd been no such providential arrangement made in regard to the rest of their features though, and these were raw and pulpy from being pressed for hours at a stretch into the behind of the man in front.

I was to go through Cambridge feeling inexplicably protective of Rugby-players, and sad for them on account of how their sport seemed to slow them down and impair their capacity to enjoy the company of anyone whose features weren't as raw and pulpy as their own. But on this occasion I found them frightening. There was menace in the air. The nutritionists were up in arms. So were the historians who knew where such demonstrations led. On the other side of the quadrangle I could see the animal behaviourists grunting and pawing the ground. All in all I think I can say that even from where I stood, a little to the rear of the abstract philosophers and the fine artists, it was an ugly and distressing scene.

It mustn't be forgotten that this was 1958. There were men here who had completed their national service. (I had got out of mine, thanks to a government recommendation that people who were born in Partington had done enough for their country.) The nodding sweetness of the modern undergraduate was as yet an unknown phenomenon. As was Che Guevara intensity. And Bob Dylan perturbation. What we aspired to look like in 1958 was a country estate agent. We wore cavalry twills, just a touch short, over thick greeny-grey quasi-military socks and rustic brogues. We wore Viyella shirts with plain red ties or even cravats under Austin Reed hacking jackets. We called girls totty, and we talked about shafting them. 'Shafted any good totty lately?' was a perfectly common-place question to ask of a near-stranger crossing Magda-lene Bridge. '*Seen* any good totty lately?' would have been just as much to the point for most of us, since there wasn't any and therefore we hadn't. But we all agreed to go on pretending that it lurked not too far away and that we would shaft it rigid once it showed. It was essential to our imitation of slightly sullied squirearchy that we affect the manner of men you could trust with your prop-erty but not with your sister. Olly, olly, olly! It's not a pretty sight, a mob of country estate agents who haven't eaten well.

Many Malapert men (men is Cambridgese for boys) were to write themselves into history that afternoon. Phoenix Bowles, reputed to be the love-child of Chris-topher Isherwood and Frieda Lawrence, inveighed with stuttering eloquence against the dryness of the grilled tomato and the wetness of the sausage. Ten years later he would meet with a tragic accident at the barricades in Paris; but today he stirred us with his graceful irony and courage.

'If we're to have b-b-b-bacon like that,' he declaimed, 'I'd rather k-keep my f-f-fast than b-b-b-b-b-b . . .'

'Break it,' we all helped out.

'They serve daintier dinners at the House of Atreus,' interjected a corn-haired classicist who would one day write on wine for the *Telegraph* and the family for the *Spectator*.

'Olly, olly! Then let's go there,' answered the engin-eers.

'Closed.'

'You certain?'

'Been closed for ages.'

'Pity. Heard it was a good family restaurant.'

And so it went on, late into the afternoon – and all the while the cream of the nation's youth getting hungrier and hungrier. Where it would have ended, when or how it would have ended, had not Martinez Sjögren Léger de Pied leaped up on to the highest step of the college chapel and addressed us, I do not know. Cometh the hour though, cometh the man. Martinez it was who brought things to a speedy conclusion.

Quarter Baluchistani, one-third Paraguayan, three-fifths Faeroe Islander, and seven-sixteenths White Manchurian, Martinez Sjögren Léger de Pied was, at eighteen, the most brilliant man anyone at Cambridge had ever taught. The constant companion – some said the lover – of Maria Callas, the amanuensis – some said the private secretary – of Salvatore Quasimodo, he had argued Bertrand Russell into faith when he was ten, Teilhard de Chardin out of it when he was eleven, and was at present organ scholar at Malapert Hall, having been taught how to pull out all the stops by Albert Schweitzer as a way of saying thank you to Martinez for his example of selfless, yet practical, humanity. When the time came for him to take his exams he would, at his own request, answer every question in blank verse, with one arm tied behind his back, and in half the usual time allotted, in order to make it fairer on everybody else. On him the undergraduate gown we all had to wear hung like the cloak of some Jacobean bestialist and incest-monger. The incest went without saying. You only had to look into his burning black eyes to know how his mother and sisters would have felt, high up in their Andean *alcázar*, at that moment when they knew they were spoiled for ever for other men. He was only to suffer one setback to his wishes in the whole of his life, and that was at the hands of me – Leon Forelock, eleven-nineteenths citizen of Ruritania, the rest pure Partingtonian.

Not that I was looking for trouble. Whatever it is that I've been looking for, for the past forty years or more, trouble is not its name. None the less, after Martinez berated us for the triviality of our complaints so far – 'Why squander the fleeting hours of your youth debating the appropriate madefaction or siccity of toast?' was what he said, the pedant – and after he had warned us against treading the thorny terrain (his metaphor, not mine) of value judgements, in the company of such men as Bursars and Chief Stewards; and after he had come to the matter 'most pertinent to our struggle and alone susceptible to logical discourse', namely our freedom not to eat at Malapert if we wished not to, and our human rights to eat elsewhere; after he had got us this far and then proposed, to cheers and ollies, that we therefore march upon the Master's Lodge and inform him of our unanimous decision to boycott all dining, domestic, and cellar facilities, until such rights and freedoms were restored – well, I demurred.

Let's get this in its proper heroic context: I *alone* demurred.

A solitary voice from the back of the mob? A tiny quaking protest, in a fluted tenor voice, heard above the snorts of the animal behaviourists? Well, not quite *that* heroic. What actually happened was that Martinez led the demonstration out of the quadrangle, in the direction of the Master of Malapert, and before they had all got as far as the Fellows' Garden they noticed I wasn't with them. I can't recall now whether some natural scientist suddenly exclaimed, 'Cripes, that shafting scab Forelock's stayed behind!' but one moment they were as good as gone, and the next they were all back, drilling me with their eyes and wanting to know if I had become a victim of temporary paralysis, or some other, more unspeakable, malady.

An eerie quiet, a brutally charged hush descended on the quad as my explanation was awaited.

This is what I said to the incensed matriculants, on the evening of November 18, as bells rang out over the rest of Cambridge, calling other men to creaking tables, and the autumnal darkness, fragrant with wood fires and home cooking, fell:

'Gentlemen, I regret to inform you that much as my gorge also rises, I will not be joining you in your *protestation de cuisine*. The issue here is not food but premise. I am unable to accept the validity of the notion of "right". In the particular I do not see how I can yet have accrued any "rights" over an institution whose patronage I freely sought and which has been here for as many hundreds of years as I have been a member of it for weeks. In the general I reject "human rights", since they seem to presuppose the existence of a debt, incurred by the universe at some unspecified time, and payable to oneself by means of blank cheque whenever one is running short of privilege or protection. Where I come from there is a saying that the world owes you nowt. Forgive my rough North Country manners. In Partington we acknowledge only obligation.'

Whereupon, not entirely unpleased with myself, I turned my back on them all and walked resolutely across the quadrangle and up the steps to the Dining Hall, on the student benches of which I was to sit for ten long weeks (excluding the Christmas vacation), entirely alone, beneath the wholly indifferent gaze of the masticating Fellows of Malapert, and to the extreme irritation of the Low Table kitchen staff who might otherwise have had the time off.

Did I believe what I said? Every word of it. It's possible that in a similar situation, and were it not for the spider, I would say exactly the same again. I will be nearing the third anniversary of the bite soon, and around about that time, if the previous ones are anything to go by, I will turn into a wild thing, a passionate advocate of bombs and armed insurrection. Nothing else has succeeded, I will know in my heart, so let violence prevail. If only to vary the mixture, let's stir up the pot. But that's only on anniversaries, when the swelling comes back. In the meantime it can be a bit difficult remembering that I'm a radical now. Easier by far to recall how I felt on the evening of November 18, 1958. How much I didn't want to displease the friendly old Admissions Officer with tufts of white hair growing out of his ears, who rode past me on his bicycle, hallooing and calling me by the wrong name. It was only a short time ago that he'd welcomed me to the College and shaken my hand. How would he feel when he learned that I had become dissatisfied so quickly that I was ready to engage in mob violence? Wouldn't he have said, 'But my dear Foreplay, if you feel this so strongly then surely you should leave'? And wouldn't he have been right to say so?

Some weeks into my lonely devotions I looked up to High Table to see the Admissions Officer discussing me with the Master. The Master was offering his ear and nodding. I could understand what was being said to him. This long period of having nobody to talk to had taught me to read lips. It was the statement, 'Better watch out for what comes from Partington Grammar in the future – that Foreskin's a subservient little prick,' which had him nodding his assent.

5

YOU NEVER KNOW who you're going to please. I was
going to say, in politics, but I am not wholly convinced
that there was anything political about my refusal to
join the dining strike. (It was, by the way, strictly a
strike against the College kitchens, and not a hunger
strike. The only one who got thin was me. The striking
body of Malapert Hall gorged itself and grew fat on
jam waffles and biryani.) Anyway, I was politicized
whether I liked it or not. As time went by I found myself
the recipient of warm advances from every party, from
enthusiasts and fanatics on either side of every fence,
all of whom saw my action as quintessentially express-
ive of their cause. I was a hero of the near right because
I had supported reason, authority, and the rule of law.
I was a hero of the far right because I had forced the
Chanmugans back into Indian restaurants, where they
belonged, and thereby given the British vegetable – I
supposed they meant the white cabbage – back to the
British. I was a hero of the left because I had refused to
be swayed by that aristocratic puppy, Martinez Sjögren
Léger de Pied, whose father had been a virulent op-
ponent of Perón (Martinez was quarter Argentinian),
and who had himself founded a Cambridge Society
called Gli Eletti – The Chosen. Christians sought me
out because I had looked within and acted upon what
I had seen. The Cambridge Nietzscheians turned up
with officers of the Existential Club, because I had acted
without fear. And an assortment of mystics padded
softly up my staircase and knocked inaudibly on my
door, on the assumption that someone who would

willingly eat in Malapert Hall had no interest in the pleasures of this world and was therefore one of them.

But I wasn't one of anyone. Up until Dinmont Manifest's 500 cc BMW magically crumpled under the front wheel of my bicycle, by which time I had officially left the University anyway, and was just staying away from Partington, I had made a point of rebuffing all overtures from people who admired me for what I'd done at Malapert. Although I didn't know what that was, I knew it wasn't what they thought it was. Dinmont never actually referred to my role in the famous strike, but I had learned how to recognise even secret regard; and I would have rebuffed him had he not been offering me – had he not at least *seemed* to be offering me – Australia.

'Our remote southern brothers, with their wonderful felicity, what you might call their queer happy knack, for living life boldly' – who were they if they weren't Australians?

There is always, in exclusively academic towns such as Cambridge, a detachment of camp-followers and dreamers and has-beens which, while not enjoying any recognised status in the University, closely rivals the official student body as to size, social ambition, and intellectual curiosity. There are the drunks who gather around the fountain in the market-place in order to swap quotations from Yeats and Dylan Thomas; there are those who could never get their degrees or for some other reason could never bear to leave, who haunt the parks and college gardens, reciting to themselves, like itinerant poets in a barbaric land, the sad sagas of their lives; and then there are the cheerfully robust interlopers who gate-crash lectures, ask pertinent questions during what are meant to be silent seminars, and start up promiscuous conversations in coffee shops. Father Dinmont Manifest was one of the last. I had noticed him around Cambridge for years, looking for book bargains at David's, shouting for both teams at Fenners, punting an empty punt down the river to Grantchester. What made him stand out from the hundreds of others who did the same was the extraordinarily dashing figure he was able to cut despite the limitations necessarily imposed on personal bravura by the clerical garb. There weren't many girls at Cambridge in the late fifties – not much totty, as we used to say (except that we used to say there was loads of it) – and those there were had, as my friend Ramsay used to put it, 'the souls of librarians'. Ramsay – I can't remember whether that was his first or his second name – would actually one day become a country estate agent, perhaps as a consequence of his massive sexual disappointment as a student. 'I suppose they go to bed dreaming of Dewey,' I recall him speculating. I knew how he felt, but he was almost certainly wrong. The girls of Cambridge went to bed dreaming of Dinmont. And when they rose in the morning they whispered of him amongst themselves, asked the unaskable, thought the unthinkable, and wondered what, since the Devil got the best tunes and God got the best men, was left over for them.

As for me, I merely saw him here and there and supposed he was on some long-term sabbatical from the Jesuits. Since I hadn't heard of the CIA or Freedom Academy International, it was unlikely that I would connect him with either.

And now I suppose you want to know about the shower?

Well, it followed hard on the fog. Fog in those days wasn't the feeble merely misty thing it is now. Fog in 1962 had guts. It left its calling card. When 1962 fog wrapped itself around your hair, thrust itself into your nostrils, and took you by the throat, you didn't argue with it. You choked quietly. By the time Dinmont Manifest had led me, spluttering helplessly, back to his place – it was a perfectly acceptable custom, in

Cambridge, to visit unattached priests – I was in need of a sit down, a brandy, and a wash.

'You look as if you've been rolled in a newspaper,' he said.

I ran my hand through my hair and shook out something very like printers' ink. '*The Times*, do you think?' I asked.

He had his back to me. He was pouring brandies out of cut-glass decanters. 'Could be,' he said. 'Or the *Sydney Morning Herald*.'

This is what I mean about the sense I had that I was being obscurely tempted.

I looked around his room while I was waiting. I hadn't really been able to see where he had brought me in the fog, but I was pretty certain that we were in one of those inexplicable colleges for the godly which spring up close to universities. No teaching ever seems to go on in them. They're more like gentlemen's clubs. Not such a bad life, the single one, I found myself thinking, as I took in the oak panelling and the comfortable chairs and the silver-topped decanters. Actually, I'd been living the single life myself for the last three years at Cambridge, and not as a consequence of any vows either – *I* didn't even have Christ for company – but I was thinking in the long term.

'Nice place you've got here, Dinmont,' I said. It was a bit of a Partington sort of thing to say, I know; but I've never been able to resist telling people what I think they want to hear.

He was busying himself about his room; his rooms, rather, since he had a suite of them. 'Yes, it's all right,' he said. Then he added, rather throatily I thought (but then he'd been out in the fog, too), 'Oh, and call me Dinny.'

He had taken off his jacket, which meant that I could see the usually hidden workings of the dog collar and the clerical dickey. The suggestion of subterfuge at the nape of the neck and the tapes tied in bows behind his back made him resemble a surgeon taking time off for a smoke, or a snooker-player. That's if you can imagine a snooker-player with the noble head of Henry James.

He dropped into a chair at last, opposite mine, and we talked, over our brandies, about this and that, about items in the news, and especially about the Cuban missile crisis which had brought all the old Cambridge liberals – many of whom had been thought to be dead – out on to the streets. Duffel coats and cable-knit sweaters – the early sixties uniform of protest – had been everywhere in evidence for days, and if fog had not descended on Parker's Piece this very evening, a delegation of doom-fraught dons would have done so. The word was out that Raymond Williams himself had a warning to impart.

'That ought to make J.F.K. think twice,' I said. I always used to be very easily amused by the contrast between the dissent of the weak and the doings of the mighty. Of course I know now, now that I am a radical, that I shouldn't have been.

'Why's that?' Dinmont asked. He didn't have too much sense of humour, even for a priest.

'Just a joke,' I said. 'I was just being knowing.'

It's not easy for me to do justice to what Dinmont said next, but it was something like, 'You know too much – that's what may, on occasions, make for difficulties for you. When you don't at least – I hope you won't think me forward – know too little.'

I stared into my brandy, which I was swirling around and which, as a consequence, was leaping out of my glass. 'About what?' was all I could think of saying.

'I see in you – and the struggle for me to say this is not (as you might imagine) in itself all that pleasant – I see in you a credulity – not without its charm I am sure, for those who know you better than I do – but which in a sphere other than the social, might, I fear, show as a' – he hesitated here, to get right what it might show as, and to reach behind him, while he was at it, and untie the tapes of his false shirt-front – 'a laxity of the critical spirit.'

I had been sucking the brandy off my knuckles and licking it up from the leather strap of my wristwatch through most of this; but when I realised what I was being accused of I jerked up my head and stared fiercely into the eyes of my accuser. Critically lax? Me? Had he forgotten that I had a double-starred first in the Moral Decencies, which was as good as an official guarantee that I was austere, unforgiving and relentless? There wasn't a single newspaper in the country I approved of. There wasn't a single poet or painter whose work I liked, or had bothered to get to know. And I hadn't been back to Partington to see my mother and her sisters once, not once, since Mario Lanza died. How much more critically un-lax could a person be than that.

Dinmont – I have never felt entirely happy calling him Dinny – put up a placatory hand, as much as to admit that he had only been sounding me out, feeling my texture just to check if I were a man or a marsh-mallow. 'It's simply that I don't make jokes about Liberalism myself,' he said. 'I have seen too many of the consequences of the liberal disposition – the compromised freedoms, the moral confusion, the erotic despondency – to regard them with mirth. I am sure we are as one about this. Perhaps you would like to clean up now.'

This time it was only the last sentence that threw me. For a moment I thought he was asking me to Hoover his room. Then it occurred to me that it was the whole world he was talking about – the world which had been muddied by Liberalism – and that he expected me to ride out into it, with a dust-pan and broom, like the Knight of La Mancha. It was only when he brought me a towel that I was able to breathe with relief. I was so relieved in fact, so grateful for a chink of comprehension, that I didn't think twice about going into his bathroom and getting under his shower.

Shall I say that I was a *bit* surprised, two minutes later, to discover that he had followed me in, was leaning with his back against the opposite wall, and was staring at me, unashamedly, through the imperfect protection of a small plastic shower-curtain?

I wasn't wholly unfamiliar with the experience of showering in the presence of other men. It had been a regular occurrence at Partington Grammar, every Wednesday afternoon after the cross-country run. That's to say, since there was no country in Partington to cross, after the trudge through the backstreets and alleyways. But the boys at Partington Grammar didn't pay much attention to one another's bodies – they were all Partingtons and all Partingtons looked the same – nor did they say such things to one another as Father Dinmont Manifest said to me.

As for example: 'You have, to a wonderful degree, my dear Leon, what the French call the *sentiment de la pose*. Were it not that I know I do not possess such a prodigy, and would not be so irreverent as to keep it in my bath if I did, I would take you for Donatello's David.'

'Oh, yes,' I said. I tried to pretend that I was listening to the day's idle gossip, Cambridge chit-chat. I might even have added, 'That's nice.'

'You do, though, I see the more I study it, show a sturdier leg than I remember on the Donatello. I wonder if you might not, after all, recall Cellini's Perseus rather more.'

I was jammed, by this time, into whatever corner the shower arrangement could afford. I had discovered that far more fog had entwined itself in my hair than I had originally thought, and I was now into my sixth or seventh shampoo. Moreover, I had turned on both taps as far as they would go, in order to provide maximum volume – sound as well as quantity – although this brought the temperature of the water down to several degrees below zero.

Nobody had looked at me from top to toe, for the whole time I'd been at Cambridge, and if I really did resemble Cellini's Perseus and someone else's David (as I'd always had half a suspicion I might), then those had been tragically wasted years, not just for me but for whoever had missed out on beholding me. Throughout my lonely sentence in the cold flat town – it feels even colder and flatter from Vaucluse – the phrase 'a great prince in prison lies' revolved monotonously in my head. Well, whatever else the prince was up to on this occasion, at least he wasn't lying unwashed and unvisited in some musty oubliette. I'm not saying that I suddenly turned coquettish, but when Dinmont offered to scrub my back with a very long bath-brush an odd strangulated sound escaped me, from high up in my throat, not unlike the desperate mirthless laugh that used to issue from Hester and Nesta if someone unexpectedly spoke to them on a tram, and – well, and I didn't say don't.

I kept talking though, and of course – as it would have been wholly irresponsible of me not to – I kept my back turned. 'This erotic despondency you were referring to earlier,' I said, 'cannot surely be blamed entirely on Liberalism.' You can see what I was doing: I was trying to pretend that we were still reclining in armchairs, at a sensible distance, drinking our brandies. 'Surely men – men and women – knew sexual disappointment and satiation long before there were any liberals to bring it about.'

Dinmont – Dinny – was sitting on the edge of the bath now, plying his brush. It was travelling in a circular motion, first over my right shoulderblade, then over my left. 'Ah, you mistake me,' he said. 'Did you suppose I was referring to the immemorial sadness?'

I twitched my back for answer, sending, I hoped, a vibration down the wooden handle of the brush.

'No,' he said, 'I don't blame that on liberals, although they are not wholly innocent of the sin – the social not the theological sin – of compounding it. But where they are plainly guilty, and most to be resisted, is in their promulgation of the cult of passion. I mean that version of world-renouncing love – prized as a concomitant of all their other freedoms and relaxations – before which the claims of family, children, marriage, country, and even God himself, are as mere discarded lumber in an attic.'

'I see that,' I said.

'Leon, there is abroad a new religion of the feelings –'

'I see that,' I said.

'– and nothing less than a metaphysical refulgence, itself more dazzling than the thing it must oppose, will win away its adherents and soothe the ravages it makes in the hearts of men.'

'I see that,' I said; but as I didn't in fact see it at all I thought I'd better add, 'though I'm not entirely sure who you are thinking of. You know. In particular.'

Musing over it now, I am aware that that might have been the moment when I was not found acceptable to Freedom Academy International (funded by you know who), and not given my free passage to Australia. But Dinmont was exceedingly patient with me. I can only suppose that I was looking more and more like Perseus under that shower with every second.

'If it's names you want,' he said, 'Ingrid Bergman and Roberto Rossellini. Frank Sinatra and Ava Gardner. Nearly – very nearly – Princess Margaret and Peter Townsend.'

These seemed to me to be unlikely heroes and heroines of the left, but then I realised that they were just symbolic runaways, martyrs to the liberal ideal of personal fulfilment at any cost. In which case the list could have included my father and Trilby, who had therefore taken the disease with them to Australia. And it might just as easily, if we were headed backwards, have taken in Héloïse and Abelard, Lancelot and Guinevere, Tris . . . Of course!

'Good grief,' I cried, swinging round unthinkingly in my excitement. Dinmont had been scrubbing me hard, and what with the effects of that and the stimulus of dawning intelligence, I might be said (as he would have put it) fairly to have bristled with exhilaration. 'You're describing Tristanism!' I announced, as if I were now ready for my prize.

He was smiling at me radiantly. A shrewd intelligence lit up his eyes. I don't think I'd ever seen him more Jamesian. But I don't know how much that had to do with my having grasped the terrible meaning of Tristanism at last. His gaze travelled up and down my person before coming finally to rest more or less midway. 'So here it is at last then,' he said, 'the distinguished thing.'

You have to stick with what you're good at. 'Ah, sweet mystery of life at last I've found you,' I sang back.

They stood me in good stead for Australia, my three or four days with Dinny. I don't just mean in the sense that they gave him the opportunity to brief me fully on what I would find when I got here – and I could have gone elsewhere, incidentally, had I wished, to Bolivia or Botswana or Bali, where Tristanism wasn't so far advanced; which offer I declined on the grounds that I wanted to meet it at its worst – no, it was for what it taught me about the characters and the needs of men of God that my friendship with Dinmont proved so invaluable. Whether there were in fact more fallen and imminently falling priests in any one Australian pub at any one time, than in the collected works of Graham Greene, I don't know. But it felt as though there were. Certainly the seminaries were seething when I arrived. Had it not been for knowing Dinmont I can't imagine how I would have understood such commonplace

ecclesiastical catastrophes – Partington hadn't prepared me for them – as sudden losses of faith over a
beer, hysterical compulsions to rip off collars in public
places, assorted leaps from balconies and yachts, expressions of radical personal uncertainty in the presence of the very young, various prostrations, emotional
or physical, before unworthy objects, and sundry acts
of highly publicised absenteeism in the company of the
nearest available layperson's wife. These last, I seem
to remember, were very common. There are not many
women in Australia who have not writhed at least once
in a sacerdotal embrace.

I should talk.

6

Dɪᴅ I sᴀʏ that until Father Manifest, nobody in Cambridge had 'looked' at me? That's the truth. The only way I could make it truer would be if I said that until Father Manifest, nobody in Cambridge had *willingly* looked at me.

That's not meant to imply that I shinned up the drainpipes of women's colleges and drew open my academic gown every time I came to a window. My idea of what one was at Cambridge for was more conventional than that. But there was one shameful instance, not of coercion exactly, but of my bringing, as you might say, the mountain to Mahomet, which now that I have owned up to Dinny, there is no good reason for me to conceal.

The Mohammedan reference isn't entirely fortuitous. Though whether the woman in question was in fact Muslim rather than Hindu I never ascertained. I couldn't be expected to know everything about her. It was enough that I knew she was Indian, that her name was Ankhesenamen, that she was tall, haughtily beautiful (in the vulturine style of Indian princesses), wore a sari that showed a band of skin the texture of *crême brulée*, and painted her sharpened nails the same colour crimson as my desire. What more did I need to know? That her aristocratic bearing made Trilby – in retrospect – seem like a Lyon's Corner House waitress? That she spoke a sonorous and perfect English rarely heard in Cambridge, and beyond all wild surmise in Partington? I'd already had a hard time of it at the hands of nobility from East of Aden. The Malapert

Chanmugans had effortlessly convinced me, with barely a flare of chocolate nostril, that England was much more their country than it was mine, and I had handed over to their care, without a struggle, our prized English manners, customs, prejudices and every last intricacy of our caste system. But it was only when I heard Ankhesenamen speak that I realised I had no rights to the English language either.

She was named Ankhesenamen, naturally (this was the kind of thing we just *knew* in Cambridge), after Tutankhamun's widow. Superior Indian families place a high value on their descent from distinguished Middle Eastern ruling oligarchies. However, she herself chose to be called Aglaonice – the ancient meteorologist from Thessalia who believed she could control the motions of the moon; while we gave her the nickname Anorgasmia, as a tribute to the one thing (this might also have been lunar) she had the reputation for being incapable of.

For someone like me, in flight from the image of flattened femaleness fostered by Hester and Nesta, Anorgasmia represented near-ultimate attainment. If she'd been Australian she would have been perfect. I was never foolish enough actually to imagine winning her (the language of victory wouldn't have been appropriate in my case anyway), nor, therefore, did I put my mind to the logistics of taking her back home to meet the folks; but if I had dared to fancy such a thing, nothing less than a triumphal procession through the streets of Partington, led by elephants and flanked by panthers on jewelled leads, would have sufficed.

I think I was unusual at the time for being quite so tropical in my tastes. Most Cambridge men in the early sixties aspired to Swedish looks and that functional idea of romance that is necessitated by a cold climate. I remember my friend Ramsay spending hours at the railway station waiting for any girl with blonde hair to get off a train. Since he was near-sighted and just a little bit colour-blind he would sometimes ask me to accompany him and give him advice. It was me who was responsible for his meeting and falling in love with an albino girl, for which, once he had discovered it through someone else – he would never have noticed himself – he refused to forgive me. But this was unreasonable and faint-hearted of him. It was also illogical. Albinoism, in fact, was the final and most perfect embodiment of Ramsay's erotic ambitions.

As Anorgasmia was the final embodiment of mine.

I won't go into all the details of how I first met her and where I used to watch her perform her magic. Anyone who was at Cambridge during these years will have run into her outside the Copper Kettle on King's Parade or at any of the river pubs in summer months, and they will still remember her deep contemptuous laughter and the way she moved her long brown fingers in the air, as if those incarnadined talons were themselves instruments for making erudite distinctions. I myself preferred to take her in, from a safe distance, at lectures. Here, beneath the drone of one or other of the pre-genital and mainly malignant hebephrenics who prepared us for life, I was able to savour my appreciation of her and imagine what it would be like to spin her out of her sari. The idea of taking hold of one end of the material and pulling hard, so that whoever is inside is unravelled like a bobbin – such an idea, once formed, is difficult to dispel. I'm not safe from it to this day, whenever I see the garment worn, no matter who is wearing it. I will never forget the enormous honour accorded me during my more successful years in Australia – I don't consider it an honour now, now that I am a radical, but I considered it one then when I was a reactionary fascist hyena – of being introduced to Mrs Indira Gandhi. We discovered in the course of our brief conversation that she was as much an admirer of my journalism as I was of her character and policies. I had reason to hold the woman in a double esteem is what

I am trying to convey, but it was still only by the greatest effort of self-control that I was able to resist making a lunge for the loose end of her sari. And who knows, looking back, but that the late Indian premier might not have thanked me for my restraint. You can't have a lot of fun in high office. It's certainly unlikely that you often get the chance to enjoy being whirled at several revolutions per second out of your ceremonial robes.

Did I just say 'revolutions'? Is it possible that my desire to unravel Indian women of rank was all along only repressed closet Bolshevism?

It's doubtful. Quintuply doubtful, considering the parts of Anorgasmia I liked the best, and considering what I wanted to do to them. I am referring – as anyone who has loved a woman from the Indian subcontinent will immediately understand – to her toes. Charred, musky, independent, with the air of having lived in some dark spicy place for a thousand years or more, Anorgasmia's toes protruded from the hem of her silk sari like ten little scarabs.

I don't know whether scarabs are sacred exactly, or just highly prized; but Anorgasmia's got me thinking about religion – the base kind I mean, the kind that demands you flatten yourself on the ground and never get up again – on the one occasion she brought them (or when they brought her, if you like) into my room. Watching her rearranging herself in my chair, now swinging her legs over the arm, now putting her feet under her, now drawing her knees up to her chin, I prepared myself for acts of obeisance every time either set of five appeared.

Not that she would have known that from what I was saying. From what I was saying, and from what I was doing – pulling hairs out of my scalp, rubbing my eyes blind, pounding my fists into my neck: the usual Moral Decency student's accompaniments to thought – she only knew that I was strenuously opposed to her interpretation of the terrible tragedy of Paolo and Francesca, the two lovers consigned by Dante to a perpetual hell in each other's company. It was Dante, actually, who had brought us together. We weren't studying the same subject. Anorgasmia was reading Belief Systems, and I had already formed the impression, from what she'd said, that she'd been going through them sequentially and finding them all wanting. She was pausing briefly at Dante to get late thirteenth-century Christian-Platonism out of the way, and I was studying the *Inferno* as part of the Punishment component of second-year Moral Decencies. Chance, or whatever power it was that looked after these things, had farmed us out to the same Dante tutor, and he had suggested that we get together and teach each other, since our views were so strikingly divergent and since he had lost the will to get out of bed. That was how I'd been able to ask her round, pour her Earl Grey tea (I thought she'd particularly appreciate that), and toast her crumpets on my sputtering single-bar gas-fire. As pleasing an illustration of warm international relations in as cosy a college setting as you could hope to find – except that we were marooned without prospect of rescue in the second circle of Hell.

Which was where, she felt I needed reminding, Dante's carnal sinners were sent.

'I don't know about "sent",' I said.

'Then how do you suppose they got there?'

'I think we are meant to understand that that is where their actions lead them.'

She shook her head wonderfully and made her feet vanish, as if by necromancy, underneath her. 'I think we are meant to understand,' she echoed – only the echo was a vast improvement in timbre and assurance over the original – 'that that is where Dante prefers them to end up.'

'Dante was a great tragic poet,' I said. 'I don't think his chief creative spur was spite.'

She laughed at me. 'Rubbish,' she said. 'In his attitudes to sexuality he was a conventional pre-Reformation Christian puritan. It was historically impossible for him to do anything but disapprove of adultery.'

'Rubbish,' I said. 'He depicts it with tenderness.'

'Rubbish,' she said. 'They're in Hell not in Paradise.'

'Rubbish,' I said. 'Their Hell is simply the very fulfilment of their desires. They wanted each other at all costs, and now each other is all they have. Hell, in passion, is nothing but getting what you want.'

'Rubbish,' she said. 'Hell is a place invented by Christians for storing fornicators in.'

You can get sick of someone saying 'rubbish' to you. I didn't like her references to Christians either, as if she were in possession of some more magnanimous belief system involving a green God with fifteen arms. I must have been getting quite angry. I had burned all the crumpets. 'Fuck fornication,' I almost certainly shouted, 'it's the emotional enervation that's important.'

She had stopped shifting about in my armchair (she had the only armchair) and had attained to what I can only call a starry stillness. I noticed that there were no signs of perspiration on her cinnamon midriff for all the heat of our discussion, and that there was no other evidence, on the skin or below it, of excitation. If my midriff had been exposed it would have been blotched and heaving. 'Which emotional enervation is this?' she asked, in a way that seemed to imply that such phrases were for her to use, not me.

'Paolo's. He never stops crying, does he? All the while Francesca tells her story, Paolo cries. Why do you suppose that is?'

She made what I took to be an Indian joke, in a voice that was low and as it were crouched, like something feral. 'Could it be because he isn't happy?'

71

I waved the beast away. 'Yes, yes, but *why* isn't he happy?'

'Would you accept, because he is in Hell?'

'No. He is crying because he has become a thing of tears, as do all lovers who seek their perfection in sentiment.'

'It seems to me,' she said darkly – I was meant to understand that she'd stopped toying with me now and was ready to conclude her business (death in the afternoon) – 'that you are reading Dante Alighieri as if he were a modern psychological novelist, and the *Inferno* as if it dealt with a merely internal landscape.' She cut circles out of the air with her fingernails as she spoke, and regarded them with satisfaction as if they were little moons – little hell-less moons – of her own making.

'We've come around to Christian cosmology again I see,' I said. It wasn't the best thing I've ever said but I was distracted – she had swung her feet out from under her again and the dung-beetles were back, all ten of them.

'That's where Hell pre-eminently exists,' she told me as if I didn't know.

'Well that's not how I read the novel,' I said.

'There you are – it's not a novel, it's a poem.'

'That's not how I read the poem either.'

She was up on her feet, looking around her for the room to which high-caste Indian priestesses go when they wish to straighten their saris. I pointed her in the direction of the evil-smelling cubicle I shared with Ramsay. 'You're not the first Northern Englishman I've met,' she said, before closing the cubicle door behind her, 'who finds Dante's primitive cosmology to his liking. I'm told that the belief that fornication should be punishable by eternal damnation is not uncommon the further one travels north of London.'

She did wonders with the word 'London', appropriating it to herself as if it were a small poor village to which she sometimes distributed alms; but that was still nothing compared to what she did with 'fornication'. She gave it legs, and scales, and flaming nostrils, and a fierce flaying tail. A bit of a brute, it seemed to me, to be sent on such an innocuous errand. I listened to the swishings of her silks in the next room. I think you can tell something about a person's erotic confidence from the way they slip into or out of their clothes. Anorgasmia, I was convinced, didn't have any. Confidence, I mean. That's why she protected herself with ten little scarabs below, and ten vermilion claws above. Coming from her, the charge that we couldn't handle fornication in Partington was especially galling. There was my father's reputation to avenge, as well as my own. And of course Dante's. I can't recall now how long she was away, but it was time enough for me to prepare a little surprise for her return, a tableau vivant, a solo pantomime, what you might have called a dumb show, except that I spoke. Call it what you will – when she pushed open the door to my room this was what she found:

Me, standing on the table, wearing absolutely nothing but a sooty complexion achieved by rubbing burned crumpets all over myself, and holding aloft the toasting fork I'd bought from Woolworths in order to entertain Anorgasmia that very afternoon.

'Welcome t' blackest pit o' Hell,' I said to her, in the nearest a Partington accent could approximate to Mephistophelean English.

I'll grant her this – she didn't rend her clothes or put her eyes out. She didn't even (not immediately anyway) turn on her heels and run. What she in fact did was stand her ground, take her time, and survey me. (Breeding, you see.) But her retort, when at last it came, didn't seem to me to be all that educated.

Though of course she pronounced it impeccably. 'The proverb which states that the man who sups with the Devil needs a long horn could hardly, in this instance, be more inapposite,' she said, just before she left.

I couldn't have had a sweeter victory. 'The phrase is a long *spoon*,' I called after her. I even jumped off the table and followed her out, shouting down to her as she descended the staircase, 'Easy to confuse our English sayings and proverbs. It always surprises me how many people who appear to speak the language with fluency come a cropper with the proverbs. Funny thing a culture.'

I was still yelling when Ramsay came up the stairs. I never knew where he got to in the afternoons, but he invariably returned with red circles on his cheeks and brand-new stains of egg yolk and brown sauce on the camel waistcoat he wore buttoned tight above his Viyella Young Tory shirt. He was surprised to see me standing naked and slightly burned-looking on the communal landing; the more especially as he had been earlier surprised to see Anorgasmia go sweeping past him in the quadrangle.

'Shaft her?' he asked.

I threw him the only what-do-you-think look available to me in the circumstances.

His eyes swept over me comprehensively. He was clearly puzzled by my burn marks. He seemed not to know that things could ever get as hot as that between men and women.

'Did she come?' he asked finally.

I nodded.

'How many times?'

'Repeatedly.'

He looked obscurely disgusted. 'Filthy animals,' he said.

'Women?'

'Pakis.'

I laughed. I'd never thought of her quite like that. To me she had been Ankhesenamen, Queen of Egypt, widow of the great Tut. Ramsay's gross contempt was my deliverance from slavery.

Still naked, and still holding my pitchfork, I shook

with laughter. While Ramsay, encouraged by my response, went through his usual vile, splenetic, liberating routine.

I wasn't free for long, of course. As witness my feelings towards Indira Gandhi. It would be another twenty years before something even more poisonous than Ramsay – the Redback – would deliver me again. From? Oh, from everything.

7

It took about three months for Dinmont Manifest to OK me with Freedom Academy International, for Freedom Academy International to OK me with the CIA, for the CIA to OK me with ASIO, and for my P & O ticket to arrive safely at my digs in a registered envelope, which must have meant that I was also OK with the GPO. I spent most of that time filling in forms and writing READING, WALKING, VISITING ANCIENT MONUMENTS, LISTENING TO OPER-ETTA, and GENUFLECTING, in the space marked 'Hobbies'. As I've said, I supposed I was simply apply-ing for a job in the usual way.

Once Dinny had completed his vetting of me, our meetings became more and more infrequent and then stopped altogether. I can't deny that I felt a trifle peeved, not to say used, especially on those evenings when I would stroll home across Parker's Piece and see him and his motorbike being helped up out of the mud by a young man as fresh-faced as I had once been; but I tried to be grown-up about it. There were giant issues at stake hereabouts (or rather – since my every second thought now was Australian – *there*abouts), alongside which what was merely personal looked pygmy. The truth is that if I had a reasonable complaint at all, it was only that they were taking so long to get me out to the country that needed me, while Tristanism was sweeping across it like a bushfire.

A couple of days before I was due to leave (on the *Gloriana*, from Southampton, at midnight) I decided to make one last trip up to Partington. Decency, loyalty, and something that felt like affection dictated that I do so. Besides, I would be talking to my father soon, in deck-chairs arranged around his swimming pool, from which Trilby, even with her mouth full of water, would call my name and make it long again; and I thought that it would help, should he ask me quietly how my mother was, if I could tell him. So I pushed my way through the crowds of undergraduates waiting to see if there were any Swedish girls getting off trains today, and I bought a ticket. The journey wasn't too bad; I read Patrick White in preparation for where I was going soon, and didn't think too much about where I was heading now. The moment the train arrived at Partington Central, however, my nerve went, and I sat on a bench in the waiting-hall wondering whether I oughtn't to go straight back. All around me Partingtons with sandy hair scanned the arrivals and departures board and looked perplexed. I did the same. Had there been a return train to Cambridge that afternoon I almost certainly would have caught it, so reluctant was I to see what my aunties had poked into their chins and up their cardigans in the two or three years since I'd last looked upon them, so incapable was I of realizing that had they been in the Patrick White novel I'd been reading they would have been spiritual heroines. Anyway, the matter was out of my hands. There had already been a train *from* Cambridge today, you couldn't therefore expect that there would also be a train *to* it. People in Partington like to take their time and get their bearings; they don't hold with too much coming and going.

Scoff at such morality if you will: it none the less ensured that I did at least see my mother before travelling to the other ends of the earth. And I'm glad about that, considering that I haven't seen her since. Even if she did send me off with an atrocious haircut.

But then that was my fault. I had worked out that if I wanted to avoid Hester and Nesta (and I did – may the Goddess of Aunties, may Patrick White himself forgive me – I did) then the best way to approach the house was on my belly and through the *salon*. I was so desperate to achieve my aim of slipping in and slipping out again unnoticed that I even considered camouflaging myself as a bush, like one of Malcolm's soldiers on the road to Dunsinane, that was until I remembered that the sudden appearance of a bush in the middle of Partington – a stationary let alone a walking bush – would be an event of such novelty that it would excite the very curiosity I was hoping to prevent. If I could disguise myself as a canister of industrial waste now . . . The *salon*, though, once I got to it, promised sanctuary. Hester and Nesta never went near the *salon*, for the simple reason that the basic underlying principle of *salons* – that's to say the improvement of appearances – was wholly inimical to their philosophy. It was also, now might be the time to say, inimical to my mother's practice. But at least *she* tried. As I had tried, in the school holidays, when I used to wait with a miniature dust-pan and brush to sweep the curls up even as they fell. And as my father had tried – really tried – before me. Just how much harder still my mother had to go on trying now that all her little helpers had hopped it, was brought home to me, even as I ducked and dodged towards the shop which had once been our parlour, by the words freshly painted on the window: UNISEX HAIRDRESSING. Yes, that's the extent to which my poor mother had been forced by circumstances to succumb to the ravening sixties. I was distressed to see it. One wants one's home, even when it's a shop, to be a kind of bulwark against the times. UNISEX indeed. If I'd come home from school with that word a dozen years before, my mother would have handed me the dictionary, open at the usual place. So what, if that limited my vocabulary? At least I knew there were two attitudes to everything and that there was such a thing as disapproval, alive and kicking in the world. The only consolation I could derive from my mother's new-fangled acceptance of androgyny was of a practical kind: it meant that I could now go in there for a cut myself. And that was how – mumbling through the scarf I'd wound around my face, and pretending to be a customer – I ended up on the chair beneath her scissors. The plan was that once the scarf came off and the head came up and the towel went round – hey presto, what a big surprise, Leon back from Cambridge!

It's never a good idea to try to surprise one's parents. That's been my experience anyway. I didn't time my mother, but I would guess that I was a good twenty minutes in her hands, having my head twisted this way and that way, being rinsed and rubbed and clipped and brushed, before she recognised who I was. And even putting it like that flatters her powers of observation. What I should say is that it was a good twenty minutes before I could take the suspense no longer and gave her a clue: 'Ma. It's me. Leon.'

But at least she recognised the name. 'Ln!'

I didn't get too excited right away, just in case she followed this with 'Ln who?' Does that sound bitter? It's not meant to. I perfectly understand, I perfectly understood – I always had, even when I was nine – what had made her go vacant. She was no nearer than she'd ever been to working out whether she'd been wronged or not. It hadn't been good for her, allowing herself to be impressed by the social standing of the woman my father had left her for. It robbed her of her right to rage. A person needs to know the difference between an injury and a favour. We all must have someone to hate. My mother was most probably thinking these very thoughts herself, mulling them over along with all the other moral puzzles that preoccupied her, even as I was sitting unrecognized in her chair.

'You could have said it was you,' she complained, after she'd kissed me with dry lips on the forehead and taken off half my ear with her scissors. (That used to be another of my *salon* jobs as a boy – fetching the sticking plaster and mopping up the blood.)

'I thought you might spot the Malapert scarf,' I said.

'The what?'

'Forget it,' I said. 'How are you?'

She looked as though she could take a long time getting to the bottom of that one. And I had trains and boats to catch. 'This is a flying visit,' I said. 'I won't have time to see Hess and Ness, so you'll have to give them my love.'

'Oh Ln, they'll be very disappointed. They're Rangers now.'

'They're what?'

'Rangers. You know, very big Girl Guides. Hester is a hill-walking supervisor already. She hopes to be made a Deputy District Commissioner next year.'

'That's nice,' I lied. I knew I shouldn't have come.

'And Ness is putting on *Maid of the Mountains* with them for Christmas. She was hoping you would be able to see it.'

'Well, you must tell her that I would have loved to, but I won't be here. That's why I've dashed up to see you. I'm going away. I've been offered a terrific job in Australia.'

'Australia?' I could see that she was dimly aware, somewhere at the back of her mind, that she'd heard of it. 'What kind of job?'

'Oh, you know, a bit of this, a bit of that. It's a kind of consultative post I suppose.'

I was glad that she didn't say, 'What would anyone want to consult *you* about?' But I could tell that the question was swirling about with all the others. And to be perfectly truthful, I myself found it difficult sometimes, without Father Manifest there to remind me, to remember just what I was going to Australia for. I was only sure that it all felt right as long as I didn't attempt to put it into words. Which is the best you can say about any political activity.

But the issue of what I was going to do was of far less significance in such a context as this, it seemed to me, than the question of who I was going to see. 'Of course,' I said, as casually as I could manage it, 'I expect I'll be running into Dad.'

She took my breath away – 'And Trilby.'

'Yes, yes I expect so. I expect Trilby will – um – be – ah – with him.'

'They've got a lovely house, by all accounts.'

I wondered how many accounts she was in receipt of. 'That's what I've heard too,' I said. I was grateful to my head for being bent forward, and to her for being busy with the clippers, so that our eyes did not have to meet.

'Well you make sure they look after you – turn your head this way a bit – and don't be frightened to ask for anything. They've got plenty.'

Was that resentment or was it pride? At the cost of half my other ear I sneaked a look at her. It was impossible to tell. Her face was smooth and impassive, just as it had been since 1949, with one corner of her mouth turned down as in bitter frustration, and the other ever so slightly curled as if in triumph. Resentment or pride? She didn't know, either.

We exchanged only a few more remarks on the subject. 'Can you swim?' she suddenly asked me.

'A bit.'

'Make certain you use their pool then.' It was the nearest I could remember her ever coming to delivering me an order.

Since I wasn't going to stay and I knew there was no train back, I spent the night at the Grand Central Partington Hotel, which was irresistible by virtue of its being both the hotel closest to the railway station and the only hotel in town. It might, for all I know, have been an excellent establishment. I didn't notice it. I had eyes only for my own remorse. I could hardly believe that I was holed up in my home town like a fugitive, ready to flee at the first sign of dawn, rather than spend another minute with my mother or chance running into the aunties who had brought me up from a fatherless boy. I tried telling myself that I would have stayed to see Hester and Nesta after all if only I hadn't discovered they were now Rangers; that it was their Ranger Interest Certificates I couldn't bear to look at, not them; that it was their badges and aquamarine Terylene cotton blouses and perky Ranger optimism that I couldn't face, not their essential selves: but I didn't fool myself for a second. I was a monster and I knew it.

I looked at my reflection in the mirror and was shocked by what I saw. I was under no illusions about how bad things were within and I was even prepared for some outward signs of my moral monstrosity to show, but I had calculated without my unisex haircut. I didn't expect blood and bits of hair congealed on both my ears. I didn't expect to be cropped on one side like a conscript, or to have soft swaying curls, like a lascivious gypsy's, on the other. And I certainly didn't suppose I was going to find a little clearing, a perfect fairy circle of monastic baldness, on the very crown and summit of my head.

Did my mother do this to me on purpose? Was it the going-away present she had been denied the opportunity of giving to my father? At the time I thought absolutely not. No to both. Now I am less naïve. I've learned that one should never underestimate the degree of anyone's resentment, or their willingness to extract from B the satisfactions they are unable to get from A. I wasn't just any old passing B either. I also happened to be the son of A. And there's a long tradition of not discriminating between sons and fathers when it comes to doling out chastisement.

Whatever my mother's motives, I arrived in Australia four weeks later on a boiling-hot afternoon which, as it was a public holiday, the whole of Australia had taken to the water to enjoy. I too would have abandoned myself to the hedonism of it all had I not been compelled to wear a beret pulled down around my monkish tonsure, and a Malapert scarf wound thrice around my lacerated neck.

Fortunately that was the look favoured by most Englishmen arriving in the country for the first time and I didn't, as a consequence, excite more than the usual derision.

8

IT'S NOT REALLY SURPRISING that I arrived here on a long weekend; you'd be pushed to find a way of arriving in Australia on anything else. By my count we've had five in the last fortnight, the most recent being to honour the thirty-fifth birthday of the Queen's thirty-sixth cousin. This is observation, not complaint. Now that I am radicalised I wholeheartedly approve of holidays for the people. The more especially as they give me a brief respite from the attentions of ASIO, whose officers enjoy the same democratic privileges as the citizens they are sworn to protect.

However, now that the Nation is back at work, so is the funereal Mercedes. Only this time it isn't looking all that funereal. Either it has come directly from the beach, or we are entering a new and more sinister stage of inconspicuousness, because there is a roof-rack on it today, and on the roof-rack are three sets of water-skis, a surfboard, and one of those polystyrene drink-coolers which I still cannot bring myself to call an Esky.

If that's not sinister, then it's insulting. Insulting to me, I mean – I'm not concerned for the car. If I am to be watched then I want to be watched properly. It's not only the paraphernalia on the roof that's upsetting me. Unless I'm very much mistaken two of the agents are still wearing wet-suits. And from the way the third has his elbow hanging out of the window and drums his fingers on the wing-mirror you'd think he was a chauffeur from a luxury limousine rental company waiting for the bride to show, and not . . . well, and not what he is supposed to be. You would certainly never guess that he had a spare-time trendy-tolerantizer tin-whistle obscurantist intellectual dwarf bullshit apparatchik of the fascist left to keep an eye on.

It was *The Black Sail* – the magazine which I helped to edit in my early days here (the hoisting of a black sail did for Tristan, you will remember) – which only recently described me in those terms. I go on subscribing to it for old times' sake, and I even sometimes send the present editors articles of the kind I know they couldn't possibly print. I suspect it was what I had to say about ASIO and the police state in the latest of those articles that drove them to compliment me with their abuse. Or rather *my* abuse, since I was the one who more or less invented it. The art of vilification was in its infancy in Australia when I first arrived. There was a certain rough native idiomatic vitalism around sure enough, but it was of a kind that could easily make detraction sound like flattery; it was a coarse, affectionate, bachelor style of disparagement, and it needed to settle down in the company of some cruel European contempt. I, if you like, officiated at the wedding. So I was pleased to see, from the attack mounted against me, that the marriage is soldiering on. Just. The irony of my ending up the object of my own sarcasm didn't trouble me, though the further irony of being adjudged a member of the fascist left by the fascist right, while still being treated as a stalwart of the fascist right by the fascist left, did. I wasted no time getting the abusive piece from *The Black Sail* photocopied and sent to every one of the revolutionary organisations I had been trying for months, and without any success at all, to join. I didn't know what other proof they could require that I was one of them. But I took the precaution anyway of reviving my long-forgotten first name and signing myself, Comrade Karl Leon Forelock. Then, this very long weekend just gone, I decided to use the occasion of the desertion of the city by its capitalists to follow up my letters with telephone calls. Hi, this is Karl, don't mean to hassle, but did you get – that sort of thing. Employing, of course, whatever was left of my Partington dialect. But my luck wasn't in; that's to say every Sydney Syndicalist, Althusserian and Spartacist was out – presumably on the beach celebrating the Queen's cousin's birthday. The only person who was both there and prepared to let me come and talk to her was Norelle Turpie, the Secretary of the Eastern Suburbs New Hegemonists. And all she wanted, as I should have realised, was to see me sweat.

I'd written a piece about Norelle Turpie for *The Black Sail* years before, when she was a Senior Tutor in Women's History at the Coryapundi Swamp Institute of Meaningful Technology and famous throughout Australia for her flat refusal to teach any historical event which had a man in it. For the purposes of satire I invented a character called Noel Turdie who took a similar stand on behalf of *his* sex but couldn't find a single significant historical event with a woman in it to refuse to teach. I was fully aware at the time that this *jeu d'esprit* was on the unfair side in so far as it made light of Boadicea and Florence Nightingale, to say nothing of the girl who squatted on the Oxford under-graduate, the woman who ran off with my father, and Mrs Indira Gandhi; I thought it was reasonable enough, though, in so far as it made light of Norelle Turpie. But then I never imagined that I would one day be petitioning to join her party.

I suppose I shouldn't have gone to see her at all, but I now see that I most definitely should not have gone to see her in a suit. Shorts, thongs, and a blue artisan's vest, frayed as if from labour, would have done fine. It was just that I regarded her agreeing to talk to me as a granting of a kind of interview, and I have never been able to shake off the Partington conviction that a suit is what one goes for an interview in. And that one bones up on current affairs. If you want to know whether I did any boning-up for Norelle Turpie, before going to visit her in the house in Woollahra which she shares with giant man-eating cockroaches and diminutive crow-eating boys, the answer is yes. Only I didn't bone up on the names of current British Cabinet Ministers and the policies of visiting friendly Heads of State, the way I did before my interview at Malapert Hall. Not likely. I wasn't a complete drongo. For Norelle I did uranium, Aboriginal land rights, American bases, corruption in Queensland, East Timor – the obvious. But of course one never does enough.

'How do you see the gender division of labour pervading the new computer-based non-productive service sectors?' she asked me.

I ought to have been able to have a shot at that. I knew I would kick myself once I heard the answer. But I felt ill at ease on account of my suit, and especially self-conscious about my Pierre Cardin tie, which would have been enough in itself, in Partington, to get me elected President of the Chamber of Commerce. I sensed that my hair was too well groomed also (after my experience under the hands of my mother I have become very particular about who cuts my hair), and there could be no doubt that my Givenchy aftershave was a mistake. The ideological soundness of Norelle's toilet was guaranteed by its inattention to detail and its declared reliance on common domestic implements. A twist of fuse wire hung from each of her ears. Her own hair had been not so much cut as grated, and then, I thought, perhaps peeled. And I felt certain that she washed herself each morning with an abrasive scourer, just in case any substance or essence not native to herself had dropped upon her in the night. There was the same innocence of influence and intention about her clothes. The transparent cheesecloth shirt through which I could inspect every pore and pigment of her scoured nipples was a problem for *my* politics, not for hers.

'Could you repeat the question?' I asked.

'What is the inevitable effect of identifying the machine with masculinity?' she tried again impatiently, as if that were indeed a repetition and not, as it seemed to me, an even more daunting obfuscation.

I scratched my head, which had the effect, since I'd shampooed with sandalwood, of loosing opulent oriental perfumes into her room. A couple of cockroaches coughed and ran for cover. I stared at her hopelessly.

'It perpetuates the nexus,' she said, as she couldn't wait any longer, 'between technological and sexual hegemony.'

I slapped my thigh in frustration. I knew it. I knew I would want to kick myself once I heard it.

'It was on the tip of my tongue,' I said.

'I don't think you are quite ready for us yet,' she told me.

'I am,' I said. 'I am a changed man. I have a few of the old surface habits left, that's all.' I flicked at my tie contemptuously, so that it flew in the air and landed on my shoulder. 'Underneath I'm unrecognizable.' And I began to tell her about East Timor and West Timor too, what I thought of Joh Bjelke-Petersen, and how I believed the Americans could be made to relinquish Pine Gap.

She caught me looking, during my demonstration of my conversion, into her shirt. 'You still strike me,' she said, 'as essentially unreconstructed in your heterosexualism.'

I took a gamble that this was a bad thing to be. 'I'm not,' I assured her. 'You've no idea to what extent I'm not.'

Wherever else we'd been, we were now where I was most convinced of my transformation. But how could I possibly convince her? By explaining that I was no longer sleeping between Venie Redfern and Maroochi Ravesh, the two greatest synchronized water-ballerinas Australia had ever known, and the two neatest wearers of unobtrusive underwear that *I* ever had? By assuring her that my days of abject slavery to women were at an end, and that I now didn't give a fig for any of them, but especially I didn't give a fig for privileged women of the dominant bourgeois hegemony? Whichever way I mentally shaped these sentences I knew I was never going to get them out in a form that would be acceptable to Norelle Turpie. I had a true and stirring story of emancipation to tell but she was the wrong person to tell it to.

So I fell back on the Redback. 'I think I explained to you in my letter,' I said, 'that I was severely bitten by . . .'

'Oh, yes, the spider.'

I didn't like her tone. It seemed to imply that the whole of the Australian Left knew about me and my bite and enjoyed a hearty joke at our expense. 'What do you mean, "Oh, yes, the spider"?' I wanted to know.

It was irrational of me to get irritated. The reason the whole of the Australian Left knew about the spider was because I'd told them. But Australian women can be infuriating once they abandon their instinct to please. They can fix a man with a smirk of knowing irony which is as impossible to break free from as the locked jaws of a bitch bull-terrier. So see my loss of temper as the vain death-struggle of a half-masticated man.

Not that Norelle Turpie for her part was aware of any tussle. 'I was simply recalling that you'd mentioned the spider,' she said. 'But didn't you say you were bitten nearly three years ago? Surely the effects you described will have worn off by now? Perhaps you should go back for another bite – a sort of booster – and then come and see us again.'

I didn't stay to argue. I knew that whatever came out of my mouth next would be loud, uncontrolled, and against my long-term interests. Besides, the young men with whom she shared the house – they all wore thongs, shorts, and a blue artisan's vest, as I should have done – were beginning to mill about restlessly. I doubt if they would have gone so far as to manhandle me, but I might well have turned on them. I feel a very particular aversion for boys who fuss around such women as Norelle Turpie, like drones servicing the queen bee. (But then I would, wouldn't I, being myself a drudge and bondsman from way back.)

'What's he want?' I heard one of them asking her, before I'd even left the house. 'Isn't he the one who used to write jokes for Malcolm Fraser?'

'I don't think he wrote them as jokes.' I heard her laugh – or rather I heard her smirk snap shut. 'That was just the way Fraser told them.'

'So what's he pissanting around here for?'

'He thinks he's got left-wing politics.'

'And you think he hasn't?'

'I think he's got the itch.'

'Perving bastard.'

You can see why it's important to my self-esteem that ASIO does its job properly and addresses itself to the threat I pose to national security with the appropriate seriousness.

Those *are* rubber wet-suits two of the agents are wearing. I've been out on my balcony to check. I still can't make out the identities of who's inside them, but I wouldn't be at all surprised if it turns out to be Vaughan Cantrell and Doug Kiernan. As for the driver, my money's on Hungarian Rudi. I remember all three of them, as I would like to think all three remember me, from Human Values 1.

They were good boys in the days I used to mark their homework. They cared about their parents, their country (their *new* country, I trusted, in Rudi's case), democratic government and the rule of law. But more importantly, for me, they had that faraway look in their eyes, that characteristic Australian squint which partly comes from having shot up too quickly, from having outgrown their squat European forebears and in some cases the strength of their own bones and structures, as a consequence of so much sun and vitamin and blood-red meat. I used to take it as a kind of mute appeal for help, when I first saw it, that fright on the faces of young male Australians as they soared skywards by a propulsion seemingly not their own. I was struck, too, by its uncanny resemblance to those expressions of tribal perplexity habitually worn (in popular and commercial art I mean) by Aborigines gazing out across the Nullarbor, as if the purpose of some errand they'd been sent on, a hundred thousand years before, steadfastly eluded them. Spiritual uncertainty was what I saw – a bewilderment, an amnesia of the soul even – and although I didn't believe I could always help them to remember whatever it was that they'd forgotten, it became important to me to try to get them to turn their heads my way and to favour me with a smile of recollection. They might have been shy flowers in a greenhouse, the Australians of my first acquaintance, so hard did I work to coax their petals open. No matter what the CIA expected of me, no matter how much passionate energy I put into the task of writing articles and speeches, training agents, and saving the Australian family, my social ambitions were more botanical than political. I was a propagator not a propagandist. Does that sound arrogant? It shouldn't. Like all gardeners I was the one in the state of slavish dependency. I just required something living to notice I was there; I just wanted some native shoot to respond sensitively to my obsessive dibbling.

Even now, a quarter of a century later, my heart breaks when some beach bum from Cronulla with skin cancer and a degree in metallurgy and a shuttered gaze relaxes his expression and inclines his head my way. Infinitely touching I still find them, these lost Australian tribesmen – even the three lunks in the Mercedes – far gone in abstractedness and inexpressible detachment.

No wonder the women of Australia have lashed themselves into articulated spite and fury, so impossible have they found it to locate or lay a hand upon their men.

I'd still appreciate it, though, if Vaughan Cantrell and Hungarian Rudi could summon up a bit more professional enthusiasm, or at least stop playing Paper, Stone and Scissors in the front seat of ASIO's best Mercedes.

9

WHEN THE GOVERNOR-GENERAL of Australia is of the Blood Royal introductions should be made to him thus: 'Your Royal Highness, may I present Mr Karl Leon Forelock (say).'

When the Governor-General is not of Royal Rank, however, the introduction must run: 'Your Excellency, may I present (though you won't thank me for it) Ms Norelle Turpie.'

(Under no circumstances must the words 'Sir' or 'Madam' be substituted for 'Your Royal Highness' or 'Your Excellency'.)

I picked up this indispensable information – don't scoff: I was to use it by and by – out of Noreen Routledge's *Etiquette for Australians*, published by Dymock's Book Arcade, Sydney, in 1944. It was one of the few books I had with me on the long voyage out from Southampton, and the only guide to Australian rules of conduct that I'd been able to find in the whole of Cambridge. And I wouldn't have found that had I not ambled into a church jumble sale and accidentally knocked over an orange-box containing old copies of *The Lady* and it. I don't know if the situation has changed at all, but in the early sixties the only books you could obtain in England that even mentioned Australia were by Patrick White, and they offered a rather specialised view. They certainly weren't of much help to intending settlers like me, who wanted to know how many pullovers to take and whether one would ever need an umbrella. What surprised me was that the CIA and ASIO had not got together to provide a brief pamphlet for visiting agents and propagandists, let alone the general public; but according to Dinmont Manifest there wasn't the demand. 'The traffic is all, as it were, the other way,' he told me. I must have looked alarmed. 'And that, my dear Leon,' he quickly reassured me, 'is part of the very problem we look to you, with bounding hearts, to felicitously resolve.'

Thank God, then, was all I could think, for Noreen Routledge.

She was never out of my hands for the entire journey. While the other passengers searched Aden and Colombo for duty-free dishwashers and wooden elephants with real ivory tusks, I stayed in my cabin and absorbed her every word. 'Never, when in company,' she advised me, 'talk in whispers, be contentious, be witty at another's expense, nor enter into religious discussion.' I promised myself that I wouldn't. Nor, since I wanted Australians to like me, did I see why I too shouldn't keep my language 'crisp, clean and simple', avoiding all 'extravagant adjectives and superlatives'.

Dinny's observation, that more people were at this time leaving Australia than were going to it, was verifiably true. I saw about fifteen other liners on the Indian Ocean alone, and they were all pointing the other way. Sometimes they would steam dangerously close to us, so that we could wave to them and they could stare in astonishment at us. On one afternoon alone I waved to Sidney Nolan, Diane Cilento, Randolph Stow, Clive James, Clifton Pugh, Germaine Greer, Barry Humphries, Thomas Keneally, Robert Helpmann, Brett Whiteley, the young Bob Hawke, Robert Hughes, Barry Tuckwell, Brian Hayes, Nigel Dempster, Carmen Callil, the future Princess Michael of Kent, and scores of minor poets and essayists all of whom would return from Oxford and Cambridge ten years later to take up Gough Whitlam creativity grants.

I had absorbed every word of what Noreen Routledge

had to say about the delights of the Australian picnic-party (she didn't call it a barbie), at which 'a sense of fine comradeship prevails, happiness and fun forming two of the finest guests'; but as I hung over the rail of the lower deck and counted the boatloads of Australians heading for where I'd just come from, I began to wonder whether there'd be anyone left to enjoy the delightful camaraderie of an Australian picnic with. I date from this journey the sensation which still intermittently assails me of being forever in the wrong place at the wrong time. So it was a relief to round the heads at Sydney at last and find the harbour full of gambolling indigenes. Decked in the brightest of colours and sporting the briefest of fun wear, honking and hooting and hallooing, hanging out of slow-moving craft and pirouetting behind fast-moving ones, they flew under us and around us in their thousands, gybing and yawing as a matter of necessity, careening and spinnakering as a matter of spectacle. Despite the one-way traffic jam on the Indian Ocean it was impossible to believe that the population of Australia was depleted by a single sensual soul. Either those were phantom ships I'd passed, or it was only the thinkers and dreamers I'd seen leaving.

I would have felt more of a participant in the carnival myself, as I think I've said, had I not had to conceal my mother's act of vicarious vandalism under a scarf and beret; and I was not at all certain, either, that I had done right to wear my tweeds, for all that Noreen Routledge had recommended them as much the best thing for travelling (though to be strictly avoided – this accorded with Partington practice too – at any occasion with an official atmosphere). But fortunately, not every Australian was out catching skin cancer on a boat or a board; and although I can't say that I saw any other berets ashore, I was most certainly not the only one in long trousers. Well before we berthed – even as the tugs were turning us around – I caught sight of a gloomy gathering of agoraphobics on the quay, clothed in the uniform of mental adventurers, evincing Dracula-like distress at being out in the fresh air and the daylight, and only risking it, clearly, to meet someone off the *Gloriana*. I felt pretty confident that this was 'our side', the anti-Tristanist movement in Australia, the intellectual 'right', and that the someone they'd come to meet was me.

At our farewell encounter in the middle of Parker's Piece Father Dinmont Manifest had briefed me as to the welcoming party I could expect. 'Will Menzies be there?' I had asked.

'Unlikely.'

'The Governor-General?'

'Mm – I doubt it.'

'Joan Sutherland?'

'Possible – but I suspect, ultimately, not. Probably touring.'

'Touring? I thought you said there was a national emergency out there.'

'Not everyone senses it the same way, Leon.'

It shouldn't come as any surprise that I lost my temper. I was due to sail the following day, and most people are tense before a journey. Besides, I was still out of sorts as a consequence of my failed trip to Partington. 'So who the hell will be meeting me, Dinny?' I asked. 'Rolf Harris?'

He looked at me reproachfully, his eyes full of a dumb creature's pain. I hate that look from priests. It makes me feel like a moral hit-and-run driver. He defied me to leave him lying on the road, without a word.

'Well,' I said feebly. 'Well, I mean . . . Put yourself in my place.'

He glistened at me. Now that I wasn't a callous pet-murderer I was St Francis of Assisi. That was the other thing I hated about priests. Their extremism in matters of good and evil. He put an arm around me, as it were from on high. 'Leon,' he said, 'the best men often lie in unvisited graves. And the best deeds are often unmarked by a plaque or a memorial.'

It was looking as though I wasn't even going to get Rolf Harris. 'I know that,' I said. 'I'm not expecting a fanfaronade.' (I was of course, though I wasn't going to admit it.)

'The people who will be there to meet you, Leon, are the unsung heroes of any battle for the retention of the civilizing amenities. Editors, administrators, professors, columnists, educators, balladeers, wives – you know the kind I mean?'

'Hearts-and-minds men,' I ventured. I suppose I could have sounded more thrilled. Especially as I was a trained hearts-and-minds man myself – a minds man anyway – and it wasn't costing me anything to go out there and meet more of them.

'Precisely. The warriors of the spiritual underground. The stormtroopers of slow change. And of course there will be the odd foreign fulminator, you know, exiles from Hungary and such places, to bear witness and lend passion.'

'How will I recognize them?'

'Oh, don't worry. They'll recognize you.'

And they did too. They picked me out at about the same time I picked out them, and although we didn't wave or jump up and down, as others on the boat and the quay were doing, we did exchange narrow looks and barely perceptible nods of the head, which for us were just as cordial.

The familiarity of their appearance had a calming effect upon me. I had been suffering agonies of apprehension, which even Noreen Routledge had been unable to assuage, ever since leaving Southampton. It was good to know how to address the Governor-General, for all that Dinny had assured me that he wouldn't be there, and comforting to learn that it was no longer considered discourteous to refuse a cocktail from him, provided that one's refusal was made graciously. It was a help, too, to know that I would be met by the unsung retainers of the civilizing amenities. But I was still essentially in the dark. How big were these people going to be? What colour? In what language and employing which arcane forms would they greet me? Noreen Routledge had not implied that one put forward anything but one's hand when the time came for it to be shaken, but was that only because she assumed everybody knew it was one's foot? Now, at a stroke, my terrors were dispelled. I knew these people. Nervous and yet aggressive, introverted and yet histrionic, gauche, grey, ghostly, and cataleptic, they might just as easily have been teaching Moral Decencies at Cambridge. Only the Eastern European émigrés had a more wistful and agitated air, and they reminded me of the men I'd seen going in and out of the Partington Polish Circle – the Polskie Kolo – in the days when my father used to point it out to me from the tram and tell me what he could only have learned from some widow, that it was the best place for cheap bortsch outside Cracow.

Whether my hosts were as relieved by my appearance as I was by theirs I couldn't say for sure. I suspected they were alarmed by my beret but found the rest of me – my Cecil Partington travelling suit, my deferential stoop, my reserve, my manifest air of hierarchical modesty, and my passion for operetta and gothic ruins (these things show) – to their liking.

What I didn't of course realize, because no one had told me, was that it was of no account, really, what I looked like; it was enough, simply, that I was an Englishman, because Australians in the early sixties doted on Englishmen, believing them to possess all the secrets of urbane existence and multiple answers to every riddle of the universe. It goes without saying that this slavishness wasn't openly acknowledged, but I was soon to perceive it in the eagerness with which anything I said would be listened to and sometimes even copied down; and there was no other explanation for those boatloads of young and avid pilgrims I had crossed, at the rate of one every thirty minutes, on the Indian Ocean. They were off to visit the Oracle at Delphi situated in west London. So I was a winner even before I landed. The fact that I looked a bit like Webster Booth, held myself a bit like Ivor Novello, talked a bit like the Hallé Orchestra, and held a double-starred first in the Moral Decencies from Cambridge – this was just icing on the cake.

'And this,' said Orel Rosenfeldt, 'is my wife, Nonie.'

'Thank God for that,' I said. I was standing in the Rosenfeldts' kitchen, having met everyone else's wife drinking Pimms No. 1 in the Rosenfeldts' garden. I'd been driven straight here, after a minimum of preliminaries, from Circular Quay.

'Thank God Orel has got a wife?'

'No,' I said. 'Thank God you're called Nonie. All the others are Judi.'

She thought about it. 'Henry's wife is called Yolanda,' she said.

I smiled. 'Yes, I know,' I said.

'And Gunnar's wife is called Hermie.'

'Yes,' I said.

'And Alex's wife is called Lobelia.'

'I know,' I said. 'I was exaggerating. I simply meant that there are rather a lot of Judis. But not all, obviously.' I was furious with myself. Hadn't Noreen Routledge warned me about hyperbolic language in the presence of Australians?

'And then there's Robin, Robyn, Robinne, and Valda. They're not called Judi.'

I looked to Nonie's husband, Orel Rosenfeldt, Professor of Pessimistic Philosophy at the University of Noonthorungee, for help; but Australian husbands don't help you with their wives – they hope that you might help them. He was busying himself with the mosquito netting on one of the windows. He seemed to have spotted a hole through which some zymotic microbe might fly with poisonous intentions towards him and his family.

Nonie herself was pressing garlic into a casserole. She had an Elizabeth David cookbook open at *bœuf bourgignon*. For the next five years I would eat almost nothing in Australia except *bœuf bourgignon*. Served to me, almost invariably, by wives called Judi. That's when they weren't called Robin, Robyn, Robinne or Valda.

'That looks good,' I said, changing the subject and being careful to avoid names.

But I hadn't been careful enough. I'd blundered into illusion and reality with the wife of a professor of philosophy. 'Looks aren't everything,' she said.

'Well I'm sure it tastes good.'

She sighed. 'Oh yes, taste,' she said. She apparently saw such depths of bitterness in the word that I wondered if it meant something entirely different in this country. I fell silent – I suppose I should say I was contradicted into silence – and watched her.

She was tall and dark, lean almost to emaciation, and pretty in a sour, weatherbeaten sort of way. I liked the way her mouth turned down at the corners. My mother could have looked like her if she hadn't shilly-shallied on the question of grievance. Nonie's sense of wrong was unequivocal, infinite, ineluctable, like an ancient Greek goddess's. I sneaked a glance at the man who had wronged, still wronged, and – I knew from the droop of her mouth – would always go on wronging her. Orel Rosenfeldt was small, round and white. His eyes were bad, his hair was thin, and his mouth was pursed up pink in a Cupid's bow. A man destined by nature to be so unattractive to women was bound, by whatever is the opposite of nature, to be irresistible to them. He reminded me a little of my father. In both the human struggle to overcome the base material was nothing short of heroic. And I was struck once again by the truth that little men make the worst husbands.

I felt the need to give Mrs Rosenfeldt my support. But I was running out of things to praise her for. I hadn't got far with her name or her casserole; and since she was wearing a kind of Indian tablecloth under her Elizabeth David apron I didn't see how I could risk complimenting her on her frock. I'd picked up frock as a word Australian women liked to use to make light of the weighty business of fashion – all Australian women are ironists - and I was keen to try it out myself. But now wasn't the time. 'Your friends seem very nice,' was all I could think of saying, instead.

She gave me a sideways look. The figure of speech is common but Nonie Rosenfeldt was the only person I've ever met who really could look at you out of the side of her face. 'Do you know my friends, then?' she asked.

'I mean . . .' I gesticulated in the direction of the garden, where my welcoming party had now divided into two distinct groups, one of women, one of men.

'Those? Do you think they're my friends?'

I didn't say anything.

'They're Orel's friends,' she said. I noticed that every time she spoke she killed a couple of house plants with her words.

I would have liked to go on saying nothing but I have never been able to bear long silences. 'I think Nonie is a wonderful name, your casserole looks superb and I am just mad about your frock,' I said.

'It's not a frock, it's a tablecloth,' she corrected me, emptying a flagon of red wine into the stew, as if it were gall.

*   *   *

101

Once I made it into the garden myself I discovered that there were not two distinct groups formed, but three – women, men, and *Irish*men. I should explain that to be Irish in Australia does not necessarily entail coming from Ireland. A sentimental attachment to the place, formed through travel, literature, or just hearsay, is sufficient evidence of nationality. It's even possible for selected southern Europeans to become honorary Irishmen on the strength of a proven commitment to the uniting tenets (emotional, political, and alcoholical-poetical) of Australo-Irish Catholicism. Which explains why it took me a moment or two, when I went over and joined this third and most voluble group, to distinguish Enrico Santalucia (the writer of charters and manifestos) from Vance Kelpie (the writer of dirges and dithyrambs) even though I'd been introduced to them separately the moment I'd stepped off the *Gloriana*.

'You know where I stand on the crass cult of vegetable sensuality,' one of them was saying.

'Yes, but it's sensuousness I am talking about – that sensuousness which is next to numinousness,' the other replied.

Although it was just possible to detect a faint olive hue on the skin of one of them, they were both essentially without colour. I didn't realise at the time how much effort was required, what precautions and evasions were necessary, to achieve the appearance of an inhabitant of a cold climate when one lived in a torrid one. But I could see that there was something more than mere Partington pallor – something, if you like, more strenuous, something more *serious* – on the faces of both of them.

But that still didn't help me with which was which.

'Fine distinctions,' the first speaker said, contemptuously. I thought I heard an operatic quality in this, a melodiousness Milanese.

But then the reply – 'My friend, do we not, as a

matter of pride, deal in fine distinctions?' – had a certain Calabrian courtliness about it also. Yet they couldn't both be Enrico Santalucia.

'Not I,' said the first. 'I deal only in truth and reason.'

'Ha – reason!' said the second. I took it that whoever he was he wasn't big on reason. Which could have made him, from what I'd heard, either Kelpie or Santalucia or one or two others besides. I'd been warned that there was a powerful lobby of irrationalists in Australia, even amongst one's own. So he wasn't exactly giving me any clues. 'I've always said that what is missing from your make-up,' he went on, 'is the intuitive. You lack the oceanic.' (I was all at sea now.)

But his friend – Vance or Enrico – wasn't. 'If you mean that I am not carried along by the tide of permissive sentiment washing down from our centres of learning and communication, and taking with it all the constraints of sense and morality, then I am proud to lack what you call the oceanic.'

I was impressed by this. If anyone ever charged me with lacking the oceanic I would know what to say. But I was even more impressed by the way the other threw open his arms in a gesture of non-combativeness. Italian warmth if ever I'd seen it.

Except that it wasn't. 'Enrico,' he said – well at least I knew now – 'Enrico, the truth is that today's young whom you so greatly and unnecessarily fear, possess an inner self-acquaintance, a sensuousness of their own natures, which we, at their age, did not.'

There was a murmur of agreement here from the three Cooney brothers – George, Bernard, and Shaun – to whom I had also been introduced earlier in the day, but who were not, fortunately, confusable with anybody else, except one another, thanks to their vast height, their intensely woeful expressions, and their habit of forming a circle around whoever was talking. I was to meet and be encircled by the Cooney brothers on countless occasions over the next years, and I was to be beaten up by them one night also. I don't hold it against them. It was my own fault. The experience lingers with me in a melancholy sort of way; it was like being pressed and saddened into submission by a herd of doleful camels. But today, as they stood around Vance Kelpie and mumbled their approval out of long faces, the only person they upset was Enrico Santalucia.

'Mere slogans!' he shouted. 'Mere catchwords. This is the sentimental romanticism of nihilism.'

'I'm not a nihilist,' said Shaun Cooney. Being excessively tall, he wasn't ever called upon to say very much. People somehow know what the excessively tall think. Shaun Cooney lectured on his own short stories (he called them *romans* and *novellas*) at the Tumbarumba School of Mines and Mineralogy, and was an active member of every political party in Australia. Like all teachers and lecturers in the country he was very popular with students who applauded even his silences and considered him a superb raconteur. None the less, this was one of the longest and most complete sentences I was ever to hear him deliver.

His interruption was enough to put paid to the conversation though. Vance Kelpie was losing interest and looking round for someone to fill his glass, and although Enrico Santalucia seemed incapable of speaking other than vehemently, what he said next was clearly a sort of valediction.

'I will not stand idly by,' he warned whichever of us thought he might, 'and allow the destruction of the fundamental biological structuring of our society by hordes of mystical hoodlums educated to believe in their right to make their own acquaintances inwardly.' He moved his plump white fingers in the air, marvellously, as he spoke; not as a conjuror might, to confuse and conceal, but in the manner of a reformed gourmandiser who wishes to show that his hands are clean, that he has not eaten for weeks. It was hard to believe that Enrico Santalucia had ever been guilty of any excess of appetite, but he took long views of such things and no doubt wished to demonstrate that he was cleansed of original sin.

Vance Kelpie put his own white fingers out to me. I was to shake them frequently in the years ahead, particularly in the late evening, at the fag-end of a party, when he would sit slumped at a kitchen table, or propped up by acolytes, and would read by the light of a half-opened refrigerator from his latest ballad, calling all scattered Irishmen to arms. Sober, his fingers would clutch hold of yours in a horrible simulacrum of Celtic comradeship; drunk, they would lie like four stillborn mice in the palm of your hand. 'Peace,' was the last word anybody ever got out of him before he fell on his back for the night. And already, although he couldn't have been drinking for more than four or five hours, he was beginning to look for an end to all belligerence. 'So tell us about the old country,' he said.

I've never been much good at dealing with that sort of an invitation. 'Well, it's still there,' I laughed. 'What would you like to know?'

'Why your government has virtually disappeared from South-East Asia, leaving left-liberal totalitarian regimes behind it, and us to carry the can,' said Santalucia.

Kelpie waved that away. 'No, no, no. Tell us about streams and meadows. Tell us about lochs and raths.'

I must have looked bemused.

'You know – the fairies. The customs of the hearth. The sacred trees.'

'There aren't that many sacred trees in Partington,' I said. I was about to shape something along the lines of, 'Fairies in Cambridge now,' but he interrupted me.

'Who's talking about Partington?' he demanded. 'It's Clonakilty I want to hear about.'

'Ah, Clonakilty,' said the Cooney brothers, in unison. And since any remark from them automatically brought all conversation to an end, I was able to get away.

10

GUNNAR MCMURPHY'S WIFE, Hermie, caught me trying to remove the black seeds from the Pavlova.

'That's passion fruit,' she whispered.

'I see,' I said.

'You can eat those,' she whispered.

'I see,' I said.

'Well, what do you think?' she whispered.

'Good,' I whispered back.

Something told me that Gunnar McMurphy didn't like to see me whispering to his wife. He hadn't been comfortable about our sitting next to each other, and had thrown her hurt looks, I thought, over the gaspacho and the *bœuf bourgignon*. Now that we had our heads together over the sweet, he seemed quite distraught.

Gunnar McMurphy taught at the Tumbarumba School of Mines and Mineralogy, along with Shaun Cooney, but whereas Shaun had been able to fix it so that the only subject he lectured on was himself, Gunnar McMurphy had been forced into sociology. A Lawrentian by inclination, training, and dark intuitive knowledge, Gunnar McMurphy ran courses on Man and the Machine, The Will as Weapon, and Blood Relations, all three of which, despite earning him the covert mistrust of those in authority and the open hatred of those against authority, were extremely popular with students. It was his wife, Hermie, who had told me all this, and when I'd asked her what she did she had answered, 'I am Gunnar's woman.' Which was why I thought it was safe enough to whisper to her.

But I didn't want trouble on my first night in Australia – not when I was a guest at the Rosenfeldts' table – so I turned, as soon as I decently could (I wanted to be decent by Hermie as well as by Gunnar), to the person on my other side, Lobelia Sneddon, wife of Alex Sneddon, President of Freedom Academy International (Australia), and Vice-Chancellor of the University of Oodnadatta, who would one day write the series of classic handbooks on benign autocracy – *Courtesy and the Campus*, *Politeness and the Police*, *Dignity and Drill*, *Gallantry and Genocide* – and be named in the Queen's Commonwealth Birthday Honours list.

Where Hermie was pink like an Englishwoman and suggestive of rolling Devonshire hills and dairy products – 'I am the mother of Gunnar's children,' she had also told me, redundantly – Lobelia was parched dry by the sun and worn thin by climatic hardship. She hadn't wizened permanently though, as by an act of the mind, like Nonie. Her mouth could still turn either way, and her eyes were still black with expectation, darting about in their sockets as if something of vital importance, carrying the promise of a Southerly change, was just out of vision. She had the habit, too, of addressing me in French – the language of her dreams, I suspected, and therefore one which she was certain was wholly unfamiliar to me. I couldn't recall a chapter in Noreen Routledge dealing with the requirement to translate all foreign words and phrases for visiting Englishmen, but had there been such a one Lobelia Sneddon could have served as a model.

'*Bon appétit* – enjoy your meal,' she had said to me when we first began eating.

'You too,' I said.

'I will, *sans doute* – without doubt.'

And then, as the courses came and went, she would lean my way and announce, 'Mm, *délicieux* – or should I say, delicious,' or, '*Superbe* – that means superb.'

'Well, that's my first Australian dinner finished,' I

said, the minute I'd polished off the passion fruit, turning to her as part of my strategy to save the McMurphys' marriage.

'And you enjoyed it, *n'est ce pas*?'

I waited for the translation, but for some reason – perhaps because she thought I'd now attained proficiency under her tuition – none came. 'I did indeed,' I said. And then I moved a little closer to her and whispered, confidentially, '*Formidable.*'

I never discovered her reaction. Something suddenly drew my attention away from her and towards Gunnar McMurphy whose eyes were now blazing with the same pain and resentment I'd noticed when I was under suspicion of being intimate with Hermie. It was unmistakable that I was under the identical suspicion now. Could it be that I wasn't allowed to whisper to *either* of them? This proves how young I was (and how un-Australian); it had never previously occurred to me that a man might even be interested in two women at the same time let alone be capable of throbbing with simultaneous, stereophonic jealousy over them. In Partington you took them one by one. Even my father knew that when you fell for a new, you discarded the old. Gunnar himself would eventually bow to the conventional niceties and do the same, fleeing Australia with Lobelia on the very day her husband was awarded his knighthood, and leaving Hermie to wonder what she was going to put to her breast next; but until then he would stand sleepless vigil over the pair of them, protecting them from themselves ('They can become desperate once they find out,' he was to tell me), from each other, and from every man who wasn't him.

Yes, I was young all right. Full of Partington pieties, and still smarting from the shame of Cambridge where a multiplicity of totty meant, on a particularly good night, one. But all that would change very shortly, and I too would soon be keeping both ears cocked just in case anyone had the mind to prise me out, when I wasn't looking, from between Venie and Maroochi. For this was a land of plenty, in which Tristanism took, as Father Manifest had warned me, like a native plant. Tristanism! It looked more like cornucopia to me this evening as I withdrew from Lobelia as smartly as I'd previously withdrawn from Hermie, and sat, with my arms folded on the table in front of me, bolt upright.

Yes, Dinny had warned me. But he had talked about the enemy. I thought I was among friends!

Call me old-fashioned, but I always feel sorry for the husband. Or at least I always used to. The Redback is no respecter of marriage and she passes on her indifference to her victims. But these are my pre-spider days I am describing, when I didn't have a single puncture on my body and knew pity for middle-aged husbands with grey hair, to whom the proper domestic courtesies had not been afforded.

Courtesy, by one of those cruel ironies which the post-spider me does not find all that ironic, was an important concept for Alex Sneddon. Courtesy and civility. He talked to me about them, after dinner, on a low sofa in the Rosenfeldts' front room. And it goes without saying that I listened to him reverentially; in those days I had a nose for imminent knighthoods and liked to put in betimes with my respects.

'You are a young man, Leon,' he told me. 'And I am an administrator. I make no bones about it. I think like an adminstrator, you may have noticed that I eat like an administrator, and I don't mind telling you, Leon, just between ourselves, that I even make love like an administrator.'

He didn't actually say, 'make love'. The precise expression he used was 'root'; but I am deliberately cleaning up the speech of all the Australians I first met so that I should not be held guilty of condescension and caricature. *I* have to go on living here. It's for the same reason that I have avoided all mention so far of such other distinctive Australian conversational practices as excessive labial vitality (that's when there wasn't, as in the case of Nonie Rosenfeldt, an absence of all oral activity whatsoever), and the raising of the voice at the end of every sentence, so that even the most brutal and dismissive assertion of opinion comes out sounding like an enquiry. You would not have wanted to be a prisoner in the dock in these days, when Australia still retained the death penalty, because you would not have known whether the judge had condemned you to be hanged by the neck until dead, or was merely wondering, as a matter of idle curiosity, how such an eventuality sounded to you. It wasn't quite so bad for me on my first evening here – I'm sure that my views on diverse matters were genuinely sought – none the less I will never know how many questions I answered that hadn't in fact been asked.

As for Alex Sneddon's language, the last thing I wish is that he should be considered coarse on account of what I have just confided. The brute sexuality of the Australian male might have been the reason so many thinking Australian women were leaving their country – who else were all those boats carrying? – but the subsequent history of our times does not report that they found any greater sensitivity on the other side of the world. Far from it. Those that stayed, stayed single; the rest went home. Better an Australian administrator's quick and breezy root, they'd learned, than an English estate agent's dismal shaft. Any day.

Alex Sneddon meanwhile, unaware, like the rest of us, of the march of sexual sociology, was warming to his immediate theme. 'You see I believe in administration,' he wanted me to understand, 'unfashionable as I know it is to do so. And do you know why? Because administration cannot be practised without the four virtues which form the bedrock, to my mind, of all civilised societies. Courtesy, civility, respect, and compliance with established procedures. Does this make me a Conservative?'

'There's nothing wrong with being a Conservative,' I said. I would have agreed with him even if he had not been patting me all over the upper half of my body while he spoke. I didn't mind the mauling I was taking. Some people touch you to force you into compliance, to make sure that you're listening, to check that you're there. Alex Sneddon touched me to check that *he* was.

'I'm glad you think so,' he said. 'Do you know, I sometimes feel a well-chaired meeting to be an expression of our quintessential humanity. I find such joy in it. These radicals or whoever they are, who go on and on about freedom and liberation, know nothing, in my view, of the true human freedom that comes from working within the structure of civility imposed by established procedures. A place in the sun is all very well Leon – I grant them their place in the sun' – he slapped me soundly around my neck and shoulders to test his magnanimity – 'but without someone in authority, someone in the chair who can decide who is to speak first, who is to speak longest, if necessary who is not to speak at all, we have tyranny, Leon, we have anarchy, not freedom.'

'It sounds like anarchy to me,' I agreed. But my attention had begun to wander to that other anarchy – the marital kind – over which no chairperson has any final say; for I had caught sight first of Gunnar and Lobelia, then of Gunnar and Hermie, then of Hermie and Lobelia, then of Hermie and Lobelia and Gunnar, in earnest and even agonized conversation in the Rosenfeldts' front garden, and I did not want to stay to share Lobelia's husband's pain. So I excused myself and went to the bathroom.

On the stairs I passed Orel Rosenfeldt, his eyes closed, his little cupid lips pursed, stroking the bare brown arms of Judi Beaurepaire, President of the Sydney Women's Committee for Censorship. In two of the bedrooms the innocent junior Rosenfeldts were sleeping soundly, protected from the dedicated anti-Semitism of the mosquitoes by nets on the windows, nets around their beds, and slow-burning coils of malodorousness; but in a third bedroom, the one which had been made over to me, the Cooney brothers had formed a circle around Judi Colebatch, the national and overseas co-ordinator for Women Who Want to Be Wives, and were looking dangerous. I wasn't looking too good myself. The bathroom mirror showed little trace of the inexperienced young person who had stepped off the *Gloriana* only a few hours before. My eyes were puffed and bloodshot, my lips swollen and stained with South Australian claret. The black seeds of the passion fruit had lodged between my teeth, making them appear old and broken and uncared for. I had red blotches on my cheeks also, where Alex Sneddon had carried out tests to check whether or not he existed. I splashed water on my face, forgetting to see if it did indeed go down the sink the other way – the water I mean – and made for the stairs. On the way down I passed Orel Rosenfeldt, still standing where I'd left him, still closed and pursed, and still stroking a brown arm. The only difference was that the arm did not belong to Judi Beaurepaire, who had gone, but to Judi Cooney, who had taken her place. I had no idea whether Orel had noticed the substitution or very much cared. I had no idea either – and still don't, after over twenty years – to which of the atrabilious Cooney brothers Judi Cooney was wife, helpmeet and friend. By now I would imagine the Cooneys have forgotten themselves, that's if they ever knew.

At the bottom of the stairs I ran into Gunnar and Lobelia. They were having a furious argument, full of suppressed longing and rage, of the kind only possible between the ardently adulterous. Every time Gunnar went away to console Hermie, he returned to find Lobelia exchanging confidences with another man.

And every time he told Lobelia off about this Hermie became upset and had to be consoled. 'It's a vicious bloody circle,' he was complaining. *'Silence, mon cher,'* she whispered to him, when she saw me coming. *'Salut* – hello,' she said to me.

'There you go again,' Gunnar fumed, as I left them.

I was trying to decide who I was the more sorry for, Alex Sneddon or Nonie Rosenfeldt, and which one I ought to go and cheer up, when I came upon the two of them cheering each other on the very same low sofa from which I had risen only ten minutes earlier, after hearing all about the joys of established procedures. Alex Sneddon – Sir Alex as he would shortly be – was patting the upper portion of Nonie Rosenfeldt's body even more vigorously than he had patted mine. What is more he was patting it under the Indian tablecloth I'd mistaken for a frock. I knew that if I was to be consistent I should be as pleased for them both now as I had been distressed for them before. But it was a bit soon for consistency. I considered I was doing well enough by them just leaving them to it. I would have been within my rights if I'd pulled them apart with my bare hands. Wasn't that what I'd been sent here for?

I crept from the room and took a look at what was happening in the kitchen. It was quiet. A small blue flame still flickered on the gas-stove, the only light by which, a half an hour before, Vance Kelpie had incanted his ballad of the diaspora of the old Celtic genes. But now he was collapsed across the table. So too, arranged in an arc around him, were the Cooney brothers. This struck me as near-miraculous, since I had seen them upstairs, surrounding Judi Colebatch, only minutes earlier. This wouldn't be the last time I would have cause to wonder whether there wasn't more than one trio of Cooneys, or phantom sets of them scattered across Australia.

The only person conscious and on his feet was Henry Dabscheck, the presiding genius and phrasemaker of

Freedom Academy International (Australia), and he was scrambling himself some eggs.

'In the four long years I was interned by the Nazis,' he told me, 'and in the three even longer years I was held by the sociopathic left-wing totalitarian madman, Joseph Stalin, I kept my hopes alive by scrambling eggs. Now, in the midst of this moral debauchery, I do the same.'

Henry Dabscheck was of the same size, colour and rotundity as Orel Rosenfeldt, but whereas Orel's mouth was a little pink rosebud of self-indulgence everything about Henry's face bespoke a passionate abstemiousness.

'You wouldn't scramble me one, would you?' I asked.

'You like eggs?'

'I like eggs tonight,' I said. Does that sound like crawling? Maybe it was. I'd always admired men who were austere and unforgiving not by temperament but by choice. I wouldn't have read Moral Decencies at Malapert had I not esteemed the eremite above the sybarite. But I could also see no virtue in giving away what you didn't want. Henry Dabscheck looked to me as though he could name all the pleasures.

'Sit,' he said. 'Sit, sit. And move the drunk.'

I eased Vance Kelpie's elbows gently from the middle of the table. He stirred fractionally in his sleep and muttered, 'Peace,' without waking up.

Henry passed me a plate of something yellow and pulverised. 'You have these,' he said. 'I'll make myself some more.' I wouldn't hear of it. He wouldn't hear of my not hearing of it. 'The exercise is good for me. I don't get enough. Yolanda does everything for me. This is a rare privilege, to cook for someone.'

Not that rare, as I later learned.

I wondered where Yolanda was but didn't dare ask. There was always the possibility that she was at the bottom of the garden with three more Cooney brothers. Henry watched me running through the permutations.

115

'I've sent her home,' he reassured me. 'We have a rule when we come to dinner at Orel's' – he pronounced all his words gutturally, but Orel's name he rolled around the back of his throat as if it were a gargle he wanted to spit out – 'Yolanda goes home at ten. I don't like her to stay for the depravity.'

'So why do you stay?'

'I'm an old man – do you want more egg? – I've seen worse. When you've survived Nazism, Stalinism, Zhadnovism, Castroism, Modernism, Cubism, Maoism, and Andersonian Libertarianism, the domestic degeneracy of the Australian clerisy isn't too difficult to take. Don't mistake me, I do not approve of sexual fidgets in anyone over the age of eighteen, but I have yet to be convinced, even by Enrico Santalucia, that there is a clear cause-and-effect relation between wife-swapping and Marxist–Leninist socialism.'

'I am relieved to hear you say that,' I said. I was too. 'But I have to confess that I expected something different. Especially from' – I was a bit hesitant here, on account of my being a visitor and a guest and all – 'especially from people' – and on account of their being Henry's friends – 'who are themselves—'

But he couldn't wait. 'You think they're bad? Wait until you meet the others.'

'The others?'

'The other side. The enemy. The Stalinoid junta.'

'Oh, them,' I said.

'The moral delinquents of the left-liberal press. The totalitarian lackeys of the unions. The intellectual pogromists and pea-brains, with their scream-squads of love-mongering mystics who have taken over our educational institutions. The ear-ringed obscurantist riff-raff of the arts.'

'Oh yes, them,' I said.

'The phoney-pacifistic spiritual jargon mongers of the church. The fellow-travelling orgiastic fantasists who call themselves our intelligentsia.'

116

I couldn't keep saying 'Oh yes, them'. So I said, 'I haven't been here very long, Henry,' instead. And just in case that didn't quite follow I added, 'No doubt I will come face to face with the people you are mentioning very soon.' I didn't really know what I was talking about. I think I was a bit frightened. Dinny had not said anything about Stalinoid juntas.

Henry seemed to understand me though. He did a comical imitation of a fanatic. At least I think it was an imitation. 'What are you asking for?' he screamed. 'The right to make up your own mind?' I think he was mimicking a broken European accent, but as he already had a broken European accent it was hard to be sure.

I laughed anyway. 'I only said I haven't been here very long,' I reminded him. 'I didn't say I vanted to be expelled from ze party.' I don't know why I bothered. I have no gift for mimicry. A *v* for a *w* and a *z* for a *th* is the best I can manage, regardless of the nationality.

This time Henry switched to an impersonation – though with nothing like the same verisimilitude – of a man of reason. 'Judge for yourself,' he said. 'I give you a week. No, take ten days. Listen, take a fortnight. Then come and tell me that we are not an island surrounded on four sides by a sea of human rubbish.'

'Peace,' murmured Vance Kelpie, dreaming of Clonakilty.

On the stroke of midnight exactly, to the accompaniment of much scraping of furniture and the opening and closing of many doors – as if a vast game of musical chairs had suddenly begun and just as suddenly ended – the angel of propriety re-entered the Rosenfeldt household. Only Gunnar McMurphy had trouble dismounting his golden coach and returning to his pumpkin.

The last people to leave were the Sneddons. Alex was civility itself. Not a hair of his neat grey head was out of place. I sneaked a look at Nonie Rosenfeldt

117

and she too betrayed no sign of lingering passion, no memory of an embrace. The droop of her mouth was as resolute as it had been all night. I marvelled, as I shook their hands, at the ability of these Australians to begin a brand-new life every half-hour or so. Such things were unimaginable in Partington. Only Lobelia seemed to crave consistency. '*A bientôt*,' she said to me, 'if you know what that means.'

She was right to raise the query. I was a long way from home and I didn't know what anything meant. If I wasn't entirely mistaken I was still vaguely sea-shaken, the guest of some people called Rosenthal, and probably drunk. Thus ended my first day in Australia. And I rounded it off, as I was to round off hundreds more, by wondering whether I was the man for the job, whether I had it in me to hold back the Tristanist tide of luxury and demoralization on which the Chinese communists would otherwise roll in on surfboards, and by being violently sick in someone else's bath.

And I still didn't remember to check which way it went down the plughole.

11

 OREL ROSENFELDT was addicted to three kinds of tobacco and a little water in his whisky. These consolations – they were not pleasures: no Professor of Pessimistic Philosophy acknowledges the possibility of pleasure – were self-administered in a strict order of rotation. First a cigarette (Disque Bleu), then a little whisky and water, then a small cigar or panatella, then a little whisky and water, then a pipe, then a little more whisky and water, and then back again to the cigarette. In the course of a one-hour seminar Professor Rosenfeldt could get around this circuit of consolations twice.

Of course it was necessary, if the Professor was not to be forever jumping up and down, for the arms of the armchair from which he taught to be broad and flat, so that they could balance his dry necessities, and for there to be a table by his feet, on which to balance his wet. Thus provided for, he would wave in the students privileged to attend the only class he gave each week, remove his spectacles, massage his eyes, and ask, through a blue film of smoke, 'Why is it that man was born to suffer?'

I myself was invited by Orel to sit in on one of his Tragic Condition classes a few days after the dinner-party at his house. I knew that a drive to the University of Noonthorungee was imminent, since Noonthorungee had been selected, along with Oodnadatta and Tumbarumba, as an ideal campus for me to have a room on; not to conduct original research or receive pupils in – I had not come this far to be an academic hack – but for purposes of keeping an eye open, looking around me, and generally forming a sense of what was what and who was who. (The dirty wash of Australian society principle, remember.) But when Orel mentioned over breakfast that he was about to take a spin out there, it being his teaching morning, I was more than a little surprised by his casualness. I had looked up Noonthorungee in young Søren Rosenfeldt's school atlas and had calculated it to be about a hundred miles from Broken Hill, which was itself (as you could tell by the sound of it) at least a thousand from anywhere else.

'Isn't it a bit far?' I wondered. I didn't want to sound too amazed; I'd heard that Australians had a different attitude to distance.

Orel puffed at his pipe. He forwent his whisky and water during breakfast but not his pipe. 'Not really,' he said. 'Twenty minutes, half an hour, depending on the traffic.'

In order to make sense of this I had to juggle a number of possibilities – that Orel was some driver; that he drove some car; that there was more than one Noonthorungee in Australia; that the junior Rosenfeldts were learning their geography from scandalously approximate atlases. 'Is there usually a lot of traffic on the Noonthorungee road?' was all I could think of asking.

Orel saw to the bottom of my difficulty. Perhaps he saw the eleven-hundred-mile tail-back that had formed, in my mind, on those eleven hundred miles of dirt-track. 'I think you're confusing the university with the township,' he helped out.

'You mean they're not in the same place?'

'Not quite.'

'Not quite that's what you mean, or not quite in the same place?'

'The latter.'

'So where's the university?'

'Twenty minutes down the road.'

'You mean the University of Noonthorungee is in Sydney?'

Orel seemed to think he was under some kind of attack. Whereas, as should have been obvious, I was just trying to get my bearings in a foreign country. 'It's common for a major educational institution to be outside the town it serves,' he said.

'A thousand miles outside?'

Perhaps I sounded a touch too surprised. Orel looked at me and then at the contents of his pipe, as if one of us were spoiling the other. He pushed his spectacles up on to his forehead and rubbed his weary eyes. 'Who'd go to the University of Noonthorungee if it was in Noonthorungee?' he challenged me to tell him.

'Who'd go to study there, you mean?'

'Who'd go to study there? Who'd go to teach there? Who'd go to clean there? Who'd go to do anything there?'

I couldn't be expected to answer that. I'd only just picked the place out of Søren's atlas, with the help of Immanuel's magnifying glass. On the atlas nowhere in Australia looked like a good place to go to. But I had a question of my own. 'So why is it called the University of Noonthorungee if that isn't what it is?'

'That *is* what it is.' I'd brought out the pedant in him. 'It just isn't *where* it is.'

'All right then: why isn't it called after where it is?'

'Because there already is a University *of* Sydney, and a University *at* Sydney, and a University *near* Sydney. Sydney has oodles of universities. The only way there was going to be money for a new one was under rural redevelopment. And Noonthorungee needed redeveloping. The only catch was—'

'I know,' I said, 'nobody would go there.'

'So better a University of Noonthorungee at Sydney—'

'I know,' I said, 'than no University of Noonthorungee anywhere.'

Orel smiled at me, cleaned out his pipe, and lit himself a Disque Bleu. He was a teacher to his fingertips. He loved it when, under his feather touch, the whirligig of reason came to rest at truth.

'Just one thing, though,' I said. 'If there are oodles of universities in Sydney, and no one wants one in Noonthorungee, why have another one at all?'

Orel's mouth fell open, causing his lit cigarette to drop like a little incendiary bomb into his lap. For a minute or two he was too astounded to retrieve it, too stunned even to feel pain. My words must have reached Nonie in the kitchen also, because she too was suddenly before me, her eyes staring, her usually locked lips prised apart and hanging loose like an imbecile's. A second later the three junior Rosenfeldts had arrived as well, each one – Søren, Immanuel, and Judi – in as identical a state of stupefaction as its parents, each one regarding me as if I were a breaker of homes or a maker of orphans.

Why hadn't Noreen Routledge warned me that you don't go around venturing it as your opinion that there are enough universities already in the hearing of an Australian academic and his growing family?

Funny thing though. Eight or nine years later when the campuses of Australia became, in Henry Dabscheck's words, Marxist-Theological Seminaries and Arsenals, and in their own words, Counter-Ideology Collectives, offering courses to themselves on Constructive Anarchy and declaring every day but Melbourne Cup Day a Day of Outrage, I wrote a series of articles outlining contingency plans for systematically closing them down. I won't go into the details here of what I recommended, short of saying that I pinned my hopes on stormtroopers and riot-police and low-flying B52s. Orel Rosenfeldt was one of the first to congratulate me on my

122

proposals. QUITE RIGHT TOO STOP, he telegrammed me to say, NOT BEFORE TIME STOP IN LIFE LITTLE TO BE ENJOYED AND MUCH TO BE ENDURED STOP BUT NOT THAT MUCH STOP SHUT THE LOT STOP orel. The telegram was sent from Washington where Orel was heading a Cerebration Unit charged with exploring methods of lowering the threshold of human expectation for the Nixon administration. Closing down institutions of learning was one of the methods he was exploring.

Which just goes to show that timing is of the essence in politics; that it is not what you believe which determines which side you're on, but when you believe it.

Take me as an example. There must have been a time when an act of gross discourtesy towards a rich and pampered female member – I daren't say which – of a powerful land-appropriating royal family – I really *daren't* say which – would have drawn the plaudits of all those who cared for freedom, justice, and emancipation. But who can I find to reward me for it today? Today, apparently, a woman is a woman before she is an aristocrat, and woe betide the man who would seek social revenge upon a woman. It's just my luck, of course, that she-reverence should be all the rage the moment I lose my taste for it.

But then it was just my luck to get bitten by a spider.

'There's no such thing as luck,' Gunnar McMurphy used to say. 'We call our own fates down upon ourselves.'

Well, he was in a position to know. I haven't seen Gunnar for a dozen years or more. The last I heard of him he was in Europe with Lobelia, giving readings from a new D. H. Lawrence novel he'd discovered. His ambition was always to refer to the most private parts of women's bodies in the most public places that would allow him to do so. If they are permitting him to say

'Eh, tha's got lovely cunt, Connie' (or whoever's cunt it is that he's unearthed) to cheering audiences in every Common Market country, he mustn't be able to believe his luck. Except that there's no such thing.

If he were here now he wouldn't accept that I had been accidentally bitten by the Redback. 'You chose to sit where you sat,' he would inform me. 'A bite is a transaction between two parties – a biter and a biteree. You sat in wait for that spider with every bit as much purpose as he sat in wait for you.'

I know what I would say. 'It wasn't a he – it was a she. Only the shes are venomous.'

I'd be calculating, you see, on the extraordinary effect that the word *she* has always had on Gunnar McMurphy. *Her* is another one.

But he'd hold back the sweat and the tears just long enough to say something like, 'You knew what you were after. Somewhere in the black inchoate centre of you, you needed that bite.'

Perhaps I did. Who am I to argue? I was just the one whose testicles came up like ostrich eggs and who tossed around for three hellish weeks on a bed of vain priapic frenzy. And who is due, any day now, a recurrence of those very symptoms, since, like stigmata, they never forget their own anniversary.

But if that's what I need, that's what I need.

I might have learned something more about needs in general, viewed philosophically that is, had I paid stricter attention to Orel Rosenfeldt's line of reasoning on that one occasion I sat in on his Tragic Condition seminar. I have a feeling that somewhere between the cigarette the whisky and the cigar he had some pretty scathing observations to offer on the subject of needs. But I found it difficult to attend. My thoughts were elsewhere. Because although this was my first experience of the to and fro of Australasian dialectics in a place of higher Australasian dialectology, it was also my first glimpse of the apprentice-dialecticians – the verdant Australasian young – and I was as beguiled of my senses by them as if they were the sirens and my ears had not been stopped. Does that mean that Orel Rosenfeldt's students were all young women? Not quite. There were three or four obligatory boys dotted about, for the look of the thing, boys who would have been Gods in some other place (in Cambridge, for example), but who were crushed into insignificance here both by the indifference of their professor to everything they had to say and by the glaring superiority – numerical, intellectual, ornamental, casuistical, structural, you name it – of the other sex.

Forgive me if I rave retrospectively; nothing that had happened to me in Partington or Cambridge (not even Anorgasmia) had prepared me for such a reversal of the usual arrangement as to girls and boys, that's to say as to the enforced scarcity of the former and the predomination, in matters of personality, of the latter. That this was a microcosm of Australian society, and not merely the way Orel Rosenfeldt preferred to arrange his classes, I had no way of knowing at the time. It would be months yet before I came to realise that the Australasian male was everywhere in hiding from the Australian woman rampant, in awe of her assurance, in fear of her quick tongue and vast vocabulary, in mortal terror of her rampaging wit. I had come armed, naturally, with a few thoughts of my own about Aussie mateship, but it would be some time yet before I understood that it was not an aggressive system for the ritualistic exclusion of wives and daughters but the sad defensive huddle of a threatened species, alone as upon a darkling plain, frightened for its life.

I was frightened myself, I don't mind admitting, by all those big bright brash girls darting out their answers to Orel's elaborate conundrums – a credit to the nuns who'd educated them. Or at least I *was* frightened until I suddenly comprehended why Orel *wasn't*. I don't know what enabled me to grasp this so soon, unless it was the amount of vying for his attention and approval that I perceived, but by the end of the hour I knew why self-satisfaction sat on Orel's skin like a rich unguent from Arabia. *He* wasn't an Australian. *He* wasn't high and broad and golden and afraid. *He* was a European. He might have been born in New South Wales. His father might have been born in New South Wales before him. That didn't matter. What did matter was that Orel was soft and white and ovaloid and *un*afraid. Unafraid of the dashing girls, that is. As a consequence of which, of course, the dashing girls could enjoy the novelty of being afraid of him.

Only the day before I had got up late, still ship-lagged, and watched Orel pottering about the garden in his shorts, looking for deadly insects, or anything smaller than himself, to destroy. I had been struck by the bluey whiteness of his legs, their abbreviation, and the degree to which, with their pretty dimples and cute creases, his knees resembled the baby Jesus's. How did such podgy flesh go down, I had been foolish enough to wonder, in a country that could boast so much physical magnificence? Well, I was in a position now, watching Orel struggling to reach his whisky with his chubby arms, his feet not quite making it to the carpet, the cream of Noonthorungee maidenhood hanging on his every postulate – I was in a position now, all right, to answer my own question. It went down, as we used to say in Partington, a bloody treat!

I never got very close to Orel Rosenfeldt. No man did. He left the business of getting close to other men to real Australians. But he did me a great favour on my first day at Noonthorungee (the institution not the town). He taught me that there's nothing in the world Australian women love more than clever little bastards with crumpled babies' knees and restlessly enquiring minds. Actually, there isn't anything wrong with *my* knees and in Partington I was always considered tall, but Orel's example stood me in good stead anyway, at least until the black widow cornered me in a country shithouse and cleaned me out for ever of all personal curiosity as to *what* Australian women love.

12

'So you've been pondering the necessity of suffering for the last hour?'

'Yes. Though I can't say I allowed the problem to overtax me.'

'Your mind was on higher things, perhaps.'

'I don't know about higher.'

'Lower, then? The Rosenfeldt lovelies?'

'Oh, they're not lower. And they *are* rather lovely.'

'Mm, they're a taste I suppose. If you like them North Shore.'

'North Shore?'

'That's Sydney for middle-class.'

The speaker was Frank Whiling, described to me in advance by Orel Rosenfeldt as a snuffed-out volcano, an inactive activist, a sort of soporiferous socialist who quarrelled with his own bedclothes and hailed from my part of the world. The drooler talking to him – 'I do, I *do* like them North Shore' – was of course me.

Orel had introduced me to Whiling in the back bar of the Ultima Thule, a vast yawning green-tiled beer-palace into which the young and old of Noonthorungee Uni spilled for the afternoon, and into which we spilled with them for a spot of lunch and in order that I should see where the malcontent Sydney Poms hung out. Orel didn't stay for lunch himself. He didn't really see the point of pubs, as I've said, since he could find better (and broader) shoulders to cry on than those of his own sex. But he had an apple with him and he sat with us for the ten or fifteen minutes it took him to prepare it for consumption. It was a privilege to watch Orel dissect an apple, akin to witnessing, close up, a famous surgeon's farewell operation. First he held it to the light, twirling it by its stalk, examining it for possible bruisings, discolorations or contusions, all the while expounding the beauties of the apple in general (as a genus) and the special virtues of the Jonathan in particular (as a species); then, with a fine fastidious precision, and employing a pocket penknife which he carried for the purpose, he peeled it – yes, he peeled it, taking care (for reasons of aesthetics) that the peel should come away in one unbroken spiral, but ensuring also (for reasons connected to his own hopes of longevity) that nothing which harboured germs or any other agent of the 'silent spring' should make the journey to his lips; after which he quartered it and cored it and seeded it; and only then, when every last possibility had been removed that he might suffer the discomfort of a single pip, only then did what was left of the fruit of the *Pyrus malus* itself enjoy the privilege of sliding through that other rosy miracle of Nature, Professor Orel Rosenfeldt's soft and plashy mouth.

Which ceremony completed – though not before he had taken me aside and warned me, 'He's a poisonous little rat, but of course you'll make up your own mind' – he left me to the company of Whiling.

The Ultima Thule was what was known in those days, and in those parts, as a Push pub. That's to say it was where Jean-Paul Sartre and Simone de Beauvoir would have gone to discuss *le néant* ('That means nothingness' – Lobelia Sneddon) had they lived in Sydney, but as they didn't the Sydney Libertarians, those tropical *fleurs du mal* of post-war Australia, went there instead. It was the kind of pub in which theories of amoralism were openly propounded, in which a woman might look directly into the eyes of a man not her husband, in which artists found their models, poets their inspiration, and where, in the back bar, querulous English migrants like Frank Whiling couldn't quite bring themselves to admit how lucky they were to have landed far from home in a country that paid them well and took them seriously.

'You'll notice,' Whiling said to me, 'that this room is tiled from floor to ceiling. Every other room's the same. And the outside. Do you know why that is?'

'Why?' I asked.

'So that they can hose it down at closing time.' He gave a tubercular sort of laugh and pushed his plate from him. He was thin and frazzled, feverish even, and hadn't attempted a single mouthful of the huge steak he'd ordered. He'd made the odd aggressive jab at his peas with his fork and those that he caught, he ate. That was his lunch.

But he drank freely. I went to the bar when it was my turn and was surprised to see that the system of hosing he'd referred to operated as a means of pouring beer into glasses as well as swilling it off the walls. Not being cultured myself in these matters I was rather impressed by a facility which enabled a barman to fill up to a dozen glasses in a single squirt. 'Nifty idea,' I said, when I returned. The beer was so cold that it anaesthetised my teeth and gums. I could have bitten off half the glass and not noticed. But I wasn't looking to be critical. 'Nice drop,' I said.

Whiling had snaked himself around his chair and was scratching his ankles. I could see that the mosquitoes had ganged up on him in the night. 'It's piss,' he said. 'But at least it's cold.'

The climate – the heat and the humidity – and the torments associated with the climate – the mosquitoes, the cockroaches, the thirst, the weariness the fever and the fret – occupied all Whiling's attentions. There was never a moment, throughout our desultory conversation, when he was not engaged in scratching or slapping or mopping some part of himself. Even when he was sleeping – and he was capable of dropping off during one of his own sentences – he was never still, and he would cuff himself awake suddenly, in pursuit of some imaginary malaria-bearing protozoon crawling up his leg.

'You working for Orel then?' he asked me, after he'd caught and murdered something high up in his trousers.

'Oh no,' I said. 'I'm no philosopher.'

He arched one of his scraggy eyebrows, as who should say, 'Is Orel?' But what he actually said was, 'So what will you be doing?'

Dinny had of course coached me in what I should say when the inevitable question arose. 'I'm here on one of those Commonwealth exchange things,' was how I seemed to remember it went. 'You know, I float around these parts for a few years and spread the good word about the old UK, and then, when I go home, I do the same for this place. Furthering cordial Common-wealth relations and all that. I'm afraid it's a bit of a lurk.' And I let out one of those self-deprecating little laughs designed to make a lurk easier for those not lucky enough to have found one.

But the gesture was wasted on Whiling. He didn't need to be spared. He'd found a lurk himself. He'd found Australia!

Nor was that the only reason my precautions were superfluous. 'I see,' he said. 'You're working for Free-dom Academy.'

I began to feel a bit itchy on my own account. I flicked a frozen corpse out of my beer, threw a look of disapproval at the juke-box – the Rolling Stones had just made it to Australia – and decided against an outright denial. 'I'm not exactly *working* for them,' I said.

'I know, I know, they just happen to be paying you.'

'I'm on a scholarship, if that's what you mean.'

He couldn't be bothered with that. 'I assume you know just who happens to be paying *them*.'

I didn't, as I've already explained. But I was always

prepared to believe that there was bound to be something bad behind all organizations, as behind all men. Wasn't that partly why I wasn't a socialist? 'All money's dirty if you trace it back far enough,' I answered. 'We'd all starve if we were particular.'

As soon as I'd said that, I knew he was going to reply, 'Thousands already do'.

'Thousands already do,' he replied.

I took a long look at him. He had a sharp pointed face, like one of those dogs the sporting working classes of Partington used to let off leads at weekends to chase rabbits down their warrens. But if he had a nose for trouble I doubted that he'd ever dirtied himself underground. He looked to me as though he'd seized his opportunities in a good grammar school in the Malvern Hills prior to nine slow terms at Oxford. I decided that his clothes were casually expensive also, for all that they were crushed and wet and blooded with a thousand tiny deaths. 'But you're not one of them,' I said.

He fainted clean away for a moment or two, as a consequence of the heat and the alcohol and the acridity of the air in the Ultima Thule; but when he came round he wasn't looking especially triumphant. 'No, I'm not one of them,' he agreed. He let me see that he thought life had dealt him a low blow however, spilling him out into the back bar of this hell hole.

'So what do you do?' I thought it was time I enquired.

'I used to work for Orel.'

It was my turn to arch an eyebrow. 'You a philosopher?'

'I said *used*.'

'I gather from your tone that you fell out.'

Whiling wiped his throat with his handkerchief. It was a thin, miserable throat. Which was perhaps why thin, miserable sounds came out of it. 'Orel is not what you might call dispassionate when it comes to marking examinations and awarding prizes. What would you say the chances are of the Robert Menzies Medal for

Philosophy and the Burke and Wills Overseas Travel Fellowship both being fairly awarded, five years running – that's to say since Orel took the chair – to the daughter of a judge?'

Some phrases carry, for some persons, an inexplicable potency. You couldn't, for example, say 'Nordic beauty' or 'Mrs August Strindberg' to my old friend Ramsay without his instantly buckling at the knees. And I was affected similarly by the phrase 'the daughter of a judge'. To put it at its bluntest, it made me want one. And I had no trouble imagining why Orel might have felt the same. If he'd been fortunate enough to find one I could see why he wanted to go on rewarding her. Though five years running, as I conceded to Frank Whiling, was perhaps overdoing it.

'Not the same daughter of the same judge,' he snapped. He looked as disgusted by me as he was by everything else.

'Oh I see,' I said. 'Orel has awarded ten medals and fellowships to ten *different* judges' daughters.' I hadn't realised there were that many judges in Australia. But naturally the news was not unwelcome to me. 'And you're asking me what the chances are of ten judges' daughters being worthy winners?' I didn't really have to think about it. 'I'd say, reasonable.'

Whiling blew his nose and stared into the contents of his handkerchief. 'You'll hit it off fine with Orel,' he said.

I decided not to be stung by that. 'I hope so,' I said. 'I'm only sorry that you didn't. But you still haven't told me what you do now.'

From the frantic raid he suddenly made into his own shirt I fully expected to see him bring out a family of scorpions, but his hands were empty when they reappeared – bleeding but empty. 'Did you just ask me something?' he remembered.

'I asked you what you're doing now, as you no longer work for Orel.'

'Now?' He managed another of those death-rattle laughs from the wreckage of his lungs. 'Now I do what you do.'

I very nearly said, 'What, work for Freedom Academy International?' Which would have been pretty stupid of me, considering that he obviously didn't and that that would have been tantamount to a confession that I obviously did. What stopped me was not my own circumspection but the distraction caused by a party of malcontent Pommy migrants falling through the open doors of the Ultima Thule, recognising Frank Whiling, and seating themselves, to the accompaniment of sundry minor moans about the heat and the humidity, around our table.

As was the case with Whiling, they were none of them, I noticed, fully able to hide the shame of having come to good only in another country; and yet they were none of them, at the same time, prepared to spurn the happy fortune that had brought them here. They were going to stay, but they weren't going to stay with grace. It struck me that it couldn't be easy, not knowing whether you believed yourself failed or favoured; and I could see why they turned to Whiling's brand of sulking self-satisfaction, his irked narcissism, to explain their condition to themselves.

Whiling, I was soon to learn, had only recently made the journey back to the old country – a permanent return it was meant to be too; books packed, friends farewelled, all that – but he found the folks back home so uninterested in him, so incurious as to where he'd been, so unhelpful as to what he'd do, and so indifferent as to who he *was*, that he caught the next boat back. He wasn't the first Englishman to be trapped in the cruel dilemma of being thought interesting only in a country that bored him stiff.

Which might be why he seemed to take such savage pleasure in introducing me to the new arrivals one by one, lingering over their names and occupations, gloating over the details of their exile, so that it was impossible for any of us to determine whether the butt of his humour was them, me, himself, insolicitous Britain, or gullible Australia.

In this spirit I met Margaret who had been a secretary in Saffron Walden but was now, according to Whiling, the roughest root in Randwick; and I met the Haygarths from Exmouth, who spoke so softly it was impossible to hear them, and who streaked their hair to match their cats, cats being, according to Whiling, the only living things besides each other they could bear to live with; and I met Sefton Goldberg from Manchester, who was a world authority on shy girls in Dickens and always wore a leather tie (even in bed, according to Whiling); and I met Hugo from the Midlands, whose father was National Front candidate for Nuneaton South and who was living in a terraced house in Ultimo with one of Australia's foremost spokesmen on Aboriginal affairs – it was a subject for ribald conjecture, according to Whiling, which aspect of Hugo's new life his father would find it more difficult to swallow: his lover's colour or his lover's sex.

'The funny thing is,' said Hugo, 'that my old man paid for me to come out here because he thought the White Australia policy was a guarantee, no longer certain in England, of the colour of his grandchildren. He had a vision of Australia as an Aryan haven. He just forgot the Abos.'

'Most people do,' Whiling drawled.

This was a cue for a little spasm of righteousness to shake the whole company, and even the normally indecipherable Haygarths could be heard agreeing that the Aborigines were too often tragically forgotten.

I thought this was rich coming from a people whose ancestors had hunted the indigenous inhabitants of Australia down for sport, or at least I *would* have thought that had the spider got me earlier and rendered me a radical then, when I had the strength for it, instead of now, when I am past posing threats.

The question of my radicalism, that's to say, the question of my lack of it, was due to come up the minute we stopped lamenting the plight of the Aborigines, because now that everybody had been introduced to me, it was my turn to be introduced to them. And I couldn't see Whiling begrudging himself the pleasure of telling them what he'd more or less accurately guessed I was here to do.

Though in the event I wasn't prepared for the promptness with which he got around to it. 'And this is Leon Forelock,' he said. 'Leon works for Freedom Academy International. Leon's come to save us all from drugs, pornography, the communists, and the little yellow devils from the north. Haven't you, Leon?'

I made a decision on the spot (and I haven't once reneged on it) never to look for subtlety from Frank Whiling.

'I see that you like to stir shit,' I muttered.

'Like I say,' he said, 'I do what you do.'

I made another decision too, and that was to break the pattern of this conversation. 'Let me get you all a drink,' I offered, and without bothering to ask them what their poison was I pushed my way past them to the bar.

I was relieved to find it busy. That gave me time to compose my thoughts. I didn't yet have any experience, remember, of undercover work. And as I hadn't yet done any work to cover over, I couldn't tell whether I felt foolish for being found out or foolish for having nothing to be found out for. But I knew I was in no hurry to get back to the pious Poms. So I didn't rush the barman. I made it easy for him to miss my eye. When he came to my end of the bar I dropped my change, or suddenly remembered that I needed to wash my hands. 'Hose me a dozen beers,' I said at last, when there was no one else but me waiting. The barman struck me as having a pleasant Australian face; dented and put upon, but not intimidated. From the other end of the room a woman with a Spanish comb in her hair was giving me the sort of look for which the Ultima Thule was famous. I suddenly decided I was going to like it here. 'And hose yourself something, sport,' I added, doing my best not to let that sound like an afterthought.

13

'LEEE-OHN! Leeeeorrhn!'

For all her air of wonderful surprise at finding me standing in her portico in my new oatmeal tropical suit, Trilby was expecting me. I had thought it best to warn my father and the woman with whom he had run all the way from Partington to Vaucluse that I was here, in order to spare us all the embarrassment of their not recognizing me. It was years since they'd last seen me, and I liked to think that I'd made some progress in that time from the wide-eyed nearly-nine-year-old in short pants who'd watched them sprint off. It's true I was in short pants once again, but these were stylish, the bottom half of my new summer suit, worn rather rakishly above long pure-white socks pulled up to the knees, Governor-General aide-de-camp fashion. So I'd dropped them a line from Suez to say that I was on my way, and another one from Colombo to say that I was getting closer, and then I'd rung them from the Rosenfeldts' to inform them that I was on their doorstep. In other words this was a strict and long-standing appointment I was keeping, although you would never have known it from Trilby's finely crafted spontaneity. Breeding, you see. Its radiance undiminished by time or distance. I hadn't realised how much I'd missed it. I immediately felt that it had been worth circumnavigating the globe just to hear my name made long again.

My father wasn't home yet. He was emptying the tills of their three *boutiques* – the one in Elizabeth Bay, the one in Double Bay, and the one in Rose Bay. They were all called *Trilby's* and sold only European *haute couture.* There was of course – there still is – a great demand for French or Italian labels in the Eastern Suburbs of Sydney. It helps to allay the terrors of distance to have words like Paris or Milan stitched into your clothing. It reminds you of who you really are and where you really come from. Years later, whenever I was flush and wanted to demonstrate my affection for Venie and Maroochi, I would take them to *Trilby's* at Double Bay (that was the most exclusive) and fit them up with something tight and shiny and just in from Florence. I used to love shopping for clothes with those girls, especially Maroochi who had so much static electricity in her hair that you could hear it crackling in the changing room the minute she raised her arms. I made no secret of my family connections with the business. Venie and Maroochi both knew that I was good for fifteen per cent discount. And they didn't think that took anything away from my generosity. It was understood that I had to make economies some-where, with the two of them to support. I'm not saying that they didn't contribute practically to the manage-ment of our household themselves; but synchronized swimmers had to be very careful, in those days, to protect their amateur status.

Apart from its greater exclusivity, the other reason for patronizing the Double Bay *boutique* was that my father himself was usually in personal attendance there. I didn't especially enjoy the spectacle of him in his little velvet suit, bent so low in the name of respectful service that the ends of his waxed moustaches tickled the gilded ankles of his clientele, but I didn't think it was fair to withhold Venie and Maroochi from him. Remem-bering his innocent enthusiasm for electricity I put my finger to my lips the first time Maroochi went into the changing room, so that nothing should interfere with his enjoyment of listening to the sparks fly. A faint smell, such as might come from the kitchens of an expensive restaurant, of top-quality flesh browning, filled the shop. The minuscule epicurean who had given me life leaned against a rack of Christian Dior nightdresses and inhaled. If that had been his last moment of sensuous existence we would both have been content. But I had another treat in store for him. 'Maroochi is the daughter of a judge,' I told him. I'll never forget the look of shimmering collusive ingratiation which crept across his face. His pale impermanent eyes only once shone with a greater and more abject love for me, and that was when I told him that Venie was the daughter of a Liberal State Premier.

Liberal in Australia, incidentally, means Conservative (unlike in England where it means nothing very much in particular), and is not to be confused with Labour, which also means Conservative only not to quite the same degree.

I don't mean to be splenetic. Blame the spider. The miracle is that a country with so many better things to do with itself should have got around to thinking up names for political parties at all. Politics was certainly far from my mind – even Tristanism receded – as I sat with Trilby beside her pool, drinking ice-cold orange juice enlivened with sparkling white wine, watching the ferries transporting heat-stunned hedonists from one paradisal cove to another, and the yachts, careless of time or destination, shuddering like summer lovers to the faintest sigh of the breeze. An alabaster cherub held out an unshaking tray to me on which I rested my glass when I wanted to smoke or nibble macadamia nuts or savour guacamole or merely stretch and whimper. It occurred to me that this was a perfect setting for one of Orel Rosenfeldt's seminars on the Tragic Condition of Man.

'Well,' said Trilby, after she'd refilled my glass a couple more times, sliced me more guava, iced me more paw-paw, and failed to get any sense out of me on the question of what I was doing here, 'how you've grown!'

I'd often thought, while I was still growing, that as soon as I'd grown completely I would travel out to Vaucluse and show myself to the fine lady who had patted my head and stroked my cheek in the park in Partington, just as, presumably – since he was no bigger than I was – she patted and stroked my father. 'What a man you've become, Leeeorhhn,' I had imagined her saying, still looking down upon me only not from so great a height. And my anticipation of this moment was so exquisite that the hairs I had not yet sprouted rose and trembled on my narrow chest.

So why, now that I really was grown (I assumed there was no more of me to come) and Trilby really had noticed, why wasn't it all as good – it was good enough, don't mistake me – but why wasn't it *as* good as I'd always thought it would be?

Of course Trilby too had grown. Grown older and grown rounder. But I don't think that was the problem. I've never been against age, particularly in women, whom it in the main improves; and Trilby had never loomed in any of my imaginings as anything less than substantial – as massive and as immovable as her class (how my father had had to tug at her to get her moving that last afternoon in Partington), as grand and as monumental as those hotels and opera-houses through whose vestibules and loggias I used to picture her, my father a mere shadow at her side, shouldering her furs. Her furs! There was the difference and the change. Many and varied were the scenes I'd put together over the years, in which Trilby would welcome me to Vaucluse, marvel at the man I had become, and once again take my name and prolong it in her mouth – exactly as she was doing this afternoon; except that not for one single moment in those slow-moving dramas of my soul did she appear without that very glass-eyed fox, in which she had secretly met and finally run off with my ferrety father, wound around her throat. Here in Vaucluse, at the water's edge, in the Sydney heat, she was denuded of her symbolism. A whole harem of silkworms might have expended their yellow labours on the loose flowing robe which kept her cool, but no bristling creature, slaughtered expressly for her, sat like an immemorial right to spoils upon her back. No fox, no beaver, no sable, not even a dead dingo.

In short, Trilby in Australia was not as unimpeachably aristocratic, to my eye, as Trilby in Partington. Even the Vaucluse villa, with its swimming pool and cherubs, its French provincial furniture, its eighteenth-century watercolours of Scottish grouse moors, and its commanding views of harbour and ocean and mosaic'd verandas, failed to match the quiet certainty of Trilby's Georgian ruin in the Wirral, whose ancient wiring my father had attended to with his little box of silver screw-drivers all those years before. You could feel the argument for money out here but you couldn't remember the case for class. Like everybody else in Australia who aspired to manners and sophistication, Trilby looked trumped-up.

Mind you, trumpery has a charm all its own. Pretension and imposture can carry a heavy charge of sexuality. Whose pulses ever race for what is natural? And if Trilby was no longer the *lady* I'd remembered since I was nine, she was certainly still the *woman*. Put it this way: I couldn't possibly feel, in sight of Sydney Harbour Bridge, that Trilby conferred a title on me every time she used my name, on the other hand I would willingly have pushed under the Manly Ferry any man (except my father) whose name she used instead.

Although, for some reason, growth had quickly become the theme of our conversation while we waited for my father, we didn't – more's the pity – confine our talk to how big *I'd* grown. Other things were growing hereabouts also. The population was growing, so was the

142

economy, so was violence. According to Trilby it wasn't safe to walk the streets of Sydney at night if you were a homosexual. Or even if you weren't. Only a few months before my father had been set upon in The Rocks because his fairy tread of universal servility had been misconstrued.

'He came home black and blue, Leeorhn,' Trilby told me, 'in an ambulance.'

Trilby wasn't to know, of course – which of us were? – that these poofter-bashings of the sixties were just the final heroic effort of an essentially homosexual culture to deny itself. The love that did not dare to speak its name, aware of a new and overpowering impulse to volubility, tried *felo de se* as a last resort. It didn't work. Now, when we speak of poofter-bashings in Australia we mean being bashed by poofters.

It goes without saying that I take back, today, everything I wrote for *The Black Sail* about the dangerous, morale-sapping effemination of Australian society. 'The Marxist–Leninist totalitarian powers do not themselves officially tolerate androgyny,' I wrote. 'But they are not beyond encouraging it to flourish in the Western and Pacific Democracies, understanding that it will work its way through all levels of free communities like a moral myxomatosis, undermining that matrix of family and inter-personal loyalties which for so long has been our strength and our glory.' Yes, despite my three lost days with Dinmont Manifest in a Theological Seminary in Cambridge, I lent my weight to the great monosexual crusade. No lover of children, couples, nuclear families or any other hellish domestic units myself, I none the less became their most articulate champion. Such is the power of self-suppression conferred by a degree in the Moral Niceties from Cambridge. But all this was before the spider got me. Now I give a little inward cheer whenever I see a couple of strapping Australian boys walking arm in arm down William Street; and if I don't find a rough and hairy companion of my own it is only because the spider has ruined me for *all* affairs of the heart.

This, though, was not the growth area that was of most urgent concern to Trilby. She was much more immediately interested in the way Vaucluse was growing: denser and noisier and higher, so much so that she was concerned for her space (she called it her *lebensraum*), her peace (she called it her tranquillity) and her watery view (her panorama, her prospect, her vista). She pointed towards some new tower blocks, as yet uncompleted, already a dozen storeys high and still climbing. 'They call them Home Units,' she told me. Our eyes met in keen European disdain for Australian vulgarity. 'You know what I call them?'

I didn't. But I waited for her to tell me. I expected her to call them something pretty damaging.

'I call them' – she paused infinitesimally here and curled a fleshy nostril, exactly as I'd seen her do on the tram in Partington in 1949 when the conductor gave her trouble, a contemptuous curl of complete animal assurance which made me loathe Hester and Nesta who shrivelled into little hairy balls of shame before conductors – 'I call them . . . flats!'

It was even more damaging than I'd expected. I had always had an idea that there was a correct attitude to that system of living on top of one another practised in Partington by the poor, that's to say – given that everyone in Partington was poor – by the very poor, but I had never suspected that the correct attitude was quite so severe. Flats. Oof! I was glad that I wasn't a few miserable tons of concrete masquerading as a Home Unit myself, with someone as withering as Trilby looking on, knowing what I really was. Funny then that I should have ended up living in one of those very tower blocks that Trilby pointed out to me that afternoon. Funnier still that it should have been Trilby's money that acquired it.

But I'm running too far ahead. I haven't finished yet

with growing things. Or at least Trilby hadn't. There was still my father to talk about. My father, growing? Not in size, obviously. But in years, in wealth, and in love. It seemed to matter to Trilby that I understand how much more my father loved her now, even than when they ran from Partington for thirty days and thirty nights (for that was how I had imagined it) without ever once unlacing their fingers each from each. And how much more, come to that, she now loved him.

'I'm pleased it's a love-match,' I said. I felt a passing twinge of bitterness on my mother's behalf, but I was as pleased as I said I was.

Trilby looked dissatisfied with my phraseology. Clearly 'love-match' didn't fully get it. 'It's a grand passion,' she said. She had heavy, even pendulous features like the English royal family's, Germanic, Habsburgian, and she showed me a profile as solemn and as regal as anything I had ever seen on the back of a penny.

'You make it sound tragic. Aren't grand passions generally fatal?'

'Ah, Leeorhn, Leeorhn,' she said, allowing gravity in both its senses to have its way with her head, 'fatal, I fear, is the only word.'

I waited for what else she would say but she remained silent. Her face was averted and I wondered if she was crying. I let the cicadas screech uninterrupted for a while and I diluted my orange juice with some more sparkling white wine. Then I thought I'd better ask, 'Are you ill?'

For an answer she rose from her deck-chair and stood before me, confident and colossal, bourgeoise and blooming, trumpery for all the world under a patina of coarse Australian health.

I saw my mistake. 'My father then?'

She nodded. She possessed a technique for allowing her features to drop, at will, so that her already long

145

face became an exaggerated mask of mournfulness. For some reason I associated this melancholy elongation, too, with high birth. She was standing with her back to the harbour and behind her another liner was pulling out, carrying the insatiable away to discomfort and disappointment. 'Your father is very sick,' she said.

And when I stared up at her enquiringly she added, 'Lovesick. Sick unto death with desire for me.' She waved away objections that I hadn't offered. 'I know, I know – I should take it as a compliment, me an old bird in her fifties. But it's killing him. Look, here he comes. Look at him, the lovely man. He's emptied all the tills and locked all the shops and done all the banking and he's carrying me flowers. He's brought me flowers every day for fourteen years. I have to throw them away when he's not watching. You can scarcely breathe in the house for living things – his love-offerings. Can't you see, Leeorhn, his devotion is sapping his vitals?'

That evening, after *bœuf bourgignon*, I sat with my father by the pool. Trilby didn't join us. She had invented a number of transparently implausible domestic tasks for herself so that a long-lost father and his boy should have time alone together. I suspect she was grateful for the opportunity to get in some surreptitious destruction of the latest flowers. Every now and then I would catch sight of her slipping out of the house carrying black plastic refuse-sacks, and once, out of the corner of my eye, I saw her jumping up and down on what looked to me suspiciously like the severed heads of white carnations.

My father was just as restless. He was in and out of the pool. Whenever the heat became too much for him, which was every ten or fifteen minutes, he would untie his towelling robe, beneath which he wore only his little boy's bathing trunks, and dive in. Despite the final promise my mother had extracted from me, that

I would make the fullest possible use of the adulterous pool, I didn't dive in with him. I couldn't feel that we were familiar enough to be gambolling about in the water together. Besides, Trilby might have been telling the truth when she said he was dying, and the last thing I wanted was to be involved in some terrible aquatic tragedy with a father I hadn't seen for fourteen years. When life comes at you with that kind of brutally obvious symbolism you owe it to your own self-respect to back away.

In fact he seemed little changed to me from how I had remembered him. He looked dreadfully fragile, it's true, but that was certainly not ascribable to his devotion to Trilby: he had looked just as wispily insubstantial when he loved my mother, and he had not died of love of her. I did notice this, though: he was stiller than he used to be – yes, he was in and out of the pool, but I never once heard him say, 'I'll be off now' – and he was sadder also. I admit I was on the look-out for some such deterioration. He'd disappointed me, you see – speaking impersonally now – by staying with Trilby. It had been stabilising for me, over the years, knowing where he was, and it was good seeing him again; but I think I would altogether have preferred it, enjoyed a more abiding sense of pride, had I heard that he'd hopped it to Mount Isa with an heiress.

'It sure is staggeringly beautiful here,' I said to him, during one of his dry periods. I was overcome by the rich sweet smell of blossoms I hadn't yet learned to name. Lights flickered on the water. A string quartet played Borodin a few villas down. I don't mean on record either. When it stopped I could hear the applause of about two hundred culture-crazy overcompensating Australians. I too wanted to clap, and not only the music – but the night, the stars, the bridge, the end of journeying, the infinite promise.

'Yes, but it's a bit far from everything,' he said.

I'd just come from everything. So I didn't find the argument all that compelling. 'A bit far from what?'

'Oh, I don't know. Home?'

'Home?'

Maybe my surprise was greater than it should have been. It was undoubtedly more explicit than I'd meant it to be. Without actually naming them I'd as good as said, 'What, Partington? Hester and Nesta? The *salon*? My mother?' Which was perhaps why my father didn't answer me but unloosened his robe and slipped into the pool instead.

He was so light that he was able to float a centimetre above the water, like the gnats which had arrived thinking they'd found a river. My father's presence didn't seem to deter them. He was just one more mouth to feed. But if it had come to a fight between him and them it was certain he'd have lost. So I kept an eye on him. And I persisted with my surprise. 'Do you really get homesick?'

He did three lengths of the surface of the pool, barely causing a ripple, then he flitted out and dried himself on a towel the size of a pixie's handkerchief. When he was back in his wrap he took me by the wrist. Apart from our initial handshake this was our first physical contact. The lightness of his touch upset me. But I could understand how, for the ladies with wet hair in my mother's *salon*, it might have seemed like an electric charge. 'Let me show you something,' he said, leading me up marble steps to the highest point of what Trilby called the *property*, a tiny turreted folly which Trilby called her *belvedere*. 'Look around you. See all those boats in the marinas, see all those fine houses and gardens, see those tennis courts, those swimming pools, those Roman verandas, those garages big enough to hold five cars – how many do you think are owned by Europeans who came here so recently they are still struggling with the language?'

This was not the kind of thing I was clued up on.

Migration patterns was not a component part of Moral Decencies. Journeys of the soul I knew about; I hadn't studied where bodies go. But most questions have their answers buried in them. 'I suppose lots,' I said.

'You suppose right. Lots. And do you know what happens to a suburb like this when Boris Rubaschkin or Galina Vishnevskaya comes to sing at the Sydney Town Hall?'

I was astonished that my father had heard of such people let alone was capable of pronouncing their names. Then I remembered the opera-scarf he had worn, even for breakfast, during his last days in Partington. It was the opera-scarf that had finally turned Hester and Nesta against him.

'Well I suppose it empties,' I guessed.

'It empties for the night of the concert. But what does it do for a fortnight afterwards?'

He had me there. But I gave it a go. 'It sings Russian songs?'

My father still had hold of my wrist and he tightened his grip on it. 'It throbs, Leon. Living in the Eastern Suburbs of Sydney for a month after a recital of songs from the old country is like living inside a giant cello. There are some streets in which you can feel the pavement vibrating with emotion beneath you. This is a sentimental country. Everybody is a long way from home. There are pools winners here, Leon, lottery winners, refugees, runaways, people who have come thirteen thousand miles bent double in the boot of a motor car with their fortunes hidden in protective wrappings in their small intestine. They have risked everything to get here. This is the fulfilment of their dreams' – I could tell he was speaking from the heart – 'and still they cry. Sometimes I've stood on this very spot, here, where you and I are standing now, and I've heard the sobs of grown men and women from as far away as Perth and Adelaide. The whole country shakes nightly; but in Vaucluse, after a recital of folk-songs in

149

the Sydney Town Hall, feeling is so strong it registers on a seismograph.'

I stood by his side and listened with him to the night. I tried to hear beyond the merely haphazard noises of the harbour, the clinking of the boats, the lapping of the water, the irritable coughing of the mermaids. And at last, even though there hadn't been a recital from a Russian baritone for months, I made out the low moaning threnody of fourteen million souls in exile.

'So don't ask me,' my father concluded, 'if I'm homesick.'

Just before we went inside he held me back to enquire whether I was the bearer of any messages from Partington. I led him to the light and lowered my head, so that he could see the bald circle, still not fully grown over, which my mother had given me, once she knew I was off to Australia, as a farewell cut. 'Just this,' I said.

He inspected the damage thoughtfully, in the manner of someone digesting the import of a letter.

'Fair enough,' he said at last.

Which I took to mean that he wasn't going to bother replying.

Trilby wouldn't hear of my returning to the Rosenfeldts' that night. She had made up a bed for me in the spare room and I lay in it, wide awake, for hours, listening to my father driving her to the borders of Climaxos but seemingly never quite able to take her across. The noise issuing from Trilby was very similar, in pitch and desolation, to that which I had made out earlier, standing on the *belvedere* with my father, as coming from Australia's waifs and strays. Trilby too was a long way from home.

The sounds of other people's erotic labours had never held much charm for me, and I would have far preferred it if I could have got to sleep. But it worried me that my father should be striving so hard, after all these years, to see Trilby safely over. Now I understood why he had not shot through with an heiress from Mount Isa. He still had unfinished business with Trilby. And this was presumably what Trilby meant when she told me that he was dying of devotion. He hadn't got the better of her yet and the effort to do so was killing him. I could actually hear his breathing through the intervening walls. I could hear his little heart beat.

Orgasms are funny things. I know all about them after what the Redback did to me. Three weeks of unshrinking verticality in the serious bites ward of a Wangaratta infirmary will turn the most unthinking of brute instinctives into a philosopher. Take my word for it, then, when I say that the great paroxysm towards which we all tirelessly labour – whether on our own behalf as an entitlement, or for other people as a favour – is every bit as pure an act of the mind, as exquisite a tremor of the intelligence, as a thought is. My father failed to get to the bottom of Trilby, failed to escort her to the bottom of herself, for the simple reason that he chose to believe she was bottomless. Infinity and mystery live in the single sexual eye of the infinitely mystified. Even after fourteen years in her company my father still thought he was wrestling with an unattainable aristocrat. Which was why he brought her home flowers each night as an act of obeisance and began afresh, where he'd originally started, on his knees. Small wonder he made no progress. He was Sisyphus and Trilby was his rolling stone. His gemstone. His grindstone. And finally his tombstone.

But I couldn't be expected to understand all this as I lay awake on that first night in the villa in Vaucluse. I wasn't so smart then. I was a Redback-virgin. And the sound of my father hastening his death in pursuit of an unreachable Trilby he himself had put out of reach only engaged me, as it were, on the side of his ambitions. If anything happened to him, I thought, I would take over where he left off. Because I too needed to know what it was like to tip an aristocrat over the edge.

14

THERE ARE ABOUT four hundred species of reptile surviving in Australia, ranging in size and malevolence from the retiring water-skink and the common merely barking gecko to the twelve-foot deadly taipan and the mountain devil (the *Moloch horridus*) which can kill a grown man with a single wink. Leaving aside the platypus and the echidna, which are monotremes anyway – the missing link between the crawlers and the hoppers – there are about three hundred species of marsupials, plus four or five dozen other ratty specimens which make do without a pouch. I can be reasonably precise about the numbers because I have intimate knowledge of every one of them. All seven hundred and fifty, and a few more besides, were regular visitors to the North Shore waterside garden studio flat I moved into on CIA money the minute I could see I was overstaying my welcome at the Rosenfeldts'.

I had only been there four nights, one of which I'd spent with my father and Trilby in Vaucluse, but it was obvious that my presence was inhibiting Nonie's expressions of bitterness. If I was Orel's guest then Orel had to stay at home to entertain me, and if Orel stayed at home to entertain me he couldn't simultaneously stay away. It stood to reason therefore that if Orel couldn't stay away, Nonie couldn't castigate him through closed and drooping lips. I was interfering badly with their domestic rituals. The peace in the house was upsetting the children. I had to go.

The North Shore was the obvious place for me to choose to settle after what Frank Whiling had told me about the number of judges (and therefore judges' daughters) who lived there. But he had omitted all mention of the wildlife. The only warning of what might be waiting to slither under my door was given me by Nonie and Orel on the morning they drove me, at great speed, over the Bridge and helped carry my luggage down the cliff-face to my new home. After they'd gone I discovered that they'd left me a cardboard box containing a few basic provisions – milk, Weetabix, apples, and chocolate spread – together with an assortment of aerosol sprays, anti-mosquito coils, netting, antiseptic ointments and adhesive plaster dressings. It was very kind of them. But if you have ever tried to hold off a giant tree-climbing iguana twice the size of your father with nothing but a can of fly-spray, you will understand what I mean when I say that the Rosenfeldts might have done even better by me. They might at the very least have left me a brace of pistols.

As things turned out it was only the jar of chocolate spread that got me out of a tight corner. I don't know if all goannas have a sweet tooth (goanna, by the way, is an affectionate Australian corruption of iguana), but mine fortunately did.

He was waiting for me, on the phone, when I got back from my first acclimatizing walk around my adopted neighbourhood. I'd only been out about an hour, generally taking my bearings and looking out for my first judge. But that was time enough for him to break in and make himself at home. I say he was on the phone but he wasn't, of course, ringing anybody up. Unlike just about everything else in Australia goannas are not great conversationalists. He was simply using the receiver as a handy item of furniture for taking the weight off his stumpy front feet. He was propped up on it leaning forward as a man might recline upon a lectern. He resembled, both in his indolent attitude and in his colouring – dark brown with yellow stripes was the colour of the Malapert sporting jersey – the Rugby-

154

playing engineers whose pulpy features I used to be so touched by at Cambridge. Certainly his shoulders were as powerful as theirs were. And he had the same look of slumbering menace. If he'd shouted 'Olly, olly!' at me and shown a little less intelligence in the one eye he bothered to keep open I could well have thought I was back on the river at Fen Ditton, enjoying Bumps Week.

I'm the sort of person who must always have someone to blame when he's in trouble. Even as I stood paralysed with terror, afraid to turn and make a dash for it in case the goanna came after me, and unable to use the phone because he was on it, I ran through the long list of those responsible for getting me into this. I won't bore you with all their names, but they included Frank Whiling, Orel Rosenfeldt, Trilby, Hester and Nesta, Mario Lanza, God, Father Dinmont Manifest, the captain of the *Gloriana* and, obviously, Noreen Routledge whose guide to getting on in Australia had been my Bible during the voyage out. Where was the good of knowing how to say no to a cocktail mixed especially for you by the Governor-General if you hadn't been told what to do when you come eyeball to eyeball, in your own room, with a ten-foot lizard who might never himself have seen anything quite so succulent as the soft skin of an Englishman fresh in from Partington?

I can't now remember what I thought I might achieve with the aerosol spray. I can only be certain that everything I did was dictated by blind panic, fear for my life, and metaphysical shock. I knew that the cardboard box was still where the Rosenfeldts had left it, by the front door; I knew that the can of spray was still in it; and I knew that I could reach it without having to make any sudden movements. In the circumstances, considering that this was the first dinosaur I had ever confronted, and that the previous biggest animal I had ever seen out of a cage was a Partington whippet, I call that lucidity. I believe that I even had the presence of mind to shake the contents of the can, surreptitiously, behind my back. Then I flipped off its metal cap, dropped to one knee like a marksman, and using both thumbs for maximum pressure I sprayed him between the eyes.

I suppose I ought to have been a few feet closer. By the time it reached the goanna the Mortein was only a fine mist. For all the discomfort it caused him he could have been out in a light summer drizzle, he that was built to withstand cataclysms. He didn't care much for the smell though. He opened his jaws, showing me a flat bluish tongue on which a whole tribe of Aborigines might have fed for a week, and he spat. I can still visualize the gesture. It signified complete boredom and something pretty like contempt.

In the meantime it was me that the pressurised pyrethrum was choking. The goanna watched me wheeze for a while – he even opened his other eye to get a more panoramic view of my distress – then he brought his tail around from behind the telephone table and thumped the floor with it, an unambiguous expression of goanna mirth, without any doubt at all a goanna's way of shouting, 'Encore!'

It was the movement of the tail that caused me to lose my nerve altogether and to throw the can at him. The tail has always seemed to me the most frightening part of any animal. Partly because of its apparent capacity for independent action, and partly, I presume, because I haven't got one myself. Call it a form of penis envy if you wish. Though I suspect that women would have even more vexed relations with the penis than they already deny they do if men carried it behind them and could thump the floor with it. Or if they could shed it altogether, as a distraction, the way many of my goanna's smaller relatives were to do when I attacked them with garden spades or broom handles during the five or six years I was to stay on the North Shore, waging singlehanded war against every warm-

or cold-blooded thing that wasn't instantly recognizable as a judge's daughter.

I missed him with the can, but he responded to my change of tactics with a few variations of his own. He reared back. He knocked the phone over. He tried to climb the wardrobe.

I didn't want him up there. I am blessed with a reasonable amount of self-knowledge and I knew that I would not sleep well at night with a goanna on my wardrobe. I threw apples at him, I threw the milk, I threw the packet of Weetabix, and then, because I had nothing else to throw, I threw the jar of chocolate spread. That caught him. On what I suppose you'd have to call his knee, rear nearside. And with sufficient force to smash itself and to cause him to lose his footing. I've since learned that goannas frequently fall out of trees, many of them a lot higher than my wardrobe, but I knew nothing of this congenital clumsiness at the time and thought I'd dealt him a blow that was either mortal or of a kind to make him now turn really nasty.

He landed with a thud and a crunch of glass on the far side of my bed. I stayed where I was, with my back to the door, unable to see anything of him but the round of his shoulders. If I'd just come in I would have wondered why there was a large, old-fashioned lady's handbag on the floor by my bedside. And then I would have wondered why it was making a slurping noise, such as comes from sucking at an empty straw. At first I thought he was licking his wounds, but when I heard glass being crunched and a couple of gravelly burps I was able to put two and two together. After about five minutes he came waddling out from behind the bed, his dewlap rippling with contentment. He was limping slightly but he knew his way around the flat. He crossed the carpet to the french windows without so much as a backward roll of the eye in my direction. He pushed aside the glass door with his front foot, just like a

Malapert Rugby-player fending off a tackle, banged once with his tail, and was gone.

I never saw him again. But every night before I went to bed I would leave a jar of chocolate spread at the bottom of the garden, just under the wooden pier the yachtsmen used to tie their rowing boats to, and it was always polished off, glass and all, by the morning.

The description of how I fortified my flat – how I built barricades and set traps; how I lit flares and put down poison; how I fought bare-knuckled with a homicidal bush-tailed possum, and wrestled for two hours with a four-eyed tarantula hairier than Hester's chin – all this belongs to the conventions of adventure narrative and can have no place in the story of a spiritual conversion.

But I will repeat here the advice I gave a young Englishman I found scratched and shaking in a North Shore bar several years after my duel with the goanna:

'Buy yourself a vacuum cleaner. Not the upright kind but the one that comes with a long sinuous hose. The longer the hose the better. You'll find that there's nothing more efficient for getting the huntsman off your curtain rails and the praying mantis out from under your bed. Have you got a garden? A water frontage? Good, then make sure you buy a generous extension lead. That way you'll be able to clean up the bull-ants and the funnel-webs and suck the cicadas clean out of your jacaranda-tree. I've even found the brush attachment useful for pushing back the sharks. They break their teeth on it and they hate the noise.'

I met him again a few weeks later in the same bar. His skin had healed up nicely but he was still shaking. He had taken my advice and everything had worked out exactly as I said it would until he had tried to vacuum up a snake, tail first. He thought he'd been successful too, and was just rewarding himself with a stiff brandy when the hose started to move. Slowly at first, but then with more vigorous convolutions. For two hours he had to look on in horror while his vacuum cleaner writhed around the room, wrapping itself about the furniture and spitting poison.

Which just shows that you should never take an Englishman's native intelligence for granted. How was I to know he needed telling that you don't Hoover up a death adder?

I realize there are questions to be asked relating to my vendetta against the indigenous creatures of Australia. Such as: Was it really necessary for me to want to exterminate them *all*? And: Had I never heard of such a thing as harmony, man and beast living in peaceful concord and reciprocity? And: Did I suppose that the bandicoot and the snapping turtle were what Freedom Academy had in mind when they brought me out and paid me handsomely to identify the enemies to Australia's progress?

Yes to the first. No to the second. Booh-sucks to the third: I killed in my own time.

I was born, don't forget, in a town that filtered one industrial city for another and vice versa, and I lived there for the first seventeen years of my life. What did I know of animals? I was twenty-one before I stroked a cat. Apart from the odd depressed whippet that blundered into our cul-de-sac in an escape bid from its owner, and the black beetles that bred between the bricks in our backyards, the only things that could be said to have adapted to the toxic air of Partington were Partingtons. I didn't have any pets. It's possible, had I not existed, that my father would have acquired a little stunted something that needed regular outings in the Municipal Gardens and whose cuteness would have opened conversations with grieving war-widows from good families. But since he had me there was no reason for him to trouble the Superintendent of the Home for

Strays. Except of course when I was the one who had been left out all night.

As for my mother and her sisters, they were immobilized by terror of whatever moved differently from them.

'It's the way they scuttle,' my mother used to say.

'It's the way they crawl,' was how Hester put it.

'It's the way they look at you,' Nesta would shudder.

And this was just their neighbours and acquaintances they were referring to, two-legged upright carnivores fashioned in the same image as themselves. When it came to the even more brute level of creation their timidity was boundless. I clearly remember Hester refusing to climb the mound to Okehampton Castle with me, although we had travelled all day to get there and had studied its history together for weeks, because there was an old sheep grazing on its ramparts. And I remember, too, how Nesta had to be carried screaming from the front row of the dress circle on the first night of the Partington and District Amateur Operatic Society's production of *The Desert Song*, when Albert Partington, alias The Red Shadow, came on stage riding a real camel.

They were zoophobics, my aunts Hester and Nesta, morbidly afraid of what wasn't human because they were morbidly interested only in what was. See what happens when you let diffidence circumscribe your experience: mysteries gather around your own nature, the commonplace becomes charged with wonder, you weep for an unknown past and pant for an impossible future, and before you know it you are an idolater of your own species. That was what lay behind Hester's passion for gothic ruins and Nesta's love of operetta. They were both humanifreaks. Hester might have drawn my attention to unusual details over rotting doors and windows as we tramped through one ransacked monastery after another, but we both knew that we had really packed sandwiches and caught the bus from Partington Central in order to imagine what it must have been like to be a happy medieval friar, making mead and silent friendships in a tranquil place. And when Nesta and I let the music take us deep into the Vienna Woods we were no more thinking trees than we were spotting birds over Heidelberg, on that moonlit night when one solitary chirrup told Mario Lanza that his royal blood bubbled for the local barmaid. People, that's what we'd saved our money and got dressed up (an extra pillow under the jumper, in Nesta's case) and taken our seats to hear about. People. Ladies and gentlemen. Boys and girls. Doctors and nurses. Men and totty.

Operettas aren't for animal-lovers. Even when there are cats in the cast they are only pretend cats, putting human emotions to tawdry human tunes. They don't write operettas for *actual* animals. Or at least they didn't until the night Albert Partington came riding in on a camel.

I like to think that my mother was less exquisitely anthropocentric than her sisters, and I can certainly remember her saying, not long after my father bolted, that she had so little feeling left she would neither mind nor notice if a family of rats ran up and down her body. But I can see that there was an element of hyperbole about this, and that her idea of the very worst torture she could prove herself immune to was itself a bit of a give-away. It was rather too like the very worst torture she had *not* proved herself immune to, when a colony of daddy-long-legses (forget the spelling; think of the horror) marched and fought and for all she knew conducted initiation ceremonies upon the convex slopes of her naked belly (I was inside, causing the convexity, choosing my moment), while she lay helpless in a country maternity hospital, her nightdress rolled up to her neck, her legs in the air, the bombs dropping on Manchester and Liverpool, my father nowhere to be found, and not a nurse in the ward who could comprehend her abhorrence, who could distinguish a scream of aversion from a scream of pain and think of flicking the insects on to someone else.

No one in the family gave me any chance of coming out of such an early shock to my psychology unscathed. My earliest memory is of my mother and her sisters clustered round my cot, scanning me for signs of trauma. And when at last they caught me shrinking from a crane-fly they exchanged looks of eager corroboration bordering, I thought, on connivance.

A tyrant then – all the worst tyrants are flinchers first – I was bound to be, wherever I set up home. Fly-paper hung from the ceilings of my rooms at Cambridge, for example, like curtains in a kasbah. But Australia – where beast-life had been pushed back only a few feet; where re-encroachment is unremitting and often instantaneous: the sharks nibbling at the shore, the spiders slinging their hammocks back across the toilet seat the minute you vacate it; and where every morning flocks of garish and satiric birds fly by your window guffawing – Australia couldn't fail to call out the hunter in me.

If you're thinking that the Redback was therefore quite within her rights to get me where she did, that she owed me on behalf of all her hacked-down furry friends, remember that you're only anthropomorphizing. Redbacks aren't motivated by principles such as justice or revenge. They're just naturally nasty bastards.

15

But whether I killed or catered – leaving out jars of chocolate spread where the Harbour lapped my rocky garden – I altered the ecological balance of Australia, as I have already explained, in my own time only.

However, lest you think I didn't earn my keep, that (God forbid) Freedom Academy International and the CIA didn't get their money's worth, here's a list of the more significant operations in which I was actively engaged during my first three or four years here – what might be called my teething time, my pre-Vietnam, pre-Whitlam, pre-Women's Disenthralment (them from men; me from them) and, incidentally, my pre-Venie and Maroochi period:

PROJECT POM
No specific time allocated to this. And no specific duties, beyond a willingness to put oneself around, raise the tone of gatherings and get-togethers, keep an ear open for language abuse and intellectual parochialism, and be prepared to talk slowly or repeat sentences when Australians were copying down what one said.

MONITORING AND COUNTERACTING AGITATION ON THE CAMPUSES OF NOONTHORUNGEE, OODNADATTA AND TUMBARUMBA
My bread-and-butter drudgery. Unglamorous, time-consuming, thankless, but not at all dangerous in the days before Ho Chi Minh and Norelle Turpie became common campus names, since agitation was limited to grumblings about the high level of library fines and the

163

unreasonableness of being expected to read more than one book a month in good weather, and monitoring it consisted of sitting in pubs all afternoon. Counteraction, as I conceived it, meant providing a living example in one's own person – the word 'model' was not yet in use – of the benefits of uncomplaining study. Personality politics, in other words. Pay your fines and be like me. Effective, as anyone who has tried it knows, only if one is charismatic. So please note that there wasn't a single sit-in at Noonthorungee, Oodnadatta or Tumbarumba until, on the same afternoon, Marshal Ky and his beautiful wife flew into Sydney, Orel Rosenfeldt awarded the Menzies Medal for Material Philosophy to the psychomotor-retarded niece of the Chief Justice of NSW, and Alex Sneddon, acting as a husband and a Vice-Chancellor, sacked a whole department of modern linguists for gross academic discourtesy after they refused to confer a *baccalauréat honoraire* ('That's an honorary baccalaureat') on Lobelia. Events, I can assure you, quite beyond my control; though I too saw no reason for withholding common courtesy, whether from the unfaithful wife of a senior and soon-to-be-knighted administrator, the afflicted niece of a revered jurisprudent, or the smiling inscrutable representatives of a puppet government which was as innocuous, to my mind, as the chorus of *Chu Chin Chow*.

CACA (Campaign for A Cleaner Australia)
I wasn't a founding member of CACA. It was well established long before I arrived, but I sympathized with its aims and hit it off with its officers from the start. Some of my happiest memories dating from this time are of long hot afternoons beside a pool or on a shaded patio, discussing the New Modishness and shaping plans to decelerate the trendification of modern Australia. My own contribution to this deceleration campaign was necessarily limited. No outsider can possibly take the measure of all that constitutes the

'trendy' for an Australian. In Cambridge it meant owning your own screw-apart punt-pole or being able to order your drinks in ecclesiastical Latin; and in Partington we weren't trendy enough to have heard of the word. But for Australians it described anyone from a wearer of bell-bottomed trousers to a person who had lesbians for friends. I kept out of this semiotic quagmire and brought what I like to think was a more international flavour to CACA, persuading the State of Victoria to ban Mary McCarthy's *The Group*, and pulling off an Australia-wide with Stephen Vizinczey's *In Praise of Older Women*. I supported continued prohibition of a few flagrant oldies also, carnal classics such as *Ulysses* (Tennyson's poem as well as Joyce's novel), *The Rape of the Lock* (Pope's), *Venus and Adonis* (anyone's), *Leviathan* (it sounded like *Decameron*), and *Self-Help* by Samuel Smiles, a handbook to personal self-sufficiency which Australian Customs officials were particularly reluctant to let fall into the hands of their countrymen.

My only real failure with CACA related to the unexpurgated paperback *Lady Chatterley's Lover*, a work I was anxious to keep out of Australia on social rather than sexual grounds, believing it was likely to give animal husbanders, farriers, shearers and bushwhackers in general ideas beyond their station. I was opposed in this by Gunnar McMurphy, himself an active if sometimes divided member of CACA and Chairman of the Steering Committee for Restoring Reverence to the Word Fuck.

'Here is a book which will give Australian women back their cunts,' he said.

Few of the Australian women present looked properly grateful for this.

'It's a question of class not hrrumph,' I maintained, substituting a grunt for a cunt. 'I strongly resist the implication that coitus is improved by impoverished surroundings and the expression of explicit endearments in a rustic tongue.'

You can see why they paid my passage out. This kind of dead-fart Pommy irony could silence any Australian in those days. There wasn't one of them that didn't shrivel beneath its scorn. Distaste – that's what did for them every time. And they were never able to do it back. They lacked the confidence. They were too far from the Delphic mysteries, always behindhand with the latest oracular news. Expectant, wide-eyed, agog. And you can't practise distaste with your mouth hanging open. Whereas I was still fresh from Cambridge where I had heard for myself from the old women on three-legged stools. I knew what was what and who was who. I could go forward, wrinkling my nose and jutting my jaw, secure in the knowledge that I was protected behind.

'Put a book like this into the homes of ordinary Australians,' I continued, 'and the toe of the Peasant will soon be scraping the heel of the Courtier. As for whatever other part of the Peasant will be doing what to whatever other part of the Courtier's wife – I leave that to you to imagine.'

Not bad, eh, for a hairdresser's lad from Partington?

Because I was only joking (sort of), because I couldn't really be talking of Peasants and Courtiers in Australia, even at a meeting of CACA, Gunnar McMurphy could only puff and pant and go red and mutter a few true but ineffective things about my supposing that fucking was better if you had a degree.

But that wasn't the end of the matter. Gunnar turned up at my place that very night with the three Cooney brothers lined up in ascending order of melancholy menace behind him. I invited them in, found myself instantaneously encircled, and offered them a beer. It shouldn't be forgotten that apart from the odd fine detail and the Cooneys' mysterious tergiversations – more a wanting universally to please than a betrayal – we were all essentially on the same side.

McMurphy, however, waved away all pretence that

166

this was a social call. Much to the disappointment of the Cooney brothers, who would be anybody's friend for a beer.

'Sign this,' McMurphy said. He handed me a sheet of CACA notepaper, embossed with a map of Australia showing an invasion of yellow arrows (denoting Chinese communism) from the north, an invasion of red arrows (denoting Russian communism) from the west, and an invasion of black arrows (denoting impure thoughts) from everywhere. I used this paper regularly myself when writing to magistrates or senior Vice Squad officers, urging greater resolution. But this wasn't addressed to any individual workers in the field. It was addressed, as far as I could make out, to humanity. AFTER CAREFUL RECONSIDERATION, it said, I AM NOW OF THE UNSHAKEABLE CONVICTION THAT THE AFOREMENTIONED NOVEL (its title was typed at the head of the page) IS A WORK OF THE HIGHEST MORAL INTELLIGENCE. And there was a space for my signature, marked with a pencilled cross, followed by the words, IN THE PRESENCE OF GEORGE, BERNARD, AND SHAUN COONEY, followed by a space for their signatures.

'You expect me to sign this?'

McMurphy nodded. He had a big round red face which I was sure Hermie and Lobelia (separately, of course, and unbeknown to each other) cradled.

'And if I won't?'

The Cooneys reduced the circumference of their circle. It was a dispiriting experience. The pain and the indignity of being roughed up by them was as nothing compared to the contagion of their lugubriousness. They were, all three of them, unutterably sad. My father was right when he said that Australia was a sentimental country. I could tell that the Cooneys would have much preferred to be sharing a beer and a few genuine tears with me. Their punches had no back-swing. They kneed me without follow-through.

They ground their knuckles almost fondly into my eyes. 'Hit him where it won't show,' McMurphy suggested. But it wasn't necessary to encourage them. They'd upset me into signing long before they had me doubled up on the carpet.

Which is how you come to be able to buy *Lady Chatterley's Lover* with all the reverential fucking left in from any newsagent in Australia. And why there is even a popular edition that carries a recommendation from me on the front cover: A WORK OF THE HIGHEST MORAL INTELLIGENCE: LEON FORELOCK.

BOLSHOI-BASHING

'It is an incontrovertible truth,' I once said, in a famous after-dinner speech to visiting Asian Freedom Academy delegates, 'the irony of which will not be lost on those who make it their business to observe the sociology of Bolshevism, that no one sinks sooner into the softness of corruption and luxury, is more exacting in his requirements as to comfort and service, or more high-handed in his relations with those whose job it is to serve, than a visiting Russian virtuoso sent to show the Western Fascist-Imperialist Dictatorships what Marxist-Leninism can do on a fiddle, or how well Collectivism looks in ballet tights.'

My dead-fart Pommy prose style and my appalled, even somewhat nauseated delivery – as if evil smells were emanating from my own upper lip – went down especially well, as I remember, with those Indonesians and Malayans who had been educated in the ins and outs of wit in England. They banged the tables and threw back their heads and flashed their strong white teeth and all but shouted 'Olly, olly!' as I completed every cadence.

I delivered many speeches in this vein, to Chambers of Commerce, Democratic Unions, Croatian Separatists, Special Branch Study Groups and the like, whenever the Moscow State Circus or the Red Army Male

Voice Choir or the Bolshoi Ballet itself came to Australia. I was a mine of what you might have thought was inaccessible information. I knew how many Western lipsticks the little ballerina bought herself at Myers. I knew how much lobster the cossacks consumed at Doyles. I had photostat copies of bills. And sworn statements from hapless hotel-desk reception staff who had been subjected to gross Moldavian liberties. It was me who masterminded some of the great anti-Russian tabloid scoops of the middle sixties. Remember NAUGHTY NIKITA IN PRESTIGE PENTHOUSE PANTY-PARTY ROMP? IVAN NOT SO TERRIBLE SAYS MOTHER SUPERIOR AFTER PERTH LITTLE SISTERS OF MERCY SPANKING SPREE? VODKA VIOLINISTS: CAIRNS COUNTS THE COST? Mine. All Mine.

I assume that it is not necessary for me to point out the essential good-naturedness of this satire, or to insist my innocence of anything so low as political propagandizing. Whatever those who made use of my gifts might have thought, I myself did not suppose for one moment that I was delivering body blows to a system of which I was largely ignorant anyway. The main purpose of discrediting Russians, as I saw it, was to restore a bit of morale to Australians. Their economy might have been booming, they might, individually, have been growing bigger and stronger by the second on blood-red meat and sun-rays, but as far as their collective morale went – their national pride, so to speak, their corporate identity – they were, as they themselves were only too willing to put it, up shit creek. Their entire navy, consisting of two vessels – the aircraft-carrier *Melbourne* and the destroyer *Voyager* – had contrived, despite several thousand miles of empty coastal waters, to crash into itself. Dawn Fraser had gone for an indiscreet midnight swim at the Tokyo Olympics and shown the wrong kind of attitude to the Japanese flag. More and more photographs of Sir Robert Menzies curtsying to remote members of obscure European royal families were appearing in the newspapers. And in west London pubs and restaurants, and camper-parks all over the Continent, the myth of the unruly, overconvivial Australian was gathering credence. I just thought it would make them feel better to be reminded that they weren't the only ones who couldn't keep their heads or hold their liquor in the excitement of foreign travel.

I hope it will be remembered of me – both by the secret servicemen in the Mercedes outside my window and by the élitist Trotskyites who won't let me join their party – that when Australia was up shit creek, I offered myself as a paddle.

But if there was nothing political about my attacks on high-spending visiting communists, there was nothing personal either. I actually rather liked Russians and had as warmish a regard for their culture as a lover of operetta might be expected to have for a country that never managed to compose any. The idea of brotherhood ruined them, of course, for a genre that thrives on subtle social graduations. But some of their gypsy music had the power to touch my heart by reminding me of better days in other places, which is the stuff of nostalgia, when all is said and done, for conservatives and socialists alike. So I regularly accompanied my father and Trilby to Boris Rubaschkin concerts, where I clapped and whistled and wept with the rest of Vaucluse. I went with them to the circus also, and to watch the baby gymnasts, and to hear Rostropovich play Shostakovich. I drew the line only at Yevtushenko. But that wasn't political or personal either. It was because he was a poet, used too much alliteration, wore natty suits, had sunken cheekbones, and drew bigger audiences than I did.

THE PIERS PLOWMAN PLOY
Speaking of alliterative poetry, it was me who hit upon the idea of the Prologue to *Piers Plowman* (Text B) in

response to the Commonwealth Government's request for an appropriate language test to be taken by problematical migrants and dubious visitors.

'No foe shall gather our harvest nor sit on our stockyard rail,' the poet and patriot Dame Mary Gilmore had promised all Australians during the darkest days of World War Two, when the Japanese had got as close as New Guinea in pursuit of the ancient Samurai ambition to reach Bullamakanka and lounge around on stockyard rails. And she had kept her word. The Japanese had not got through. But now, in peacetime, there were other foes trying to enter Australia, by more conventional routes and methods it is true, but still with the same intentions towards the old stockyard rail. It wasn't really possible to refuse them access simply on the grounds of their obnoxious views or clashing colour. Where was the point of being a democracy if one acted like that? On the other hand, there was nothing to stop even the most welcoming of countries from ensuring that its intending settlers possessed a passing proficiency in the local tongue – in this case, basic Australian. So they were given a little test to sit (devised by me) the moment their boats and planes disgorged them.

If you'd been a black Maoist, flying in from Cuba in 1964, you would have been ushered through immigration into an empty room furnished only with a picture of the Queen (whose language basic Australian was) and an old school desk. Here you would have found waiting for you a blotter, an inkwell, a scratchy fountain pen, a piece of blank paper, and the following extract – though I should say that the comprehension questions you would have been required to answer, after reading it through twice, were of the simplest:

In a somer seson   whan soft was the sonne,
I shope me in shroudes   as I a shepe were,
In habite as an heremite   unholy of workes.

Went wyde in this world   wondres to here.
Ac on a May mornynge   on Maluerne hulles
Me byfel a ferly   of fairy me thoughte. . . .

You'd be surprised how many Indo-Chinese don't
know the average May mornynge temperature of the
British Isles, or where the Maluerne hulles are, or how
many shepe they support, or the quickest route to them
from Chipping Norton during rush hour, avoiding
Stow and Tewkesbury.

HOISTING *THE BLACK SAIL* (or, Throwing Back the
Red Herring)
I am not going to list here all my early contributions to
the only Australian journal of ideas Major-General Idi
Amin was said to read from cover to cover. I am prepared to admit that most of them – the piece attacking
the liberal habit of insisting there are two sides to every
question for example, or my panegyric of Ivor Novello,
or my advocacy of Mururoa as an ideal nuclear testing
site (I didn't know where Mururoa was, but Frank
Whiling did and was against it, which was enough for
me) – are now of antiquarian interest only. Serious
scholars of this period of Australian cultural history can
always look them up in the annual indexes of the
magazine, at least one set of which can be found in
the Library of the National University of Canberra, in
the reading room of the Australian High Commission
in the Strand, and presumably in the President's Room
of the National Cultural Centre, Kampala.
    But if you are wondering what happened to Tristan-
ism, it is time for me to admit that a lot less was looked
for from me in relation to that social scourge than Father
Dinmont Manifest had led me to expect. In fact Dinny
was out of touch and out of date. Tristanism had ceased
to be a major preoccupation with any but the most fanati-
cal members of the Australian Right several years before
I arrived, and although *The Black Sail* retained its original

172

anti-Tristanist title, it now had other wars to wage. Even Enrico Santalucia was compelled to concede, in an important interview, that while he could never condone adultery he was prepared to admit that as long as it was sincere, indoors, and unaccompanied by marijuana it was not *necessarily* a conduit for communism.

This was a lot further than I was prepared to go in my first fervid months here. I bombarded *The Black Sail* with crusading articles which they made lame excuses for not publishing. I turned more and more to Henry Dabscheck, whose abstemiousness I had so admired on my first night at the Rosenfeldts', until I burst into his office one afternoon, enraged by another rejection, and found him feeding his secretary. She was sitting in his chair and had a tea-towel tucked into her blouse. Henry was standing behind her, fondling a breast with one hand and spooning her something yellow – it might well have been scrambled egg – with the other. On his desk was a plate of Polish sausage, some marinaded herring, and a bottle of plum brandy. I didn't stay to see what they were having for dessert.

This left only Vance Kelpie amongst the senior editorial staff whose personal behaviour seemed to me at all commensurate with what I still regarded as the magazine's essential credo. I saw a fair bit of Vance for a while, on account of our doing a Freedom Academy-sponsored tour of New South Wales country towns together. He extemporized Celtic ballads, I showed slides of ruined fortresses in old north Wales, and a girl from Adelaide, called Montserrat Tomlinson, gave readings from William Blake.

'And Priests in black gowns were walking their rounds,' she would declaim by way of polishing off our little entertainment, and sending one final frisson of confessionalism through the tiny timbered town-hall, 'And binding with briars my joys and desires.'

The residents of Yass and Nowra, knowing precisely how both Blake and Montserrat Tomlinson felt, would then warmly applaud, while we inclined our heads in acknowledgement, closed our folders, rearranged our slides, and thought about the bland lobster which would be waiting for us, under a topping of cold melted cheese, in our motel dining room.

I had no doubt whatsoever that all Montserrat Tomlinson's readings were chosen to heat the blood of Vance Kelpie. She made no secret of her vast regard for his poetic genius, and when he was on the platform she would make it her business – opening and closing curtains, experimenting with switches, draping shawls over naked bulbs – to ensure he had the right amount, and the right quality, of light. She dressed for him too, keeping us waiting for our lobster while she changed into the sort of outfit a well-brought-up provincial Australian girl of the late fifties would have worn for a first-time pre-theatre dinner date with an English engineer. Her skirt fluffed out with layers of petticoats; her legs strong in deadly sharp but not too high stilettos; her waist pinched by a broad plastic belt. Only the curling orange hairs which she always forgot to brush from her black woollen sweater gave her away as a lover of poetry.

In any place at any time Montserrat Tomlinson might have been accounted a temptation, but in the Mudgee Homestead Motel at midnight with one small candle (lit by her) burning on our table, she was witchery itself. And yet Vance Kelpie never once succumbed to her. By fifteen minutes past midnight he was in his room, she was in her room, and as I can truly vouch because I was in my room in between, they neither of them moved until morning.

I made two further country tours with Vance Kelpie and Montserrat Tomlinson, and what was true of the first remained true of the others. Only once, when we got very drunk and Vance passed out briefly at the table, did I bring up the question with Montserrat of the briars that bound her joys and desires.

'Fleshly men take mistresses,' she told me in a whisper, so as not to break the flow of what might be coming to Vance Kelpie in his sleep. 'Men of ethereal genius require spiritual consolation.'

I looked around the room. We were in Moree, if I remember rightly. And the orange-juice reps were taking an intense interest in our conversation. There isn't a lot else for a rep to do in Moree.

'And that's all right with you?' I didn't have much else to do myself except ask.

She suddenly saw a tightly curled red hair on her sweater and took a long time to pluck it off. Then she raised her eyes to mine. 'Love seeketh only Self to please,' she said, 'To bind another to its delight, Joys in another's loss of ease, And builds a Hell in Heaven's despite.'

I waited to hear what else she had to say and was alarmed to discover not only that she had finished but that she was expecting a reply. 'Yes, well I reckon love can be a bit like that,' I managed at last, lowering my head and scratching it, the way I had been taught to do at Cambridge to express ruminative if not wholehearted sympathy.

'I reckon it can too,' I heard one of the orange-juice reps saying to the others. And for a while the whole of the Moree Haven Motel Restaurant sat in contemplative silence, swaying over its drinks, reflecting on Love and Self, remembering Heaven and Hell.

Finally Vance Kelpie woke up, said 'Ye may roam i' the hills, ye may clamber o'er the raths, but the days o' the clans are nae more,' and permitted us to lead him to his room. We opened his door and pushed him in. Then Montserrat retired to her room and I retired to mine.

So you will understand why I felt dimly uneasy when, during the last days of our final tour, I noticed that Montserrat had taken to leaving off her plastic belt and was looking progressively less *svelte* around the middle. And why I felt obscurely betrayed when, on the train back, Vance Kelpie poured us each a paper tumbler of whisky and proposed a toast to the new life stirring not so very far from here – a warrior boy to be, he had no doubt, a wild colonial lad whose name would be Maeldune. I can't believe I would have been crass enough to ask how and where the wee Maeldune had been put together, but my whole expression must have evinced some such stupefied curiosity because the moment Montserrat rose, flushed, to visit the women's portion of the carriage – 'Men are requested not to loiter at this end of the car' a notice warns you, if you are a man, on Australian trains – Vance whispered to me that although Maeldune was his, he had had no hand in his being there.

I narrowed my eyes at him. He was leaning back in his seat, deathly white as ever, but at peace with the world. Above his head there was a framed picture of a bit of unpeopled scrubland, not unlike what was passing monotonously outside the window, entitled 'Hibiscus Tree and Goanna'. My eyes were like the slits in Ned Kelly's tin helmet.

'You've observed the arrangements,' Vance Kelpie reminded me.

I had. And I had done more than that too. I had remarked upon them to all and sundry. I had turned interminable jokes back in Sydney about the Bard and his Spiritual Bride. Of which Vance Kelpie also didn't scruple to remind me. 'A powerful force, the spirit,' he said.

'Not *that* powerful,' I replied. I was displeased. I hadn't fixed myself up with any excitement in Yass or Goulburn because I had believed that we were in the business of having a dull and uneventful time together. I had been impressed by their restraint and modelled my own behaviour upon it. Hence the sensation I was unable to dispel that I had been duped.

Vance Kelpie got in one more sentence as we both

watched Montserrat returning carefully down the swaying carriage. She was blooming. She had put on at least another pound while she'd been away, where no men were meant to loiter. Her breasts had grown rounder also. In anticipation of Maeldune.

'The fairies, you see,' he said. 'Never mock the little people.'

I was in a spiteful mood. 'Tell that to your wife,' I said.

'Oh, I don't need to,' he replied. 'She's a believer. Ours is not a marriage that precludes colloquy with the sacred stones.'

That pretty well finished me for anti-Tristanising. You can lose all stomach for a cause if you don't get support. Just before I'd gone on this last tour Orel Rosenfeldt had sat with me on a bench outside his room in the main quadrangle of Noonthorungee University, discussing this and that but mainly trying to temper that crusading zeal of mine which was becoming such an embarrassment to *The Black Sail*. I remember the afternoon clearly, although I don't remember all Orel said, because of the exceptional heat, the brevity of the students' swimming costumes as they passed us on their way to lectures, and the unbroken spiral peel of Orel's lunchtime apple which he had placed on the arm of the bench and which had so much sap left in it that it rose and fell and quivered like a mechanical spring. 'I am myself a moralist,' I can still hear Orel saying, 'but I look for no mere practical application of morality in the behaviour of my fellows. I am what you might call, when it comes to the doings of chaps, an equivocalist.' He smiled at me here, threw away a cigarette in order to make room between his cherub lips for a cigar, and pushed his spectacles up into his hair. 'Not to be confused,' he managed to sigh and twinkle all at once, 'with an equivocator.'

I twinkled back. I knew the difference, with my education, between an equivocalist and an equivocator.

177

Had I only known that Australia was ready for such a thing – had Dinny only prepared me properly – I would have declared myself an equivocalist the day I arrived.

Well, Orel's words came back to me when I needed them. After what Vance Kelpie and Montserrat Tomlinson put me through I embraced the principles of equivocalism unequivocally. I preached order and moderation in public and threw my personal life into a chaos of concupiscence. By 1968 Australia was fully committed in Vietnam, the young were chanting on the streets, and I was the country's leading ambigamist, an ambivalentier of style and swagger, sporting Venie on my right arm, Maroochi on my left arm, and writing with a pen fixed between my teeth against the greed and moral degradation of the times.

16

Vast deserts, like limitless expanses of black space, vex the finite imaginations of men. We have trouble with the idea that there is only more of the same out there. And so we go in search of a single green tree, or a settlement of green Martians – some token of benevolence, some friendly message in a bottle left by God.

The explorer Charles Sturt had a more grandiose conception: he set out to find the great inland sea – the New Mediterranean – whose basin had to be the burning navel of Australia. For thirteen months he trudged into the uncharted centre, pursuing the blue mirage, the cool waters on which God's bottle bobbed; enquiring of every native he passed whether there was surf or good beaches hereabouts, befriending anyone prepared to swear he'd heard swans honking in the night.

He came back ill, near-blind, and disappointed. If the continent of Australia possessed an inland sea it wasn't where he'd looked. The best he'd found were a few broad creeks, the odd indigo pool, a lagoon visited by seagulls, and one wholly unexpected source of running water – seven Aborigines, weeping inconsolably in the wilderness, their tears pitting the desert and drying as they fell, in one hundred and fifty degrees of heat.

Sturt was not able to fathom these bitter, unremitting tears. The great explorer could not discover why they flowed, nor could he devise any means to stop them. There is no record of his trying out his best jokes on the heartbroken Aborigines, supposing there to have been jokes in Australia in 1845; but whatever his discourse consisted of, the men kept up their sobbing and the women maintained their howling, throughout it. Realizing at last that they weren't in any condition to direct him to the New Mediterranean, even if they knew its whereabouts, he left them to irrigate the scrub with their sorrow.

Whether there was any particular occasion for this show of overwhelming grief, or whether Sturt had merely happened upon a tribe which wept perpetually and in the natural order of things – as more foolish men smile – from the cradle to the grave, we shall never know. But it is my suspicion that all Australians, Aborigines and white settlers alike, weep buckets the minute they are alone. Some are just unable to conceal their anguish, even in company.

This is a sentimental country all right, as my father told me the night we stood together on Trilby's *belvedere*, looking out over the Roman-tiled terraces of Vaucluse. He was wrong, though, to attribute such national emotionalism entirely to the experience of exile. Those Aborigines Sturt encountered were not crying for their infancy in another place. It's just possible that home for them had not always been Australia, but even if they did originate from somewhere else they hadn't heard word of it for a hundred thousand years or more. So it was much more likely to be God they missed – the old consoling message in a bottle – than Partington or Vladivostok. There are corners of the earth that God appears to have lost interest in, or to have washed His hands of altogether. When this happens – as in the case of Partington – the abandoned residents develop a surly, stoical demeanour. They bear a grudge, but they are not broken. And they often do well in life, spurred on by rejection, like the children of divorced parents. But there are also localities whose desolation is owing not to God's abrupt decampment but to His never having set foot there in the first place. Australia is one of those. It is a country which does not bear a single treadmark of divine visitation. Which is why everyone is so lonely here, and looks so sad.

I don't except myself. Long before the Redback brought the tears to my eyes with a vengeance, I had become a seasoned blubberer. I find it hard to recall, looking back, a single dry forty-eight hours in the first fifteen years I was a willing exile here. Though one afternoon does stand out in my memory for its unparalleled lachrymation. This was when I rolled through the main street of Albury, over the border between New South Wales and Victoria, and into the neighbouring town of Wodonga, in what can only be called a wrestling embrace with the person who is now Australia's foremost Flexible Marxist, but who was then just dear old Ruddles Carmody, product of the Christian Brothers at Bendigo, and my good friend from the Bureau for the Obtainment of Overseas News and Gossip (BOONG) in Melbourne.

Most Australian Intelligence Obtainment is done in Melbourne. The more temperate climate and the greater sobriety of its citizens have made Melbourne the Number One choice for work requiring mental agility. I didn't have a lot to do with BOONG myself. As I've said, I was never a spy. But I would visit the offices in St Kilda Road, just across from Luna Park fun-fair, once every three or four months, to help decode the latest batch of socialist journals just in from London. My work in relation to *Tribune* and the *New Left Review* was especially well regarded, and I once carried off the monthly Transliteration into Plain Australian Award for what I did with *limitless centripetency*, the *scourge of macrocephaly*, and the *heteroclite disparate gamut of bourgeois strata*.

It's possible that modern technology has at last found its way into St Kilda Road, but in my day BOONG functioned perfectly well without electronic gadgetry.

181

I never saw any screens or aerials, and I never heard of anyone planting bugs. We didn't even have a transistor radio. The intelligence collected came entirely from newspapers and magazines, so that the most highly valued informant was the paper-boy who would park his bicycle outside the front gate every morning – the Bureau was, of course, to all intents and purposes an ordinary private house – and spend a good forty minutes stuffing *Pravda* and the *Peking Post* and the *Straits Times* and the *Lucknow Pioneer* and the *Hanoi Herald* and *The Black Dwarf* and the *British Journal of Bad Industrial Relations* and *Slimmers' Weekly* and *Melody Maker* into the tubular tin posting box, before blowing his whistle and cycling off to the offices of ASIO and the Special Branch a few doors down.

I used to enjoy my periodic calls on BOONG. Melbourne itself wasn't up to much, being in something like the same relation to Sydney (benefiting by association, suffering in comparison) as Partington was to New Brighton. But St Kilda had a dilapidated charm, what with its scruffy beach and its views over the oily waters of Port Phillip Bay and its Continental cafés busy, at all hours, with deracinated Eastern Europeans playing chess at Formica tables and spying on the spies. As for the latter, the boys who worked in the Bureau itself, I cannot adequately descibe them without first introducing the indispensable Australian word, *dag*.

Strictly speaking, dags are the locks of wool clotted with impacted dung which hang from the rear end of badly house-trained sheep. It isn't at all difficult to trace the process of association which turns a dag into a certain kind of Australian, though precisely *which* kind depends at any one time on such imponderables as the prevailing attitude to sheep, or the current state of national self-esteem. Thus, when Australia decided to be charmed by its own simplicity, 'a bit of a dag' was someone who cut a dash rather, an incorrigible wag who could make the girls laugh and the boys remember him nostalgically. But with the development of the cities and the growth of pride in urban sophistication – entailing an inevitable alienation from the rear ends of all farmyard animals – being a bit of a dag carried a bit of a stigma. It meant you were conventional, unfashionable, lacking style, out of touch, without that very swagger which was your pre-war appeal. Most successful politicians and all prime ministers in Australia have been dags, with the exception of Mr Hawke who is a bodgie, which is another kind of anachronism again.

The Bureau, being a short first step towards a career in politics or the Public Service, was of course staffed entirely by dags, using the word in its widest applicability. The nerve centre of the whole operation, into which I was admitted as a sort of visiting dag *d'honneur*, was the Upper Information Extrapolation Room. Here dags from some of the daggiest private schools in Victoria (itself a daggy state) sat about in solicitors' suits (the height of dag) and read aloud to one another from the morning papers. I've recently heard the Bureau referred to as a pack of dags immersed in rags, but at the height of its influence it called itself the ears of Australia, and I can avouch that few things took place outside its walls that this room didn't get to hear about sooner or later.

I happened to be there, to cite only one example, on the day Sukarno's overthrow was decoded. I was struggling in a corner with a couple of paragraphs from *Curtains*, the Actors' Revolutionary journal, trying to decide whether there was to be an invasion, led from Stratford-upon-Avon, of the Cocos Islands, or whether the Redgraves were just thinking of bringing out *The Three Sisters* on a short tour, when Noel Preen, who would one day be the Liberal Party's youngest ever Deputy Leader and earn himself the nickname, the Whelp from Warragul, suddenly broke into the after-coffee quiet. 'Jesus,' he said, in the daggy nasal drawl that would make him a favourite with the farmers, 'fucking Suharto's grabbed power.'

It was a particularly steamy morning. A heat haze rose from the bay. It was hard enough to pick our own papers up without having to put them down to listen to what was in someone else's. It was a morning for private, silent deciphering, if ever there was one. On the other hand, Suharto *had* grabbed power.

'Who's Suharto?' a voice asked at last, civil rather than curious. We had all read Alex Sneddon and we all valued civility.

'Some bastard,' said Preen ruminatively, without raising his head from his paper. He was taking his time, tracing the words with his finger slowly, although they were English, not wanting to jump to false conclusions.

'Some bastard from where?'

Preen looked down the page. 'Djakarta.'

'Where's that?'

Preen looked down the page some more. But he didn't seem to find the information he needed. 'South of Cuba, I think.'

'That's Djamaica, shithead.'

'So you tell me where's Djakarta, fuckwit.'

I helped out here, since no one else could. 'Isn't it on one of those vertebrae-ish bits at the top?'

'At the top of what?'

'At the top of Australia.'

'You mean New Zealand?'

'No. Isn't that at the bottom?'

'Fiji, then?'

I shrugged. I'd only meant to go for a paddle and suddenly I was up to my neck in the Pacific. (I think it was the Pacific.) I didn't know where Fiji was. What's more, I had just decided that the Redgraves definitely were planning to liberate the Cocos Islands and I didn't know where *they* were either.

'All right, let's solve this by a process of elimination,'

Noel Preen suggested. He had folded up his paper and taken out a Platignum fountain pen. Already the qualities that would make him a leader were apparent. 'What shape eyes have these dagoes got?'

Despite the torpor of the morning, Preen's question brought a powerful response from the Bureau. Papers and periodicals were thrown to the ground and in seconds the room was a United Nations of face-making. Some of us pulled our eyes downwards like Laplanders, others pulled sideways like Charlie Chan. We bulged like Peter Lorre. We drooped like Harold Macmillan. We were all opened wide like Mississippi minstrels and singing 'Way down upon de Swanee Ribber' when Ruddles Carmody – dear old Ruddles – came in from the balcony where it was his wont to stand dreamily by the hour, staring out beyond the refineries on the bay, imagining it was the South China Sea. 'That depends on which ethnic type you're talking about,' he said. 'But if you mean the Deutero-Malay, of which the Javanese proper form the majority, then the eyes are a limpid brown, set straight but with the most delicate almond sway.' You wouldn't have picked him, from his own heavy, even orang-outangy appearance, as a connoisseur of delicacy, but the very incongruity authenticated his appreciation and made it touching, like King Kong's.

He silenced us, for a minute or two anyway. And left us wondering what we were doing with our fingers in our eyes.

'They are also hairless,' he added. 'With fine complexions and well-developed cheekbones. Though they are not as hairless' – here he sighed – 'or as finely contoured' – here he sighed again – 'as the Chinese.'

Ruddles was not a trained Indo-Orientalist but had become one as a consequence of a series of abruptly truncated love-affairs with the dainty-cheekboned daughters of well-to-do Hong Kong and Singapore Chinese businessmen who were not so well-to-do that they could afford to send their girls to Switzerland instead of Melbourne to finish their educations, but who were not so hard-up that they couldn't reverse their decisions once they learned how much of Ruddles Carmody finishing an education in Melbourne entailed. The reasons why a hirsute dag from Bendigo should have seemed such an unwelcome choice of son-in-law are locked away in the mysteries of Chinese family lore. Suffice it to say that while all of the daughters wanted him, none of the fathers did. By the time I met him Ruddles had reduced a once profitable traffic to a trickle, and was now confined, for company, to those ordinary Aryan Australian girls whose coarse complexions and lumpy features he could not abide. He did all his own cooking, stewing water chestnuts in bean curd, removing the veins from lotus leaves with a single chopstick while sitting cross-legged on the floor, and was the first European in Victoria to own a wok.

He put us right on the geography of Djakarta, explained the complex ethnic composition of the islands of which Djakarta was capital – making fine distinctions between the bone structures of the Javanese, the Sudanese, and the Madurese – expressed his concern for the future of the Chinese minority, and told us who Suharto was. 'I think you'll find,' he said, favouring the weighty, judicious mode he had acquired from the Christian Brothers, 'that the Communist Party, the PKI, will soon be outlawed in Indonesia. In fact I'd be most surprised, knowing Suharto' (that's what he said) 'if there are any communists left in Indonesia to be outlawed.'

Noel Preen was excited by this. His handsome sun-burned face shone with the promise of promotion. 'You mean the bastard's one of us?'

He wasn't to know of course – which of us were? – that he was addressing a person in whom the devils of disloyalty had already been unloosed, and that the

name of Ruddles Carmody would one day be synony-
mous with Flexible Marxism, and therefore dirt the
length of St Kilda Road.

'One of us? Suharto?' Ruddles looked as com-
placently inscrutable as the fat Chinese fathers who
had ordered their daughters home. 'I suppose you
could say that, though he has a much finer skin texture.'

'One of us *ideologically*, arsehole.'

Ruddles only nodded and once more turned his face
towards Port Phillip Bay, as if he might finally see
Singapore if he looked long enough. I suppose it should
have been clear to us that capitalism, oriental abacus
capitalism, had kicked him below the belt and that he
would never be upright again. But we were young,
male, and frisky, and we thought disaffection merely
described the way one felt after two days with the same
girl.

We also had our careers to think about. 'In that case
I'd better get on the blower to Canberra,' said Noel
Preen. 'It's my belief that Holtie ought to know about
this.'

Which is how, to the best of my knowledge, the
Australian Government came to hear of the suspension
of the Communist Party of Indonesia, and how Canberra came to hear of Noel Preen.

Eighteen months later I was in the Bureau when the
news came through that Holtie himself had walked
into the surf at Portsea. Once again it was Noel Preen
who was first with the story, having decoded it from
an obituary in the *Amateur Snorkler and Diver*.

I stayed with Ruddles Carmody whenever I was in
Melbourne, and whenever he came to Sydney he
stayed with me. I won't go so far as to say that our
friendship began as a consequence of his begging me to
take him under my wing, but his Bendigo uncertainties
were still clearly showing when we first met and I don't
think there can be any doubt that he was awed by my

Englishness and ground into abject submission by my double-starred first in the Moral Decencies from Cambridge. He had heard of everybody who had ever taught me, kept signed copies of their most obscure pamphlets – so obscure that they themselves would not have known they'd written them – wrapped in newspaper in a shoe-box underneath his bed, and would frequently touch me, when he thought I wasn't looking, just so he could say he'd more or less touched them. If Cambridge had had its own cuisine Ruddles would certainly have become expert in it, serving Sirloin Sidney Sussex in a pungent Malapert sauce on crested college china.

Such a powerful urge to express discipleship was not uncommon in young men who had been brought up by the Brothers, but whereas most apprentice Australian votaries at this time lacked robustness, were really only seeking refuge from stereotypical male casting and found their fulfilment, at last, at the feet of the women's movement, Ruddles Carmody was absolutely at his ease in the role of drunkard, storyteller, cricketer and clown. There was an uncertainty, it is true – an old-fashionedness such as you find in renegade ecclesiastics or New Zealanders – about the way he put himself together: his grey trousers (they really were flannels) worn a touch too high, his belt pulled a touch too tight, the navy blazer fastened on one too many buttons. (A bit of a dag in short.) But what he had a dim idea he lacked in style, he was confident he made up for in natural gypsy virility. A fresh black stubble appeared on his chin only seconds after he'd finished shaving, and the hairs on his back and shoulders grew like pine-needles, forcing their way through the very weave of his short-sleeved shirts. If you wrestled with him, as I did on the streets of Albury/Wodonga, you had first to suffer a thousand tiny pinpricks before you could get close enough to try a throw. And it wasn't difficult to imagine the Chinese girls rolling off him, in mock dismay, their voices tinkling like bell-birds, while Ruddles minutely examined the punctures in their perfect skin.

Ruddles Carmody was a wholly acceptable person, in other words, to have as an admirer. Brother Wilkes and Brother Hanrahan hadn't minded, the Controller of BOONG hadn't minded, Mary Thong hadn't minded, so why should Leon Forelock object to having Ruddles Carmody hobbling behind, wanting to go wherever he was going, wanting to see whatever he saw. Later on, as Flexible Marxism began to take supple shape and Ruddles himself, by a cruel irony, grew more and more to resemble the plump Buddha-like entrepreneurs he had never forgiven, he was to be seen shuffling a little to the rear of the left shoulders of Frank Whiling and Norelle Turpie. We weren't friends by then – Vietnam had done for us – but I wrote to him all the same. 'If it moves follow it, eh Ruddles?' I said, though I should have known he wouldn't reply.

A week later the spider bit me and I too was struggling towards the light.

However, our tearful fight through the streets of Albury/Wodonga – our tumbling embrace I suppose I should call it – had nothing at all to do with politics. I'd say it had to do with women, except that that's not true either. Let's settle for its having something to do with love, and beg the question of just who was in love with whom.

For all that he couldn't bear to look upon the pitted complexions of white Australian girls – 'They might just as well have smallpox,' I remember him telling me – Ruddles Carmody had been forced to live with one once the other kind dried up. As a rapacious adherent of alien cultures (alien to Bendigo) and imported ideologies (imported from the British Library and Peking) he was badly in need of someone to adhere to him. Someone who would shave his chest and trim his shoulders and with whom he could share the contents of his wok. I am not going to describe the particular example of gross Western womanhood he selected for these functions – the more especially as it is her *un*importance to this story that is important – beyond informing you that her name was Dreena, that she was a legal secretary, and that she was pleasant.

Some equally rough description will suffice of the girl I'd entrusted my needs and wants to at the time – I had no wok to share, but the goanna expected feeding when I was out – whose name, as chance would have it, was also Dreena, who also was a legal secretary (I hadn't found my judge's daughter yet, since Orel had taken most of them, but I was looking), and who was also, just like Ruddles's Dreena, pleasant.

'Nice girl,' Ruddles used to say to me after he'd stayed with us in Sydney for a month or so, 'your er . . .'

'Dreena, I think,' I'd remind him.

'Remember me to whatsername,' he would say as I was ready to leave his place.

'Same name as yours,' I used to tell him.

'Give me another clue,' he always asked.

'Dreena says to say hello to . . . Oh gosh,' I would say if I rang him on some matters.

And, 'Ruddles Carmody and Friend' I would write on the envelope of any letter I sent him, remembering to add the Friend in pencil only as I reached the post-box.

Have I said enough to convey our total lack of interest both in our own and in each other's Dreena?

In that case will it surprise you to hear that when I turned up at Ruddles's place one evening, as arranged, and learned that he was at that very moment turning up at my place, some six or seven hundred miles away, also as arranged, I was unable to stop myself taking Ruddles's Dreena in my arms and telling her that I had wanted her ever since I'd clapped eyes on her, yes, and even for some time before that?

And will it surprise you to hear that although he

would most certainly have been reeling with distaste from her open occidental pores, Ruddles was saying the very same thing, yes, and in the very same voice, to the Dreena who was mine?

Surprise or not, it is the case. He confessed his petty misdemeanour to me himself. And I confessed mine to him. In person. In one hundred and ten degrees of heat. In a milk bar. In Albury.

If you're going to drive from Sydney to Melbourne, or vice versa, and you don't have the time to go across the mountains and do a bit of skiing, or to go along the coast and fish at Bateman's Bay, then you take the Hume Highway, stopping at Gundagai and Wangaratta for petrol, Goulbourn and Euroa to repair your shattered windscreen, and Albury for a milkshake. Driving in from opposite directions, Ruddles Carmody and I arrived at Albury within fifteen seconds of each other, parked our cars at adjacent meters and found ourselves at the same table ordering an identical double dollop of ice-cream and extra caramel.

'Good trip?' (It doesn't matter who said what. We were interchangeable.)

'Not bad. You?'

'Not bad. Look, I've something I want to say to you.'

'Me too.'

'You first.'

'No, no, after you.'

'It isn't easy.'

'Mine neither.'

'I saw your er . . . whatsername last night.'

'Dreena. Yes, I saw yours.'

'My what?'

'Dreena.'

'Ah, yes. Did you? Mm. Well. Have I mentioned that I saw yours?'

'Yes. Just now. Look, I don't know how to say this.'

'Then maybe you shouldn't.'

'Why shouldn't I? So that you don't have to?'

191

'I'm not afraid to say what's on my mind.'

'Say it then.'

'I fucked Dreena.'

'Yours or mine?'

'Yours.'

'I know.'

'How do you know?'

'I rang her up from Benalla. She told me.'

'And you fucked mine.'

'How do you know?'

'I rang her up from Cootamundra. She told me.'

What we next said, we said together.

'You bastard!'

Then, because it was hot, because we hadn't slept much, because we were young, because we were friends, and because this was Australia, we leaped at each other across the Laminex table and took each other by the throat and stuck fingers into each other's mouth and precipitated ourselves out of the Albury Star Milk Bar and Grill and rolled down the main street towards the bridge, each straddling the other, scratching and biting, unable to break free, unwilling to let go, until we tumbled over the New South Wales/Victoria border into Wodonga, where we came to rest at last, under a flowering jacaranda, and were both not at all surprised to discover that we were sobbing in each other's arms.

Ruddles's hopelessly old-fashioned tropical shirt was torn across the back, and I dried my eyes on a tuft of his shoulder hairs. He wiped his nose on my sleeve.

'You all right?' we both asked together.

'Fine,' we both answered, our faces shining like roof-tops just washed by rain.

We stayed in Wodonga for three or four days, swimming without our cossies in the Murray every morning, taking walks into the bush in the afternoons, and getting plastered at night. We talked about our boyhoods in Bendigo and Partington, how his family had wanted him to take the cloth, how mine had wanted me to be another Nelson Eddy. As we searched for yabbies in the creeks he repeated some of the vows the Christian Brothers had extracted from him, and I sang the Indian Love Call from *Rose Marie*, including the soprano echo which brought the yabbies to the surface of the water, on their backs, quivering with bliss.

We formed a darts team of two and pulverised the locals. We ate steaks pizzaiola and washed them down with claret from Rutherglen.

'Here's to the best time I've had,' said Ruddles, raising his glass, 'since I was a kid in Bendigo.'

'I didn't have your advantages,' I reminded him. 'I grew up in Partington. So here's to the best time I've *ever* had.'

When the hour came for us to return to our respective cities we parted with thumping breasts. Ruddles was compelled to borrow my sleeve again, and I rubbed my eyes into the vegetation sprouting from his shirt.

We banged the bonnet of each other's car a few times before we got into them, and once inside we flashed our lights and tooted our horns.

'Been good, mate,' Ruddles said, winding down his window.

'Too right,' I said, winding down mine.

Then, with one last toot, we parted.

And the Dreenas – his Dreena and my Dreena?
Who?

17

I RANG RUDDLES only recently on a number that promised to find either the private man or the public figure, depending presumably on who one was and how one made him feel. He knew who I was instantly, which might account for why I found the public figure.

'Ah, Leon. Leon Forelock, yes. Not a name we hear much of these days.'

The 'we' wasn't royal. Ruddles Carmody had been a republican for some time now. But the communistical 'we' can be just as exclusive.

I told him that nobody had heard much of me these days. That I'd been lying low and ruminating. But that I was now ready to join his party, if he'd have me. Sorry – I remembered just in time – if *they'd* have me.

I heard a sharp intake of breath on the other end of the phone. Which didn't really surprise me. I knew I was chancing my arm a bit after the things I'd said about Flexible Marxism over the years, but I thought that being under surveillance by the security forces five nights a week constituted a recommendation, was a guarantee of my good faith, proved how much I'd changed.

'And is this ASIO or ASIS we're talking about?'

I was prepared for the scepticism in his voice, and I wasn't unfamiliar with the mandarin gravity, but the statesmanlike imperturbability caught me on the hop, until I recalled that he'd just returned from Peking. And that reminded me that I'd once referred to him, in an article for the *Queensland Countrywoman*, as a little pink bunny, a nursery flexi-doll whose rubber neck was bent this way and that by the Gang of Four.

'I don't know,' I said. I thought he'd like to hear me imply that his enemies were all alike in their iniquities. 'One or the other.'

'That was always the trouble with you, Leon. You were always vague. You made a virtue of approximation.'

I gave an approximate little laugh. I didn't like being told what the trouble with me had always been. But if that was the price of being allowed to join the party I was prepared to pay it. I had to get out there and meet somebody.

'You used to say the trouble with me was that I put personalities before issues,' I reminded him, just to show how many troubles with me I was willing to acknowledge, just to show how prepared I was to pay. 'You once accused me of arguing with the proponent instead of the principle.'

'Which you hotly denied.'

'Of course I denied it. I had to argue with you, however much I knew you were right, precisely in order to vindicate your charge. I've always been obliging, Ruddles. Had I suddenly addressed myself to the principle instead of to the personality you would have accused me of being perverse.'

I gave another little laugh, which wasn't returned. Ruddles had been losing his sense of humour for some time now. This happens when you put issues first.

And when you marry at forty.

I can't bring myself to say much about Bev Belladonna, except that she was the opposite of everything Ruddles had always admired and wanted, being neither petite, graceful, almond-eyed, close-pored, soft-skinned, finely sculptured, sweet-voiced, calm in manner, temperate in views, amiable, amenable, or nice to Ruddles. The only other detail of their marriage worth recording is that Belladonna is not her real name.

195

It goes without saying that she couldn't call herself Bev Carmody on the day she put a ring on Ruddles's finger and got him to promise to obey her – no even moderately militant modern Australian woman assumes her husband's name, and Bev Belladonna stood, as it says in her entry in *Who's Who in Victorian Activism*, 'in the very front line of the ceaseless bloody battle between the sexes'. The trouble was that she couldn't retain her maiden name because that, by one of those cruel coincidences which posterity – women's posterity – would never credit, just happened to be Carmody also. She chose Belladonna, after going twice through the Melbourne telephone-book, for its association of female beauty with poison.

'So why do you think you're being watched?' Ruddles asked me, once he was certain that all merriment had drained from my voice.

'I can only suppose,' I said, 'it is because they fear I am going to write my memoirs. I would of course be in breach of my duty of confidentiality owed to the Crown, to Canberra, and to the White House, if I sought to publish information or knowledge gathered during the course of my duties.'

'And do you intend to publish such information?'

'I can't say over the phone,' I said.

'Leon, do you *possess* such information?'

'I can't say over the phone,' I said.

'You rang *me*, Leon.'

'I was hoping we might discuss it over lunch. Steak pizzaiola, I thought.' I heard myself go a bit throaty here. Which was a pity. I didn't want to sound sentimental. Or lonely. Or desperate.

'I am pretty busy at the moment,' he said.

Maybe he was. It must have been time-consuming, getting on with leftists and rightists, reconciling unilateralists to multibelligerents, explaining russophiles to sinophobes. But I had a vision of him, grossly overweight now, and as bald as a Buddha, sitting around in his kimono in the kitchen – the headquarters of Flexible Marxism in the Southern Hemisphere – swilling aromatic floral teas without milk, balancing extremism with moderation by thinking he should take a knife to his fanatic helpmeet – his and his party's other half: she the ism, he the Flex – and then thinking maybe he shouldn't.

Some friend, either way.

'Don't blame yourself if you hear that I've been wiped out,' I said, not even bothering to try to hide my hurt this time. 'I wouldn't dream of bending you or your party from your already flexuous courses. I fully realize that the complaints of a mere put-upon Pom from non-tribal Vaucluse—'

He interrupted me. 'The trouble with you, Leon—'

So I interrupted him. 'Is that people think they can tell me what the trouble with me is,' I said.

'There you go again,' he said. 'I don't mean you as you, I mean you as you promote yourself in the public domain – you as *texte*.'

Sometimes I think there is more French spoken in Australia than in the whole of Hampstead. '*À bientôt*,' I said, just before I put the phone down on him, 'if you know what that means.'

It was Vietnam, as I've mentioned, and not Bev Belladonna – who was yet to flower in Ruddles's garden – that came between us. By the late sixties Ruddles had become an acknowledged expert on Indo-China and could go back a couple of hundred years before Christ in his denunciations of imperialist atrocities perpetrated on the indigenous peasant population of what was then Nam Viet; whereas I – well I was what Ruddles rightly accused me of being: a personality rather than a principle man, incapable of seeing the argument for the arguer, hopelessly *ad hominem* when all around me was history. I had dined alone for ten weeks under the dead eye of the Master of Malapert, without a soul to talk or

197

pass a roll to, purely because I objected to the syntax of Martinez Sjögren Léger de Pied, and I became a passionate advocate of Australian military involvement in South-East Asia not because I knew where South-East Asia was, or what justification anyone who wasn't South-East Asian had for being there, but because I hated Frank Whiling. The moment I saw him standing on an upturned mango-crate in the middle of the lawn at Noonthorungee, giddy with vertigo and agoraphobia, faint with sunstroke and neurasthenic megalomania, but just able to stay up long enough to twist his fingers into an arthritic fist of victory, to contort his hunched and hollow shoulders into the first famous fight-back of the turning worm, and to give an example to draft-resisters everywhere by setting fire to his Australian driving licence – the moment I beheld all this and heard his nerveless, malarial drone – 'They tell us we must make Vietnam safe for democracy; but *whose* democracy must we make it safe for?' – my loyalties were fixed, and I was ready to fly low over enemy jungles, dropping cans of fumigant and flame.

The rights and wrongs of the conflict were quite beyond me, but you couldn't go far astray, I believed, if you found out what Frank Whiling thought, and thought the opposite.

I still adhere to that view today, incidentally, even *post Lactrodectus mactans*. Some obstinacies of character even a spider bite can't alter. If Frank Whiling were to appear on the steps of the Opera House tomorrow, pleading the cause of the starving, I would instantly remember a thousand compelling arguments in favour of malnutrition.

Fortunately it won't happen. Frank Whiling has grown plump and quiet. His moment came and went, and even El Salvador doesn't rouse him now. He made it up with Orel Rosenfeldt when the latter returned from America after the project for lowering the threshold of human expectation ran out of money. I don't know what they found to reunite them, but conciliation was in the air in Australia – Bob Hawke had just come to power, ushering in the era of the strange bedfellow – and now they are in Canberra together (the academic equivalent of being put out to graze) where they take turns running the Futility Unit. They accept no students and encourage no research, since these would breach the spirit of the discipline. I'm told time hangs heavy on both their hands; that Orel – abandoned by his wife once the doctors ordered him off cigars, French cigarettes, whisky and judges' daughters – can be found drinking shandies in the company of public servants; and that Frank Whiling is talking of retiring prematurely to a smallholding in the Maluerne hulles, failing which, Queanbeyan.

But if you think this gives me any satisfaction you are mistaken. Vengeance is just one of the many pleasures normally stored up for middle age which the Redback robbed me of. It is a desolating experience to be bitten. Long after the pain goes and the swelling subsides and even the shame abates, you are left with melancholy reflections and a dim view of what usually passes for consolation. It is no longer possible for me to believe, for example – not with a small angry puncture in one of the most secret recesses of my body it isn't – that the fact of now, when obscurity settles over Frank Whiling like dust, can obliterate the fact of then, when no candle-lit procession, no demonstration, moratorium or vigil could call itself competent until he'd blessed it. Time's whirligig, the spider teaches, does *not* bring in its revenges. Poetic justice is for prosaic minds. Whiling stands for ever on his upturned mango-crate, address-ing the nation's babies, and there's nothing I or fate or irony can do to topple him.

Those were tough times for me, when the streets were given over to a ceaseless carnival of righteous youth. Not least because I was young myself. It was still well short of thirty years since the crane-flies had organized their own charivari on the slopes of my mother's belly, just inches from where I lay curled like a spring, or one of Orel Rosenfeldt's spiral apple-rinds, poised to make the great bound of my life. But young in the way these bronzed and bouncing Nazarenes were young I had never been.

I had a mistrust for all forms of revivalism for a start. Not because I didn't know what it was like for one's heart to pound in unison with a thousand others, but because I did. Ever since my first morning assembly at Partington Grammar, when the sound of five hundred Partingtons singing *Gaudeamus Igitur* moved me so profoundly that I wept on to my new school shoes, I had turned my back on that part of me that would be a crowd, and had made a decision in favour of solitary emotion. It's true that I still wept, in the privacy of my darkened bedroom, at Mario Lanza's version of my old school song, but at least I was out of harm's way, off the streets, free of that bewilderingly upsetting sensation that comes with being roused into fellow feeling with people you don't even like.

But it wasn't just fear of the throb that had kept me away from mass expression, it was also discomfort with the daemon. However conscientiously those chanting kids had mastered Indo-Chinese history – in contradistinction to me who had only mastered Frank Whiling – however genuinely they felt the suffering of an oppressed and distant peasantry, it was above all the violence of their own energy that stirred them, the unstoppable exuberance of their own youth. When one hundred thousand people in the prime of life link arms, the great cause that binds them is themselves. The first impulse in any revolution is the exhilaration of revolt – the daemon of disobedience – and for revolt itself, revolt pure and youthful, I was too much of an idolater of grown-ups (I only *hid* from Hester and Nesta, I didn't mutiny) to have any taste.

And so I missed out on the best and longest outdoor

party Australia is ever likely to throw. It was the pick of picnics. The barbecue to end all barbecues. I watched it for four years from the windows of the offices of *The Black Sail*, conveniently situated for party-pooping at the corner of George and Barrack Streets, overlooking Martin Place, where Frank Whiling summoned what always promised to be his last breath in order to shout, 'Victory to———', and the demonstrators responded with whatever took their fancy: an army, a Chinaman, a racehorse. Yes, like an angel of virulence I stood at the window and watched it, grinding my forehead into the glass with fury, swallowing pencils whole with indignation, flaying the very skin from the back of my hands with the rage of unspent vehemence. For I, too, you see, was in the prime of life and in need of letting off a little steam. And although I had my own quiet little socials and shindigs to attend – this was a busy time for Freedom Academy and the CIA, as you might imagine – there could be no doubt whose the big do was and where the good times were. I hated to the bottom of my soul what was happening in the streets, but I hated even more missing out on it. I believe that I would have exploded, literally blown apart from the inside, and taken the whole of *The Black Sail* and half of George Street with me, had I not, at the eleventh hour, found an outlet for my energy, a buttress for my crumbling faith, a sign – as potent as a rainbow or a burning bush – that the God of operettas and gothic ruins was still in his heaven, that he had not capitulated yet to the Beelzebub of street babble, and that he still loved me.

Two signs, to be exact.

I am referring, of course, to Venie and Maroochi.

201

18

'HAVE YOU NOTICED how much time Australian men spend scratching their dicks?'

I had to say – although I was at that delicate early stage of a relationship with a woman, when one doesn't want to admit the first suggestion of disagreement or discord – that I hadn't.

'Oh, come on,' Venie said. 'You've been to the cricket. You've seen what happens the minute an Australian batsman comes to the wicket.' She made a gross, ape-like grab for herself under the tablecloth, causing the ashtrays to empty, and the water in the pretty little vase of flowers to jump. For a second or two it looked as though she was going to stand up and grubble about in the area where her penis would have been giving her trouble had she been an Australian cricketer.

I looked quickly around the room. We were in a crowded Swedish restaurant in Kings Cross, waiting for someone to come and help us with the menu. Every dish seemed to be *med agg*, which we guessed meant with egg, and as Venie didn't eat eggs (for some secret synchronised swimmer's reason) I was already – our topic of conversation apart – beginning to have second thoughts about my decision to bring her here. I badly needed nothing to go wrong. We had met only a couple of hours earlier on the fringes of a moratorium, both accidentally caught up in a crush occasioned by a police-man's refusal to accept a frangipani blossom from a boy in a beard and a cheesecloth shirt. Like me she had been standing idly by, appalled, nauseated, but minding her own business. By the time I heard her

202

mutter, 'That's it, flatten the freak,' the policeman had been sitting on the boy for a good five minutes. So she couldn't be accused of inciting anything. Except me.

'Isn't that just first-ball nerves?' I wondered.

'First-ball nerves? What I'm describing lasts all through the innings.' She made a further illustrative lunge under the tablecloth, as if she were scooping up fleas, by the handful, from her lap. 'They're still scratching when they've reached a double-century, although you wouldn't believe they had anything left to scratch by then.'

'Surely that's only because they're wearing boxes.'

I didn't know Venie well enough yet to look her in the eyes while I pronounced the word box, so I looked up at the wall above her instead, where there were blown-up black and white photographs of the Swedish royal family, and Greta Garbo reclining on satin sheets, her eyelids heavy and her lips wet, as if she had just eaten a little too much of something or other med agg.

'They *all* wear boxes,' Venie said. I thought I detected the sort of confidence that only comes with inside knowledge. 'But it's still only the Australians who get stuck in there.'

'So if I were to say I'd once seen the Nawab of Pataudi . . .'

'. . . I'd say you were misunderstanding me. I'm not talking about the odd quick adjustment which all men find necessary from time to time. We're dealing with compulsive, obsessional behaviour here. You're not going to understand the significance of dick-scratching amongst Australian men without going into the whole question of their psycho-socio-erotico needs.'

I leaned towards her, my elbows firmly on the table. She had a soft golden down on her cheeks and green eyes and a mouth whose fullness reminded me of Trilby and breeding. There was a faint fetching indentation on her nostril which intrigued me and which I learned later came from the nose-plug she had to wear so that she could breathe under water, while practising her inverted verticals. But what I most liked about her appearance – I'm talking about the whole razzle-dazzle now, the bright colours, the make-up, the plumage, the fun jewellery – was the way it made me think of dessert. Most Australian women look like afters of some kind. Maroochi, for example, whom I would hear of for the first time any minute and meet by and by, was a rich dark chocolate cake, crumbly rather than chewy, with a bitter aroma of molasses and cocoa. I would always know when Maroochi was home because it was as if there'd been baking in the house, and the oven door was just opened. But Venie was more than merely another sweet. Venie was the great Australian indulgence itself. Venie was double cream and icing sugar and marshmallow and kiwi-fruit and passion-fruit and strawberries and peaks of stiff meringue. Venie – and please note that naming desserts after women is not my idea – Venie was a Pavlova.

The Pavlova – for those who have never left Partington – is a versatile extravagance and sometimes takes the place of a birthday-cake. That said, I trust I will not be misunderstood when I confess that there were times in the company of Venie when I wanted nothing so much as to turn down the lights, put a candle in her and blow her out.

Tonight, though, in the first hot flush of our acquaintance, I was content just to sit and hear her talk. I wanted to know who she was and where she came from and what she had been doing where I found her, on the fringes of a moratorium. I knew we were going to have a good time countering the counter-culture together. And of course I wanted to hear more about the psycho-socio-erotico needs of the itchy Australian male.

'Do you reckon the heat's got something to do with it?' I asked. There seemed to be all sorts of as yet unrevealed advantages to me in establishing that all

Australians suffered from acute tinea of the prepuce.

She shrugged and smiled, so that white creases of her original skin showed suddenly, around her mouth and eyes, through all the tan and make-up. I was to grow very fond of those silver fault-lines which would appear across the face of Venie Redfern only when she was amused, giving a quick glimpse of the girl beneath the glitter – for all that I loved the glitter.

'There are three principal methods of scratching your dick in this country,' she said. 'There's slapping' – she pulled her chair back from the table and cuffed herself, with a rapid raking movement, where her napkin should have been – 'there's prising' – she delved in the air with one finger, as if trying to reach the last olive in a jar – 'and there's tweaking.' She didn't feel that she needed to demonstrate tweaking. 'Of these only prising can be directly attributable to discomfort caused by heat. The others are nervous disorders connected with anxiety and distress. My father, for example, tweaked himself stupid just before an election.' I couldn't have guessed at the time that she was referring to a Liberal State Premier. 'Just like this fellow here.'

I looked up. A waiter was heading for our table at last. I wouldn't have known for certain whether he was Australian or Swedish had his fingers not been plucking at his penis as he approached us.

'See,' Venie whispered.

I couldn't look. I kept my eyes on Greta Garbo instead and explained our problem with the menu to *her*. 'I'll have whatever you recommend,' I said. 'But my friend would like something medout agg, if that can be arranged.'

During periods of intense concentration it is possible to receive those sensory impressions we call sight through just about any part of the epidermis. Greta Garbo, who herself had always made a virtue of looking out upon the world from behind a film of gauze, surveyed me now through drooping lids; and although I returned her gaze unswervingly, I was still able to know, thanks to the great eye my whole body had become, that Venie Redfern's lovely face was criss-crossed with the silver fault-lines of amusement, that the waiter, who was pointing to the menu with his right hand, was still paddling in his privates with his left, and that every Australian male over thirteen in the restaurant was, with greater or lesser urgency, doing likewise.

'See,' Venie repeated, once the waiter had left us and I could relax my stare.

'See? I doubt if I will see anything else again.'

'It's a problem,' she said, 'if you are a girl, knowing where to look in this country.'

I adopted a serious sociological demeanour, so as not to appear too smug about coming from Partington. 'It's country-wide, then?' I asked. 'Not just an affliction caused by the hectic pace and humidity of Sydney?'

'I can assure you it's worse in Melbourne. And as for Perth.'

We both peered, for a moment or two, into how bad it was in Perth.

'So where *do* you look?' I asked at last.

She measured her reply expertly, as if she knew to the centimetre just how deep a dive she needed to take. 'Overseas,' she said.

Only she didn't say it like someone who was planning a long trip.

I swallowed hard. A voice I didn't recognize as mine but which definitely originated in my throat said, 'Then look no further.'

We threaded eye-beams. 'I won't,' she said, as two vast open egg sandwiches stuck with little flags and paper umbrellas arrived in front of us.

We scarcely noticed them.

'That's settled then,' I glistened. And I want it to be clear that I still didn't know she was the daughter of a Liberal State Premier.

206

'It is,' she glistened back.

I was so excited that without giving it a thought I reached beneath the table and scratched my penis.

Over coffee and dessert – we had one Coupe August Strindberg between the two of us, and Venie ate the best bits – we discussed all the other ways in which I was appealingly un-Australian.

'You don't screw up your eyes, you don't look as though you'd rather be in the pub with your mates, you haven't got flaking skin, you haven't got chapped lips, you don't sport a cancerous scab on the upper fold of each ear, you're not covered in freckles, you don't have broken purple veins on your nose as a consequence of the time you've spent in the pub with your mates . . .'

I could not remember ever having been the object of so much negative appreciation. 'So what *do* I have?' I asked, emboldened by what I didn't.

'A dirty face,' she said.

I made a startled grab for a serviette.

'No, I mean you look bad.'

'Evil, you think?' It's possible I sounded a touch eager.

Venie thought about it. 'Your face is a map of low desires,' she said.

At a later date she would tell me that the area from the bridge of my nose to the slight cleft in my chin reminded her of a hitherto undiscovered sexual organ. But she made no mention of this tonight, presumably because she felt she'd gone as far as she could with the subject of organs on a first meeting. As for me, I was more than content with her description of me as a map of low desires. Don't forget the context. The streets had been full of goodness for the last three years. You were no one if you didn't come up each morning looking like an innocent flower on a fragile stalk, just washed by the dew. It must have been bad everywhere – I'm told it was awful in France and Germany – but in Australia where there was already a powerful temptation to pretend you were the first children of creation, stammering out the names of all the wonders of another Eden, the artlessness movement of the late sixties – the beatification of the nymph and shepherd – had an especially deleterious effect upon the national character. To this day an extravagantly high value is attached to naïvety in Australia. Mothers dress like their baby daughters. Fathers are more enthusiastic than their sons. And no politician who fails the test of boyishness can count his seat secure. So to be told, in the very thick of it, that I was bad, that I looked dirty, that my face was a map of low desires – and to be told by a girl who encouraged policemen to sit on hippies and whose wrists jangled with gold – why, that was very heaven.

'And,' she said – yes, there was more – 'and you don't seem to me to be the sort of bloke who would be jealous of Mooch.'

'Mooch?'

'Maroochi. Maroochi Ravesh, my swimming partner.'

I had gathered that Venie was a synchronized swimmer, but there hadn't been time for it to dawn on me that there was therefore someone she achieved synchronization with.

'No,' I said, 'I'm certainly not the sort who would be jealous of your swimming partner. Are many people?'

'You've no idea,' she said, folding her hands upon her chest in perfect imitation of a butterfly, a big bejewelled butterfly, settling. It was a movement I could easily imagine figuring in her routine – *their* routine – and earning top marks from every judge.

'Men are possessive,' I enjoyed reflecting.

'Especially Australian men.'

I shrugged like one who couldn't be expected to know. Or shouldn't be expected to say. I really was having the most terrific time.

'Why do you think that is?' I pretended I was curious to learn.

Venie didn't even hesitate. 'No confidence in their masculinity,' she said. Her voice, when she was being bright, rang like bone china under sniper fire. You could hear it pinging all over the restaurant. 'It goes back a couple of hundred years to when there were no women in the country. They had to be shipped over specially, while the men stood at the water's edge, waiting and peering. Which is why they all still squint and look longingly into the middle distance.'

'So you think they're frightened that at any moment the ships might return to take the women back again?'

'Mooch's theory exactly. She reckons Australian men are in the same relation to their wives as they are to their dicks – they only fiddle with them to make certain they're still there.'

'It's an interesting theory,' I said.

Then, but for no other reason than that it was necessary for me to show I wasn't possessive, I added, 'So when will I be meeting this friend of yours?'

'All in good time,' Venie said, rising so that I should hurry up and pay the bill, so that we might go.

But three hours later, as we stood together at the bottom of my North Shore garden, listening to the water lapping the rocks and the goanna getting his teeth into the chocolate spread, she was more forthcoming.

'We used to train just there,' she told me, pointing to the Olympic pool across the bay.

'You and Maroochi?'

'Me and Mooch.'

I had my arm around her shoulder, or at least around as much of her shoulder as I could encircle. The memory of the width and power of Venie's upper torso is still capable of bringing a brief tear to my eye. I saw it again only recently on film, when they were showing a television clip of her and Mooch just failing to get among the medals at the Montreal Olympics, and I cried myself to sleep.

'And now?' I asked.

She leaned against me and sighed, breathing in the marvellous Sydney night. I think she must have thought – from the way she threw her head back and took in the stars – that my question was more philosophical than I had meant it. 'And now and now and now,' she murmured.

'And now where do you train?' I spelled out.

She shook a Christmas beetle out of her hair, which I crunched surreptitiously where it fell.

'Oh, over at Balmain. At the Dawn Fraser Pool. Do you know it?'

'I'll find it,' I said.

That's not entirely the end of the only evening I was ever to spend with Venie singly – not entirely the end of what I am prepared to report of it, that is. Though to go on calling it an evening is misleading, since we were still making each other's acquaintance when the light came, and with it those flocks of ironic Technicolor birds, blowing raspberries and all but laughing in our faces. In fact it was almost certainly to defend herself against what the rosellas and the cockatoos charged her with – folly, ineffectuality and absurdity – that she told me who her father was. God knows if the information impressed the birds, but it would have stopped me squawking had I been one. 'Really?' I said. 'Is he? Did he? Will he? Well!'

There are validating moments in life, call them illuminations or epiphanies or confirmations, when you understand what it is that has all along been in store for you. At such moments a man will turn his back on everything for God or art, and a woman will know in her soul that she must become a Human Rights Commissioner. In my case, as soon as I heard the name the Hon. Murray Redfern, Premier, Treasurer and Minister for Looting and Gaming, I knew that every path I'd ever taken led inexorably to his daughter.

'I know,' I said, when she told me that had she not been concentrating on her swimming her father would have paid for her to read Moral Decencies at Cambridge.

'I know,' I said, when she told me she shared a house with Maroochi in Vaucluse.

And 'I know,' I said, when she told me that she'd been born and spent her first formative years in Heidelberg.

It turned out that she meant Heidelberg, the Melbourne suburb, not Heidelberg where the Student Prince lost his heart to a commoner, but I wasn't in any mood to split hairs.

19

ALTHOUGH there was no place on earth I would rather have been that afternoon than the Dawn Fraser Pool, Balmain, I had to give it a miss. I had a long-standing appointment to accompany Trilby and my father to a fashion show – a fashion show for trade buyers only, that is – and my father was looking so fragile these days, so worn to a frazzle by love, that I treated every arrangement with him as if it could be the last.

Not that I viewed an outing of this kind solely as a duty. I loved helping to buy for the *boutiques*, even though my opinion on what seemed chic and saleable was never heeded. I have a feeling that Trilby was guided by my taste in the same way I was guided by Frank Whiling's politics. She listened in order to learn what to avoid. It's pretty certain that she thought me vulgar. 'That would be fine, Leeorhn, if we had a shop in Bondi,' I remember her saying, 'but in Double Bay? – Well, I think not.'

For Bondi I was to understand Partington.

I didn't mind. It gave me a thrill of the old kind when Trilby found me vulgar. There wasn't anybody else I would rather have remind me of my origins. And I *was* vulgar. I got excited by the amounts of money I watched her spend. I liked the sight of the scraggy models slipping in and out of makeshift changing rooms to order, trying on whatever you fancied seeing them in. And I liked the wary worldly businesswomen we dealt with – more attractive than the models because more fraught – who watched us through narrowed eyes as we fingered samples, until they remembered who we were (who Trilby was, anyway) and then snap-relaxed into professional amicability and showered us with drinks. Outside, in Martin Place, toddlers in Chinese work-sandals were standing vigil, wearing their hearts upon their placards. Some of them had stopped exchanging such greetings as 'Hello' and 'Good morning' on the grounds that they were platitudinous and hypocritical. So I would have gone to a wholesale fashion show every day, had there been one, in order to enjoy the sort of seasoned courteousness that only economic necessity can impose.

Boy, was I vulgar. The spectacle of my father confidently sizing up famous international collections, shaking his head or pausing to stand on tip-toe and whisper in Trilby's ear, filled me with sentimental pride; I wanted to take him in my arms and press my lips to his melancholy musketeer's moustache and tell him how well I thought he'd done for a man who once couldn't hold down a job as a toweller and drier in a certain *salon* in a certain cul-de-sac not less than thirteen thousand miles from here.

The show I postponed my first meeting with Maroochi for was being held in Sydney's newest and most fashionable tower block. It was the tallest building in the Southern Hemisphere, and the fourth tallest round building surmounted by a revolving restaurant – being turned around while you ate was the big thing this year – in the world. Its other feature was its spacious ground-level patio, offering stationary but outdoor bijou Continental feeding facilities. There had been a lot of talk recently about how much more sophisticated Australia might have been had the French discovered it, and street cafés were suddenly springing up in the most unlikely places, in despite of the Southerly buster which would leave kerb-side coffee-drinkers shivering at their tables in the late afternoon, watching the umbrellas carrying advertisements for Perrier Water go sailing off into the harbour. I was guardedly approving of this move towards the Continentalization of Australia myself – although I was watchful of its possible implications of disloyalty to the Commonwealth – and rather agreed with what Lobelia Sneddon said about it on national television, to wit – '*le style c'est tout* – that means style is everything'.

The show itself differed from all the others I had attended in that it was devoted solely to lingerie. Seeing pretty girls wandering about in their underwear was nothing like so sensational in Sydney as it might have been elsewhere, since underwear was more than most Sydney girls wore anyway. Nonetheless there could be no mistaking that it was precisely for the sensational element, for what she hoped might turn out to be the curative powers of near-nakedness – *other* women's near-nakedness, she meant – that Trilby had brought my father. We met as arranged at the fountain in the foyer and she wasted no time in telling me that she was still concerned about his indefatigable devotion to her.

'Just look at him,' Trilby repeated. 'He doesn't give a monkey's.'

I made the obvious polite objections. You should be flattered etc. It's a compliment to your etc.

But she waved them away. 'I'm exhausted by it,' she said. And then, just before my father joined us, she quickly added, 'We both are.'

I was unable to decide whether he looked any more exhausted than usual. I thought I could detect a faint creak, like the sighing of old trees, issuing from his joints, but then I thought I had detected something similar twenty-five years earlier when he tried to lift me out of my pram and sit me on his shoulders. The only sure signs of deterioration were these: his hair had grown thinner and his eyes, once they rested on Trilby, had grown brighter.

'You look tired,' he said, handing me my badge.

Trilby's he insisted on fastening to her himself. She

inclined towards him so that he shouldn't have to stretch. He took a small lifetime to secure it, making no attempt to conceal that he was seizing the opportunity to feel her breasts. Trilby threw me a woeful glance, as if to say, 'See? Here he comes again. Twenty years this has been going on – twenty years, day and night, in the privacy of our delightful home or in full public view, as here, in a room crowded with beautiful young women.' But I noticed that she didn't move away, and that there was an eruption of something suspiciously like pleasure, a sort of heat rash, just discernible high up on each of her cheeks.

Ashamed to be seen or associated with them, I walked ahead into the main exhibition room. Six blondes – none as spectacular as Venie, but all glowing with that isn't-it-amazing-to-be-alive animation which is characteristic of Sydney and marks it out as a country town still – were doing a can-can on a narrow catwalk. I've never taken much interest in the can-can. My old friend Ramsay, who knew about such things, once told me that the original dance was altogether more lewd than the modern family adaptation, since the dancers wore nothing underneath their petticoats. 'Yes, well I can see that that would make a difference,' I conceded. 'But I still wouldn't go for all that screaming and shouting and general high spirits.' 'You would if you saw the original,' Ramsay assured me.

I doubt if Ramsay would have enjoyed the Australian version. That combination of irony, tomboyishness, and country-town rawness which is to be found in all Australian women makes it difficult for them to throw themselves into public sexuality. The six I was watching could manage the shrieks and the splits all right, but there was no escaping the impression the minute they began to kick their feet above their heads, that one had gate-crashed an end-of-term party at a convent school, where the senior girls were indulging in a bit of horse-play before the nuns came to turn the lights out.

'Look,' I heard a voice behind me saying. 'Frilly knickers and suspenders. You like those.' It was Trilby, still trying to interest my father in lingerie.

'Wrong for our shops,' I heard him reply.

'And black fishnet stockings.'

'Nope. Not for our shops.'

'Shops, shops, shops,' she said. 'Is that all you can think about?'

I heard a whisper and then some muffled laughter. I walked on, determined not to look back. I was dead certain that if I had I would have seen my father's hand up Trilby's skirt.

As we were leaving Trilby asked me whether I had liked what had been on show. I gave her one of my I-can-take-it-or-leave-it sort of shrugs. But because I didn't want to seem ungrateful to her for bringing me, I explained, 'My mind's on other things to be frank. I think I'm in love.'

She swept me up immediately in an immoderate hug. 'Oh, Leeorhn, that's marhvellous.'

My father eyed me more cautiously. He knew, of course, what a terrible business thinking you're in love can be.

'I suppose you'd better bring her over,' he said, after Trilby had hugged me a few more times and our Fashion Buyer's badges had become entangled.

I couldn't believe my ears. This was the first fatherly thing I'd ever heard him say. I was overcome. It suddenly occurred to me that he might even be thinking of offering me advice. The prospect left me quite light-headed.

'I will,' I said. 'I'd be delighted.'

Then I remembered that it wasn't quite as easy as that. 'By the way there are two of them,' I added. I made sure that I sounded pretty casual about it.

My father's expression lightened. I thought he looked proud of me. As if I were carrying on an honourable family tradition. He seemed to be trying to let me know that numbers were no object and that I could bring a dozen if I chose. Trilby, however, looked more alarmed.

'You're not telling us you're in love with both of them?' she asked.

I date from this moment the realization that Trilby might not have been an aristocrat after all.

I pondered her question, though. I hadn't met Maroochi yet. At least not in the conventional sense of the word meet. All I knew of her was what Venie had briefly told me. And of that, nothing stuck in my mind but her capacity to make Australian men who were interested in Venie jealous. That seemed to be enough to be going on with. That and something or other about her father being a judge.

'Yes,' I said. 'Yes, I think I am in love with both of them.'

There is a small park on the western side of Balmain, a little scrubby reserve of greenery running down to White Horse Point, from where you can look out to Cockatoo Island and some of the more industrialized bays and wharfs of the Paramatta River, at Woolwich and Drummoyne. Here the pleasure-boats don't have it all their own way as they did in the discreet cove I used to overlook, but must jostle for water space with heavy shipping, boats bringing toy koalas from Taiwan or taking wheat to Russia. I had come for pleasure purposes myself, for all that I was heavily freighted with anticipation, because the other commanding view the little park enjoyed – a wooden bench had even been erected to enjoy it better from – was of a swimming pool which had been reclaimed from the harbour and fenced off from the sharks in honour of the much misunderstood genius of Dawn Fraser.

It was about four in the afternoon when I settled on to the bench and began to scan the pool, no more than

217

a hundred yards below me, for familiar shoulders. I was worried that I might be too late, that Venie and Maroochi might have had their practice swim and left. It was a rather chilly autumnal afternoon and there didn't seem to be any movement in the pool. I sat craning my neck and cursing the circumstances which had delayed me. 'Fucking Jewish novelists,' I muttered under my breath, although there was no one around to hear me. 'With their fucking hang-ups.' This wasn't racism on my part. Some of my closest colleagues in Freedom Academy International were Jews. As was Henry Kissinger whose hand I'd shaken twice, at two separate Freedom Academy dinners, and who had told me on each occasion that it wasn't often that a man could say he'd participated in turning a new page of history. No, I was no racist. But I'd spent three-quarters of the day in court, listening to a defence lawyer reading me out extracts from *Portnoy's Complaint* (which CACA was attempting to ban) and asking me if I now considered myself depraved. I told him yes. Most CACA witnesses argued that it wasn't their own depravity that worried them so much as someone else's, but I thought it might hurry things along if I owned up to being the very person into whose hands pornography should never fall. I couldn't have been more wrong. The defence lawyer stared at me in stupefaction. I seemed to be something his training had never prepared him for. 'Are you honestly telling me that having read paragraph 2 on page 115, you are now likely to go out and . . . ?' I stopped him. 'Yes,' I said. 'And that after reading lines 17 to 26 on page . . . ?' 'Yes,' I said, 'the minute I leave this courtroom.' He wasn't to know, of course, that I had a date with Venie and Maroochi at the Dawn Fraser Pool, Balmain.

It was a quarter to three before I was allowed to stand down. I'd been saying yes for almost four hours. I'm certain that the defence lawyer would have asked the court to have me followed had that not been against the interests of his client. As it was, he accused me of being slobberingly susceptible to the written word before he remembered that it was his argument that there was nothing here to slobber over.

I was still cursing, only gazing with half an eye now at the deserted pool, when I suddenly saw something break the placid surface of the water. It rose to a height of about one metre, spun, arched, disappeared, and soared again. That, I said to myself, because I had seen it only a few days before, is Venie's leg. And that, I said, when its partner appeared and did the same, is Venie's other leg. It was only when I noticed that both these legs were right legs, and that when they vanished and resurfaced they were left legs, that I realised Venie was not alone as she danced head downwards in the water, and that I had caught my first glimpse, at last, of that jealousy-provoking aqua-ballerina, Maroochi Ravesh.

I rose from the bench, forgot to test my feet for pins and needles, fell, slid down the mossy timbered steps built into the hill, and but for the turnstiles would have rolled straight into the pool. The cashier, who doubled as the life-saver, eyed me curiously. I don't mean Partington-curiously. This was Australia not England; incivility was not at the bottom of every transaction. I was a minor oddity not an irritation, another dropped stitch in life's queer tapestry.

'No towel?' he noticed.

I told him I hadn't come to swim.

'This is a pool, sport,' he reminded me.

I told him I'd come to meet some friends.

He looked at me quite hard, not moving a muscle on his face. Only in his eyes was there animation, and there little sparkling fireworks fizzed and spluttered. Moustaches were just beginning to appear on the upper lips of athletic Australians, and he twitched his at last in what I took to be a primitive gesture of male bonding.

'It's my belief that you've come to the wrong address, digger,' he said.

I waited to see if he was going to enlarge on that, but when it became clear he wasn't I asked, 'Why's that?'

His eyes were now lit up with exploding Roman candles and star-busters. He nodded his head in the direction of the pool.

'No one in there,' he said. 'It's like the Dead Sea.' A sky-rocket went off. 'Apart from a couple of old lesos.'

But he let me in anyway, because this was a free country and it wasn't for him to say how I ought to spend my afternoons.

Venie and Maroochi were practising a Neptune's Trident, or the Beast With Three Legs, when I arrived at the edge of the pool – that's to say one of them was doing an inverted splits and the other was thrusting a leg up in between. I was to learn later that this was one of the most difficult of all linked figures in water-ballet, not so much on account of its own inherent complications, but because the transition out of it – the recovery, as it was called – required a more than usually powerful turning boost. The one thing you were not allowed to do was use the bottom of the pool for thrust or leverage, though I never really got to understand how the judges could tell if you'd cheated or not. When I raised this with Venie she made me a long speech about sportsmanship, water etiquette, and professionalism. It was a speech she was to repeat, not long after Montreal, when I tried to persuade her of the virtues of anabolic steroids. But by that time we were in trouble – I was in trouble with both of them – on other grounds.

Today, though, I only wanted to marvel and award top marks. I climbed up to the higher of the diving boards and clapped and whistled, while they frolicked like twin dolphins – that's if you can imagine dolphins wearing beaded bonnets and nose-plugs – unaware of my presence. It was only when their transistorised cassette-player had completed its third and final cycle of the 'Ritual Fire Dance' that they realized I was there. Floating on her back and breathing heavily, Venie gave me a wave. Floating on *her* back and breathing even more heavily, Maroochi did the same. But since we hadn't been introduced she was a touch more formal and ceremonial in her movements. She seemed to be performing a little welcoming water-dance especially for me. She raised her thumbs. She separated her toes. She blew her lips in what I was convinced was an authentic Maori greeting.

'Come on in,' Venie shouted. I thought her voice was more nasal than I'd remembered until I realised she was still nose-plugged.

'I can't,' I called back. 'I haven't brought my cossie.'

'Who,' shouted Maroochi – and I somehow knew immediately that we were going to hit it off – 'needs a cossie?'

'He does,' said a voice. It was the man who'd let me in. He'd come out from behind his cashier's grille in order to pick up litter, and sweep away leaves, and spoil my day.

Venie and Maroochi swam towards him in perfect unison. I stayed where I was, on the diving board, not wanting trouble. The man leaned on his brush placidly. He wore a yellow T-shirt which said, IF I HAD TO CHOOSE BETWEEN PARADISE AND AUSTRALIA I'D CHOOSE AUSTRALIA, and a tiny pair of green trunks which said nothing but implied the same.

The girls climbed out of the water together, removed their plugs and sequinned hats together, shook out their hair together – Venie's golden, Maroochi's black – stuck out their tongues together – Venie's pink, Maroochi's magenta – and said 'Wowser!' in one voice.

The man smiled at them imperturbably. He seemed about to say, 'Is that the best you can do?' but checked himself and scratched his dick instead.

'There he goes,' Venie laughed.

'Making sure it's still there,' Maroochi said.

'Would you say he's a slapper or a tweaker?' Venie asked.

Maroochi didn't hesitate. 'Neither,' she said. 'This one's a born priser. You can tell from the broken finger-nails.'

'Show us your nails,' Venie dared him.

The man looked at me in mute appeal. What was I doing, he wanted to know, kicking around with a bunch of loud-mouthed lesos in the middle of the afternoon?

But I couldn't help him. There were only two questions on my mind right now. How it was that Venie and Maroochi had managed to look identical in the water, on their backs, when Maroochi was at least five inches shorter than her partner. And whether, since their swimming costumes were cut so high into their abdomens, they might consider employing the personal services of someone who'd been trained in women's barbering since he was a nipper.

As for the man who was prepared to give up paradise for Australia, he was less astute in his estimate of Venie and Maroochi. They weren't lesos. They were normal, decent, healthy Australians. Girls, as Richard Tauber would have noticed, made to love and kiss.

So who was I to interfere with this?

20

JUST RECENTLY I suffered a visit from Hartley Quibell, the present Domestic Affairs editor of *The Black Sail*, who once described himself to me as the last married man in Australia. This description was meant to reflect favourably on him and adversely on Australia, not the other way round. For a while, when Hartley and I were friends, he infected me with his hymenealatry, and since I wasn't engaged in a marriage of my own (you couldn't call what I had with Venie and Maroochi a *marriage*) I hung around his. He didn't seem to mind. He and Isadora enjoyed a conjugality so perfect that it wasn't necessary for it to be conducted behind closed doors. I was granted a kind of tacit mandate, like a UN observer; only it was understood that I was looking on for my benefit not for theirs.

They retained some essential privacies, obviously, else they would not have sustained perfection, but otherwise I was not hindered in my movements; I had the privilege of complete freedom of access and observation. I arrived early in the morning and stayed late at night, eating the food I had observed them prepare, lolling on the lawn I'd observed them mow, discussing questions of advanced morality with the children I'd observed them bring up, listening to the Deutsche Grammophon masses and magnificats I'd accompanied each to buy the other for solemn anniversaries I observed them observe. And when modernity made one of its periodic spring-tidal rolls towards them, threatening that weak spot in their fortifications where their young were housed (drugs, promiscuity, heavy rock, Tristanism), I took off my jacket, forgot I was an observer, and helped them fill the sand-bags with my own hands.

I saw less of them, as you might imagine, in the great dog-days of Venie and Maroochi. I suspect that Isadora feared the influence of my satisfied gluttony on Hartley; and I know that Hartley feared its influence on his children. They never actually said, 'Don't you dare come parading those two galumphing gorillas here,' but I knew they were unable to put their minds to the women I loved without recourse to some such animal imagery. Which perhaps was only fair seeing that Venie and Maroochi didn't scruple to think animalistically in regard to them. 'I don't know why you spend so much time in the company of mice,' Maroochi used to challenge me. 'Been Squibelling?' Venie used to ask me when I came home late at night with a thumping migraine, pale with the strain of observing a perfect marriage. A squibell, it was understood between us, was a stocky little marsupial with sharp teeth and strict morals, a hairless-nosed insectivore which hoarded its wife and family in the forks of gum-trees and, unlike the koala, grew progressively more sober on the smell of eucalyptus.

'Leave them alone,' it was my habit to reply. 'They're my friends.'

Venie was always the one who would keep it going longest. 'So why aren't you looking as though you've had a good time?'

'I *am* looking as though I've had a good time.'

'So why have you just swallowed a dozen paracetemol?'

'Because I'm drunk with merriment.'

'Is that why your eyebrows have gone grey?'

'I'm going grey all over, Vene. I'm getting old.'

'You're getting old through excessive squibelling. Show me your tongue. Say ah.'

I never refused Venie my tongue. 'Ah.'

'Look at the colour of it. It's ashen. Leon, they're making a ghost of you, starting from the inside.'

What could I say? They were blooming girls in their prime of life who had never gone without anything. How could I explain to them the satisfactions, for a poor orphaned boy from Partington, of sinking into the comforts of a North Shore house (an *Upper* North Shore house), surrounded by a couple of acres of fastidiously tended bush, in the company of a blissfully happy couple (the last in Australia) fifteen years my senior, listening to the younger Quibells (the squiblets, Venie called them) interpreting Albinoni and Telemann on their flutes and harps? It made me quite angry sometimes, having to apologize for such simple pleasure.

On the other hand I couldn't deny that I always returned from Hartley and Isadora's a pale shadow of the man who'd left to see them a couple of hours previously. But it wasn't because they were tame, as Venie and Maroochi insisted, that they were ageing me prematurely – with those two girls waiting up for me I was glad of the odd stretch of inexcitability anyway; nor was it because they reminded me in what smaller numbers and more confined spaces one was obliged to take one's pleasures if one wasn't a revolutionary – here, too, Venie and Maroochi were my solace. No, what wore me out and wore me down was their closet infelicitousness. All families are alike in that they are unhappy, but families which pretend that they are happy are the unhappiest of all. Hartley and Isadora Quibell, as co-owners of the last and most successful marriage in Australia, were on their knees with misery. Hartley, because of the seriousness with which he took his vow never to stretch out his body alongside that of any woman other than Isadora; and Isadora, because of the daily domestic insults Hartley was bound to rain upon her, seeing as he'd made such an intolerable sacrifice on her behalf. (Hartley, by the way, was the prettier of the two, and in a happy and successful

225

marriage the prettier always exacts the higher price for fidelity. Market forces and all that.)

So when Isadora said it was a lovely day, Hartley said it wasn't. And when Isadora used a word like never, Hartley told her that she meant a word like seldom.

'How nice,' said Isadora.

'I think you mean how agreeable,' Hartley told her.

'How agreeable,' said Isadora.

'Not to my eye,' said Hartley.

'Kangaroo,' said Isadora.

'Wallaby,' said Hartley.

'Lindeman's Hunter River Riesling,' said Isadora.

'Brown Bros Chardonnay,' said Hartley.

'*Riders in the Chariot*,' opined Isadora.

'*The Tree of Man*,' Hartley corrected her.

'Isadora's right,' I was once foolish enough to interrupt. It was the nearest I had ever come to forfeiting my mandate.

'Isadora's never right,' Hartley said. 'The only time Isadora ever said anything right' – and here he patted her bottom to show that passion was still alive between them for all that she was always wrong – 'was when she said yes to me.'

'Yes,' said Isadora.

I calculated that at the height of her happiness Isadora was shrinking about an inch a year. I couldn't be certain of my measurements and was never able to hit upon any method of approaching her casually with a ruler or an astrolabe. But I did once manage to make a mark on the wall above her head with my thumbnail, without her noticing, and when I next caught her in the same position three months later, I could see the difference.

I considered pointing this out to Hartley, but I knew he would tell me I was mistaken, that Isadora was in fact taller now than when he'd met her, and that the love of a good husband was rich in nutritional content.

I also thought there was every likelihood that he would go straight back and punish Isadora for what I'd said, with still more euphoria.

As for passing on my observation to Isadora herself – that was out of the question. I dreaded hearing from her own lips what I feared was true: that happiness was more important to her than size, and that frankly it wouldn't bother her if I measured her against my thumbmark one day and discovered she'd vanished altogether, provided that her marriage was still there.

Once the Vietnam war had finished, Freedom Academy Australia (of which Hartley was, for a while, Secretary) turned its attention to domestic matters. Someone had discovered a striking correlation between the number of women in Australia with further degrees and the recent serious decline in national breastfeeding. Isadora was just one of the Freedom Academy wives to speak publicly against this regrettable trend. She delivered a paper entitled *Learned but Still Ladylike*, which Hartley and I listened to together from the back of the Mosman Town Hall. As Secretary, Hartley should have been on the platform with other officials but he couldn't trust himself not to need to correct her. He left me in no doubt that he'd made the right decision. For the first fifteen minutes of Isadora's paper he kept up a stream of mumbled contradictions and amendments, even going so far as to change her punctuation. On more than one occasion people in the row in front of us had to turn round to ask us to shush.

'Hartley,' I whispered. 'Please! You'll have us turfed out.'

'That's a good idea,' he said. 'I'll turf myself out.' And he did so, allowing the door to bang to and fro behind him.

He told me afterwards that he had locked himself in the lavatory and thrown up for the duration of Isadora's talk. I must have looked at him quizzically because he took a remonstrative tone with me. 'I never claimed

227

that being the last married man in Australia was easy,' he said.

We played badminton together every Wednesday evening for a number of years. He always won. Like all husbands who are not promiscuous with their bodies he kept himself in immaculate shape, partly I suppose to drive other women wild with the thought of what they were missing, and partly to make his own continence the more excruciating to himself. I always knew when he was feeling the pinch maritally because he gave me an especially hard time on the court. On one occasion, after he'd hammered me mercilessly – I don't think I even got to serve – he mentioned that he'd run into Venie and Maroochi at an Albinoni concert. 'Lovely looking girls,' he said. He'd just stepped out of the shower. Under the friction of his towel the silver hairs on his chest stood up firm. He didn't look as good as I had on the day Dinmont Manifest recruited me – he wasn't anybody's David – but he didn't look bad. Especially for a man in his forties.

'Yes, they're all right,' I said. 'Mind you they put a bit of effort in for Albinoni.'

Hartley turned around to dry his genitals, showing me his loins. At least I think they were his loins. I've never been entirely certain, when it comes to the mystical areas of the body, what's what. You need someone like Gunnar McMurphy around to help you with things like loins. But whatever it was that Hartley showed me, it (or they) had the peculiar poignancy of non-use. Am I saying that Isadora didn't count? I'm not saying what I'm saying.

'I suppose they're a bit of a handful,' he went on.

I'd forgotten, in my absorption in his loins, who *they* were. Before our one-sided encounter on the badminton court we'd been discussing a series of articles I'd just written for *The Black Sail* on the poofter problem – a post-Vietnam issue which Hartley believed I was right to air, for all that it resulted in my getting a fair amount of stick from the country's leading exponents of un-naturalness. I assumed that it was these Hartley thought I might be finding a bit of a handful. But I decided to check. 'Who do you mean? The sexual pluralists and camp-followers?'

'No, no.' I had it all wrong. 'Venie and Maroochi.'

'Venie and Maroochi?' I was astonished. These few disjointed and apparently idle enquiries might not seem to constitute an in-depth investigation of my private life, but coming from Hartley, on whose lips I could not recall having ever heard the name of a single one of my girlfriends before, they represented a descent into white-hot confidentiality. He was obviously having a terrible time of it internally, in whatever cluster of organs houses husbandly rectitude.

I don't know why but I felt I owed him a favour. Ever since I'd watched my father bounding down the street, trying to get Trilby's motors started, I'd nursed a soft spot for dapper men. Hartley wasn't diminutive, but he was compact, cleaned off at the edges, folded neatly in a dinky presentation-box. Except that he wasn't being given as a present to anybody. So I gave *him* something.

'It's strange,' I said. 'Living with Vene and Mooch can be a lot of fun' (I made fun sound the last thing anybody could want) 'but more and more these days I catch myself wishing that I could find someone to settle down with. A man needs certainty in his life. What are the three essential achievements of manhood?' (Yes, I said manhood!) 'Writing a poem, planting a tree, and having a son? I haven't managed one of those yet.'

I'm not too ashamed of what I said. It was only a white lie. I couldn't bear to think of Hartley going another forty years wondering what he'd missed. It was no skin off my nose to help him feel that he was the lucky one, that he'd missed nothing.

He was half in, half out of his underpants – the last

clean underpants in Australia. He stayed like that for a second or two, looking a long way into what I'd said. Then he decided to accept my gift. 'Well, I guess we make our sacrifices whichever way we jump,' was his response.

'We sure do,' I agreed.

We didn't say anything else to each other until we were dressed. And then suddenly he reverted to our earlier conversation, and his earnest approval of my campaign against the androgynes. 'Do you think they actually do anything?' he asked.

I looked bemused.

'Do you think they really, you know, simulate male–female relations?'

There seemed to be no end to what he wanted from me today. But then that's what friends are for. 'I doubt it,' I said. 'There wouldn't really be much point, would there, since it couldn't end in conception.'

He seemed satisfied with that. Provisionally. But I noticed as we walked together towards Wynyard that he was unable to take his eye off the long-striding giantesses in short dresses who passed us in the street. The idea of conception had cleared up one difficulty only to leave another in its wake. I felt pretty sure when we parted that Isadora was in for a long night of contradiction and correction.

I suppose that if I'd really put my mind intelligently to what I could do for Isadora's welfare I would have lent her husband Venie and Maroochi for a weekend. But faced with a perfect marriage you don't always think of these things.

(The suggestion that Venie and Maroochi were mine to put out on loan belongs, of course, to the pre-spider me. Ever since the Redback had her way with me I've known better than to go near any tone implying possession. Just as anyone that might be regarded as a possession has known better than to go near me. But

230

I use the language of unreconstructed heterosexualism for the sake of historical – personal historical – verisimilitude.)

Anyway, my friendship with the Quibells, like my friendship with Ruddles Carmody, belongs to the past. The whole business of my defection from *The Black Sail*, from Freedom Academy, and from the decencies, is between us now. Which is why I was so surprised when Hartley called on me the other morning. Surprised, and I must say alarmed.

I hadn't seen him for eighteen months or more, and even then we'd only met by chance in the record department of David Jones. He was buying Isadora a selection of Wagner love-duets for their hundredth wedding anniversary and I was looking for a re-release of *Bless the Bride* I'd heard about to send Nesta for Christmas. We stood in everybody's way, trying to be natural, banging empty record-sleeves against our knees, discussing old friends. Hartley knew better than to ask me about Venie and Maroochi – I'll give Hartley that, he never wanted to see me cry – and I knew better than to ask him about the squiblets, all of whom were now going through a necessary period of rebellion, distributing leaflets in Belfast and Beirut. When I showed signs of wanting to be off, Hartley asked the assistant to play him a track from the Wagner and insisted that I accompany him into the booth.

'All right then,' he said, turning down the volume so that Isolde was going to pieces only in a whisper, 'who's got at you?'

I laughed. We were pressed up close together and attracting the attentions of ordinary Australians out buying Albinoni. 'Who's got at me? What makes you think anybody's got at me?'

I wasn't going to mention the spider. Not in a confined space.

'Left to yourself you wouldn't have become a Maoist.'

'A Maoist? Hartley, Maoists went out years ago. Like Chartists and Fabians.'

'You're just proving my point. You wouldn't be in possession of such fashionable factional know-how if someone hadn't got at you. Who is it? Some smart feminist?'

This conversation must have been taking place, behind steamed windows, in 1983 or 4, yet from the way Hartley pronounced *feminist* you would have thought it was the latest explosive device, about to go off any minute in his mouth. Mind you, Australian feminists don't need much to set them ticking, and they do make a big bang.

Through the speakers I could hear Isolde winding up for her final transport. She was making the kind of sounds my father had killed himself to conjure out of Trilby. 'Isadora should like this,' I said. 'I think you've made a good choice.'

Our listening-box was now impossible to see out of, or to breathe in. I turned the handle to let myself out, but Hartley kept me with him for another minute.

'It's all about choice, Leon,' he said. 'In the last resort you have to ask yourself who you'd rather live under – Stalin, or—'

'Stalin?'

'Oh, I see – you're going to pretend he didn't happen. Or you'll tell me that he happened a long time ago – thirty years being an unconscionable time for the clever young things you mix with.'

'Hartley, I don't mix with anyone.' (I wasn't going to tell him that I tried but they wouldn't have me.)

But then he wasn't listening anyway. 'I suppose your friends call him an ism and dismiss his little contribution to human misery as if it's a worn-out style of dressing, along with Maoism and Castroism, no longer favoured by those in vogue. So who is it now, Leon, who's the new hero of the hour for the trendy left? Pol Pot?'

232

Even for the Domestic Affairs editor of *The Black Sail* he was out of touch. But I was scarcely more cluey myself. The spider hadn't provided me with any names. 'I think E. P. Thompson,' I said, hoping that would be the end of it.

I'd forgotten Hartley Quibell's natural contrariness, though. 'E. P. Thompson? Well, he's been got at too. A most distinguished historian none the less. There's an Englishness about his mind, an ordered hedgerow quality, I've always admired. I think of ploughed furrows and frozen . . .'

'Hartley,' I said, 'not now. There's a mob of angry shoppers out there, waiting to hear their Telemanns. You know what Australians are like if they don't get to listen to a bit of baroque played on original instruments at least once a day.'

Actually I couldn't see whether anyone wanted our booth or not, but I knew that unless something was done to break up the conversation we'd be in there for the remainder of the afternoon, imperceptibly changing sides. Soon Hartley would be describing the peculiarly Russian quality of Stalin's mind to me, its Steppe spiritedness, its Volga energy. I was no match for him. I'd only been bitten by one spider. He'd had a lifetime's experience of wrong-footing Isadora. Once I'd even heard him expounding the virtues of Vietnamese communism to her (him, who had gone all the way with LBJ and had kept on going after that) just because she'd said what he'd said about the hated Noam Chomsky. The old yes/no black/white happy marriage principle. Intrepid these life-combatants, prepared to have it out even on the paddy-fields of South-East Asia.

Fortunately the Wagner had finished and the helpful assistant, having found *Bless the Bride* and seeing us still in the box, played us a track. I was enraptured. Back I went, pausing briefly at Partington, to The Grange at Mayfield, and then to the Café des Pommes, Eauville, July 1870. *I vas never kissed before*, sang Georges Guétary, *een zat kind ov vay.* I knew exactly what he meant. I loved Georges Guétary. He was my ideal musical European. A voice like Georges Guétary's, a stage presence like Nelson Eddy's, an appetite like Mario Lanza's, and I would have died happy.

Hartley Quibell hated my taste for operetta. Even when we were conservatives together we were different kinds of conservative. He was after order and quiet; I just wanted to be a titled Frenchman with a warbling voice. I suppose we were bound to split.

He put his hands to his ears when I turned up the volume. 'I have to go now,' he said.

I held him back just as he'd held me. 'At least wait for "Ma Belle Marguerite",' I said.

We shook hands outside the box, but before we separated Hartley led me to understand that *The Black Sail* would still welcome contributions from me, subject of course to the usual editorial provisos. Which is how I come to have been bombarding the magazine with seditious and anarchistic articles of late. I've been wanting to test the efficiency of the usual editorial provisos. So far they have held up nicely. Everything I send them – from a blueprint for the systematic bombing of Canberra, to exposés of how the Americans harpooned Harold Holt off Portsea beach when they saw him climbing aboard a Chinese submarine – they send me back with a polite postcard attached regretting their inability to use it. With time weighing heavily on my hands I've been happy to keep turning the stuff out, knowing that it must take them longer to pop it back in an envelope than it takes me to produce it. (Mainly I just copy out one of their own pieces from a recent issue, making a few slight but telling alterations as regards people and place-names.) I haven't for one moment, I ought to say, imagined that anyone at the offices of *The Black Sail* actually bothers to read anything I write. With Henry Dabscheck in the Editor's chair, Yolanda Dabscheck acting as his secretary, the oldest of Enrico Santalucia's boys, Beniamino, looking after religious matters, Vance Kelpie keeping an eye on Australo-Irish mythology, the Cooney brothers alternating the reviewing, to say nothing of Hartley himself, with the Domestic Affairs brief, *and* Isadora who now runs a wives and mothers column, I've had no illusions as to the chances of a single page of my submissions being looked at. I might not be one of them any more but I still credit them with practical intelligence.

Or at least I did until the other morning when Hartley visited my apartment and wasted no time getting down to business.

'The proprietors and editorial board of *The Black Sail* have asked me to deliver you a message,' he said.

I depressed the plunger of my percolator and poured him coffee. 'They want me to write for them again on a more regular basis?' I guessed.

He crossed his legs, displaying clean white athletic socks. He was still fit. Compact. Dinky. He could still destroy me with a shuttlecock, if he wanted.

And he wanted. 'They wish you to know that if you make any further allegations of CIA funding, they'll sue.'

'Sue the CIA?'

'Sue you, Leon.'

'They'd get more out of the CIA.'

Hartley looked at me sadly. I'm sure that if he'd thought there was any chance of the answer to the question of why I'd changed being shaken out of me he would have held me upside down until it dropped.

As for me, although – as I have always insisted – I am not political, I was struck by the extreme inconsistency of Hartley's position. He had made no secret in all the years I'd known him of his belief in the necessity for such an organisation as the CIA, and his admiration, by and large, for its thoroughness and conscientiousness. So why was he so concerned to deny that the CIA funded him? It's always possible, of course, that they didn't. They'd stopped looking after me, for example, years ago. But surely we weren't in an argument here over the mere fine print of literal truth. If I were an admirer of the CIA – all right, if I were *still* an admirer of the CIA – I would have wanted to boast that they thought me worth investing in, even if they didn't.

I put this to Hartley but he went legalistic on me. '*The Black Sail* does not receive a cent, directly or indirectly, from the CIA.' He really seemed not to have grasped my point. 'Any further allegations that it does, Leon, and we will sue.'

'We?'

'They.'

I let that go. Something else had occurred to me. 'Anyway, where am I supposed to have made these "allegations"?' I asked.

'In the last fifteen articles you sent us.'

'You read those?'

'Every word.'

'You must be mad.'

He let me see who *he* thought the mad one was. But said nothing. For old times' sake, I was to understand.

I rose and went to the window and looked out. Hartley's car was parked in the very place, beneath the very screeching gum, favoured in the evenings by the funereal Mercedes, with Doug Kiernan and Vaughan Cantrell and Hungarian Rudi at the wheel. I turned around and looked at the trim figure of the man to the bosom of whose perfect marriage I had once clung. 'Why is it,' I asked, 'that people who decide they can only live by making a choice, who must embrace a faith whose main tenet is its antagonism to other faiths, why is it that sectarians like yourself, who cannot conceive of anything but plots and conspiracies in the workings of your opponents, absolutely refuse to believe there might be so much as a mumble of machination in your own? The conviction that there's a Red under every bed, a Russian under every cushion, is basic to your philosophy; but let me once suggest that you're in the pay of the Americans or that ASIO parks outside this apartment every night, to keep an eye on what I'm up to, and you'll accuse me of wild fantasizing, and yet not hesitate, either, to threaten me with your solicitors.'

'Why should ASIO be parked outside your apartment?'

(See what I mean.)

'To keep an eye on what I'm up to.'

'Why should ASIO be concerned about what you're up to?'

'Why not? You are.'

Hartley shook his head. I think he was genuinely distressed to see how far I'd embraced the fanaticism and paranoia of the other side. 'Leon, I can't imagine any of the secret agencies of this country—'

I wouldn't let him finish. 'Hartley, why then did they break into the Sheraton Hotel in Melbourne, indiscriminately frightening seventy party-minded Bass Strait oil-rig workers, to say nothing of the Australian Olympic Committee who were trying to choose a team, when I was in the honeymoon suite with Princess ———?' (I obviously cannot repeat the name I gave to him.)

He looked at me in silence. His face was disfigured with distaste and disbelief.

'Or,' I went on, 'are you one of those who still maintains it was a training mission, a practice run for rescuing the next defecting Soviet fleeing from the agents of his own country who, as we all suspect, are dotted all over Melbourne? Nothing fantastical about that, naturally.'

Hartley had pushed aside his distaste to make room for more of his disbelief. 'You don't expect me to accept that such a person would spend the night with you in the Sheraton Hotel.'

I was surprised by his naïvety. 'Hartley, everyone knows that's the only reason European royalty come to Australia. It's common knowledge that they especially like it over here because of the climate and the eager willingness of the natives. Why do you think we see so much of them? And anyway, who said anything about a "night"?'

Hartley made as if to leave, but I could tell that I held hold of his credulity by a thread.

'How did ASIO know you were there?' he asked.

'How do you think? From her husband.'

'Prince ———?'

'Well he has to talk to somebody about her predilections.'

There was a moment or two of silence, during which I watched Hartley pitting his curiosity against his common sense. Then he turned to me with burning eyes. 'What are her predilections?' they pleaded with me to divulge.

Anyone else in my position would have left Hartley Quibell to stew in his own unplumbed imaginings. But I've always been a loyal friend when it's absolutely necessary that I should be; and I considered that at sixty Hartley might just be ready for what I had to tell him. So, employing the tantalisingly formal narrative method of *The Story of O* (a book which I'd slaved hard in my time to have banned from every home in Australia), I took him through *The Story of X*, explaining in some detail (but formally, formally) the precise angle she preferred the chair on the bedside table to be tilted, the direction in which she insisted I point the reading lamp, and the name of all the various royal knots she taught me how to tie.

By the time I'd finished – and of course I'd eked it out in prose that was scrupulous to a fault – Hartley's face had shut up shop. The lights had been turned off in his eyes and his ears were shuttered. He was closed for business. From a little chink between his lips, though, he said this:

'Male fantasy.'

'You think I've made it up?'

Again as if someone else were speaking through him (Isadora granted a voice at last?) he said, 'It's the kind of thing men do make up.'

'Like CIA funding and homosexuality?'

He wasn't going to argue with me. He knew what he knew. All over the world husbands were curling up nightly beside the one woman – usually untitled – they'd ever loved. Every now and then, for no reason other than that they were misguided, the likes of Stalin, Mao and Chomsky came along and made things uncomfortable for everybody else. Quieten them down, send them away, discredit them in the pages of *The Black Sail* and the nightly monogamaniacal curling could placidly resume. The rest was fantasy, hallucination, make-believe.

Well he might have got it right on this occasion – it *was* make-believe.

But what, in that case, was he so bitter about? What, if it was *all* make-believe, did he fear that he'd missed out on?

21

I RANG dear old Ruddles, as soon as Hartley left, to tell him that as well as ASIO, ASIS and whoever else felt like parking outside my flat, I now had Freedom Academy lawyers and perhaps even the CIA itself on my back. But I got the operator, who gave me another number, and when I rang that I got Bev Belladonna.

'Oh, hi Bev,' I said. 'This is Leon. I see you've changed your number. Does that mean they're on to you as well?'

I could hear the icebergs massing on the other end of the line. The phone even went cold in my hand.

'Leon who?'

I knew there was no point in saying, 'Come off it,' or 'Do me a favour,' to Bev Belladonna, so I said, 'Leon Forelock, Ruddles's old pal,' instead.

'Mr Carmody isn't here,' she said. 'And this isn't a private number. This is Party Headquarters.'

Scratch a revolutionary, I thought, and you spill the blood of a bureaucrat. But I didn't say that either.

'Does that mean you've moved house?' I asked. I swear that my question was innocent of any meaning except its apparent one. I simply wanted to know where I was to find Ruddles if Party Headquarters were no longer situate in his kitchen. However, I should have remembered that Bev Belladonna was famous for her ability to hear what wasn't intended. It was said of her in her prime that she did for the Women's Movement in Australia what radar had done for the British fighting Hitler. The comparison was flattering to radar. *It* could

240

only pick up early warnings of attacks that had actually been launched.

I listened helplessly to the sizzle and spit of Bev Belladonna's aerials. 'Do you suppose that we could have gone on providing for the educational needs of three young children *and* staffing a Rape Crisis Centre *and* running a major force in Australian politics from one small terrace house without a garden, a mile and a half from the nearest post office, hospital, crèche or nature strip?'

The answer I would have liked to give was, 'No,' but I could suddenly see so many dangers in the word that I held it back. Not that it would have come out anyway. My mouth was hanging open and almost certainly wouldn't have worked.

'Oghh,' was the best I could manage.

'I can hear that you think we have taken up residence in a mansion in South Yarra. In fact we are in an unrestored artisan's weatherboard cottage at the non-trendy end of Collingwood.'

As I remembered, from my few flying visits to Melbourne to help out at BOONG, to see Ruddles, and to see Dreena (his Dreena), all ends of Collingwood were non-trendy. But I didn't say that. I said, 'Oghh.'

'Cheap point,' Bev hissed. 'We have no intentions of calling in architects. We like the original features just the way they are, including the outside dike. That doesn't bother me. I was brought up in the bush by a bastard of a father and I can squat down in the middle of Hoddle Street if I have to.'

"Oghh,' I said. 'Oghh, oghh.'

'No, there'll be no air-conditioning, and no central heating either. And since we believe in sitting on the floor there'll be no chairs. And now you want to know how much it cost? Seventy-eight thousand bucks, which is considerably below the average for a house of this type in this area. That satisfy your curiosity?'

My curiosity! All I'd wondered was how I could speak

to my old mate Ruddles. I was so dumbfounded that my mouth began to work again. 'Not entirely,' I heard it say. 'How much do the rates amount to annually?'

She told me, of course. You can get anything out of Bev Belladonna. It's not easy being your own armed forces *and* your own secret service.

I shouldn't be so hard on her. I guess it's only inevitable that Ruddles has told her what really happened between us in Wodonga, after we'd cleaned up the locals at darts and returned, through the dark sweet-smelling streets, to our motel. A man can't keep that kind of secret from his wife for ever. And in dear old Ruddles's case, wouldn't want to.

Dear old Ruddles.

No wonder she doesn't like me.

I needed a lie down after this call. It wasn't all Bev's fault. I had needed a lie down after Hartley's visit.

The idea of the number of people who wanted me watched or even silenced filled me with a strange exultation. No sooner did I lie down than I shot up again. I tried to ring Norelle Turpie – that shows how distracted I was – but she was engaged. I walked to the window, knowing full well it was too early for the Mercedes, then I walked back to the phone and dialled the Council for Civil Liberties. They were very polite and most intrigued by my story but I could tell they thought I was unusually buoyant for someone whose personal freedoms were being violated. They also thought I was vaguely familiar to them, which wasn't surprising given how frequently, in my rabid years, I had begun an article with the words, 'I don't see the Council for Civil Liberties rushing to defend the rights of . . .' (inserting the name of someone who'd planted a bomb in the offices of the Australian Labour Party, or gone berserk with a machete at a gathering of peace marchers). I made an appointment to see them the following day, but I knew I wouldn't keep it. It was *now* I wanted someone to talk to. I tried Norelle Turpie's number again. This time I got a recorded message. *There is no one here at the moment . . .* the voice with the twang of death in it rose to that maddening Australian interrogative inflection . . . *But if you'd like to leave your name and number . . .* and rose again. I put the phone down. For the first time in over twenty years I was overcome with nostalgia for Partington, where people didn't think vitality was an effect achieved by peppering their conversation with misplaced question and exclamation marks. In Partington you knew when you were torpid. You kept your eyes down. You moved your lips less. And because you knew when your friends were torpid also you didn't give them nicknames like the Big Feller, or Captain Miraculous, or Norelle the Norks.

I was overexcited, obviously. I'd been made to feel hated and important, and then hated and unimportant, in the space of a couple of hours. I thought about trying another lie down but plumped for a shower instead. Naked – in the old nuddy, as Maroochi used to say – I investigated the progress of my spider-stigmata. Coming along nicely, I thought. The small, hard tumour re-forming. The reddish stain spreading. The yellow circle – I never really liked calling it an aureole – just beginning to appear. Only another few days to go, if previous experience could be relied on, before the stiffening proper.

Proper?

No wonder I was already mordant and melancholic, by turns.

I dried myself on a large luxurious towel that was also the Australian flag, and sprinkled powder in the area of the bite. Then I sank back in my armchair, saw that it was four-thirty, and estimated that I could close my eyes for fifty minutes. Then it would be time for me to throw on some clothes, jump in my car, and drive to *Trilby's* at Elizabeth Bay where there were three tills for me to empty.

I had been well provided for by my father and the woman he'd died still trying to get to the bottom of. They didn't leave me the house with the swimming pool and the *belvedere* – a couple of obscure nieces of Trilby's turned up at the eleventh hour, stirred primitive obligations in her, and got that – nor could they stretch to bequeathing me all three of their shops. But one was more than enough for me to cope with anyway, and there was also the high-rise home unit – the 'flat' – into which Trilby had moved once she was alone – 'Memories, Leeorhn, memories' – and where I was now in hiding from ASIO and the CIA.

I don't like emptying tills. There's something about the action of scooping up change into a bag that fills me with detestation. I feel almost as badly about sorting and counting notes. I fear that at any time a camera might catch me in one of these activities and there I will be, freeze-framed for ever, in an attitude of money-grubbing.

I trust the women who work in the shop. I could easily have them money-grubble for me. But my father emptied the tills himself, religiously, every night, and I do the same in memory of him.

On this particular evening I was especially impatient of handling cash. I left the silver where it was and stuffed the dollars in my pocket. Then I went for a walk around Kings Cross. If someone attractive had accosted me I might easily have parted with the lot. Not for passion, and not for spite, but just because it seemed to me that *something* ought to happen in the second half of a day which had begun so promisingly. You can't have the CIA – well, *sort* of the CIA – tell you to button up in the morning, and not feel the need to let your hair down at night. Dread of anticlimax, after all, explains most of the wild things that people do.

244

Nothing wild, however, came my way. And I don't suppose I really expected that it would. The Cross suffers still from its origins in English ideas of vice. There's a half-heartedness about its sinfulness. The junkies go the whole hog all right, but the rest take no pride or pleasure in their work. It's a question why the Anglo-Saxon peoples try to take up depravity at all. As with the rest of Australia, Kings Cross would be a happier and more alluring place if the Italians or the French had found it first.

So the shop takings stayed intact in my pocket. I walked up and down for about an hour, then collected my car and drove, in response to some other impulse, in the direction of my old North Shore residence. I was melancholy and wanted to make contact with the past. If I'd found the goanna I would have patted his head and ruffled his scales. But nobody I used to know was around. There were new people here. Even the cicadas had changed and didn't run for cover when they saw me. The only thing constant was the harbour: man and nature – urban man and metropolitan nature – in perfect harmony; sea and sky and bridge still in a tumult of competing agitation; the lit-up ferries still promising louche destinations; nostalgia for some other place and some other time still heavy in the beauty of the here and now.

I gave it up. There was nothing you could do with such exhilaration or such loveliness; there was nowhere you could put them. I climbed back into my car, drove back into the city and then west, towards Vaucluse and the Pacific.

When I got home it was quite dark and the Mercedes was already parked in its favourite position. I was struck by the fact that my invigilators had not been deterred from their business by the unusual occurrence of my lights being out. I had half-expected an intensi-fication of surveillance after Hartley's visit, and here was immediate proof of it. Now they weren't just watching me, they were waiting for me. I brushed close to their window so they should know I was back. Had I been convinced of the seemliness of such an action I would have rapped on the bonnet by way of greeting. As I passed I heard an odd gurgling sound from within, not unlike a radiator boiling over. I looked inside. The front seats were in full recline position and their occupants were fast asleep and snoring, their heads thrown so far back beyond the head-rests that only someone laid out horizontally in the back – as, indeed, someone was – could possibly have recognised them. They were as oblivious to danger as babies, except that the smell which issued through the air-vents of the Mercedes was of the gin-palace rather than the nursery.

This time I didn't hesitate about rapping on their bonnet. I banged with both my fists, and when those were sore I continued with a stone. But I couldn't stir them. I returned to my apartment at last thinking how fortunate it was for Australia, with a secret service as somnolent as theirs, that I wasn't even more of a threat to national security than I had decided to be.

Though by the time I'd drawn my curtains and fallen back into the very chair from which, only hours earlier, Hartley Quibell had threatened me with the law, I was toying with the possibility that I might look again at that decision.

22

'FORGET NORWAY. Forget Holland. You can even forget New Zealand. Not one of them sells as many books, per head of adult population, as Australia. You wanna know the most literate country in the world? You're fucking standing in it, sport.'

Thinking about my old friends on the staff of *The Black Sail* has reminded me of the time the Cooney brothers encircled me in the back bar of the Ultima Thule. This had recently been renamed the Whingeing Pom, in deference to the disposition of its clientele; and although I was not a regular exactly – being reluctant to risk running into Frank Whiling – I would still lob along there every now and then when Venie and Maroochi were too much for me, when I felt homesick and in need of a good complain in the company of fellow bellyaching Brits.

'The thing about Australians,' I always enjoyed saying to Sefton Goldberg, the nineteenth-century-heroine authority from Manchester, 'is that they lack restraint.'

He never let me down. 'And decorum,' I could absolutely rely on him to agree.

He was having the time of his life in Australia. Just as I was. But he needed to prevent his enthusiasm for the country toppling over into infatuation. Just as I did. So we slagged it off, between cold beers, in the name of the Lancashire proprieties.

'They don't have an adequately matured sense of social distance,' I used to say. 'They're too curious about their fellow-beings. They have yet to acquire metropolitan indifference.'

'Couldn't agree more,' Sefton invariably chipped in. 'They're babies. You walk into a room out here and they all gather round, wonder who you are, and instantly want to get to know you better. In Manchester it's understood that the people you haven't met are bound to be every bit as uninteresting as those you have. We eschew awe, by and large, in Manchester.'

'Same here,' I never missed the opportunity to concur. 'We eschew awe in Partington also.'

Which is why, of course, we were both in Australia, soaking up the indecorum and having the time of our ungrateful lives.

But at least we didn't complain about the butchers and the price of books and the colour of the traffic signals and the height of the pavements and the texture of the water and the pressure of the gas and the standards of caring in the catteries, like the Haygarths. Nor did we quarrel with the resident beta particles, like Frank Whiling.

The Cooneys could no more be called regulars of the Whingeing Pom than I could; so I supposed, on the night in question, that they were half-cut and cruising, on the look-out for the three C's of Cooney consolation – Camaraderie, Combat, and a Cry.

That can be the only explanation of why, after they'd encircled me for a while, indistinguishably hangdog, seeming to want me to help them tell themselves apart, one or other of them suddenly delivered himself of the observation that Australia was the most fucking literate country in the world.

It wasn't an aggressive statement. I doubt if George or Shaun or even Bernard raised his voice above a whisper. No Cooney that I'd encountered was ever assertive. None the less, every puling Pom on the premises picked up what he said. Exile, like paranoia, can do wonders for your hearing. And these *were* difficult times for us. Ever since Whitlam had come to power, impoverished the doctors, and restored national self-esteem, we'd been forced to swallow the provocations of a rampant Australia. The phrase 'the world' was suddenly on every Australian's lips, no longer as in the sentence, 'I am saving all my dollars so that I can travel and see the————', but precisely as the Cooneys had used it, as the only suitable yardstick for measuring how much bigger, better and more fucking literate Australia was. Even the Aborigines, hitherto discreetly hidden away on the grounds that no one could be interested in a people who had not come up with anything even remotely resembling a wheel, were now a proud heritage: the oldest race in the world.

(And who needed a wheel anyway when you were in possession of some of the most astonishing arts of survival known anywhere in the you-know-what?)

So you can see why habitués of the Whingeing Pom might have felt they'd heard enough. They booed and jeered and whistled. They? *We* booed and jeered and whistled. 'If you're so fucking literate,' we shouted, 'and you read so many fucking books' – the Cooneys, I noticed, had dropped into their catatonic crestfallen stage, which was always a sign that they were thinking of bypassing Camaraderie to get to Combat – 'then why don't you write some of your fucking own?'

There was a brief pause, calculated to a nicety to give the Cooney brothers all the time they needed to look down the short desecrated corridor of Australian literature.

'Instead,' we added, 'of always reading fucking ours?'

We? *They*, rather. The moment I'd seen the blood-hound jowls of the Cooneys begin to droop and quiver – I was not exactly unfamiliar with the signs, remember – I'd begun my own instinctive response to trouble. And I was well out of it, with one hand already pushing open the saloon door, when it began.

I stayed just long enough to make sure the contest was fairly balanced. Ten whingeing Poms and three

Cooney brothers seemed pretty right to me. I walked out into the clammy night, strolled half a block, then came back and put an eye to the window. I was surprised to discover that the Cooney brothers were not employing their usual methods of elbowing and nuzzling and exerting the dead weight of their lugubrious personalities but had actually figured out a way of curling their fingers into fists. I was also distressed to see that they were using them.

'That's for Henry Handel Richardson,' I heard Shaun say.

'And that's for Katharine Susannah Prichard,' said either George or Bernard.

I winced, certain that the Katharine Susannah Prichard was unfairly low.

An old-timer joined me at the window. 'Got forty-five cents for a beer?' he asked.

I hate it when beggars are precise. 'I'm busy,' I said.

'Wha's going on in there?' he asked. 'A bit of a ding?'

'Three Australians are beating shit out of a dozen Poms,' I told him.

He wasn't surprised. 'Gamest buggers in the world,' he said.

It's true, by the way, about Australians and the printed word. They are prose junkies. Philobiblics. Gluttons for typeface and newsprint. Mad Max only became a biker so he could subscribe to a hundred biker monthlies, and I often thought that Venie and Maroochi only put themselves through their rigorous training routines so that they could come home at night, put their feet up on me, and read *The Synchronized Swimmer and Double Diver*.

That wasn't the only colour magazine devoted to S/s either, but it is the one I remember most fondly. Not least because it paid well and punctually whenever I sent them a piece on Venie and Maroochi. We even made the front cover, the three of us, at the time of the

250

Montreal Olympics, and my profile of them – 'Aussie Golden Girls: At Home with the Refulgent Naiads' – took up half the issue. Here's an extract from it – it won me a nomination for the award of best sportswriter of the year on an Australian subject:

The climax to any of the world's great aquatic duets is reached when the two swimmers sink without warning from our view – create the fear in us that they are gone, drowned, reclaimed for their beauty by the old gods who guard the sea – and then, at the very peak of our despair, soar up again in boosted verticals, one leg each breaking the surface of the water, in marine-mimesis of that moment when life itself with painted toe-nails first rose from the inundated land.

Does this mean that synchronized swimmers take a Darwinian view of creation? In the case of Venie Redfern and Maroochi Ravesh, yes and no. Whether they execute their final figure to the music of Eric Satie or de Falla, they are somehow able to evoke both the long arduous struggle out of slime and the wholly unexpected eruption of flesh on earth. Their singular achievement is to pay simultaneous tribute to the two great contra-dictory orthodoxies of our time: their duet justifies God to Darwin and makes Darwin palatable to God. Whatever marks the Canadian judges choose to award them for technical proficiency, Australia's golden girls have already made a unique contribution to sporting culture. Thanks to them, ambivalence has arrived in our waters with a vengeance.

Yes, I loved those girls. For very nearly a decade, for nine and a half hot years – hot as in stuffy more than hot as in anything else – I slept between them, never

251

once knowing what it was like to wake in the night and feel a cool breeze on my back.

When they finally rejected me – that's to say when I finally rejected them and they made no attempt to get me to change my mind – I went into a cold shiver, an icy judder of all my extremities, an instant bitter freeze-up of the seats of my affections, from which I didn't recover until the spider bit me and warmed my blood with poison. Now I'm never cold.

But I have more to say about daily life with Venie and Maroochi before I turn my attention to such solemn subjects as the Redback and the present.

We ran a highly cultivated household – I want to make that clear. Because we were unconventional in number and in pairing system that doesn't mean we wallowed in the flesh all day like pigs. In fact we were always up and showered by seven. We took a ceremonious breakfast at a table invariably set the night before for three. We passed the butter formally, poured the tea with solicitation, and sliced the heads off our googies with one stroke. Breeding, you see. In Partington we used to give them compound fractures with the back of a teaspoon and spend the rest of the morning spitting up shell. But in this house (I'd moved of course, moved to theirs in Diamond Bay, Vaucluse) we had other things to do with our mornings. Vene and Mooch wrote letters to their families on personalized paper. I had CACA meetings and *Black Sail* editorial conferences to attend, I had secret agents to educate and women's groups to address (I mean *proper* women – wives and mothers), and I had the no-longer-docile campuses of Noonthorungee and Tumbarumba to prowl. I left the house at eight in a crisp and freshly ironed shirt and returned at six for sherry. Whether we had guests or dined alone, whether we went to the theatre or stayed in and played three-handed euchre, it was always at least twelve o'clock, the house had always been

252

Hoovered and dusted, and Telemann had always revolved for at least an hour on our stereo equipment, before we went to bed and began handling one another's genitals.

Our life together was a model of consonance and conservatism. We were spotless, orderly, softly spoken and considerate, and we harmonized our actions with the place and with the hour. I sometimes wonder how many families in Australia who do *not* practise three-way sex can say the same.

Have I rendered the essential *seriousness* of my relations with Venie and Maroochi? It frequently happened, after I'd written an especially colourful attack on drugs, youth, or feminism for *The Black Sail*, or succeeded in getting some Oodnadatta sociologist seconded for sleeping with his students, that I would receive letters, anonymous phone calls even, charging me with hypocrisy, sometimes Tartufferie no less. Meaning that degeneracy was the last subject I was in any position to comment on. Now I don't mind admitting that the charge of hypocrisy has never seemed to me to be anything but an empty one, whatever the circumstances. I don't see why a man has to be good before he can proclaim his neighbours bad, and I suspect that I would have been no less conscientious a campaigner for the moral niceties even if I *had* spent my days as my detractors imagined, wallowing like a pig in shit. But I was doing nothing of the kind. Anyone peering through our windows would have seen the life of the mind in action. Venie teaching me how to mix gouache; Maroochi taking me through logical atomism; me singing to them from *King's Rhapsody*; them educating me in the history of the baroque. Do you know, those girls taught me how to tell Bach's sons apart. 'Who's that?' Venie would ask, hiding the record-sleeve and turning up the volume. I would stand at the window, looking out across the Pacific to where they'd shown me Fiji was, and guess: 'Johann Christian?'

'Why don't you listen?' Maroochi would say. 'Does that sound better suited to the piano or the harpsichord?' I'd listen. Then, 'Carl Philipp Emanuel!' I'd shout, and they'd both smother me in kisses. You see, it was like a little university in there, a gymnasium, a closed conservatoire, a long summer seminar with Socrates's sisters.

We used to test one another with tiny segments from great paintings. A dozen art-books would be brought to the table, one of us would cut a shape like the letter O from a big piece of cardboard – say one of Venie's shoe-boxes, flattened – and then we'd begin. Whose hand of God was this? Whose ears of alien corn were those? Whose cherub's dimpling cheek was that? And we had dating sessions too, each taking it in turns to read out extracts from the *Oxford Book of English Prose* which the others had to assign to a period. I've since seen experts hot from Oxford or Cambridge colleges sit and play this and be pleased with themselves if they can narrow a gobbet down to a century; Venie and Maroochi allowed themselves a leeway of only five years either side. 'If you can't get the decade,' Maroochi used to say, 'you're not a dater's bum.' She was a consummate chronologizer herself. A real mega-dater. 'Pre-Romantic but definitely post-Johnsonian,' she would pronounce, running her hands through her hair and setting off her static electricity. 'Jane Austen hasn't happened yet but Fielding definitely has. A mind antithetical by manner rather than instinctive bent. I can hear faint cracklings of gothic in the vicinity' (I could smell burning myself) 'though the social assurance is still unruffled. Urban, elegant, *haute bourgeois* rather than aristocratic. I'd say the early 1780s. Probably Fanny Burney. Though not, I think, *Evelina*.'

God, I loved her.

After I'd taken them to meet Trilby and my father for the first time – we were neighbours now, of course;

254

everything I loved on earth was where I wanted it, in Vaucluse – my father walked me up the stone steps to Trilby's *belvedere* and had me stand with him in silence for a while, looking out over the lights of Sydney, across the impossibly propitious harbour to where the Bridge was winking. I felt certain that he was once more going to tell me what a sentimental country Australia was, but Venie and Maroochi's dazzling performance over dinner – they'd even given him a taster of their Aussie dick-scratching routine – disposed him to reflect differently. 'They're clever over here, aren't they,' he said. 'Not just bright and quick, but actually cultivated.'

'More than in Partington, you mean?' I don't know why I said that. It must have been some tic of guilt. I could never get through an evening in my father's company without mentioning Partington.

'Sheesh, Partington!' he said. Even in the darkness I could see his face fall.

But I was driven. 'Wouldn't you say that Hester and Nesta were cultivated?'

He gave himself time. We were standing close together and I thought I could feel an increase in his pulse rate. Certainly something small and pump-like was overworking in his body.

'Hester and Nesta,' he said at last, 'used books and ruined monasteries to make themselves miserable.'

I gave a savage snort.

'All right – *more* miserable. Isn't that the English way? Isn't culture just another method for ensuring maximum hostility and discomfort over there?'

I wasn't sure whether he was right, but I was reminded of how much I didn't want to go back. Partington? Sheesh!

'Whereas here?' I asked. I needed to hear him enthusing over Venie and Maroochi again.

'Whereas here they really yearn to be civilized,' he said.

Only he made that sound depressing too. Suddenly I couldn't remember what Venie and Maroochi looked like. Or what they said. Or what they did. Or why they bothered. Lit up and vast and balmy, Sydney resembled a set for a film about a lost planet.

'Sad, isn't it?' I said.

My father didn't reply but I could tell that he agreed with me. We had come around again to our usual position. Sentimental place, Australia.

Venie and Maroochi didn't talk much about death, but Sunday was the day they always set aside for flesh tests. Some morbid uncle of Venie's had passed on to her information relating to the springy properties of the flesh which she found so unnerving that she had to pass it on to us. 'Apparently,' she explained, 'your skin starts losing its resilience from the minute you are born. You can test for elasticity by depressing a soft bit with your thumb and seeing how long it takes for it to come up again. When you're young it jumps back up immediately, but the older you get the slower its reascent.'

'And when it doesn't come back up at all?'

Venie knew all about it. 'Dead,' she said.

So every Sunday, after our usual formal breakfast and, in Maroochi's case, a weekly self-abnegation boost at Our Lady Star of the Sea, we would fall to proving one another's tensibility and recoil. God knows how many hours I must have spent in all, consulting the stopwatch I carried in my right hand while I carefully prodded them with the thumb or forefinger of my left.

Venie's fear of that moment when the depressed flesh would stay depressed was deep and silent. Maroochi's terrors were more immediate and voluble.

'How long was that?' she'd cry, as the circle of skin that contained her birthmark seemed to take a lifetime to reassert itself.

I'd check the watch carefully. 'A hundredth of a second,' I'd say.

She'd look at Venie. 'Is that good or bad?'

Venie's reply didn't vary. 'It can never be *good*, honeybag,' she said, 'but in the circumstances—'

'What circumstances?'

But we all knew what the circumstances were. We weren't as elastic as we'd been, not one of us.

Myself, I preferred the pencil test, which required no other participation from me except observation and applause.

There were two halves to the pencil test and two apparently contradictory objectives. In the first, which consisted of Venie placing a pencil under each of Maroochi's breasts, and then Maroochi placing a pencil under each of Venie's, the idea was for the pencil immediately to hit the floor – if it didn't, that proved that the breast that held it soon would. In the second the girls would place the same pencil between their thighs, about halfway between the pelvis and the knee, and here the pencil was expected to stay gripped as in a vice. A pencil held when it was meant to fall, or dropped when it was meant to stay, and that would have been the end of all our contentment. But never once, in all the years I sat cross-legged on the bed and watched my felicity hang on a strip of graphite, did I fear for the consequences. Venie's breasts rose up and away from the rest of her and nothing, not so much as a feather, had any hope of finding lodgement under their airy sweep. Even my kisses could not adhere. As for Maroochi, although she was heavier, although it took a hundredth of a second for her skin, when pressed, to spring back into place, her breasts too were buoyant and optimistic and pointed heavenwards, like aspirants to God.

I won't speak about the retentiveness of their thighs. I live alone now and have my peace of mind to consider.

Enough that I still remember every detail of their eve-of-competition preparations – the clipping and the trimming and the waxing and then the moment when they would spread a towel underneath themselves and allow me, with my creams, my lather and my razor, to complete their readiness and shave them to within an inch of decency.

Sometimes, if they were relaxed and confident of success, and if I had played my part well, not giving either of them the smallest nick or worry, they would wash my brush out in the sink and dry my razor on their towel and – if I was really lucky – 'Now it's your turn,' they would say.

23

REMEMBER the expression, *cherchez la femme*? You don't hear it much any more. The notion that there's a woman behind every catastrophe is too hot for modern man to handle. It's socio-political dynamite. But for several thousand years it was quite a popular idea. The phrase itself enjoyed so much vogue that it even made it as far as Partington, a place that had always proved resistant to the English language never mind the French. By calling the room in which she destroyed people's pride in their appearance a *salon*, my mother effectively ensured that she would never do much business. The only other French noun the Partingtons of Partington had heard of was *abattoir*, and it wasn't entirely their fault if they confused the two. Nonetheless, on two evenings a week in Partington's only nightspot – the Aluminium Fingerbowl – an entertainer who called herself Shea Shea Lafam danced and did conjuring tricks for the civic elders.

It's possible she'd be there still, plucking lit cigarettes out of the air with her toes and guessing what her audience had in its pockets, if the women of Partington had not organized a petition – We'll Have No Tarts in These Parts – to get her stopped. A ruled exercise-book was kept by the till of every shop in town, and you weren't expected to make a purchase without signing. Hester and Nesta, I remember, used to spread their shopping so that they could get their signatures down in a dozen different books a day.

What's brought Shea Shea Lafam back to me are the admissions of former CIA agents I've been reading. At the end of the sixties there wasn't a publisher's office anywhere that didn't have dozens of these apostatic operatives queuing outside, as urgent to unload as Catholics at a confessional; and although it was my job at *The Black Sail* to discredit each testimony as it appeared, arguing that bean-spilling, like VD and heart disease, was a symptom of the moral incontinence of our times, I have never until now actually got around to finding out what any of them had to say. I'm suddenly curious, of course, after Hartley Quibell's visit. Who knows? I might have a story to sell myself. Mine, though, it's becoming increasingly plain to me, would have a significantly different plot. And I don't just mean because I was only ever on a scholarship and never rose to active field-operation status, never learned to work a portable encryptograph, or how to inject the enemy with Venezuelan equine encephalomyelitis. No. Shea Shea Lafam. Much as I hate to say it – precisely because it's what I *did* say before I bothered to read them – there does seem to be, behind every one of these defections, a beautiful Cuban with a tragic past. Got at – got at they all are, by love and sex and pity, just as they were got at by hope and patriotism and ambition when they were green Harvard boys a score or more years before. A man has to be unusually get-attable to become an agent or a spy in the first place; so it's madness to look for constancy from him. These are leaky histories of impressionable men, these CIA conversion tales. They went to sea in a sieve they did. And when the sirens sang, they answered. See how that's not my story? There were no rocks fatal to my loyalties between me and Venie and Maroochi. The day was calm. The sea was flat. And grinning dolphins escorted me ashore.

Wasn't it lucky for me that the girls who whispered in both my ears at night weren't agents for a foreign power, had no designs upon my principles, and only wanted me to be the way I was, and maybe even more so?

Wasn't I blessed?

*   *   *

260

I've said that Venie and Maroochi got me through the domestic horrors of the Vietnam war – kissed me better and made it up to me in a thousand little ways for missing out on the biggest street-party Australia had ever thrown. But that was nothing – mere molly-coddling, home-helpery, meals-on-wheels – compared to the support they gave me in the aftermath when counter-ideology hit Australia, bringing Whitlam into power, Norelle Turpie into prominence, the Royal Commission on Human Nature into being, and every gay-baiting bullshit élitist US crow-eating imperialist in the country (I wasn't the only one) to his knees.

I didn't like the seventies. Speaking purely from the point of view of dialectic now, and leaving aside my plenteous store of consolations in Vaucluse, the seventies agreed with me even less than the sixties had. For a start, my social comforts fell away. The campuses of Noonthorungee, Oodnadatta and Tumbarumba, once innocent playgrounds across which I had strolled like a popular senior prefect, known to be strict but known, also, to enjoy the odd fag himself behind the lavs, became smoking battlefields, not safe for me to be seen on without a military escort. At Oodnadatta, after Sir Alex Sneddon had delivered a famous speech in defence of formal grammar, insisting that the paragraph was the last bastion of civil discourse, the Students' Union banned punctuation and declared every day until the end of the century a Day of Outrage(.) At Tumbarumba there was a powerful and vociferous response to my proposal to close all fringe theatres in Australia pending an agreement on the prohibition of gratuitous stage swearing. Groups of golden-haired teenagers from good homes gathered outside my room wearing T-shirts which said, WE ARE ALL FOUR-LETTER WORDS, and chanted SHIT, FUCK, CUNT, until I could bear it no longer and had to be helicoptered out. Even Noonthorungee, for so long the least threatening of all Australian academic communities provided

261

you got away before five, the hour when gangs of marauding single mothers collected their symbolic statements from the crèche – even Noonthorungee went the way of the others at last, changing its name to the Ulricke Meinhof Memorial University and proclaiming the principle of a wholly Cock-Free Campus. I arrived one morning to find my drawers ransacked, my pigeon-holes violated, and my office in the hands of five women philosophers and a lady surgeon all dressed in dungarees. They pushed me around for a few minutes so that I should understand what it was like to be a woman. Then the lady surgeon explained the terms under which my room would be returned to me. 'Let's see what you're made of,' she challenged me. 'Do you have the courage to be a woman or are you a mouse?' 'Keep the room, I'm a mouse,' I assured them, and ran, without once looking back, all the way to Vaucluse.

Meanwhile, at airports all over the country, those same essayists and poets who had passed me going the other way on the Indian Ocean, ten years before, were now arriving back – this time in jet planes – to see whether Whitlam had kept his promise and made Australia truly a land fit for scribblers.

It was Venie and Maroochi, travellers themselves, who spotted the first of these prodigals slinking through Customs.

'You can't miss them,' Venie said. 'They've got a guilty indoor look. They're pale and rheumatoid. You can tell they haven't moved out of their rooms in South Kensington since 1963, where they've been writing rejected articles for small magazines on the impossibility of living in philistine Australia if you're an artist.'

'And now back they come,' said Maroochi.

'Wanting a steak and a shower,' said Venie.

'And a handout,' said Maroochi.

It was the handouts our house especially objected to.

'Australia has got hundreds of thousands of miles of unprotected coast,' Venie exaggerated.

'And oil going to waste in the sea,' Maroochi added.

'And uranium rotting in the ground,' Venie said.

'And now here we are,' they both said together, 'dishing out freebees to fair-weather freaks, fuckwits and fantasists.'

I always knew when they wanted something from me.

'So what do you want from me?' I asked.

'Stop the bastards,' said Venie, sounding just like her father.

'Pour shit on 'em,' said Maroochi, sounding for all the world like hers.

I can't pretend that I needed much encouragement. On the other hand I have always been fair-minded. 'There is a sense,' I said, 'in which I might be considered to be on the receiving end of charity myself.'

I'll never forget the look they both threw me. Or the Telemann cantata that accompanied it. It taught me, in less time than it took a depressed circle of Maroochi's flesh to return to normal, how a man must feel when he has failed his family, betrayed his friends, abandoned his country, squandered his fortune, and forgone for ever his turn with the nose-plug.

'Where would you like me to start?' I asked.

'By going squibelling,' said Venie.

'And going CACA,' said Maroochi.

'By ringing up all those Judis that you know.'

'And then ringing up all those Kerris.'

I looked puzzled. 'What Kerris?'

'You know. Kerri, Kerry, Kiri, Kerrie, and Carrie. The Women Who Want to Be Wombats or whatever.'

I was punctilious about the people I knew. 'They Want to Be Mothers, Maroochi.'

'Right. Those. And when you ring them tell them they've got to get over to their nearest airport to boo

263

whoever they see coming off a plane that looks like an artist.'

'Tell them to chant, PROSPERITY BEFORE PROSODY,' Venie said.

'And, PANZERS NOT STANZAS,' said Maroochi.

'And now we're going to bed,' Venie said.

'And you can join us when it's organised,' said Maroochi.

Curiously enough, while it wasn't difficult to get Kerry and Judy to write letters to the papers, complaining about this shameful misappropriation of public money, the only people I could persuade to join me in an actual show of strength at an airport were the Cooney brothers, even though they themselves were already planning to fly out to London and back again in order to qualify for repatriation creativity grants. For three afternoons running they helped me to jeer at every jet that landed at Kingsford-Smith, and then suddenly, just as the final call for a long-haul Qantas flight was being called, they said 'Excuse us,' and disappeared. Forty-four hours later I happened to be demonstrating outside the Customs hall, shouting MANGIARE PIUTTOSTO CHE SCRIVERE at the last of the passengers off an Alitalia DC10, when the Cooneys emerged through the same door. They looked tired and dirty and had no luggage. I calculated that forty-four hours was just time enough for them to have flown to London and back, provided they didn't leave the plane. I noticed that along with the two bottles each of liquor they were bringing in they also carried copies of the previous day's London *Standard*, to prove where they'd been. They lowered their heads when they saw me and kept on walking until they reached the Returning Talent reception-desk, situated where you couldn't miss it in the middle of the main public concourse. I watched with my mouth hanging open as they were welcomed back, photographed, given three cheques and three fellowships, and handed the keys to a rent-a-car. The next day, in despite of double jetlag, they were out protesting vigorously with me once more. BETTER A PATRIOT THAN A POET, they chanted into their chests. I decided not to make any reference to their absence. You needed whatever support you could muster in Australia in the seventies.

In the long run, although we never shamed a single prosodist or proser into turning back, our campaign enjoyed a sort of success. A satisfaction, anyway. Three years later Camelot was disbanded. Gough Whitlam – Australia's first Arthurian legend – was ceremoniously bundled out of office and defeated in the ensuing election. Blame the CIA for the bundling, if you like. Even if they didn't actually, they would have liked to. But blame Whitlam himself for not managing a triumphant return. It was his own system of bursaries for bohemians, if you ask me, that embourgeoised his natural supporters and turned them overnight into self-interested Liberals.

Shea Shea Lafam – She She Lefeofee.

But there was another long-term effect of our household's private war on Mr Whitlam. It made me look again at Venie and Maroochi, and it made me think again about myself. Not to beat about the bush, a horrible feeling began to dawn on me that I was turning into an extremist. I could hear extremist poisons bubbling through my system. I was becoming hooked, like all extremist junkies, on the sensation of experiencing savage emotions; I was high on the expression of immoderate opinion.

I'd been called a reactionary and a revisionist and a fascist and a shit-eater for as long as I could remember. After my decision to dine alone in the Great Hall of Malapert someone had even hissed 'lickspittle' at me as I strolled across Parker's Piece. But none of this had ever worried me. I hadn't known the meaning of most of the things I'd been called, and accepted reactionary as a fair description of me for the simple reason that I thought it meant a person easily stimulated into opposition, someone like Hartley Quibell who needed to say no only because someone else had said yes. It had never occurred to me that I could be seen to be acting on behalf of vested interests; even when I had used the pages of *The Black Sail* to heap scorn on the Tristanists, the Free Lovers and the Androgynes, I hadn't actually put it to myself that I was shoring up the confidence of every married moral coward in Australia. In other circumstances, had *they* been the ones grabbing the headlines and frightening children in the parks, I would have turned on them. I was a reactionary. I reacted.

I saw myself, in the most romantic light, as a free-ranging spirit, a vigilante of the decencies, a scourge with a smile and a song for everyone, like the Maltese tenor, Oreste, in the Paramount movie of *The Vagabond King*. So what, if the CIA bought my horse and paid my singing lessons? Someone had to.

Now, though, with Venie and Maroochi to answer to, I couldn't be absolutely certain that I hadn't compromised my impartiality. Left to myself I would undoubtedly have spat bile about such matters as the unseemly helter-skelter dash back for maundy bread and trinkgeldt made by Australia's dispersed and hitherto unpatriotic intelligentsia. But I doubt whether I would have been quite so appalled by the thing as spectacle. I was not without experience of the cruel political bias of aesthetics. I still hadn't made it to my ninth birthday when I first understood that Trilby in motion looked better than my mother in motion for no other reason than that she was obviously richer. I didn't put it to myself in so many words, but I could see perfectly clearly how harmony and symmetry and fluency favoured whoever already had, above whoever needed to go out and get. The language of beauty, like the language of law, is all on the side of those for whom greedy going out and getting is no longer necessary. So I found it difficult to witness Venie's outraged fastidiousness ('Look at *him* – do you think some people are *born* with their hands cupped?') and Maroochi's rabid connoisseurship ('Have you noticed how habitual supplication finally lines the face?') without remembering that their fathers, or their fathers' fathers, had done their gross supplicating for them; that a graceful demeanour, like a large country estate, rests solely on the robust indifference of your forebears to the aesthetics of plunder. Does that sound socialistic? Well, don't forget that it's possible to know all this and still remain a dedicated decency-and-decorum man. It takes a spider with a fat sac of poison to come along, and sink her fangs all the way up to her gums in you, to reconcile your disparate elements, to make you whole, harmonious, and unhappy. But yes, even before she cornered me and made me howl, I was beginning to lose my ambivalentier strut; the signs were there, for whoever cared to observe them, that I was starting to crave consistency.

Does that *still* sound socialistic? Then I'll admit to something else. After I'd lived in close proximity to Venie and Maroochi for six or seven years; after I'd gone hot-air ballooning in the Blue Mountains with the Redferns and camel riding outside Alice with the Raveshes; after I'd shot crocodiles in Mataranka with Venie's dad and swum in underground thermal pools in Coober Pedy with Maroochi's mum; after we'd all ski'd down Perisher together, and gone gambling in desert casinos and sniffed wild orchids on Dunk Island and cruised on lakes above volcanic craters (the oldest in the world) and marvelled at mangroves and wine-tasted at wineries and fed sharks in sharkeries (the hungriest in the world) and been to every opera, ballet and seafood restaurant in Australia; after I'd at last got to refuse a cocktail graciously from the Governor-General ('Thank you, Your Excellency, but I'd prefer a

267

tinny') and fought back the urge to spin the Prime Minister of India out of her ceremonial sari; after I'd twice pumped the soft white hand of Henry Kissinger and grovelled, in a Canberra garden, at the feet of Imelda Marcos; in short, after I'd more or less done all that I'd fallen in love with Venie and Maroochi to do, I reached a clear conclusion about the rich. Come close so that I might whisper it. *They smell.*

Of? That's not for me to say. I think it behoves every serious student of society to track it down himself. But if you haven't yourself experienced it I'll tell you that it's altogether more of a nursery smell than you'd expect. Milkier. Soapier. Ruskier. More Miltonic. (Of the sterilizer, not the poet.) More strained apricot and mashed banana-ish. And there's an obvious reason for this. Once you become very rich you can only put your functions into reverse. The most that has ever been done for you was done when you were a baby. That was the ultimate in pampering. And so babydom becomes the model for your future wants. Which of course is why British cabinet ministers (wealth and influence being interchangeable) can scarcely wait to assume office before they're off to the backstreets of Streatham to have their bottoms talced.

Marriage is prostitution, Norelle Turpie made herself famous for saying. And who except Hartley Quibell would bother to deny it? But there are other far more interesting contemporary confusions of sex, commerce, and the family. Such as, prostitution is motherhood.

I don't know whether Venie's father had some equivalent of Streatham to slip away to. It's possible he didn't. I'm quite prepared to believe that, along with so much else, pre-oedipal regression is still in its infancy in Australia. But he cried a lot in public, as do all senior Australian politicians, and he was painstakingly and self-consciously cute – which is *de rigueur* for political survival outside Queensland – vitalising his conversation with the usual abbreviations and diminutives of pram-talk. He started his day with a beaut brekkie, said G'day to the postie on the drive, made a speech on Laura Norda at the Uni, earned big bikkies at the office in the arvo, and satisfied his adult needs with a quick naughty with some drac party worker in the dunny of a BYO.

I'm not being critical. I liked Venie's father. He was a big, amiable, brutish sort of baby. He wasn't at all sinister, as his English counterpart would have been. When you caught him with his hand in another baby's money-box his face would light up with comic mischief. 'Look, I'm bad out of animal high spirits,' his expression said. 'There's no malice in me.' And it was impossible to argue with him.

But I didn't want to play with him. And more and more I realised that I didn't always want to play with Venie and Maroochi either. For years I had slept between them and never felt a moment's trepidation before the task of keeping them content. Task? It had been a joy and a privilege. I had laboured lovingly over them nightly, and when, perchance, after a difficult day denouncing deviants for *The Black Sail*, I tired quickly, they laboured lovingly amongst themselves. The question all men wished to ask me – which even Hartley Quibell had once gingerly approached – how I er . . . whether I er . . . if I um . . . was simple to answer. Easily, sport. No worries. A doddle. But then – I suppose it must have been about the time Malcolm Fraser made his famous life-isn't-meant-to-be-easy speech – I began to notice a certain waning of enthusiasm in myself, a distinct diminution of powers. I knew that something was gravely wrong between me and Venie and Maroochi from the minute I found myself having to fake my orgasms.

24

IT'S A PITY that at the time I was faking mine, my father wasn't faking his. If he'd had any talent for dissimulation at all he might have been around to keep me company today. But he had always been literal- and single-minded, and he groaned his last, as we all feared he would, still trying to get to the bottom of Trilby's mystery.

It was from Trilby that I learned the news. I was on my own in the house in Diamond Bay, Venie and Maroochi being away for a competition, when she rang. It must have been about three in the morning. The immemorial grieving hour.

'It's happened,' she said.

There was a wild calm in her voice. The sound all men dread hearing from all women. Full of ancient Greek instability, auguring not just death but betrayal, outrage, or frenzied devotion. For a second or two I was utterly confused and thought she was my mother. At least she isn't alone, I thought; at least she's got Hester and Nesta to take care of her. Then, when I remembered she wasn't my mother, I couldn't work out whether that made me sorrier for her or sorrier for my mother.

'I'll come over,' I said.

I threw on some clothes and ran into the street. It was my intention to take the car but as soon as I smelt the night I kept on running, made strong by that strange exhilaration that can sweep over the living in the near presence of death. It was a night of the cruellest beauty. All around me I could hear water sucking at the land. Boats clinked. Shingle beaches exhaled a wet, gravelly content. In the trees creatures of fearsome appearance rubbed their back legs together and smacked their lips. Clouds were on the move, and behind them a moon as sharp as a cutlass sailed the skies like a corsair. Hard to believe it was the same moon that moped over Partington, off colour and mis-shapen like a boy with the mumps. But harder still to believe that my father and Partington were parted for ever now, and that he would never again blow in my mother's customers' ears or deposit me in a wastepaper-basket in the Municipal Gardens.

Exile is a powerful idea, even when it is only exile from the East Lancashire Road. And my face was wet with tears when I arrived at Trilby's, from reflecting on how far from his cheerless native soil my father would be buried.

A young man was getting into a sports car outside Trilby's gate. I took him to be the doctor. He was carrying a bag and wearing shorts and whistling to himself. By the inside light of his car I could see that he had golden skin and freckles. A bag of golf clubs, a squash racket and a single water-ski were jammed into the small back seat. It's hard for someone accustomed to the funereal style of the profession in England to get used to the rude health and jollity of Australian doctors. In the surgery at Partington one uncovered oneself for Dr Partington as if one's body were a nest of sordid secrets. Whereas out here the body is a shared and much loved joke. Even a corpse in Australia gets more laughs than living flesh in Partington.

Trilby and I hugged each other in silence for a long time. I was shocked by her appearance. I don't know what I expected. To see her in elegant black crêpe, behind a spidery veil, heartbroken but composed, like an operetta widow? Perhaps. I certainly hadn't antici-pated her looking so like death herself, her eyes chalk white and unflickering, her hair so thin I could see her scalp through it, her skin dry and cold as if the blood had given up running in her veins too.

'Do you want to see him?' she asked, once we'd at last drawn apart.

I shook my head.

'You should see him,' she said. 'He looks happy.'

I was sitting on one of Trilby's wide winged-back velvet chairs, my chin sunk into my chest. I shook my head again. I was Partington born and bred – the idea of anyone looking happy, even my poor dead father, upset me. I also knew that I wouldn't be able to bear how diminutive he looked. That sense of acute poignancy occasioned by the death of an infant – the fragility of the body, the smallness of the coffin, all the unfinished business – would, I was certain, seize me and prove too much for me the moment I went near him.

'I can't,' I said. 'But I'm so glad he was happy.'

Trilby raised her eyes to mine. Happiness was not the half of it, they seemed to say.

I felt that she was looking to me for some statement. So I made her one. 'You gave him everything he ever wanted,' I said. 'I've never seen a man so replete with pleasures.' But I didn't add that I'd never seen a man made so hungry by what he fed on, either.

She left her chair and came and knelt by mine. She lowered her head on to my knees. I stroked her hair, dismayed by how thin it was, and how insubstantial for all her bulk, how unmysterious, she suddenly seemed.

I don't know how long we remained in this attitude, her with her face buried, me gently stroking the cold nape of her neck, but we were still together when the light came. It was the garish jungle birds who broke our trance, mocking us, as they needed every morning to mock someone, for our idolatry of our own species. I was startled to see where I was. Once again I realised that I'd confused Vaucluse with Partington, imagining that this was my mother's head I'd been cradling, that it was her sorrow I'd been meaning to soothe.

I thought much less about Trilby and my father over the next few days than I did about Partington, and Hester and Nesta, and my mother. I contacted them of course. And wasn't surprised when a terse telegram of condolence came back. My father had died to them years ago. This latest development was just a formality. But it was precisely because my mother's grief had grown old and callused that I felt a loyalty to it. Trilby's mourning, by comparison, lacked depth and shade and history. And so I went frosty on her, at the very time she needed my friendship, so as not doubly to betray my mother.

I had alway experienced difficulties with the inevitable contrary pull of affections – never knowing how to love A without thereby despising and destroying B – until the spider came along and solved my problems for me. Once you've been bitten you don't bother loving anyone.

We buried my father in the Botany Cemetery in Matraville. We liked the idea that he would be able to look out over Botany Bay to the historic site of Captain Cook's landing place. We had no reason to believe this was a spot my father especially venerated, but there's something about death that makes its celebrants suckers for nautical or wayfaring imagery.

I didn't call Venie and Maroochi back for the funeral. You can see that as significant if you like. I rang them in New Zealand, where they were entertaining the quaint old-fashioned population of that country with their turning boosts and verticals, and told them what had happened.

Venie wanted to know how he'd died. 'As he lived,' I told her.

'What – selling frocks?'

You see what I mean about her? I'm absolutely certain that she had been genuinely fond of my father and that my news upset her. But she couldn't escape her background. Her family kept sheep, and for some reason keeping sheep in Australia destroys you as a social being.

Maroochi was altogether more sympathetic when I explained that my father had died manifesting his devotion.

'Oh, how lovely,' she said. 'That's just how I'd like to go.'

I was filled with a consuming desire not to see them for a while. 'Whatever you do you mustn't so much as contemplate cutting short your tour,' I said. 'My father would have hated the idea of needlessly inconveniencing you. And I'm all right, really.' I even suggested that once they'd finished in New Zealand they should go on to Fiji, since they knew where it was.

As soon as I was able to feel that I had sufficiently made it up to my mother by not being too nice to Trilby, I felt that I had to make it up to Trilby. If Venie and Maroochi had been home I might have made it up to Trilby by not being too nice to them, but as they weren't – as they were still wowing Rotoruans with what they could perform on the pinnacles of boiling geysers – I was left with no realistic option but to make it up to Trilby by not being too nice to the memory of my father. Which isn't to say that I slandered him. Or in any way spoke slightingly of him. Or failed to ensure that there were fresh flowers on his windy Botany grave. No. I just went wooing the woman he'd loved – making up in order to make it up – a little earlier in the piece than perhaps I should have. Before the funeral baked meats . . . and so on.

It's possible to be too squeamish about post-mortuary sex. Take a long-range anthropological cyclic seasonal attitude to it and it looks not only natural but needful. The king is dead, long live the king. Royalty, you see, doesn't hang about. There's a roaring populace out there that must be stilled; and a demanding carbon-cycle. Viewed in the light of what we learn from ancient

274

ritual Trilby and I actually let the natural order down rather. We allowed seven whole weeks to elapse before we laid a fertile finger each upon the other, and even then what came about was not so much a ploughing and a cropping as . . . well, consolation – consolation on her part – and the satisfaction of an old curiosity on mine. Mental pleasures, in other words. So the worst that can be said of us is this: that less than two months after my father began his long stare at Captain Cook's landing place, we – his common-law widow and his only son – cerebrated without our clothes on in his bed.

With Venie and Maroochi away, and Trilby on her own, it was only to be expected that we'd spend some time together.

'Come back with me, Leeorhn,' she suggested, on the morning we completed the necessaries at Botany. 'Come back with me and I'll prepare you lunch.'

I was haggard and wretched and found it difficult to tear myself away from the cemetery. Trilby, on the other hand, was how I'd half-expected her to be when I first went round to comfort her: black-veiled and wholly competent in the social desiderata of tragedy. She knew how to deal with the drivers of black cars and the assorted ghouls and harpies who make their living despatching the dead. She tossed in her little shovelful of dirt with a wonderful bravery, whereas when it came to my turn I could only blubber and cover my face. If I wasn't mistaken I even saw her slip a couple of five-dollar notes to the gravediggers and exchange pleasantries with them. 'Yer a lady,' I thought I heard one of them attest. 'I should hope so,' I thought I heard Trilby reply. In short, her breeding was back.

I lingered among the carnage, spending ages inspecting the elaborate sepulchres erected to the children of distraught Italian families. The photographs set into stone showed little angels with black eyes. I was struck by how many Italians seemed not to be able to make it beyond the age of sixteen in Australia.

'Why do you think there are such a lot of them?' I asked Trilby.

She took my arm as she was meant to do. 'It just seems a lot,' she said. She was worried about me, feeling that I was becoming morbid. Which she was meant to feel.

'I like this custom of using photographs,' I said. 'It perpetuates you more efficiently than a mere chiselled rhyme. I think I'd like a photograph.'

Trilby tightened her grip on my arm.

I stopped in front of the mausoleum of little Carlo, who had given it away just twenty-four hours short of his ninth birthday. 'Look at this one,' I said. 'A small bundle of Neapolitan bones, deposited thirteen thousand miles from where it properly belongs. He opened his eyes in Australia, he closed his eyes in Australia, but apart from that what is his connection to the place? Look at the lustrousness of him. Look at the olive softness of his skin. He was climatically as well as culturally at risk. No wonder he rejected the idea of growing old here. I tell you, Trilby, people should stay where they were born. Wherever that is.'

I resisted her attempts to move me away. 'Just a kid,' I said. 'Not even nine years old. Exactly the same age I was when—'

She cut me short. She knew what was coming. 'Oh, Leeorhn,' she said, and having got us back to where I wanted us to be, having restored our old sensitive serving lad and grand lady relations, I consented to be taken home and given a whopping lunch.

I saw Trilby constantly over the next weeks, sometimes staying the night in the spare room from which I'd reluctantly listened to my father putting intolerable pressure on his heart, more than fifteen years before. We talked and talked, though just what we talked about I now find it impossible to remember.

'We know so little about each other really,' I do recall

Trilby saying, so I suppose we tried to remedy that by divulging our innermost thoughts.

I've never been very skilled at that sort of intimacy. The moment I'm expected to *really be myself* all sense of who I actually am deserts me entirely and I have to make myself up on the spot. Nor am I able to honour the *other person* with the appropriate attention. I ask the most searching questions – because that's what's expected – then I fail to remember to listen to the answers. This was especially the case during the long evenings of mutual reacquaintance Trilby and I put in together. To be honest, I had no desire to get to know who Trilby really was. She had a symbolic function in my life. Her role was as fixed as that of the fairy godmother in a pantomime, or rather – since I aspired to something higher than farce, and more vexed than wish-fulfilment – the dowager-duchess in a Viennese operetta.

Now that I have spider venom running through my veins and can therefore speak as one who has observed mankind with passing malevolence, both from high ceilings and from cracked dunny-seats, I am able to pronounce on the contemporary cult of communication. Give it away. It only confuses you. You don't have as much to find out about one another as you think you do, and what you do discover you won't like. Return to the old mute archetypes of your ancestors. Mummy, daddy, lover, mistress, rich man, poor man, beggar man, thief – what more do you need?

When it came to Trilby, anyway, I knew that the fine details of her personality would interfere badly with who I required her to be. So I didn't listen. I let my eyes glaze over as if in intense concentration. I put my hand to my mouth and bit my knuckles white and sank lower in my chair in order to suggest an almost too excruciating involvement in what she told me. Then suddenly, during what, for all I knew, might have been the least remarkable episodes of her self-narrative, I

277

would leap to my feet and have to pace the room, have to walk out on to the balcony or thrust my shoulders through an open window, so that she would think I was overwrought and overwound and overheated, in need of air and respite, like Homer's auditors when they heard Book 1 of the *Iliad* for the first time.

These ruses, as anyone who has resorted to them will confirm, are much more flattering to the storyteller than any genuine attentiveness could ever be. Who would want an audience sitting still and upright with an ear cocked when you could have it raging around your sitting room, biting its flesh and throwing itself out of windows? Not Trilby. She couldn't wait for darkness to come again to Vaucluse so that she could pour the wine and dim the lights and carry on where she'd left off the night before, making my eyes roll in crazed fascination with her account of how she'd damp-coursed her Georgian mansion without help from anyone in 1948, and was just about to do her own wiring when she ran into my father in the park. It brought us closer together, you see, my faked absorption, and finally – because Vene and Mooch were due back and Trilby wanted, just once, to drink her power to bewitch me to the dregs (it can't be necessary for me to restate what I wanted) – it brought us to her bed.

'This is the greatest moment of my life, the consummation of all my desires,' I told her, when she took me in her hands at last.

It was too. I wasn't exaggerating. No one else had ever unwrapped me as tenderly as she did, seeming to weigh me and feel my softness, as if I were a bunch of costly fruit, so easy to bruise and damage that I must be handled with the feather-tips of the fingers. It's my belief that only someone who has known you a long time embraces you like that. Say an old friend of the family. Or your father's wife.

'I can't believe how soft your hands are,' I said.

Softness and smoothness was our theme. We both

278

couldn't believe how much of both was in the bed with us.

'And you're so smooth, Leeorhn,' she said.

'Not as smooth as you're soft,' I said.

She weighed me once again with her feather-fingers.

'Oh,' I sighed.

'Like little whortleberries,' she said.

I didn't know what whortleberries were, but I knew how they must have felt when Trilby picked them.

'So light,' she said.

'So soft,' I said.

'So smooth,' she said.

Does this sound as though we talked a lot? Well, we had plenty to talk about. We had been friends since 1949. It was now nearly thirty years on from that. If you do a few simple calculations, taking into account who did what when, you'll conclude that Trilby must have been making steady progress through her sixties. And you'll be right. Which was something else we had to talk about, in between the weighing of the fruit: how smooth and soft a woman making steady progress through her sixties can be.

'Your belly is so smooth,' I said. 'Your breasts are as soft as a young girl's.'

'That's the saddest part of growing old,' she said. 'Not that you decay, but that you don't.'

I chose not to think about it. She was a revelation to me, a mockery of everything I'd ever heard about the brevity of beauty, but I needed to see her as an exception, a prodigy, a one-off. Now wasn't the time for me to be imagining that the world was full of lovely bodies hidden away under granny clothes, going to waste, just as mine had gone to waste in Cambridge, in pensioners' clubs and old people's homes. I was here to get to the bottom of an aristocrat not to bleed for humanity.

'You are timeless,' I told her. 'You are just as you were when you couldn't stay for my birthday party.'

I suppose I shouldn't have reminded her of that. It distressed her. 'Ah, Leeorhn,' she said, 'I couldn't run as fast now as I did then.'

One little tear, a mere half-droplet of grief, appeared in the corner of her eye. I took it away with my tongue. 'You don't have to run anywhere,' I said, and gave the lie to her age with such gentleness and ease and even, I must say, propriety, that it was hard to imagine how notions of sin could ever have become entangled with such a thing. Sinners? We were babes in arms – she in mine, me in hers.

'You remember when you took hold of me and I said it was the greatest moment of my life,' I whispered. 'Well I was lying. *This* is.'

She didn't tell me that this was the greatest moment of *her* life, but I didn't mind – she had been alive longer than I had, and I wasn't feeling competitive.

I'm not sure that you can call what we did making love. The phrase is too active. Make love not war, the generation I turned my back on used to say, as if the same ferocious energies could be expended equally on both. Trilby and I had no aggressions to rechannel.

'Oh, that's so sweet,' Trilby said.

And although I had never used such a word in my life I used it now. 'It is,' I said. 'It is unutterably sweet.'

We scarcely moved. We quivered together like some very early form of plant life. Don't think the less of us for that. Without those first palpitating jelly-fish there'd have been no love between the anthropoids. There's an argument, too, for the superior satisfaction of the zoophyte – the sponge or the coral or the sea-anemone – which after my night pulsing in the arms of Trilby I would never want to deprecate. Sweet, sweet, unutterably sweet it was, and when she could feel that I was unable to bear the sweetness any longer she eased her hips towards me infinitesimally – 'Oh, how smooth!' she cried; 'Oh, how soft!' I cried back – until I was thrust from the ocean floor, heard the waters recede, and lay spent like a starfish on Ararat.

'I suppose,' said Trilby, in the morning, 'that a night with one woman must be rather unadventurous for a chap who is accustomed to two.'

I was sorry that she said this. I didn't want her to show me her uncertainty. Weren't aristocrats meant to be fearless and impervious?

'Trilby,' I said, 'whatever a chap is accustomed to, he isn't accustomed to what happened last night. You melted my bones.'

She was in a housecoat that had lace edging to it, and she looked more feminine and more pliant than I wanted her to look. She tugged absently at the elbow of my shirt, a clear signal somehow of the restraints which had once more to be imposed on our intimacy. 'You melted mine, Leeorhn,' she said.

It was true. We had melted each other's. We had seared the pith and marrow, as Gunnar McMurphy might have put it, of our several vertebrae and ossicles. As a consequence of which we neither of us would ever be entirely steady on our feet again.

Does that sound like a perfect mutuality? Well don't forget that nothing is ever equal between men and women. It's in the nature of their conjoining that one will always be on a more urgent mission than the other. And in this case the busy missionary was me. It wasn't Trilby who for nearly thirty years had sought to sound the stops of *my* mystery, it was me, following in my father's dainty footsteps, who had striven to plumb the depths of *hers*. Behold, then, the intrepid traveller returned. Now that I had, so to speak, heard the echo from her bottom, I knew the emptiness that accompanies the fulfilment of ambition. What was before or below me now? I wondered. What did I aspire to? What was I after?

And I felt some backward-looking sadness also. What

was it that my father had laboured so assiduously over Trilby to discover? Had he really believed that this generous compliant woman possessed some inaccessible reserve of forbidden satisfaction? Or had he knowingly invented her rather than face acknowledging that there was a limit to how much anyone could please him? It worried me that I couldn't make up my mind whether he'd been an oaf or a hero; it worried me that I couldn't decide whether he'd been cruel or kind to Trilby; and it worried me that I couldn't therefore sort out which I'd been.

But soon Trilby would go into a decline and I would realise that she couldn't do without my father's extravagant idea of her, and that she badly missed living in his head. Living in someone else's head, I came to understand, had quite a few things to be said for it. But that didn't stop me setting about emptying mine of Venie and Maroochi, or them from taking retributive action, and emptying theirs of me.

25

'HE DID *WHAT*?' said Venie.

I'd told Maroochi first, to make it easier, and now, with me still in the room, she told Venie.

'I'll leave,' I said.

'You'll stay right where you are,' said Venie.

'He made the beast with his *de facto* step-mum,' Maroochi repeated.

I wasn't going to have any talk about bestiality. 'Forget the animals,' I said. 'We were about as wild as a pair of molluscs.'

Maroochi snorted.

White fire flashed from Venie's eyes.

'Everyone knows,' said Maroochi, 'that Poms root like rattlesnakes.'

'And everyone also knows,' I answered, 'that Australians fuck like their own fauna.'

'Rattlers aren't Australian,' said Maroochi.

'And besides,' said Venie, 'we aren't talking about us, we are talking about you.'

'Because if we were talking about us,' said Maroochi, 'we'd have a few things to say about what we did *not* do while we were away.'

'About the temptations we did *not* succumb to,' said Venie.

'And the fun *we* could have had but didn't,' said Maroochi.

'Come off it,' I said. 'You can't have fun in New Zealand.'

'You can in Fiji,' Venie said.

'In Fiji you almost can't have anything else,' Maroochi confirmed.

'Whew, Fiji!' Venie said.

'Breaks your heart just bloody thinking about it,' said Maroochi.

'I'm sorry,' I said, 'if you feel you made intolerable sacrifices on my behalf.'

'Given,' said Venie, 'that you didn't make any on ours.'

I sighed the deep sigh of the eternal exasperated husband. I know, I know, it was my own fault. I had no business confiding what was after all a sacred family secret to a pair of romping girls who were only not strangers in the sense that I'd lived with them for about eight years. But I wanted the trouble. And of course I got it.

'Isn't it incest?' Venie asked.

'Technically,' Maroochi said.

'Incest my Aunt Fanny,' I said.

'Don't tell me what is and isn't incest,' said Maroochi. 'My father's a judge.'

'Isn't it imprisonable in Western Australia?' asked Venie.

'It's imprisonable everywhere,' said Maroochi. 'But in Queensland they hang you.'

'By the dick I hope,' said Venie.

'Naturally,' said Maroochi. 'Joh knows how to run a clean state.'

'I'm off,' I said.

'You stay where you are,' said Venie. 'You little shit.' Only, because she had just come back from New Zealand and had picked up the accent, she pronounced it, 'shut'.

Every man should know what it is like, just once in his life, to be called 'a luttle shut'.

Me – I found it mesmeric, and stayed where I was.

'And so you've been living over there the whole time we've been away,' Venie said.

I might have been mesmerized but I was still a lover of truth. 'I haven't been *living* there at all. I went around to keep her company. And to have company myself. We were both bereaved, don't forget.'

'So you went to comfort her?'

'And to be comforted,' Maroochi reminded her.

'And while you were there drying her eyes you thought you might just as well –'

'– since you already had your hankie out –'

'– and she was too upset to notice –'

'– and the opportunity was too good to miss –'

'– slip her a length.'

'That's if molluscs have lengths.'

'They have palps,' I said.

'Same difference,' said Venie, 'then you passed her a palp.'

'And she being,' said Maroochi, 'rather long in the valve –'

'I think the phrase is, stiff in the shell,' said Venie.

'– she no doubt grasped your palp thankfully.'

'Because, God knows,' said Venie, 'she wasn't likely to be given another.'

That was the end of it for me. 'You're pathetic,' I shouted. 'You're pathetic, the pair of you. You claim to be women of the world, and look at the fuss you're making. And if you think Trilby a little too weathered to be enjoyed, then why the jealous tantrums? She can hardly be competition, can she, by your account? She can hardly be taking from your stock of pleasures.'

All Venie's features had somehow managed to assemble in an ugly crush at the front of her face. The silver fault-lines I loved her for appeared like laces, pulling her skin taut. 'I don't think *a little too weathered* does justice to the singularity of your taste, Leon,' she said. 'The woman must be seventy.'

What was I going to do? Fall to bickering over years? Would Venie's expression clear if I could convince her that Trilby was not a day over sixty-three?

'Seventy-five,' I said. 'And improving every minute. Shall I describe to you the firmness of her flesh? I suppose you thought that after thirty a woman's breasts start to sag? Well let me tell you something, after seventy they start to rise again.'

'Shut up,' Venie warned me.

'There's another myth about crones that needs dispelling,' I went on. 'Trilby was so tight—'

'Shut up,' Venie warned me again. 'You make me sick.' And to prove she wasn't exaggerating she actually put her hand to her mouth and ran retching to the bathroom.

Maroochi stayed where she was, looking thoughtfully through the window. I paced the carpet, listening to my chest thump. Intermittently the sound would reach us of Venie throwing up in the sink.

'Is her flesh really firm?' Maroochi asked me at last, without turning her head.

'Let me put it this way,' I said. 'You know how quickly yours returns to normal after the thumb test? Well Trilby's has got so much spring in it that you can't even press it in.'

She swung around, distraught. 'You can't even press it in?'

I shook my head. 'Nope. The resistant force of life beneath the skin is far too strong. You can feel it pressing back at you.'

She looked down at her own arms. I decided to leave her with them. As a boy who grew up in a nest of aunts I had a highly developed sense of privacy. I knew that you got out of the way when a girl wanted to check whether her flesh had the elasticity of a woman of seventy-five's.

On my way out of the house I passed Venie in the bathroom. She was still hanging over the sink. She raised her head when she saw me and wiped her mouth on the back of her hand.

'You'd lie down with anyone,' she said.

I made a couple of blowing noises with my mouth. Venie was to understand that this was the sound my patience made when it was running out. 'Trilby's not anyone,' I said.

'Oh yes – I'd forgotten – anyone provided she's bereaved, a friend of your father's, and old enough to be your granny.'

'I won't argue with any of that,' I said. 'I think that more or less gets it. Except, perhaps, in so far as it doesn't entirely catch my versatility. I once lay down with a priest. Do you want to know how old *he* was?'

I was hoping that I might hear her being sick again, but she closed the door on me.

Out in the street some boys were throwing cicadas in the air to see if they would open up like parachutists on the way down and break their own fall. One landed badly by my feet. 'Australian wildlife,' I muttered to myself, 'who wants it?' And I trod on it, pretending it was an accident, but enjoying the crack and squelch beneath my foot.

I was disappointed in Venie and Maroochi. Disenchanted might be a better word. I had supposed that in matters of sexual relations they were equivocalists, ambivalentiers like me. Wasn't that what our own irregular but highly formalized arrangement implied? We were clean, decent, law-abiding, and in the privacy of our lovely home initiated one another in unspeakable rites. Wasn't that the idea? Weren't we meant to be disapproving of everyone except ourselves, conventional in regard to everything except what really mattered? That's how I'd always understood what we were up to anyway. But after what they'd said to me about poor Trilby, after they'd charged me with deceit, infidelity, incest and gerontophilia, I found it hard to see anything unconventional in them at all. For all that we'd been through together they were proper

Australian girls from proper Australian backgrounds. They hailed from a world where you weren't expected to show excessive devotion to your stepmother, where it wasn't done to palpitate like a jelly-fish in the arms of a woman twenty-five years your senior. Fine for them, if they consented to such limits placed upon their moral options, but this was no place for me, was it, who had done sterling service by the decencies in the pages of *The Black Sail* and who was therefore owed a hefty backpay of what, if I'd become a leftist and not a rightist, might have been called deviationism.

As I've said before, I was never political. I hadn't worked out any programme for how far I would like to deviate. I knew only that I was a pillar, if not indeed the architect, of middle-class articulate Australian society – hadn't it been me who had taught the useless dickheads which books they ought to ban? – that I was the scourge of every poof and pervert, every lout and long-hair in the country; that I was the lucky lover of two impeccably connected synchronized aquaballerinas who put rust-proof *diamanté* head-pieces in their hair and travelled miles to hear the speeches of the Honourable Malcolm Fraser; and that I was wondering whether I wouldn't have led a happier and more useful life if I'd chosen to be a bohemian.

You can see now how accurately Gunnar McMurphy might have diagnosed my condition had he been here to discuss the spider with me. It takes two to make a bite, he would have told me – a biter and a biteree. Spot on, Gunnar. That Redback had seen me coming miles away and years before. She just sat there in no hurry, waiting for me to call.

So yes, Vene's and Mooch's rabid orthodoxy in the matter of my one sweet night with Trilby was the beginning of the end all right, but our wind-down – or our wind-up, depending which way you view it – took its time.

First there were the weeks of silence and the months of reconciliation to be gone through. When I say silence I mean silence between me and them; between themselves they became fiendishly vociferous. This was my punishment for my tasteless lapse. We didn't have a spare bed. I'd demanded that they get rid of it when I moved in with them years before, as a symbolic statement of what we were about. So I lay only inches from them, my back turned, a pillow to my ear, while they made a needlessly noisy meal – dinner strictly for two – of each other's choicest parts.

'Hooley dooley,' said Venie, because there was no let-up in the conversation, even when they'd finished, 'that was beaut.'

'A ripper,' said Maroochi.

'A snorter,' said Venie.

'Who needs the other?' asked Maroochi.

'Not I,' said Venie.

'Nor I,' said Maroochi.

'Nor I,' said I, into my pillow.

Of course it wasn't long before this had the effect it was bound to have and I was disporting myself between them like a pasha from Partington once more, marvelling at their inventiveness and unconventionality. Again I set my stopwatch for the Sunday-morning skin tests. I wielded my razor. I accompanied them to competitions. And they, in return, egged me on in my paper war against the new Australian woman with the scoured face and the grated hair and the enraged and enraging nipples. 'Shame!' I shouted when the judges held up numbers that did scant justice to my girls' boosts and tuck-outs. 'Too right!' they called from the back of the Vaucluse Town Hall, when I denounced lesbianism as an abomination unto the Lord and a threat to the future of an already seriously underpopulated Australia.

For a while it was like old times – Venie and Maroochi not what they seemed, or seeming what they weren't;

me preaching into the very teeth of all I practised. But we were only papering over the cracks. We weren't the skilled ambigamists we looked. Soon the baby smell of rusks and mashed banana – the odour of the purlieus of privilege – would rise again into my nostril; and soon the wicked whispers from Bohemia would blow like kisses in my ear.

It was one whisper in particular – louder than all the rest and delivered, if I wasn't mistaken, in a familiar voice – which finally woke me in the night and bade me follow. Though by then it was all up with me and my spangled aqua-ballerinas anyway. We'd as good as said our last goodbyes. As is usual, the argument that once and for all finished us was only a pretext; we would never have split over the issue of anabolic steroids had nothing else been wrong.

You'll have deduced from my tactful silence on the subject that Venie and Maroochi had stopped winning medals at Olympic Games. And it won't have escaped your notice either, from the other clues I've dropped, that their professional fortunes must have taken something of a dive if they had to travel to New Zealand and Fiji for audiences, and if I had to shout 'Shame!' every time a judge raised his arm.

Poor Venie and Maroochi. Water-ballet can be a cruel sport. It can take you up and spit you out, with as little sympathy for your feelings as life itself. They weren't a wholly spent force as a water duo – don't mistake me – but their career had entered that phase where they heard themselves referred to as 'veteran competitors', where other ballerinas started to show them affection and esteem, and where they were increasingly giving back more silver cups than they were bringing home.

Hence my suggestion that they put themselves on anabolic steroids.

'Why not?' I said. 'Your mothers put themselves on gin and aspirins. Your fathers put themselves on freebees. We're none of us as fit as we were. We all need something to help us through.'

'So put yourself on them, Leon,' Venie said.

We were sitting on a bench at Manly Wharf waiting for a ferry to take us back to the Quay. We'd been enjoying an ordinary day out at Manly, body surfing, eating crab sticks, promenading, and listening to a choir of high-school children – the winners of the Dawson Memorial Shield for Indigenous Australian Bird Imitations – rendering the dawn chorus in the Corso. Maroochi was much taken with the boy kookaburra, but Venie and I, perhaps remembering our very first morning together in my North Shore garden, had been especially struck by the three third-year girl galahs. The noise had driven us away at last – forty different species clamouring for applause. Even from the wharf we could still hear the playground ribaldry of the sulphur-crested cockatoo.

I didn't respond to Venie's proposition. I wasn't prepared to say that *I* hadn't just returned from a swimming fiesta in Lake Disappointment having come ninth out of nine in the Invitation Duet. So I paced the wharf and tried to see if I could spot the ferry coming.

But when I returned to the bench Venie was waiting for me with a question. 'Do you know what anabolic steroids do to you?' she asked.

'They help you to win cups,' I said.

Considering that these were shark-infested waters I suppose I was pushing my luck.

'They inhibit the pituitary gland's ability to produce the hormones which stimulate the ovaries into producing oestrogens,' she said.

'And they can damage the genetic material in the nuclei of the cell,' Maroochi added.

I stared at them both. I hated science. 'So?' I said.

They stared back. 'Pity the poor foetus,' Venie said.

'Oh,' I said, 'it comes around to babies, does it?'

'I think what Venie is saying,' said Maroochi, 'is that it almost certainly doesn't.'

'Well you can't do everything,' I said. 'And they don't give cups for mothering.'

I had a feeling that in Queensland they probably did, but that didn't essentially affect my point.

'They also cause carcinoma of the breast,' said Venie.

I had nothing to say to that.

'And lowering of the vocal register,' said Maroochi.

I had nothing to say to that either.

'And hirsutism,' said Venie.

'And abnormal clitoral enlargement,' said Maroochi.

'Hang on a minute,' I interrupted.

May I be indelicate? I have already made some quick allusion to my part in the cosmetic rituals which perforce preceded any public appearance of Venie and Maroochi in their twin swimsuits. As their custodian and champion I took my responsibility with the razor seriously, and as their lover I counted it a privilege. But to be honest I had never liked the high-cut hairless naked pelvic look favoured by synchronized swimmers and indeed, latterly, by a certain class of ordinary amateur Australian bathing beauty. It seemed to me, in its fastidious removal of all signs of efflorescent womanhood – adulthood, if you don't welcome sexual specificity – to be one more example of the will to babydom in Australia. It might be going too far to say the country's beaches are today crowded only with young women wearing designer diapers, but all things flow seawards and nothing is more apparent at the water's edge than this national aspiration to nursery innocence.

An extra-terrestrial visitor deposited on Manly might well suppose that Australia possesses a species of sphinx or female minotaur – half mother, above the shaven pelvic bone, half her own baby beneath it.

In the case of Venie and Maroochi this fanatic hairlessness became associated in my mind – and don't forget that I was a collector of curls from my mother's *salon* floor from way back – with their other habits of social and ideological orderliness. We all carry the clue to our politics and belief systems secreted somewhere about our persons, and that was where Venie and Maroochi carried theirs – right there in the long blameless V of their swimming costumes. You didn't have to look anywhere else to discover why they were both privately and publicly ungenerous, why they were unable to forgive me, for example, for making a present of myself to Trilby, and why, years later, they would be unable to forgive the Australian government for making a present of Ayers Rock to its rightful owners.

This might go some way to explaining how come I chose to halt their enumeration of the harmful side-effects of anabolic steroids at hirsutism and clitoral enlargement, and how come, with the crowd for the Manly ferry still listening to every word – the women marvelling in their cut-away baby beach-pants, the men scratching furiously at their penises – I told them what I thought of them at last.

'So I'm up to here with the pair of you,' I concluded, marking a line above the heart where fondness finished and satiety began. 'I've had you both, with your neat little genital packages, tied in pretty, matching bows, and hermetically protected from hair or odour or, Heaven forbid, enlargement. What are you fending off anyway? Proletarianisation of the pelvis? Creeping communism of the crotch? Well, I've had it. I'm off. Give me a miss from now on, any time.'

Hester and Nesta would have been proud of me.

You won't be surprised to hear that I didn't catch the ferry back with them. I stayed the night at Manly, sleeping on the beach like a hippie. Had I owned a guitar I would have strummed it and let my head shake. That's how unfettered I felt. So what, if a grey-nurse was gambolling in the water only inches from where I lay, and man-eating crabs were playing This Little Piggy with my toes? I was free. I slept badly but I was liberated.

I rose early though, sick with second thoughts. Long before the sun came up I was at the wharf, waiting for the first hydrofoil of the morning to skim me home. Normally I loved harbour travel. If man had been created to commute, then there was no finer place on earth to commute to, it seemed to me, than one side of Sydney Harbour from another. But I had no eye for beauty this morning, and I was in no mood to congratulate myself on my good fortune. We rode the water like Gods, my fellow-passengers blind to everything but their newspapers and me deaf to everything but the wild thumpings of my heart. I took a Yellow Cab from Circular Quay, pushing an elderly person aside. 'Vaucluse,' I said. 'Quick.'

I didn't look right, towards the blue ocean, or left, into the warm protected bays. I looked only at the taxi-driver's clock. When I got to the house I was relieved to find that the locks had not been changed. If they were prepared to let me in then they might be prepared to have me back. But I opened the door only to find my cases packed. There was no sign of Vene and Mooch. And no note. The cases were meant to say all that needed saying. I poured myself a glass of icy Riesling from the cask we kept inside the fridge. It was a bit early to be drinking but I needed to steady my nerves. Five or six glasses later, when I'd pulled myself together, I rang for another cab.

'The airport,' I said, tossing my bags into the boot.

The driver was a Yugoslav. 'This is the country of the future,' he told me.

'Oh yes,' I said.

'This is the only country in which I am happy,' he assured me.

'I can understand that,' I said.

294

'A man is free here. Too many strikes? – yes. But here is sunshine, good food, wine, money, beautiful girls.'

'Turn around,' I said, 'and take me to the Dawn Fraser Pool, Balmain.'

I asked him to wait for me. For a happy man he looked suspicious. I reminded him that he had my luggage – the entire material history of my life in Australia, to be exact – in his boot. 'I'll only be five minutes,' I promised him.

In fact I was only two. I found Venie and Maroochi on their backs in the water, practising their synchro-sculling. 'Look,' I called out, 'don't you think this is all pretty silly?' I was reminded of the first time I saw Maroochi, in this very pool, and of how she had favoured me with a Maori greeting. Today there was no such elaborate ritual; she merely raised her thumbs lazily and unambiguously, and then, when I didn't go away, she showed me her long magenta tongue. A split second later Venie – only hers was short and silver – did the same. Their timing really was shot to pieces these days. I hated seeing it. But there was still no mistaking their meaning. They were favouring me with a Maori farewell.

I left the pool blubbering. The heat, the emotion, and the Riesling were too much for me. On the way out I ran into the life-saver. Not the original life-saver who had warned me against Venie and Maroochi all those years ago, but he might as well have been. He wore the same colour trunks and eyed me with the same look of saddened solidarity. When I say I ran into him I'm not doing justice to the extremity of my behaviour; I actually sought the comfort of his arms. 'You know what it's like,' I sobbed into his neck.

He didn't even need to ask me what I meant. 'Sure do, sport,' he said.

If I'm not mistaken he ruffled my hair as well. They can be very understanding, Australian men.

By the time I got back to the taxi I had been seized by that cold shiver of loneliness which stayed with me until the Redback warmed me with her toothy kiss.

'As you were,' I told the driver. 'The airport after all.'

'You going overseas?' he asked me. I could tell that he wanted to treat me as though I were a new fare so that he could go through his routine again, advising me against ever leaving the only country in which a sane man could count himself happy.

'In a manner of speaking,' I said.

'Where you go?'

'Melbourne,' I said.

26

MELBOURNE is all lacy Victorian balconies, red-roofed bungalows, straight streets, and schoolteachers.

You cannot move in Melbourne, you cannot hear yourself think in Melbourne, you cannot find a spare place at a bar in Melbourne, for schoolteachers, apologists for schoolteachers, teachers of schoolteachers, and theoreticians of the teaching of apologizing for schoolteachers. How this plague of pedantry came about I have never been able to discover, though I do remember Maroochi expounding a theory to account for it. 'It's gold,' she said. 'The minute a prospector struck lucky he had to turn his children into gentlemen. Schoolies were at the top of every successful digger's shopping list.'

'Conversely,' I remember Venie adding, 'the schoolies liked to be close to pay-dirt. So what's changed?'

She had a low opinion of the teaching profession. Like her father. As a Liberal State Premier, Murray Redfern believed that teachers were the main reason his life was not an unmitigatedly happy one. 'I have a highly uncomplicated attitude to the bastards, Leon,' he once told me. 'Shut 'em up, lock 'em in, shoot 'em down.'

'Too good for them,' I said. I wasn't keen on the profession either. Especially I wasn't keen on its Melbourne representatives, who put a trust verging on bibliolatry in the melioristic properties of the pamphlet, publishing a new one every thirty-six hours and thrusting it on the only-just-arrived not-a-word-of-Australian-speaking offspring of whichever Slavs or

Slovaks managed somehow to slip through my Piers Plowman migrant-discouragement test. They always ended up eventually – the pamphlets not the migrants – on my desk at the offices of *The Black Sail*. They had titles like *Greek, Gay and Garrulous*, or *French If You Feel Like*, or *Uranium and the Uterus*, and they were all no sooner printed than they were banned. This then, so long as it wasn't Melbourne Cup Day or the Queen's Cousin's Birthday or the VFL Grand Final, provided an opportunity for every teacher in town to stop the trams and march in protest under the banner of the Eastern States Educationists for Abortion Without Pregnancy, or the Heidelberg Housemasters against Ocker Ethno-centrism.

Some of these groups had invited me to speak to them over the years, as a kind of high-camp treat, in the same spirit that the Oxford Union likes to get a look at Enoch Powell or the Reverend Ian Paisley. On one occasion I was billed to appear on the same platform as Lord Longford and Malcolm Muggeridge, but they were so shocked by what they saw of Melbourne's red-light district that they felt they had to stay and be shocked some more and so missed the meeting. I covered for them, having a fair idea of what they'd want to say. I was invariably given a rough ride anyway, so I knew what expression of celestial complacency to adopt when the chants of SHIT, FUCK, CUNT got going at the back of the hall. And I knew how to start them up again, the minute they were quiet, by taunting them with something like, 'If you are the teachers, God help the taught!' or by asking them, since they were worried about the hidden politics of the curriculum, whether their own political programme consisted of anything besides the legalisation of cannabis and or-gasm on demand.

It was the least I could do seeing as they'd been good enough to invite me and had paid my expenses at the Zebra Motel for the night. And I enjoyed all the jeering.

I had no difficulty understanding why Lord Longford and Malcolm Muggeridge couldn't get enough of it. It went back a long way into Christian history, it had a powerful mythological pull – being ridiculed for speaking the truth.

The only parts of these public shouting matches I didn't enjoy were when I had to listen to protestations of ideological faith from members of the audience. I wasn't, in principle, against confessions of conversions (haven't I been confessing as much myself?) but I have an acute aversion to sentences structured around the phrase 'in terms of' and no schoolteacher in Australia is capable of structuring his thoughts about his own or other people's belief systems in terms of anything else.

'You're not going to understand radicalism in terms of the self,' they used to say to me, 'until you see it in terms of a personal willingness to embrace a humanistic commitment regardless, in terms of cost, of cost. Would you comment please.'

'In terms of?'

'In terms of what you think.'

'In terms of what I think about your terms?'

'In terms of whatever terms seem to you to be appropriate for engaging with the question of radicalism in terms of interiority.'

In terms of age, I would feel very old sometimes, conversing with Melbourne schoolteachers. In terms of what I wished, I wished it wasn't happening. In terms of where I wanted to be, I wanted to be somewhere else.

In which case what was I doing, after Venie and Maroochi had shown me their tongues for the final time, getting the taxi-driver to drive me to Sydney, Kingsford-Smith, and from there finding a pilot to fly me to Melbourne, Tullamarine?

Remember the wicked whisper? Well I was going where it called me. Melbourne? Yes, Yes, I know – it wasn't the centre of sublunary wickedness exactly. It wasn't Hades or Gomorrah. It wasn't even Hamburg or Gillingham. But it had made the Festival of Light see red; it had given the world the Women's Movement, and – no negligible claim to infamy – it had given the world Bev Belladonna. Besides, at my age you didn't put up obstacles of preference. If a wicked whisper beckoned you, you followed. And said where you would rather have been led later. You even followed it, if necessary, through Melbourne and out again, westwards past the used-car lots and the slaughter-houses to the flat land-locked sprawl of Sunshine, that cruel suburban joke played on hapless immigrants, where the sun shone all right, so relentlessly that the tarmac bubbled in the street, so unrelieved by any breath of cooling air that the mosquitoes burned their tongues on boiling blood and the Ustashi – the resident right-wing Croatian separatists – wished they were back in Yugoslavia living under communism.

I already knew something about this part of Melbourne from the pamphlets which landed on my desk. Or at least I knew something about the problems of its schools and schoolies. Ever ready to shirk a challenge, they seemed to see it as an impediment to their teaching that their charges spoke not a syllable of Australian – so how *did* they make it past my test? – and that they themselves spoke not a syllable of Serbo-Croat. 'You cannot call this education,' one of their number wrote, as if in a despatch from the front. 'We live in a state of mute and hostile incommunicado, staring blankly into one another's incomprehension, waging wordless war.'

'Sounds like education to me,' I remember saying to Venie's father who happened to be over visiting us at the time. He was fighting funding migrant learning schemes and was glad of a bit of moral support.

'If they're finding it so difficult to communicate why don't they use sign language?' he wondered. 'I'm no linguist but I can make my needs understood anywhere in the free world. I don't know about you, Leon, but I always get what I want when I ask for it in Manila or Singapore.'

I wasn't certain whether this was an argument against teachers or against migrants but I agreed with him either way. 'They want it easy,' I said. 'They want it on a plate.'

'Whingers,' he said.

The force of his argument was still carrying me with it. 'Bludgers,' I added.

We were at the bar of the RSL club Murray Redfern liked to be recognized in when he was in Sydney. At the mention of bludgers every Returned Serviceman in the room, even the living dead on the handles of the pokies, looked up. They didn't know who I was referring to but they were familiar with the state of mind. 'My word,' they all said together.

On the way out he returned to this example of national unanimity. 'It's an undefinable quality, Australianness,' he said, taking me by the shoulder, 'but one thing I do know—'

'What's that, Murray?' I asked.

'You can't teach it.'

'My oath, you can't,' I said.

'And I'll tell you something else, Leon.'

'What's that?' I asked.

He paused, to find his balance and grab a bit more of me. 'You can't learn it either.'

He was very close to me now, breathing friendship and fatherliness and melancholy Australian certitude into my neck. He looked not unlike the young Robert Menzies when he was drunk, astute and twinkling, his mouth pursed in a small o of lethal geniality. 'So tell me this, Leon,' he said, 'if you can't teach it and you can't learn it, just what in buggery's name are schools for?'

If I'd had the room I would have shrugged. But by this time I was just about carrying him on my back.

301

Aeneas and Anchises in Artarmon. 'I'm stuffed if I know,' I said. I could sense that he'd like me even better if I swore. 'I'm fucked if I can figure it out. But I've met a few teachers in my time and I'll tell you this—'

'Tell me, you bastard,' he said. Like all Australians he was an insatiable conversationalist.

So I dug deep into my instinct to please. And deeper still into my knowledge of what was likely to please him. 'I've met a few of the deadheads in my time,' I said, 'and there isn't one of them that isn't a bit of a plodder.'

A bit of a plodder! The worst insult one Australian can deliver to another. There was nothing I wasn't prepared to say to get these people to love me.

'My oath,' Murray Redfern said, into the open collar of my shirt.

I can still feel the warm breath of his agreement, winnowing the hairs on my chest.

'My word,' he said, as I handed him over to his chauffeur.

I didn't accept a lift myself. I needed to walk off the tingling sensation in my loins.

Of course I don't hold such views on the teaching profession now. Now I have a swelling in my groin and a soft spot in my heart for all suffering humanity, even the chuntering chalkies of Victoria. And I didn't unequivocally hold such views then either, when I climbed off the plane at Tullamarine in meek submission to the wicked whisper and said 'Sunshine' to the first taxi-driver I could find.

'You a striynger to Owstriylia?' he asked me.

I shook my head. Though I needn't have bothered.

'Welcome to the grytest country in the —'

'Yes, yes, I know all that,' I said.

In the main I err on the side of subservience to taxi-drivers. I consider it to be as hazardous not to

302

humour them as it is to set up hostility with your dentist. But on this occasion I wanted to be alone with my thoughts, even if it meant being thrown around the back seat with them. I needed time to prepare myself for what I was doing, for where I was going, and for who I was about to see.

Revelations concerning the unorthodox teaching procedures of a certain Sunshine secondary schoolma'am had been outraging Australia for weeks now. The newspapers had been full of her, publishing her photograph together with extracts of her philosophy and asking their readers how they would feel about having such a teacher teaching *their* children Remedial Relationship Enhancement Studies. The majority of Australians – attaching a high value to innocence, as I've already explained, and what's more believing against all the evidence that while innocence can be aped it is to be found in its purest form in children – felt that they wouldn't like it. Even migrant children, they considered, even the children of onion farmers from Medina and goatherds just out from Naxos had a right to be protected from what was said and what was shown, or at least what was said to be said if not shown to be shown, on that particular baking Friday afternoon in Sunshine. And the onion farmers and the goatherds agreed with them. *Especially* our children have to be protected, they said, because we too, although we come from ancient cultures that should know better, believe in the innocence of the young. We have our own rituals and customs. And if we want our boys to know that the reason for their aggression to our girls is womb envy and that a woman's sex is as lovely as an unfolded flower, we will tell them so ourselves.

'Bulldust,' said the teacher – this isn't an actual dialogue I am reporting, you understand, but the abstract centrifugal pull of mighty opposites – 'bulldust,' she as good as said, 'pigs will fly – and I select from the farmyard advisedly – before you pass on such a lesson

303

to your little ones. Your boys are brutes before their balls have dropped. Your girls overcome their self-horror only to blossom briefly into black-eyed sluts and then be banished to the kitchens. What they don't hear from me they won't hear from anyone. What I don't tell them they won't find out.'

Ah yes, but had it only been a matter of telling, had the issue merely been one of verbal indiscretion, peace might have returned to the battle-front at Sunshine much sooner. The teacher might not have been suspended from all duties and her colleagues might not have stopped the trams in Collins Street until she'd been reinstated, revalidated, apologized to, upgraded, congratulated, compensated and canonized. Mere *telling* would never have led to this. So what else had she done?

'See the act in context,' she had warned an interviewer for *The Australian Women's Weekly.* 'It was a hot Friday afternoon. You could smell the blood from the abattoirs. The tarmac in the playground simmered and plopped like lava. The ink bubbled in the wells. The pupils in my class were aged anything from twelve to thirty. Some of them had too little English to tell me how old they were, others had too little sense of individuation ever to have known. They sweated and grunted in the heat. I wished to bring some poetry into their relational deprivation. When I told them that a woman's sex was as lovely as an unfolded flower they snorted. They kicked their desks over. They swallowed chalk. They leaped on to the window-sill. Some of them even braved the lava. Very well, I thought, if this is how you do things in the Adriatic I won't be fazed by you. I will show you how we do things in Australia. So I slipped my frock over my head. Look, look how lovely I am, I said to them. I am vine and fig and rose petal. You don't fear a fig, so why do you fear me? You don't laugh at a flower, so why do you laugh at me? If they ran home to tell their parents (and some of them *were* their parents), it was because the shame was theirs, not mine.'

I was still with Venie and Maroochi when all this was happening, and in fact we read the interview in *The Australian Women's Weekly* together, after Telemann.

'It strikes me,' said Maroochi, 'that a woman's confidence must be very low if she has to resort to titillating Maltese. I used to be able to heat up anybody from south of Austro-Hungary before I was ten. And Maltese even earlier than that.'

'But then you,' said Venie, 'do not resemble vine and fig and rose petal. For which you should thank whoever made you.'

Thank me, I thought to myself. I take it that it's already becoming clear why, if I was growing tired of Venie and Maroochi's fastidious containment, this story of indiscreet abundance in a schoolroom in Sunshine might have stirred some dormant passion for disorder in me. As correspondent on educational matters for *The Black Sail* I was every bit as appalled by this latest breakdown of decorum in the State of Victoria as you would expect me to have been. I even wrote a kind of Swiftian piece on the subject myself, recommending all teachers to undress progressively before their classes, beginning with a little something on Monday morning and building up to a climax on Friday afternoon. This was one method, I suggested, of improving levels of pupil interest and involvement. I subsequently heard that two schools in the Altona area of Melbourne followed my advice, reporting excellent results as a consequence in the examinations leading to university entrance. But whatever public attitudes I struck I was unable to conceal from myself the queer excitement the Sunshine episode aroused in me.

Not least, it is now time for me to admit, because I knew who the schoolteacher was. I recognized the name. I recognized the face. It wouldn't be an exaggeration to say that had they published a photograph of the vine and the fig and the rose petal I would have recognised those too.

Remember Desley? The young Australian woman with powerful mandibles, an MA in Fine Arts, and special interests in Lorenzo di Credi, Bramante, and Berthe Morisot? The squatting *cognoscente* who gave the Oxford undergraduate a night he would always remember? Well now you know what became of her. She continued with her grand ex-Australia self-improvement tour, visiting every major cathedral on the Continent and finding frescoes in Tuscan monasteries that no one else had, got married, got divorced, taught a bit, came back to Australia, got married, got divorced, taught a bit, dropped out a bit, walked around the Simpson Desert, got married, couldn't be bothered to get divorced, tried an abortion, lost weight, put on weight, thought about a baby, had another abortion, picked up teaching, and then one hot Friday afternoon took her frock off to body forth a metaphor during a class on Remedial Relationship Enhancement Studies for non-Australian-speaking migrants from mountainous areas of southern Europe, and became a national celebrity.

Thereby proving that travel at an early age is a long-term investment.

Seeing her photograph after all these years was a big shock to me. It took me back to the eager imaginings of my youth. It made me remember what had prompted Australian longings in me in the first place. And it jolted me out of my neat three-way live-in situation with Venie and Maroochi.

But you must be wondering how I knew what Desley looked like in order to recognise her in the first place, given that I had only ever heard about her in a story – a Cambridge jest at the expense of some Oxford noodle, a cautionary fen tale about passion at the other place which compensated us for not having any of our own. Had the tale-teller done his job so brilliantly that we would be able to pick out Desley's features from the dots in a newspaper twenty years later and in another country?

The truth is – or let's put that another way and keep truth out of it – the facts are that Desley stopped off at Cambridge in 1958, not Oxford; that she took tea at the Garden House Hotel, not the Randolph; that the wind ensemble was playing not in Oriel, but Malapert; and that the terrible impression she made, she made not on some Oxford noodle but on me.

So why didn't I admit all this at the outset? Why the elaborate contrivance to unload my shame on to someone else?

Come off it. Would you have been able to show the proper intellectual regard for the spiritual history of a man who, on the very first page of his confessions, confessed that he'd been shat on by an Australian?

27

EITHER BECAUSE I hadn't made such a marked impression on her as she had made on me, or because she had had a lot on her plate in the intervening years, Desley did not recognize me.

'You a journo?' she asked.

'Not really,' I said. I was hoping she might find a less public place for us to talk. I felt a trifle foolish, standing at the door to the staffroom with two heavy cases, not being recognized.

She thought she dimly knew my name though. 'Aren't you something to do with that CIA rag? Surely *they* don't want an interview.'

'No,' I said. 'Or at least if they do that's not why I'm here.'

She stared at my cases. They suddenly struck her as comic. 'You look as though you've run away from home,' she laughed. The noise she made was abrupt and explosive. In the main the Women's Movement in Australia frowns on its members giving way to laughter, but when the coast is clear for them to express mirth they are inclined to give it all they've got, from low in the chest, like Volga boatmen. I was reminded all at once of how I had fallen in love with Desley on the lawn of the Garden House Hotel in Cambridge because of the deep sounds that issued from her thorax, clearing the Cam of all its wildlife at a stroke. Though then she looked like a corporate receptionist with blue ribbons in her hair, whereas now she was convict-cropped and wore only a simple South Sea Islander's sarong, tied with a single knot between her breasts. It

308

wasn't what schoolmistresses in Partington wore for work. I had no trouble envisaging the ease with which it could be removed for a class on Relationship Enhancement. I could even hear the quick swish it would make.

I didn't say that I *had* run away from home as it so happened. Given this school's reputation for social conscience I might have found myself adopted and enrolled in the third form before I had time to demonstrate my command of the language. But since I had to say something I said what was also true. 'You don't remember me, Desley, do you?'

She peered at me. Whatever the rights or wrongs of her life-style it hadn't been good for her eyes. She scratched her head, showing me that she had not attacked her armpit with blades and creams the way Venie and Maroochi did. Lush images of unkempt nature passed before me. I saw vine and fig and rose petal. I trust I didn't show it, but I was in a tumult of changing perception. I felt like the eighteenth century being overtaken by Romanticism.

Desley, meanwhile, was making no progress. 'Should I?' she asked.

Now it was my turn to laugh. Though I didn't even try to go as deep as she had. What I was remembering wasn't all that funny.

'Cambridge, 1958,' I said.

I watched the first light of recollection dawn in her eyes.

'Tea at the Garden House,' I went on. 'Titian at the Fitzwilliam. The Oberon Wind Ensemble. The Paradiso Restaurant.'

'Holy shit!' she said, only she said it with so much violence that her colleagues in the staffroom looked up from the blank exercise-books they were marvelling over and wondered whether she was about to blow again, and precipitate them all into another stoppage.

I can't be sure, because I had other things on my

mind, but I thought they all seemed disappointed when they realised Desley had merely met someone she used to know. I formed the quick impression that they were all crisis junkies and looked to her for their supplies. I date from this brief passage my changed attitude to Australian schoolteachers. I weep for them now. How terrible to be seeking excitement still in a profession which the English have known for a hundred years or more to be the graveyard of every rational expectation.

It was only later that I realised I hadn't seen any pupils at the school.

'It's Non-Confrontation Week,' Desley explained to me.

'I see,' I said. 'Is that like a holiday?'

My question was wholly innocent, but being a man and being a Pom I had forfeited all rights of trust. I could feel Desley mentally frisking me for irony.

'No, Leon,' she said, 'it isn't like a holiday. We're all here, we just keep out of one another's space.'

I wanted to pull out the linings of all my pockets for her. Look, no sarcasm. See, no attitude. But I couldn't be certain, after where my suits had been hanging for the past decade, that there wouldn't be something offensive lurking in the corners. Coagulated crumbs of cynicism, or little furry balls of ribaldry. I'd forgotten how careful you had to be with free spirits.

'It makes sense,' I said. I developed a number of phrases of this noncommittal kind during our brief reconciliation. 'I guess that's about the long and the short of it,' I said. 'You'd be a fool to do otherwise. It all evens out in the end. It's a job to know.'

I can see now why she didn't find me much more engaging this time than she had the last. But I'll give her this: she made an effort. She introduced me to her colleagues, some of whom hadn't been born – some of whose parents hadn't been born – when we had first talked art in Trinity Street. Those who didn't wear sarongs wore twin suits and pearls. Unlike their English counterparts they seemed to believe that teaching was an activity worth dressing for. They broke my heart. Then she took me back to meet the other interestingly weathered women she lived with in a corrugated shack in Carlton. I was not so crass as to look through their transparent shirts. I possessed sufficient awareness of the cultural differences between Sydney and Melbourne to know that breasts in Melbourne bore their own distinct political significations, and pointed downwards to symbolise suffering and subjection. Wasn't it precisely in pursuit of such seriousness that I had turned my back on the soaring physical optimism of Sydney?

Desley found me a spare settee to lie on, and the following afternoon drove me out to the mountains – the Bogong High Plains – where the sisters were building a Girls Only ski-lodge with their bare little hands. 'We aren't against accepting help from men,' Desley explained, 'provided that it's understood they exert no influence over the decision-making processes and agree to sleeping in a tent outside the lodge.' You've never seen anyone understand more or agree quicker than I did. A few days in the mountains hammering nails into my thumbs and seeing to the sewage for a bunch of razorless radical femmos was just what I needed. By the time I'd dumped my cases in the back of Desley's beaten-up Torana I'd just about forgotten what Venie and Maroochi looked like. If somebody had shown me a nose-plug I wouldn't have been able to identify its function. But then where I was going you didn't need such things; where I was going you hung head first into septic tanks and breathed normally.

'Yippee!' I shouted, as we at last saw the back of Melbourne with its sweltering unswerving streets and its vista-less roads and its forty miles of milk bars and pizzerias. I drummed on the dashboard of Desley's rotting motor with my fists. To be alive and under forty was good, to be out of Vaucluse was better, but to be

311

Desley's passenger on the highway to the Bogong High Plains was very heaven. I went through every Australian traveller's song I could remember. 'Take me back to Cootamundra,' I sang. 'You can keep your Yarrawonga, If you'll let me linger longer, In Wodonga, home town of mine.'

'You're in high spirits,' Desley noticed.

I hit a couple of staggeringly difficult notes. 'In Bundaberg, old Bundaberg, I hear you calling me.'

Desley kept her eyes on the road. She was a careful driver and drove in fear of having her windscreen smashed.

'Do you know any?' I asked.

'Songs?'

'Australian songs.'

'I know a few.'

'Go on then, give us one.'

I was very gentle with her. I suspected that she didn't like singing much but had the odd basso profondo dirge about Botany Bay up her sleeve for just such a contingency as this. 'Yes, that's a lovely old song, isn't it?' I expected it would be required of me to say, once she'd trembled her way through it. In fact I was digging around for precisely some such funereal commendation – getting one ready in advance, as it were – when the car suddenly filled with what people who experience audio-epiphanies call a diapason of sound. Music. Not dead-march music either, but beefy tunes and thrilling melodies and witty syncopations. This wasn't amateur high spirits as mine had been, this was prime-time song-and-dance. You lingered a lot longer in Desley's Wodonga than you ever would have done in mine. When Desley took you to Gundagai you knew with all your senses where you were headed, and never wanted to return. You could see those blue gums growing, you could really hear that Murrumbidgee flowing. You baked under the sunny sky. And then you were off again, on The Road to Jugiong, then Down Wagga

Way, and then Back to Bendigo. She whistled. She did bird imitations. She slowed the car down, driving with one hand while she made flapper circles with the other. She even tap-danced on the pedals.

Then, just as suddenly as it had begun, it was over and she was steering carefully again, watching out for stones on the Hume Highway.

'You do know a few then,' I said.

She kept her eyes on the road in front of her. 'I love all that stuff,' she said. 'It's a great shame we've lost music-hall Australia.'

'Yes,' I said, 'yes, it is. It's a great shame.' And I settled back in my seat and looked out of my own window at the drooping landscape.

I was glad of a bit of quiet now. I wanted to castigate myself in silence for my sociological blue. Of course I should have known that Desley had to be sitting on a pretty snazzy vaudeville routine. She was Australian, wasn't she? All Australians – certainly all Australians of her class and generation – put a high value on snap vitality. This was part Americanization: every girl her own Shirley Temple; and part indigenous sentimentality: nostalgia for the good old Australia of wandering shysters and mountebanks and song-and-dance men. The more serious the Australian, the more thorough-going the nostalgia. Which was another reason why I didn't engage with Desley's remarks about the lost spirit of the music-hall. The last thing I wanted was to discuss outback showbiz, circus folk and strolling illusionists, with a girl who'd been to university.

For half an hour or so I indulged in a spot of nostalgia of my own – for Venie and Maroochi, whose politics didn't run to ratbaggery and incorrigible Australian roguishness. But it didn't last long. My nostalgia, I mean.

We stayed the night at Myrtleford, on Desley's suggestion, so that we would be able to enjoy the drive

through the Ovens Valley and up into the mountains at first light. There was no impropriety in our arrangements. We took separate motel rooms, just as Vance Kelpie and Montserrat Tomlinson had, only no divine spirit descended to unite us as we slept.

Before we separated we ate a steak in one of the pubs. We were both tired and chatted only fitfully. Desley wondered how I'd got mixed up with the Santalucia mob and I concocted a few lies, down-playing the extent of my involvement and skipping lightly over Freedom Academy and the CIA. I explained how I'd been offered what seemed to me merely an opportunity for some foreign travel while I was still at Cambridge. 'I can't say that I entirely knew what was what in those days,' I told her. 'I was a bit of a baby as a student.' I didn't look at her while I said this but I wanted her to understand that I was aware of what a little prat I'd been and that, should she ever be thinking of trying me again, well – she'd find me changed.

I can't say that I detected any sign – not any *overt* sign anyway – that she was looking to a time when she might be thinking of trying me again. But I was satisfied to plant my tiny seed and let it prosper if it would. Already, you see, I was putting my trust in Nature.

She told me a bit about herself over the fruit salad and the ice-cream. Not details. Just a rough graph of her fortunes. The lows and the highs. She resorted throughout to that psycho-meteorological vocabulary favoured by modern women when they come to describe the phenomenon of their own natures. 'I was in a state of total depression – on a real downer – really in the pits – for the whole of that winter. Then I suddenly looked up and saw X and for the next six months I floated with happiness.' It was like listening to the life-history of a cloud. A neuro-nimbus, buffeted by this wind and by that, blown miles off course, then up and away and above it all, and then again black and incalculable, ready to drop the lot on some poor passing innocent without an umbrella.

And when she wasn't a cloud – when she felt that the story of her airy self had become too lowering – she was a clown. 'So there I sat,' she said, 'flat on my arse, feeling like a total dickhead, with the tears rolling down my face' (a sad clown) 'while the man I loved drove into the sunset with my best friend.' She botched all her suicide attempts (a tragic clown), putting her head in electric instead of gas ovens and swallowing three hundred saccharine tablets instead of aspirins. 'In a moment of inspired lunacy,' she said, 'I replied to his letter and married him.' She liked seeing herself as an inspired lunatic. That way she could balance the magnetic pull of the moon with the gravitational commands of the inner woman. And still stay in touch with the circus.

She even wore a brightly parti-coloured clown's suit for our evening out in Myrtleford – baggy pink trousers ending only halfway down her furry calves, a sloppy sweater for falling tragi-comically about in, funny little elfin boots of purple suede, and an orange beret that was somehow militant and mirthful all at once.

I was glad I was not going to find it too easy getting on with Desley. I would have been disturbed had my escape over the wall proved altogether trouble-free. If you're going to betray your old loyalties you want to take a few regrets with you.

So I slept soundly to conserve my strength for the tough times ahead. Refused to go on with a dream in which Venie and Maroochi hired me as a gardener and ordered me to cut down the vine and crush the rose petal. And in the morning was driven up the mountain.

After three hours of rocks attacking our underside, but still a long way from anywhere a sociable man might want to be, Desley turned right in obedience to a home-made finger-post which said, SNEGS – 1 KL.

315

'Are we stopping for sausages?' I asked.

Desley appeared to have made herself more jagged for this leg of the journey. There seemed to be fewer spiky hairs on her head and more about the rest of her person. She looked dangerously unkempt, ferociously practical like some prehistoric farming tool which doubled, in the event of invasion, as an engine of war. 'Snegs is the name of the lodge,' she told me.

I went rapidly through the possible implications of this and could come up with nothing except that Snegs was an anagram of Gents with the *t* out and another *s* in. Out with the *t*hreat, in with the *s*ympathy? Who could say?

After we'd driven about 10 kls from where it had said 1 kl Desley decided to help me out. 'It's short for Snegurochka.'

'Oh, I see,' I said.

'The Snow Maiden.'

'Oh, the Snow Maiden.'

It sounded like the name of an operetta – Jeannette MacDonald waiting for Nelson to heat her through – but I didn't know it.

Desley could see that I still needed help. She was a schoolteacher after all, with a record of unusual conscientiousness. 'She's the daughter of Spring. She's safe from the sun as long as she doesn't fall in love. The warmth of mortal passion is fatal to her.'

'Oh, I see,' I said. 'Snegs, yes.' I had a feeling that I wished it had been an incomplete anagram of Gents after all. 'Is this an Australian allegory?' I asked.

It was my intention to empty this enquiry of all unwelcome modulation, but it's possible Desley saw what I saw: every beach in Australia stacked high with melting maidens.

She went tight and snappy on me, anyway.

'No, Leon, it originates from Russia. But I'd say it's pretty universal.'

I wasn't looking for trouble, at least not *this* kind of trouble, so I said, 'Oh shit, yes,' and was glad to discover that we'd arrived.

Every new building in Australia is, as they say, architect-designed, so I wasn't surprised to see that Snegs had been contrived to follow the contours of the mountain, to blend with the mountain, to look like the mountain, to be as difficult of access as the mountain, and to be as resistant to all human efforts to make it hospitable.

A couple of pythons watched our arrival from an upstairs window. A Bongong mountain devil slashed our front passenger tyre with his tail. A million bush-flies greeted us as if they hadn't sniffed white flesh for months.

'Of course you don't see it to its best advantage in the summer,' Desley said.

I found it hard to believe there could ever be snow here, for all that we'd passed the odd deserted chair-lift straddling blue smoking ravines, on our way up.

'Have you ever actually *been* here when it snows?' I asked.

She pointed to the roof of the lodge, some of which was still covered only in tarpaulin, but whose austere lines told you that even when finished it would never remotely resemble the cute make-believe roof of a Swiss chalet. 'I've seen snow that high,' she said.

Bullshit, I thought. 'Amazing,' I said.

She showed me around as if she were the works foreman, pointing out what needed doing. 'There's a party of us coming up in a fortnight to work on the roof, so we can forget that. How's your plastering?'

'So-so,' I said.

'Can you hang doors?'

'I can hang them,' I said, 'but they don't necessarily open thereafter.'

She took me quickly past the bunkrooms – the girls' dormitories whose secrets no man would ever penetrate – and showed me the shower area. 'Can you tile?'

'Not as well as I can grout, but I can try.'

It was agreed that I would try. Then we went around the back, where the land was uncleared and fell away steeply into a fierce tangle of vipers' nests and spiders' hideaways. You could actually hear the drone of murderous intention from the undergrowth.

'That's where you'll be sleeping,' Desley said, motioning towards a bundle of waterproofs which had been slung, apparently over a washing line, between a pair of peeling gums. 'In that tent.'

'Looks comfy,' I said.

I noticed that the ground in the vicinity of my tent was thick with animal droppings, some of them so vast in diameter that they could only have been left by giant tree-climbing buffalo. The ants grew big out here also, and were already devising a system for carrying off our feet, a toe at a time.

'There's a dunny here, too, if you want it,' Desley said.

I couldn't see anything.

'Just there.' She pointed to a wooden crate, the size of a telephone-box, further down the deadly declivity yet. It was overgrown with bracken and leaning at a perilous angle.

'What do you mean, "If I want it"?' I asked. 'What's my alternative?' I was angling for an invitation to the lodge, after dark, in the event of acute stomach cramps.

But I didn't get it. 'The bush,' Desley said, rounding her mouth around the word the way Australians do when they want to express their reverence for its unfathomable mysteries, the fearlessness of their own functions, and the close relation between the two.

Hearing itself referred to, the bush answered back with low murmurings of malediction.

*   *   *

318

It turned out that I quite liked tiling. The discipline of organizing square objects in straight lines seemed to appeal to something in my personality. I would probably have enjoyed the job even more had the tiles themselves been prettier, but this was the winter abode of the Snow Maiden and I knew not to be wanting warmth.

'Well, what do you think?' I asked Desley when she came to see how I was getting on. She'd been painting a bunkroom herself – the Holy of Holies – and had tied another knot in her sarong, this time above her knees, for freedom of movement. Her legs were heavy and brown and bruised, and of course unshaven. This is who we are and this is what we believe, they seemed to say. I was pleased to note how badly they would have done in the thumb or pencil test, and how little they would have cared. But if I'd thought through the politics I would have realized that the person who owned those legs couldn't possibly admire my tiling.

'A bit straight, aren't they?' she said.

'Tiles are meant to be straight.'

She scratched her head, putting paint in her hair. She wasn't annoyed with me, she just wasn't impressed. 'Yeah, they'll do,' she said. 'Wasn't what I had in mind, but they'll do.'

I was quite upset. Venie and Maroochi would have massaged my neck and shoulders and bathed my eyelids in rare unguents if I'd tiled their bathroom as well as this. 'So what exactly was it that you had in mind?' I defied her to tell me.

Desley pulled one of her vital-weary arch-exasperated Australian faces – the kind that are meant to win over an imaginary third party, the sort that famous Australians employ to amuse audiences when someone else is speaking. 'I don't know,' she sighed, 'something – oh, I don't know – more Italian or something.'

319

'You wanted mosaics? You wanted me to build you a Tuscan terrazzo?'

I didn't know whether there was such a thing as a Tuscan terrazzo, and it's possible that in some corner of myself I was hoping that Desley the schoolteacher, Desley the Europeanized Australian with an MA in Fine Arts, might fall to giving me an education. I was obsessed, as I've already explained, with what I'd heard of her teaching methods.

In the event I didn't get a lesson but something almost as good. I got a sudden show of mateship.

She looked pleased that she'd hurt my feelings. That seemed to equalize us in some way. She squeezed my shoulder. Comrade to comrade. 'Don't get uptight,' she said. She fetched me a beer. We leaned against the walls of rigidly correct tiles and swigged in unison. 'No negativity, heh?' she said. She drew me closer, aura-wise. She told me how she hated being criticized herself. How it fazed her. How it sent her into herself. She talked about crack-ups and mental collapses as if these were commonplace eventualities which bonded us. We drank from the same muddied waters. We were poisoned at the same well. And we obeyed the same imperatives issued by our emotions. We might have been two of the Grand Old Duke of York's ten thousand men; when we were up we were up, and when we were down we were down. In step.

Communality – wasn't that what I'd crossed over to find? Well, for one hour at the end of an afternoon's tiling, in a half-built women's ski-lodge on a remote peak of the Bogong High Plains, I found it. I breathed it in as if it were one of those cigarettes – were they called joints? – I had campaigned so hard against in my *Black Sail* column. I let its warm acrid smoke curl about my nostrils and burn my eyes. *Our* eyes. If there'd been a demo going on somewhere in the mountains I'd have joined it, regardless of the cause. The demo *was* the cause. I wanted to link arms and wave banners. I wanted to kick a cop. I swear, if there'd been anyone around qualified to do the job I'd have had my ear pierced.

I clinked my beer-can against Desley's. 'Good to see you again,' I said to her. And I could feel geniality lines I never knew I possessed breaking out all over my face.

Then there was the sound of a car arriving, followed by the deep voices of women in dungarees.

'Quick!' Desley said. 'To your tent. You know you're not allowed in here after six-thirty. Go!'

28

I KNEW THAT only extreme fatigue would induce me to crawl under those waterproofs and wait to be eaten, so I went for a long walk, sticking to the dirt-track and heading towards a small cluster of lights which I took to be the ski-village proper. No holiday resort is inviting in the wrong season, but not even a frosted beach and a rotting sea are so desolate as snow chalets abandoned to the scrub and the red gravel. Moonlight itself lent no charm to the place and I still wasn't convinced that any snow had ever fallen here.

I found a pub open that doubled as a grocery store and an equipment-hiring centre. You could buy a beer, play pool, do your late-night shopping and rent a toboggan here if you wanted. I settled for the beer.

'Not much snow tonight,' I said to the barman.

He was wearing one of those ascetic beards difficult Australians sometimes take refuge in, a fringe around his face, leaving a half-moon of chin and the whole of his upper lip bare. He couldn't decide whether I was a dill or a smartarse and just shook his head slowly at the only other two people in the bar.

They were an elderly couple, just up in the mountains for a few days I gathered, in order to enjoy some peace and quiet and to find inspiration. I twitched involuntarily at the word and took a longer look at the woman who used it. I thought she was vaguely familiar. The bony little body disappearing into boots that were the wrong size and the wrong fashion didn't mean anything to me, but the weatherbeaten face and the boy's haircut and the air of fragile complacency did. 'Aren't you Eula Wake?' I asked.

She was pleased to be recognized so far from her usual habitat, even by someone who wondered why there was no snow at the height of summer. She gave me an emaciated hand to shake and enquired whether I was one of her readers.

'Indeed I am,' I lied.

The truth was that Eula Wake wrote poems which *The Black Sail* was honour-bound to publish since they celebrated the domestic ups and downs – the sorrows and the joys, as they say – of ordinary Australians. The three adjectives her admirers used about her were 'textured', 'grainy', and 'rooted'. But what really made her popular was that she hadn't started writing until her sixty-ninth birthday, and was thus an inspiration and an encouragement to every grandparent in the country. 'Reproduce first, write later,' she told rapturous gatherings of still-unfulfilled septuagenarians who could therefore believe that they were at least halfway there.

The only old person who wasn't inspired and encouraged by the example of Eula Wake was Mr Wake. I watched his eyes glaze over when I recognised his wife. The miracle of the woman he had lived with for nearly fifty years suddenly turning out to be a poet – a grainy rooted poet at that – was clearly putting a strain on his retirement. It had to be hard, standing idly by while she found rhymes for everything they'd ever done together. Apparently he wasn't enjoying the travelling either, which Eula's popularity occasioned – nay, which her curiosity demanded.

'If it's snow yer want,' he said to me – it seemed important to him that I shouldn't think *he* was a poet – 'you oughta go to Russia. That'd freeze 'em off for yer.'

I thought I saw his wife drop into a little musing trance, looking for something that rhymed with 'off for yer'.

It turned out that they'd just come back from Russia on an all-expenses-paid fact-finding goodwill-spreading tour sponsored by Freedom Academy and the Domestic Literature Board of Australia.

'How was it?' I asked. The question wasn't merely polite. I had reason to be curious. Who could say? Once I'd joined the party I might want to go with Desley to inspect the icons at the Hermitage.

Mr Wake snorted. Russia was ratshit, I was meant to understand. The Russians were mongrels. I'd have a better time in Woop Woop.

Eula took a more considered view. She had a tiny nut-brown monkey face which she screwed up to suggest humane concern. 'Well, it was a salutary experience,' she said. 'Naturally it's hard to know what life is truly like there. Because of the restrictions and the surveillance ordinary Russians are frightened to talk to you. And of course the artists have to toe the party line or that's it – they don't get published.' She managed to make not being published sound very terrible. I had a vision of the terminally unpublished standing in their thousands in Red Square, their heads bowed, their pride in themselves as human beings as tattered as their coats. 'But what upset me most,' she went on, 'was the children. You actually see them in public places, in the big parades and so on, actually repeating what they've been taught. They stand for hours and recite and recite. Chanting like parrots.' She shrugged and turned the palms of her hands upwards, as if there were much she would like to do but little that she could. She looked up at me, meaning that I should see the milk whites of compassion in her eyes, but showing me only the nut-brown polished complacency, the righteous sheen, of the Australian home-maker. 'It's a tragedy,' she concluded, 'for children to be so impressionable.'

'Sounds like children everywhere to me,' I said. 'I've never met one yet that doesn't want to be a parrot.'

She shook her head at me. 'I won't have that,' she said. 'It's not the same everywhere. I know children. I've had several of my own. The ones I saw in the big parades in Russia were impressed. Impressed and impressionable. They were slaves to the system.'

If communist countries didn't exist, I thought, Australians would have to invent them. But I didn't say that to Eula Wake. I couldn't be bothered arguing with her. She was an old woman. And God had already punished her by putting two ugly brackets round her mouth, the deep-gouged parentheses with which He mocks and disfigures the faces of lovers of ordinary domestic life the world over.

Such marks were waiting for me, who had taken a degree in Ordinary Domestic Life, unless I could do penance.

'We're all slaves to something,' I said, remembering Desley, and I got out before either of the Wakes could reply to me.

I walked back the way I'd come at a furious pace. I needed to exercise off my exasperation. No good comes of talking to old people, especially in Australia where they strike themselves as characters. Their opinions invariably lack truth and wisdom. And when you have finished listening you are denied all the usual methods of obtaining relief: you can't really shout at them and you oughtn't really to knock them down.

By the time I found the dim lights of Snegs I was just about running. I would never have imagined that I could be so pleased to return to a house that I was barred from entering. I sat on a boulder and cooled off. Then I began to prowl around the exterior of the building, even crawling underneath it at one point, in my search for the most advantageous position for listening in to the lush harmonies of Women's – unfettered Women's – talk. It didn't matter that I was not allowed to participate. I was satisfied just to be in the vicinity of Bohemia. Citizenship could come later.

325

I heard nothing for a while. Just a few faint footsteps and some deliberately relaxed breathing. Meditation exercises, I guessed. Psyche stretches. I did one or two myself while I was waiting. Then came what sounded like the breaking of wind, followed by laughter, followed by the breaking of more wind, followed by more laughter. Farting freely is natural, I reminded myself. Bush farting is partly what it's all about. But after about fifteen minutes of it I began to get bored. It was still better than talking to Eula Wake but it wasn't what I'd run all the way back for.

I took a short walk down the mountain to see if my tent was still there, then I returned. This time I could hear talk. It seemed that one of the afternoon's interlopers was pregnant and wished to discuss the details of her condition with Desley. She was particularly concerned to win votes for her scheme for the ritual burying of the placenta in the front drive of the lodge.

'I don't envisage any difficulties,' I heard Desley say, 'though we will have to secret-ballot everybody.'

'Yuh, sure,' the woman said. She sounded content but in the mystic centre of herself unmollified. Even from underneath the house I could hear the battle raging within her between her belief in the democratic processes and her blind allegiance to the Dark Goddesses.

Conversation twisted this way and that, like the snakes on which I was almost certainly sitting, until it became unmistakable that there was some important ideological difference brewing between she who had a placenta to bury and Desley who purposefully didn't. I could tell that Desley would soon be charged with lacking reverence for the womb mysteries, and I feared that Desley would strike back by arguing that it was no act of reverence to bring a new life into a world gone mad. That was a phrase – a world gone mad, not a new life – it had long been a cornerstone of my philosophy to find objectionable. It seemed to me that nothing was easier of demonstration than that the world always had been mad, had been conceived in a moment and as an act of madness, had gone on being mad through all time, and was now, if anything, slightly less mad than before if only for the reason that madness required energy and we didn't have any left. The thought that throwing in my lot with Desley might mean throwing away my objections to this sort of language was a difficult one for me to face. I wasn't sure that I was ready to go that far. Venie and Maroochi were not easy to part with and I'd only known them for a decade; my objections I'd lived with since infancy. Please God, I wished, please God don't let her say it otherwise I will have no option but to retire to my tent.

'What freaks me out,' I heard Desley say, 'is how someone as rational as you—'

'I don't believe in rationality,' the placenta-planter interjected. 'It's the rational mind that screws us.'

'All right, I don't understand how someone as un-screwed and irrational as you can contemplate bringing a new life into a world gone mad.'

I had no option but to retire to my tent.

'Sleep well?'

'I did not,' I said. 'Every other living creature in my tent slept well, but I did not.'

'The bush is the most marvellous place to sleep in,' said Desley, 'provided you trust it.'

'What if it doesn't trust me?'

'The bush possesses no power of active suspicious-ness,' Desley explained. 'The Aborigines know that. It can only return your own attitudes to you.'

'In that case the bush had a pretty scary night.'

'You're out of harmony, Leon. You should spend a few months up here. Sort out the tangle of your emotions.'

I wanted to say, 'I don't have any tangle of emotions to sort out, thanks very much'. But the power of all accusations relating to the state of one's pneuma is such that every denial is a further confirmation. So I just went on with my breakfast which, as an unpaid workman, I was allowed to take in the lodge.

The two women who had driven up the previous afternoon had driven back first thing that morning. As far as I understood I had a whole day of Desley to myself. I wasn't counting on it – to avoid disappointment – but there seemed a chance that I might not be kicked out at six-thirty. Throughout the morning I toyed with such fantasies as being allowed to stay until seven, or even (why not?) seven forty-five.

'I'll grout today,' I said as I washed up my breakfast things, Desley's breakfast things, and anything else that looked as though it needed washing that I could find. I hadn't been expected to stand over the sink when I lived with Venie and Maroochi; they considered it demeaning in a man to do a skivvy's job. But such attitudes were behind me now. 'And then I'll attend to that blockage in the septic tank,' I said.

At six o'clock we knocked off work and shared a beer. At six-fifteen Desley told me that she planned to drive back to Melbourne the next day but that I was welcome to stay in the tent if I wanted, to do some disentangling. At six-thirty she looked at her watch and reminded me of lodge rules.

'But there's no one else here,' I expostulated.

I'm not being wordy – that's really what I did. I expostulated. I complained and pleaded and debated in an aggrieved manner.

'It's not a question of who's here,' she said. 'It's the principle of the thing.'

'What do you think I'm going to do? Desecrate one of your shrines? Rip up the placenta-bush?'

She looked alarmed, and a bit disgusted. 'Were you eavesdropping last night?'

'I happened to be passing at the time,' I said. 'Sound carries up here.'

I wondered about referring to the farting, but decided against it. On such decisions a man's happiness can hang.

'Well I ask you to honour our agreement, Leon,' she said. 'I spelled out the terms before we drove up.'

She had. I couldn't deny that. And I was a believer in adhering to the spirit of agreements. That was one of the reasons I had agreed with the Australians agreeing with the Americans agreeing with the South Vietnamese to bomb the shit out of Hanoi. 'I'll go to my tent,' I said. 'But do you think I might make use of the inside toilet before I go? In return for the work I've done on the tank?'

Desley looked at her watch. It was a man's watch of course. Or at least mann*ish*. I suddenly found myself wondering whether she'd kept it on when her sarong went swish in front of her Relationship Enhancement class. For some reason – perhaps because his watch had been similar – I also suddenly found myself thinking of Dinmont Manifest. 'You've got five minutes,' Desley said.

But I took ten. An agreement was an agreement, but I still didn't intend to be pushed around.

I didn't need a long walk to exhaust myself this evening. I wasn't exaggerating when I said I hadn't slept the night before. Desley's remarks about my inharmoniousness – implying that I sought city niceties in the bush – were unfair. My discomfort had hardly been of the order of the princess and the pea, after all. I didn't see that it made me a mincing royal just because I had an aversion to sleeping on writhing ground. Anyway, I was so tired tonight I knew I would drop off regardless, the minute my head touched the python.

It was the rain that woke me. Solitary, unrhythmical spatterings at first, as if something big and spiteful were spitting on my tent from a tree. But then a deluge, soaking me not just from above but from the sides and from underneath. Within minutes I was actually afloat, bobbing about in a couple of feet of water along with the rubber torch Desley had loaned me, my bush hat, my travelling alarm-clock and the goanna that had been curled up by my feet. I half-crawled, half-swam from the tent. I was no sooner out of it than it took off, like the *Kon-Tiki*, down the hillside. I watched it crash through the undergrowth, somehow managing to keep its shape, a ghost-tent, an ark freighted with one of every wild thing to be found in Australia. Except, of course, Desley.

I slithered my way to the lodge as best I could without my torch, following the tremendous noise the rain made on the tarpaulin. It did occur to me that if Desley had put herself to bed early and the rain had got in through the unfinished sections of roof, she could be in some trouble. It would be ironical, I thought, if the underwater skills Venie and Maroochi had taught me should be put to use rescuing Desley. Ironical and also auspicious, for then I would be able to discern purpose, progression even, in my transfers of loyalty. I wouldn't be like the Cooney brothers, lurching from one tergiversation to another.

I can't believe I was the first person to grasp at coherence in a cataclysm.

'Desley,' I shouted, as I approached the lodge, 'Desley, are you all right?'

There was no answer. I could hear the tarpaulin flapping but I couldn't see anything. I kicked my foot on a boulder. Fortunately I'd kept my boots on when I went to sleep in the tent. I felt my way around the building, still calling her name. There was water rushing everywhere, warm water carrying debris and thrashing insects.

At last I saw a light coming from one of the lower bunk-rooms. I pressed my nose to the streaming window and saw Desley sitting on her bunk reading a book. I rapped on the pane and called out, 'Are you all right?'

She looked up, seemed a touch surprised to see an amphibious creature peering in at her, nodded her head, mouthed something that looked like, 'Fine', and went back to her book.

I rapped again. 'Well I'm not,' I shouted.

She let me in, reluctantly.

I shook a gallon or two of water out of my hair, coughed up a flood into the empty Scandinavian fire-grate, and said, 'I know about the rules but I've lost my tent,' before she could remind me of our agreement.

I was allowed a shower, given a glass of wine, and after a bout of spectacular though wholly unnecessary shivering I was even permitted to wrap myself in a Snegs army-issue blanket and join her in the bunk-room, albeit on a bunk at the furthest remove from her own.

'Sorry to interrupt your reading,' I said, at what seemed like an opportune moment.

She was very good about it. 'That's all right,' she said, 'it was depressing me anyway.'

I took a look at the book. It was called *Corruption in Australia* and was very thick.

'And that's only the first volume,' she said.

I sighed in what I thought might be an appropriate manner. 'I guess there's a lot of it about,' I said.

'You *guess*?'

I shivered a couple of times and wrapped the army blanket around myself. 'I know the country's riddled with it,' I said. 'I know it's everywhere you look, but the fact of its being on the surface is its own kind of charm.'

'I don't find it charming.'

'I don't either,' I said, 'I just mean that its undisguised omnipresence is a sign of the country's naïvety. Experienced civilizations know how to obliterate the look of corruption. England is infinitely more wicked than

331

Australia but you have to mine deeper for the evidence. There are catacombs down there that have been under construction for centuries. Whereas here it's just alluvial chicanery. You can stop anywhere and scoop it up with your bare hands.'

'That's just *Black Sail* bullshit,' she said.

'It's not,' I said. 'We don't admit to chicanery in *The Black Sail*. We call it enterprise.'

'Chicanery lets it off just as much. It makes it cute.'

'Instead of?'

'Leon, there are people in this country who'd cut your toes off as soon as look at you if you stood in their way.'

'There are thugs everywhere.'

'I'm talking about elected Members of Parliament.'

I gave another little shiver. More from pleasure than from chill. This was the kind of conversation I'd come over the wall to have. Very soon I'd be ditching everything I'd ever held dear. Everyone, as well.

'Yes, well,' I said, 'I admit the two can sometimes be confused out here. But that's part of what I like: the really nice thing about Australians is their lack of interest in finding their politicians honourable. They actually prefer them dodgy. The rougher they are – the more they pissant around where they shouldn't – always provided they remember to blubber where they should – the more they're trusted. In a country that idealizes the ratbag and the larrikin, the scoundrel will always be a hero. Take Murray Redfern.'

Yes, I was off. Shedding allegiances as blithely as an Old Etonian. Only more subtly. Melbourne schoolie or not, Desley was too smart to be impressed by mere prompt capitulation. I had reason to recall her treatment of men who feebly gave in to her. So I fought and frothed and punched the bed and attitudinized in the hallowed tradition of male mastery, even as I went ever so subtly over to her side.

Only when it was very late did I subside into keen

silence and listen with a dry mouth to all she knew about deals and rackets, about the sharp practices of the dull and the low cunning of the mighty. 'So after he resigned as Director of Pine Gap he moved to ———?' I said. 'And became a close friend of ———?' I sighed. I shook my head, 'I see,' I said. 'Really? Yes. Mm. Gosh.'

And by then, with the rain still falling, and a third bottle of Shiraz polished off, there seemed no good reason in the world for me not to step out of my army blanket, not to untie Desley in one swish from her sarong – there the vine and there the fig and there the rose petal – and not to announce in a voice that had all the joy and competence and animality it lacked twenty years before, 'Lodge rules or no Lodge rules, I have come back to fuck you, Desley.'

I feasted my eyes on her un-Venie and un-Maroochi-like profusion. So here I was at last, before the tangled thicket of Bohemia. I lowered myself upon her and felt a faint but sure resistance.

'With,' I thought I heard her say.

I cocked the whole of my face at an interrogative angle. 'I beg your pardon?'

'With,' I was sure she said again.

'With what?'

'Fuck *with*, is how you should say it.'

'I wasn't planning on fucking you *with* anybody,' I explained. 'I was planning on fucking you on my own.'

'You don't fuck me, you fuck with me.'

'Oh,' I said. 'I see,' I said. I didn't actually, but I wasn't looking for an argument. I wasn't geared up, as they say, for aggravation.

I applied a little more pressure and felt an answering resistance.

'Say it,' Desley said.

'Say what?'

'Say you want to fuck with me.'

'I don't think I can,' I said.

333

'Why not?'

'I think I have an in-built cultural incapacity to.'

'Say, "fuck".'

'Fuck.'

'Say, "with".'

'With.'

'Say, "fuck with".'

'Fuck wi—' I couldn't. 'This is asking a lot,' I said. 'We're dealing here with language trapped deep in my psychology.'

'Precisely,' Desley said.

'But that means that I can't go around inserting prepositions into myself at will.'

'But I should go around being the feminine object of a masculine verb?'

I was much more democratic in the area of sexual grammar than she realised. 'Of course not,' I said. 'Once I've fucked you, you can fuck me.'

She shook her head. It would be truer to say she shook the whole of her body. It was as if a light wind had passed over a field of corn.

'You'll have to try,' she said. 'Come on, say you want to fuck with me.'

I didn't want to try. I knew that much more of this and language would be the least of our problems. But I gave it one final go. 'I want to fuck wi—'

'Go on.'

'To fuck wi – wi—'

'Go on, Leon.'

'Wi – wi – wi—'

It was no good. So far I could go – selling out on my loyalties was no problem. But embracing new ones? It seemed not.

I fell back on my original bunk.

'No fuck with?' Desley asked.

'I'm afraid not,' I said.

'Then fuck off,' she said.

* * *

I didn't know whether she really expected me to go out in the rain, tentless, but I stayed where I was. I clasped the wooden rails behind my head and fell into an immediate sleep, exhausted by the supreme effort of having failed to learn a new language in one lesson. I believe I snored. I'm sure I was covered in sweat. It's possible I was otherwise objectionable. Whether this reminded her of a previous encounter, or whether I merely reminded myself, I cannot say. All I can be certain of is that I thought I awoke, that I thought I caught her about to straddle my chest, and that I thought I threw her off with a cry.

'Oh no you don't,' I know I shouted, because I remember thinking how like a character from a D. H. Lawrence novel that made me sound. I have a feeling that I even slipped into a Nottinghamshire accent. 'Ha, not likely,' I cried, gathering my blanket around me and running out into the rain. 'Oh, no, not this time. I don't let you. Not likely. I know you. I know what you want. Well you shan't have it. Not from me.'

I had no plan of action when I ran out of the lodge. Given that I set off down the ravine it's not beyond the bounds of possibility that I meant to find my tent. On the other hand I might just have been running for my life, desperate to escape that last indignity which I knew Desley to be perfectly capable of inflicting. I can't be any more definite as to why I was howling, throwing my head back as I charged through the spouting vegetation and allowing the water to run down my face into my mouth; but there's a good chance I was calling out women's names – Venie's and Maroochi's, Trilby's, my mother's, Hester's and Nesta's. My sequence of betrayal and forgetfulness. My political slogans.

If I was looking for my tent I didn't find it. What I found instead was the redundant wooden dunny, the outdoor lavatory situated halfway down the ravine as a courtesy to whoever failed of a properly trusting attitude to the bush. The force of the rain had exaggerated still further its perilous angle to the mountainside, and my sudden fierce collision with it – I had lost my footing and come down the hard way, ricocheting from one alpine blue-gum to another – very nearly toppled it altogether. But country shithouses have their own resilience, even when their functions are cosmetic and they have no actual plumbing to hold them up. It shuddered under my weight, bent its back, and flung its little door open in what I took to be a gesture of hospitality. I didn't have to be asked twice. I made myself small and squeezed gratefully inside.

Where of course the Redback was waiting to welcome me.

29

THE CITY OF TARANTO (pop. approx. 250,000) lies a little up from the sole, a little in from the heel, and a little down from the ankle of Italy, in the Region of Apulia. A swing-bridge divides the old town from the new town and the two together divide the Mare Grande from the Mare Piccolo. Here you can sell your agricultural produce, refine oil, dredge oysters, turn your nose up at the largely remodelled Romanesque cathedral, or parade your fur coat under the palm-trees of the Lungomare. Three or four hundred years earlier, when according to Desley the world was saner, you might also have come to Taranto to cut in on the local dance – a frenzied, unflagging, morbid-hysterical Bacchanal known as the Tarantella, in deference not just to the town which hosted it but also to the noxious neighbourhood spider – the Tarantula – whose bite was reputed to be its cause.

Most of Europe was behaving strangely at this time, and an outbreak of lewd hyper-activity in a hot climate, even when it lasted for over a century, was not in itself an occasion for remark. However, if the politicians didn't care and the sociologists weren't surprised, there must have been something for medicine to ponder in the wild antics of the Tarantists because several contemporary chirurgeons and physikes of note made the journey to Taranto to observe the phenomenon with their own eyes. Amongst these was a Dr Mead, much interested in the sneaky doings of arachnids and the effect of their poisons on the fragile constitutions of man.

In the summer months, he observes, *especially when the heats are greatest, as in the dog-days, the Tarantula creeping among the corn in the fields, bites the mowers . . .*

. . . altho' the pain of its bite is at first no greater than what is caused by the sting of a bee, yet the part quickly after is discoloured with a livid, black, or yellowish circle, and raised to an inflam'd swelling; the patient within a few hours is seized with a violent sickness, difficulty of breathing, universal faintness, and sometimes trembling with a weakness of the head; being asked what the ail is, makes no reply, or with a querulous voice, and melancholy look, points to his breast, as if the heart was most affected.

During this mournful scene, all the usual alexipharmic and cordial medicines are of no service; for, notwithstanding their repeated use, the patient growing by degrees more melancholy, stupid, and strangely timorous, in a short time expires; unless musick be called to his assistance, which alone, without the help of medicine, performs the cure.

For, at the first sound of the musical instrument, altho' the sick lie, as it were, in an apoplectick fit, they begin by degrees to move their hands and feet, till at last they get up, and fall to dancing with wonderful vigour, at first for three or four hours; then they are put to bed, refreshed from their sweating, for a short time, and repeat the exercise with the more vehemence, perceiving no weariness or weakness from it, but professing they grow stronger and nimbler the more they dance.

Being an Englishman, Dr Mead alludes only passingly to that aspect of the Tarantella on which other observers tend to dwell, namely its extreme indecency. It falls to the Spanish and Portuguese doctors to record how normally modest young women abandon all their inhibitions the moment they become Tarantati, lose all shame, scream, pant, uncover their genitals, roll like beasts in the mud, and take a fancy to playing on swings. Dr Mead is more concerned to note their passion for vine-leaves, naked swords and red cloths, and to ascribe much of the excitement of the dance to the already fiery Latin temperaments of the dancers.

All observers agree though, that the building up of a sweat is an important feature of the dance and a partial explanation of its success as a cure; that the dancers are in the grip of some queer fidelity to the sort of Tarantula they believe has bitten them – thus those who have been nipped by the Tree Tarantula like to hang upside down while they sway to the music; and that the symptoms can recur on every anniversary of the bite, often with an accompanying sensation of even greater melancholia if the original music cure was not effected in good time.

The symptoms themselves, incidentally, are by no means confined to the violent sickness, difficulty of breathing, universal faintness and trembling weakness of the head noticed by Dr Mead, but can include: acute urinary retention, pulse acceleration, depression, speech defects even to aphony, delirium, severe pains of the leg and back, constipation, bluish discoloration of the skin, oedema, paralysis, incessant tinging of the flesh akin to pins and needles, a flushed and swollen face, heavy furring of the tongue, fouling of the breath, board-like stiffening of the abdomen, papular erup-tions, thirst, dizziness, irascibility, buffoonery hysteria, loss of hair and nails, hebetude and torpor, cyanosis, convulsions (general or of a single member), syncope, morbidity, more depression, extended priapism (that's to say persisting and unrelievable erection of the penis) and of course – because what other options are open to you when you have lost the power of speech, are covered in purple pimples, are foul of breath, but have a painfully erect penis? – shameless exhibitionism.

I didn't myself experience *all* these symptoms, or at least I didn't experience them all at the same time. But then I wasn't bitten by a Tarantula. That was no fat furry frightening Lycosa hiding under the rim of the wooden privy-seat, wondering what had kept me. No, my assailant was an altogether more petite and pretty sac of venom, with eight eyes, a glossy back and a little distinguishing splash of crimson – a sister-in-law to the Black Widow, of the phylum Anthropoda, of the class Arachnida, of the order Araneida, of the superfamily Argiopoidea, of the family Theridiidae, of the genus Lactrodectus, of the species Mactans. A sleek Aussie *Latrodectus mactans* in short – a murderous biting robber-baroness. A lover of dusty corners and rubbish heaps and collapsing shithouses. Not a great bounder through the corn, not a swift irascible pursuer of men on horseback, like the Tarantula.

But come a little closer and I will tell you something about the Tarantula. It's a teddy-bear. It couldn't poison a flea. As a murderer it's piss-poor. Forget about its capacity to scare you rigid with a look; in an out-and-out venom competition with the Redback it would lose, fang for fang, palps down. What actually bit the Tarantans – what turned them into sweating Tarantati – was not the Tarantula at all, but the Redback's Italian relation, waiting in the usual place to plant her toothsome kiss. Hence the priapism. Given where the Black Widow likes to sit and bide her time, it can be no surprise that the priapus itself comes in, as it were, for the lion's share of her attention. Unaware that he's been singled out for arachno-osculation, the hardy Apulian mower pulls the chain, heaves up his breeches, and only hours later, when the fit is upon him, will he remember the towering Tarantula that chased him through the field that morning and thus apportion blame, by logical misassociation, where no blame belongs.

So pity the poor Tarantula? I don't see why. You might as soon pity poor Hartley Quibell for not in fact being the recipient of a healthy handout from the CIA. In neither case is the failure to deliver a mortal blow to their enemies a consequence of informed moral choice. They both would if they could. And I am the first to agree anyway that as far as getting on with the dance is concerned it scarcely matters whose venom is in one's veins. My mother recoiled from the crane-flies and believed me to be irremediably damaged by their proximity even though not a single one of them so much as tried to puncture her skin. The simple fact of their existence, the stark reminder that she who was about to give life shared the miracle of it with them, was sufficient to cast her into a despondency from which she never wholly escaped. Similarly, the mere sight of a Tarantula snapping at your heels is justification enough – whether or not the Black Widow has already taken her slice – for a profound metaphysical dismay, a sensation of utter Godlessness, which only a frenzied dance to the death in the company of the comparably afflicted can have any hope of relieving.

The Tarantella itself has not been officially adopted by Australians as a cure for the thirst and the torpor, the papular eruptions and the sentimental morbidity to which they are subject; but what's in a name? The remedy's the same; they just call it a party.

As usual I found myself where the party wasn't.

That's not a complaint. No one had forced me into this malodorous wooden function-box angled precipitously on a streaming mountainside. There was no conspiracy to keep me from the fun. There never had been. My father hadn't meant for him and Trilby *not* to watch me blow out my nine candles; I hadn't been *made* to dine alone in Malapert; I could have been *against* the Americans bombing the bejesus out of Hanoi. And I might have tried harder to say Fuck *with* to Desley. I know, and knew, all this. Nonetheless, I wouldn't have minded finding some early-morning Apulian hoe-down, some wild Bogong High Plain rort to join in on when light at last crept under the dunny door and showed me how and where I'd been spider-violated. At the moment of the bite itself I had felt little other than a mild stinging sensation in the rough geography of

341

what Maroochi used to call 'the old manhood'. It had been no more than a tingling pin-prick such as might be caused by an irritated bull-ant or a splinter. Just to be on the safe side I had shaken out the army blanket as best I could in the confined space and had rearranged it about myself in the manner of a sumo wrestler's drawers – or, if that conjures up too aggressive an image, a Hindu mystic's dhoti. It was only an hour or so later that the shivering began, followed by a cramping pain which travelled up and down my thighs. My temperature rose. My lips went stiff and even contracted, causing my mouth to pucker up and set in an uncomfortable and I was sure unattractive oval shape, like a dead carp's. I don't know how long I sat in this condition, rigid and yet shuddering, biting the air as if I were a fish, and with no more than a fish's comprehension of time or history. But I was still there when the dawn came, bringing the light by which I could inspect the damage. I found a couple of tiny red marks at the root of my member and noted the unfamiliar mottled appearance of that part which the physicians into whose hands I was soon to fall would refer to as the glans. But these were as minor details compared to the gross enlargement – I would say to twice the normal size – of the whole caboodle. It must be that all swellings of the body, or at least all sightings of such swellings, are accompanied by sadness. My mother was big with me when spiritual anguish claimed her, divesting her of expectation when she was most expectant. And I was big with myself when rhyme and reason deserted me. I stared in horror at my discoloured and distended flesh, and had any passer-by hearing my groans knocked at the dunny door and asked if there was anything I needed, I would have answered, with a querulous voice and a melancholy look, pointing to my breast as if my heart were most affected, 'Yes, a party.'

Fat chance, though, of any pipes or timbrels on

the Bogong High Plains at first light. Considering the feverishness of my condition, and the difficulty I experienced moving, I took some remarkably rational steps towards the furtherance of alternative needs. The first of these was to get out of the box and to push it, with all its poisonous black occupants, down the ravine. Second best to a party is an act of violent revenge. And I did my own little dance, not quite a Tarantella but serving an identical purpose, as the vile receptacle broke up and vanished into the undergrowth. If it's of any interest, I unthinkingly gave the same sex to the box as I did to whatever had bitten me. That should be the end of her, I thought to myself. And her. Then I crawled up the slope – funny that I could dance but not walk – past where my tent had been, to Desley's car. I was particularly anxious not to rouse Desley, but I knew that if her car was locked I would have to smash my way into it with a brick and brave the consequences. I had no intention of driving it away – Tarantati automatically lose the power to steer – but I did want to recover my cases from the boot. The old voice of Partington respectability, still alive within me, whispered that whatever I was going to do next I should do it in something other than an army blanket. Even had I got to dance the Tarantella in abandoned company I would have kept a careful eye on what I wore.

Fortunately the car was open. I dragged my cases out as quietly as I could. Suitcases are probably the last things a man suffering the desolation of a bite from an odious species should ever go near. There were objects in those cases I hadn't seen for over twenty years. Travelling pyjamas bought for me by Hester and Nesta. A set of silver shoe-brushes which my mother had imagined might make me feel less out of place at Cambridge. And then there was a pair of blue and black Italian dress moccasins from Trilby. A stylized Rugby shirt in Australian colours from Venie. Swimming trunks cut as high as hers and bearing the logo

343

HOMME, from Maroochi. Everything I touched distressed me and only confirmed what the spider had whispered of the vanity of human affections.

I hid behind the blind side of the car, on the off-chance that Desley was awake and watching, and chose myself an outfit made up entirely of garments bearing sentimental associations. I gathered a few further necessaries and tied them inside a towel that used to be my father's. The rest I left where they fell, for the bull-ants to fight over or for Desley to build some other sucker a tent with. Then I set off down the dirt-track to the highway, that's to say to the slightly wider dirt-track, as fast as my cardboard-stiff limbs would allow me.

Travelling back to Melbourne early, in order to put in a guest appearance at the Australian Domestic Literature Board's Annual Dinner and Fellowship Divvy-Up, Eula and the word-weary Mr Wake would have been surprised to round a bend that marked the beginning of the long descent from the mountain and to find a figure wearing a paisley pyjama-jacket over mustard-yellow bathers and two-tone lounge-shoes tottering blindly in the middle of the road. Surprised but not astounded. Nothing took Les Wake's breath away any more, and Eula was used to life throwing its little tragedies her way now that she had become a published artist. They stopped the car and helped the totterer inside.

'Gone troppo, if you ask me,' Les Wake said.

His wife didn't think so. 'It's emotional,' she said. 'This is the man we met the other night who was unable to grasp the suffering of ordinary Russians living under a repressive regime. I thought he looked emotional then.'

'Pom, isn't he? All Poms are emotional. But I reckon this one's gone troppo on top.'

I sat sweating on the back seat. I tried to get my rigid oval mouth to say, 'Spider. Bitten. Poison.' But no

344

sound would come out. There was a good chance they wouldn't have believed anything I said anyway. There's no moving an Australian over forty, once his mind's made up. I wasn't too worried. The Wakes' diagnosis wasn't all that wide of the mark. And you can be overpedantic about what's wrong with you.

Did I mention, when running through the symptoms of Redback neuro-toxicosis, lassitude, heartburn, amnesia, irreligion, inconsequential jocularity, dull pain in the soft palate, swelling of the kidneys, the passing of sediment in the urine, and the spasmodic and wholly involuntary ejaculation of spermatozoa, dyed a shocking paraffin pink by the admixture of a little blood?

Each of these, together with those other pangs and irritants observed by sixteenth-century medicine, had its way with me during my extended stay in the brand-new bites and stings ward of a Wangaratta hospital, not that many miles from where I had once rolled across the New South Wales/Victoria border in the arms – much furrier than any Tarantula's – of Ruddles Carmody. But while amnesia and aphony came and went, giving ground to buffoonery hysteria which in turn ceded primacy to syncope and thence to vacancy of almost teenage proportions, the one unrelenting feature of my condition remained priapic obstinacy. For three weeks I lay on my back, under a special frame that raised the bedclothes, as if impaled by an organ that both was and wasn't mine, a victim of my body's monomania, it's single-minded egocentric determination, like many a martyr of free expression before it, to be itself.

Sad? How could I not be sad? That exhaustion of all happiness and ambition that afflicts the male of every species the moment he expels his seed – necessary, because nothing else would ever stop him – cannot go on surprising beings whose nature it is to repeat themselves. Masochistic man spiders who get only one

345

bite of the cherry might expire reflecting on the high price of such a small pleasure; but the rest of the sex knows from experience what awaits it. We are associative creatures. It isn't possible for the emptiness and the vexation of the after not to creep around and poison the before. Readiness contains all anyone needs of desolation, long before fulfilment nails down the coffin lid. And thanks to the Redback I was nothing but readiness, I was the essence and personification of readiness, I could have served, just the way I was, as a concrete monument to the abstract idea, set on a stone plinth. Like Cleopatra's Needle.

Readiness, ready for nothing. There was to be no event, and I was sad before it.

But I wasn't just sad for myself. Even when I couldn't remember who I was, I was still sad. I haven't been able to unearth any precise medical language for the sensation of altruistic hopelessness which took possession of me, not as an effect of the toxicant itself, but as a consequence of the very *idea* that I'd been bitten and envenomed – but I can best describe it as a form of species-shock. I was degraded on behalf of humanity. It shouldn't have been possible for a mere creeper the size of a cent to do what she did to one of us. By possible I mean metaphysically possible; in the great ordered scheme of things. I didn't care that she failed of a proper regard, I cared that I – *we* – failed of a proper insouciance. One eensy-weensy little bite and down we went. No wonder governments have plans not to tell us when they discover that crimson grasshoppers the size of the Empire State Building roam freely on Mars. Of course we wouldn't be able to take the news. We can't survive the horror of what crawls across our own planet. Because in its loathsome appearance we read the impossibility of a Creator, the absence of a plan, and our own randomness.

Sad? Of course I was sad.

Then, suddenly, there was word of a party. I almost

leaped out of bed with excitement. 'Will there be music?' I asked my nurse.

Two weeks had passed since I'd learned the hard way of the extreme fleshly vulnerability of man, but (or rather, therefore) I still felt an overpowering Tarantist's urge to let my hair down.

'I don't think so, Leon,' the nurse told me. 'I doubt if it's going to be that sort of a party.'

I must have looked pained. I could feel fur forming on my tongue. 'So what sort of party is it going to be?' I was just able to ask.

She looked as though she didn't want to tell me, but I tugged at her sleeve. There were probably some involuntary spasms going on as well, beneath the framed tent of my blankets.

'It's more a sort of visit,' was all she'd say.

I had to find out from the other patients – men who had been half-squeezed to death by cobras or sawn in quarters by crocodiles – that the preparations afoot were for a *royal* visit.

Why it is that touring members of British royal families must inspect the diseased and dying of other countries the moment they leave their own – whether it's a genuinely charitable attempt to bring history to the beds of those who are too sick to go out and make it for themselves, or whether it serves to satisfy a ghoulish curiosity, a blue-blooded psychic need to observe the badly off – I am unable to determine. Whatever their motives, a certain triennially touristical royal couple (I am not at liberty to disclose which) had expressed an earnest wish to get a stickybeak into the new bites and stings wing of the Wangaratta General; and their every wish being as good as a command, they were expected any day.

'Will there be dancing afterwards?' I asked the ward sister.

I didn't pay much attention to any of the hospital staff – they were all just further examples of a fallen

347

species to me – but I could see that Wangaratta, as well as life in general, had been unkind to this one. 'I think you've got the wrong idea about this visit,' she told me.

I took that to mean there would be no dancing. 'No naked swords, or swings, or vine-leaves, or red cloths either then?' I supposed.

She asked me to sit up, and then punched my pillows around a bit. 'I hope you'll be careful where you sit in future, once you get out of here,' was the only answer I got.

I thought I detected an awkwardness in her manner towards me, which increased as the day drew nearer for the couple (I said the couple, not *the* couple) to arrive. Not only did she appear to be warning me against expecting a good time, I also thought I caught her, and indeed the rest of the hospital staff, suggesting that it might be for the best if I somehow absented myself from the visit altogether.

'You're looking well today, Leon,' I was told, by everyone who passed my bed, at accurately timed ten-minute intervals. 'Nothing crook about you. You'll be up and about and off and away any hour now.'

The nurse who regularly took my temperature, and always showed me the whereabouts of the mercury, had the thermometer out of my mouth and into a bowl of icy water before I had so much as settled my lips around it. 'Fit and well,' she said. 'You should be out in the morning.'

'How high was that?' I demanded to know.

She laughed, as if dying of despair and species-shock was a laughing matter. 'Aw, about normal,' she said.

'98.6?'

'A bit higher.'

'108.6?'

She gave me the look that the ignorant give to pedants, that deceivers give to the deceived. 'Around there.'

'118.6?'

'Look,' she said, 'this is a chance of a lifetime for most of us. We don't often get a royal visit to Wangaratta. When else am I going to shake hands with a prince?'

I was astounded on two accounts. 'I thought you are all republicans out here now,' I would have said, had there not been a more urgent point to make. And that was, 'How on earth am I stopping you from enjoying your once-in-a-lifetime grovel?'

This had clearly brought us to the nub of it, because the whole ward fell silent and every nurse on duty, plus a couple of passing pathologists plus the head neurologist plus the chief hospital administrator appeared around my bed.

'What you have to understand,' they took turns to explain to me, 'is that you're a bit of an iffy case for royalty to hear about. You see there's no precedent, no existing protocol, for discussing priapism with a princess.'

I did a deal with them. In return for not being thrown on to the street, I gave my word that should the royal party pause at my bed I would not refer to any of the more iffy details of my ailment. I could go as far as pulse acceleration, stiffening of the abdomen, throbbing of the soft palate, but no further.

'What about furring of the tongue?' I asked.

'No,' they said.

'Sedimentation of the urine?'

'No,' they thought.

'Involuntary ejaculation and discoloration of the—?'

'No,' they said.

But they forgot to take account of my amnesia, my chronic unreliability, my inconsequential jocularity, and the toxic goadings of my blood to whip up a party.

*　　*　　*

349

'Satyriasis syndrome, Ma'am,' I answered, when the princess singled me out for the exercise of a spot of suzerainty and sympathy. 'It's a fairly rare condition, Ma'am, though far more prevalent in Australia than it's often given credit for. I contracted mine when I was nibbled by a Redback.'

Apparently she knew about Australian spiders from a book detailing their heinous habits which she'd possessed as a child. She gave a gracious shudder, recalling how horrible she'd found them merely from their photographs, and imagining how much more horrible still they must be in the flesh.

'Loathsome, Ma'am,' I said. I thought about discussing species-shock with her – comparing my being savaged by an arachnid to her being bitten by a commoner – but decided she might be a touch young. I didn't want to blight her hopes.

I won't say I was smitten with her – I'd made too arduous a journey into the hinterland of Bohemia to remain the loyalist I'd once been – but that old baby smell which the pampered invariably give off called out something protective in me. I would have liked to pat and powder her – no more. Then I remembered Venie and Maroochi, who smelt the same, and through them I remembered my wasted decade dancing attendance on the seemly and the satisfied; and I determined that the princess would ask me what satyriasis syndrome was, and that I would tell her.

She was obviously curious. I could tell from the perplexity in her royal blue eyes that she didn't understand why, if I'd only been bitten by a spider, I needed such a vast protective framework underneath my bedclothes. On the other hand it was equally obvious that she'd been trained never to ask too many questions. If you're going to wander in and out of leper colonies or Wangaratta sting wings asking questions, you're going to have to listen to some pretty terrible answers. So I invited her confidence by employing one of those intense, exhausted looks that expert hypochondriacs grow sick on. Ask away, my jaundiced expression seemed to say, ask away, your very questions might turn out to be my cure.

She was carrying flowers and appeared to press them closer to her diaphragm. For a moment I thought she was going to move on to the next bed to discuss Australian reptiles with the drongo who'd been sawn in four, but then she looked at my tented blankets again and inclined her head in my direction. 'What *is* satyriasis syndrome?' she enquired. But with great tact, so that I might refuse to answer if I wished. Breeding, you see.

Only now did I pay any attention to who else was with her in the ward – the attendants, the civic dignitaries, the hospital staff, and her famous consort. 'Satyriasis syndrome,' I dearly wanted to say, 'is having a hard-on as long as a polo stick.' But I couldn't do it. I lost my nerve. It wasn't a sudden attack of post-Redback aphony; my voice was still there all right, I just couldn't use it. If I was suffering a sudden attack of anything, it was deference. The old Partington malady, more deadly than any poison, impossible ever to cleanse the blood of. I felt a deep shame, even as my features fought amongst themselves, outdoing one another in the performance of those little bows and curtsies that demonstrate true servitude. Measured on the thraldom-metric system I must have been no more than a couple of flunkey-centimetres from being the kind of man who stuck photos of the monarch in an album. Some Bohemian. I was a milk-and-water revolutionary, just as I'd been a musical-comedy conservative. For the first time since I'd been bitten it crossed my mind that I deserved the bite.

Then, quite by chance, I noticed that Murray Redfern was also in the royal party, as of course he was bound to be, since this was his territory and these were therefore his official guests. Who can say where courage comes from? The overflow at last of long-suppressed resentment? I wasn't aware that I especially resented Murray Redfern. He was bad, brutal and boorish – he opposed the sacred-site claims of the Aborigines on the grounds that their heathen beliefs were incompatible with the Christian concept of salvation; he was in favour of speeding up mining by the controlled deton-ation of underground nuclear explosives; and he rec-ommended cutting off the electricity to every freak ecologist in Australia ('Let the bastards freeze in the dark') – but therein, as I had tried to explain to Desley, lay his charm. None the less, I had no hesitation once I knew he was there. 'Satyriasis syndrome, Your Royal Highness,' I said, 'for which another term is priapism, after the Greek God Priapus, the patron deity of fruit-erers and sheep farmers, means struggling under the weight of a prick as big as a Liberal State Premier.'

As far as I could remember, this was the first purely political statement I had ever made.

30

I CAN SEE NOW that there was probably no necessity whatsoever for me to have resigned my Freedom Academy fellowship after this, nor to have turned my back on all my old friends at *The Black Sail*. It's highly unlikely that any punitive action would have followed my breach of protocol, if only because no one who was there who mattered – I don't count the Wangaratta ward sister – actually heard it. There is a most wonderful natural defence system which operates for the protection of the mighty when words not conducive to their well-being are uttered in their presence. This is known as discretionary deafness and works on roughly the same principle as the aphony that follows a bite from a Redback. One hostile snap of the jaws and it's operative.

But it wasn't fear of reprisal that determined my defection, anyway. The importance of my little mutiny was wholly symbolic. *I'd* heard it, even if no one else had. And for me it represented my final deliverance from twin bondage. I had been rude to someone who was pretty, and I had been rude to someone who was rich. If I had been an Israelite I would have assembled a small gathering to break unleavened bread with me and to join me in making faces at the Egyptians. For I had rejected the wife of Potiphar at last.

As soon as the Wangaratta General gave me as clean a bill of health as was commensurate with a hardy annual affliction, I caught the train back to Sydney and a taxi back to Trilby's. I won't pretend that I had no thoughts of Venie and Maroochi as the taxi sped towards Vaucluse, but in the sum total of things those thoughts are too insignificant to dwell on. If I'd made space in this narrative for every twitch of old loyalty to which I'm subject I would never have got past my ninth birthday party – that's assuming I ever *did* get past my ninth birthday party.

I was shocked by Trilby's appearance. Not having my father to drive her to distraction with his voracious affection for her – not having fresh flowers to destroy surreptitiously each day – she had mislaid her self-esteem. Without him she couldn't remember what it was that was supposed to be so infinitely unattainable about her. She looked worn and sallow – and old.

And I didn't look much better. We were each shocked by the ravages which death and despondency, spiders and schoolteachers, had wrought upon the other. We lived together for a few months in Trilby's new home unit (yes, she'd been brought as low as that – a *home unit*), to see if we might effect some mutual improvements. No funny business. No mollusc misbehaviour. Just company. Then Trilby decided that there was no longer any reason why she shouldn't sell up and return to die in the bosom of her ancestors in the Wirral. She'd remembered what I'd said in the graveyard that contained the tiny coffin of my father, overlooking Botany Bay: she wanted to lie where she was born.

I tried to dissuade her. 'Leaving aside the fact that you're going to live for years,' I said, 'wouldn't you prefer to keep the old boy company?'

She shook her head. 'You can do that,' she said.

There was no moving her. She was going back. I could have the home unit and one of the frock shops, and she could complete that inexplicable puzzle which had been her life.

'Your father seemed to have some idea of who or what I am,' she told me as I said goodbye to her at the airport, 'but without him I'm blowed if I can sort it out.'

It was a gusty winter's day by Sydney standards and she was wearing the old fox fur – remodelled now, of course – in which she'd run the circuit of our cul-de-sac. But even seeing her in that didn't enable me to offer her any help.

As I watched her fly away I wondered, and not for the first time, whether my father had really done her any service making such a meal of his amazed appreciation of her. It seemed to me that you had a responsibility not to go around marvelling at people's infinite unfathomableness. It seemed to me that otherwise you could love them out of their own sanity.

Not that I was planning on making any such mistakes myself. You need an intact regard for your own kind before you can start falling for specific instances of the biotype. And the spider had done for me for that. What, love someone who might at any tick of the clock slip away to the ladies' room and return with an abdomen as stiff as cardboard and a mouth as oval as a carp's? No, I had no further ambitions of that kind. All I wanted was an invitation to a party.

It's hard to know, when you've been a long time out of the swim, what qualities make you desirable as a guest. When I first arrived here I could dine out anywhere merely on the strength of being an Englishman. All that was required of me was that I let them watch my lips move and hear me deliver myself of informed judgements. It's no exaggeration to say they copied down my every stricture. To this day there must be hundreds of spiral notebooks full of me and my opinions hidden away in attics and cellars throughout Australia. But being an Englishman won't buy you so much as a meatball today. As far as the likelihood of hospitality goes you might just as well be a Frenchman in New Zealand. And a degree in the Decencies from Cambridge is hardly more of a recommendation. Who in Australia hasn't got one of those? As for the architects of the new national cock-sure self-pleasure – the teachers and the sages, the exemplars and the imported social additives like me – well, they are always the most expendable members of any community. Once their lessons are learned, they are no longer needed. Ask Orel Rosenfeldt and Frank Whiling, rotting in Canberra. So you can see why, short of making it necessary for them to deport me back to Partington, I have been encouraging the Australian security forces to take a dim view of me. An urbane undesirable, I have reasoned, a putative moral terrorist, once in the employ of the CIA and now not to be trusted, according to report, in the same room as royalty – surely *this* is a man with whom you'd be only too pleased to have your other guests (bombers and leafleteers themselves, with a bit of luck) dance the Tarantella.

I am assuming that you know what I mean by the Tarantella, that you have a firm grasp by now of just what it is that Tarantati seek. I would hate to be mistaken for a mere middle-aged raver. Everything I say now is political, just as everything that I used to say wasn't. Not party-political, but personal-political. I who have missed out on great periods of social and imaginative excitement – missed out by choice, I grant you; by a deliberate cultivation of the temperament – am now ready, with spider-venom running through my veins, to dance from dawn to dusk, and dusk to dawn, the moment I hear pipes and timbrels.

I strain my ears. I come home from emptying the till of *Trilby's* and throw my veranda windows wide. Tarantati are gloomy yet optimistic all at once. So I will not be put off by the refusal of Norelle Turpie or Ruddles Carmody to strike me up a tune. And I will not allow the final disappearance of the Mercedes from outside my flat seriously to depress my spirits.

It showed up for what I am bound to acknowledge was the last time four nights ago. It was a screeching

Sydney night. You could hear the boats on the water buckling in the heat. Some species of beetle was involved in a clumsy suicide bid, hurling itself off one balcony only to land with a crunch on another. I had gone out on to my balcony to watch for those who were watching me and to hope, thereby, that I might provoke them into action. The Mercedes parked in its usual place. Turned out its lights as it always did. Sent up its familiar prying aerials. There seemed to be three occupants as ever, and as ever they were indistinguishable through the tinted – perhaps even bullet-proofed – glass. I was resigned to another evening of faceless threat and nameless promise and tuneless disappointment, when suddenly the doors of the vehicle were flung open. Simultaneously. Two at the front, one at the back. I didn't wait to see who or what was getting out. The noise and the vibration were enough to tell me that whatever it was it was big.

I rushed back inside and rang Ruddles Carmody's number. I wanted him to hear what was about to happen. I wanted to wipe that oriental certitude off his face. The phone was answered by one of Bev Belladonna's compromises with the idea of motherhood, made during a previous misrelationship. 'G'day, this is the Flexible Marxist Party of Australia,' the small voice said. 'If you want me mum and dad they'll be home later.'

'Listen son,' I said, 'this is very important. Have you got an answering machine there?'

'Where?'

'There, son. There!'

I listened to the lumbering silence of ineptitude, before the voice came back saying, 'Yeah, I think so, but I don't know how it works.'

My luck, I thought. In a world full of infant electronics geniuses I have to find a microchip illiterate. So much for the future of Flexible Marxism, I thought.

'All right,' I said, 'we have an alternative. I want you

to hold the line and to try to remember everything you hear.' Already I could hear the apartment-block lifts creaking under the terrific strain of Australian security. In another forty-five seconds they'd be on my floor, wearing party-hats and rubber masks and brandishing their Heckler & Koch automatic submachine-rifles, and coming my way. 'If you can take notes,' I added – I know, but there was no harm hoping – 'so much the better. And look – there could be a personal computer in this for you.'

I enjoyed promising the little twerp what I knew his mother would never let him possess.

I slid a pen crosswise between the receiver and its cradle, according to a method I'd picked up from a violent film I'd helped to ban, and waited for my door to be smashed down. In fact, there was a rather polite knock – one gentle rap of the knuckles – accompanied by the sound of feet being wiped on the mat. ASIO, I thought. Definitely not CIA.

So I was staggered to open the door and find the Cooney brothers standing outside – George, Bernard and if my eyes did not deceive me, Shaun.

In the time it took for my mouth to open and close again I was able to notice that Shaun had changed out of his accustomed *novella*-writer's roll-neck T-shirt into a blue real-estate agent's suit and a broad yellowish tie, shot through with gold silk. That Bernard was kitted out as usual to resemble a little boy – a Sunday School boy, not a street urchin – in knee-length white socks, powder-blue Crimplene shorts, and a lemon shirt bearing an embroidered koala over the left nipple. And that George wore his familiar white deck-trousers under a striped work-singlet. Australians who wear white deck-trousers, Venie had informed me, scratch their dicks with a frequency that puts to shame the already prodigious national average; and I noticed that there were indeed greasy smudges in the area of George's fly compatible with excessive paddling. Had they been looking a touch more cheerful, I might have taken them for a tableau, put together by a mail order company perhaps, illustrating the three phases of fashionable dressing favoured by Australian males.

'Shit,' I said, 'how long have you three been working for ASIO?'

They formed their usual circle around me, and seemed to need to check my query out with one another before they answered.

'We don't work for ASIO,' George said at last.

Pedants. Wherever you go in this country you meet pedants. 'Fine,' I said, 'that's fine – ASIS then.'

This precipitated another mute three-way consultation.

Eventually George said, 'We don't work for ASIS either.'

I waited for them to tell me who they did work for in that case, and why they had been watching me from a bullet-proof Mercedes five nights a week, but no explanation seemed forthcoming. They simply resorted to their old sad-camel ruse and nuzzled me slowly back into the middle of my living room.

There are, in any country not your own, no matter how long you have lived there, quintessentially alien moments in which you are reminded that the pulse of your patience does not beat in time to the throb of the host culture. Such moments have always occurred for me in the company of the Clonakilty Cooneys. Near to them – and you cannot be in a room with a Cooney without his being near to you – it is possible to feel that the flow of your lifeblood itself is at risk, so complete a suspension of animation and intelligence are they able to effect.

But for their close encirclement of me there is a good chance I would have swooned away. Remember that I was approaching the anniversary of my bite – an event accompanied every year by a recurrence of the old symptoms – many of them aggravated by familiarity.

359

Even without the debilitating presence of the Cooneys my body was preparing to go into shock. And that's to take no account of the keen disappointment I was bound to be suffering, after all these weeks of waiting, of not being raided by ASIO – or ASIS – after all.

So when Bernard wondered if there might be a beer going I was slow to recognize the meaning of his question, and slower still to remember where I kept my fridge. Which had the advantage of more or less equalizing things between us as far as speed of uptake went.

'Here's to 'em,' said George, when I returned from the kitchen with a four-pack. He had taken his fingers off his cock in order to wrap them around his can.

'Here's to 'em,' Bernard concurred.

'Here's to 'em all right, the little beauties,' said Shaun.

One is only as conversationally adept as the company one keeps. 'Here's to who?' I had absolutely no option but to ask.

They looked surprised that I needed to be told.

'The Vietnamese, sport,' said George.

'The Kampucheans,' said Bernard.

'The Lebanese,' said Shaun.

I couldn't say that this collocation of nationalities was wholly unintelligible to me. Had I still been writing for *The Black Sail* these were the peoples I would have been suggesting we (by which I would have meant Australians) think twice about indiscriminately admitting. On the grounds, obviously, that too much of them meant too little of us. That's putting it roughly. *The Black Sail*'s enemies were complicating matters rather by wanting to think twice about some of these peoples themselves. On the grounds, obviously, that they weren't all the broken, shambling, impoverished wrecks that refugees, strictly speaking, ought to be. These contrarieties apart though, I could see what the Cooneys were getting at. I only couldn't see why they were getting at it to me.

'Yes, well here's to 'em,' I agreed anyway.

'I'm glad you're for them,' said Shaun. 'Because they're who we're here for.'

For all that I had first-hand experience of the Cooney brothers' ideological versatility, I still found this difficult to believe.

'You can't be here for *all* of them,' I said.

They looked even more hurt than usual. 'Why not?' Bernard wanted to know. 'There are three of us.'

'We represent the interests of Croatians as well,' George said.

I set them a little test. 'Which?' I asked. 'The extreme right or the extreme left?' As far as I knew there were no extreme-left Croatians.

The brothers exchanged glances. 'Both,' Shaun said.

I made a decision against conflict. 'Well, how can I help?' I asked. I handed them each another beer-can, as a practical token of my willingness.

It fell to Shaun to begin to tell me. 'We're in a human tragedy situation, Leon,' he said. It so upset him just to say it that his eyeballs appeared to come out of their sockets and to rest among the pouches of his cheeks. 'There are people out there,' he went on, 'who are unable to get in.'

He made the problem sound very immediate. I actually sneaked a look out of my window to see if I could see the people he was referring to. What I couldn't grasp was why they might have wanted to get into my flat. 'Get in *here*, Shaun?' I thought I'd better check.

'Australia, dickhead,' George corrected me.

I suddenly remembered Ruddles Carmody and Bev Belladonna's unscientific boy, listening in to every word. 'Ah,' I said, walking towards the phone and subtly changing the modulation of my voice to extremely high, 'if it's the Asianization of Australia that we're talking about, then I'm for it. I, for one, am delighted that satay has replaced *bœuf bourguignon* as the Australian national dish. So the more the merrier, I say.

361

And the sooner the better.' I thought about referring to the superiority of the Asian complexion but decided that might be gilding the lily. 'The yellower the mellower,' I said instead, without quite knowing what I meant.

'In that case,' Shaun said, pushing an eye back, 'you won't mind giving us the answers.'

'The answers?'

'To your questions.'

'My questions?'

'On your test.'

'My test?'

I thought I could get away with this once more at the most.

'Your Piers Plowman Non-Anglo-Saxon Migrant Discouragement Test.'

'Oh, that test!'

It would be hard to say which of us was the most relieved.

For some reason, perhaps precisely to express relief, or because they were in an advanced state of drunkenness already on a can and a half of beer, they decided to imitate my accent. 'Oh, that test!' they repeated. They gave it an impossibly squirearchal, unpleasantly theatrical, inaccurately old queenish intonation. They emptied it of whatever Partington vowel sounds I hadn't emptied it of myself. I might have been peeved had I not recalled how all Australians were subjected to a parody of *their* speech patterns the minute they moved their lips in the presence of an Englishman.

'I didn't know that old thing still operated,' I said – meaning my Piers Plowman Non-Anglo-Saxon Migrant Discouragement Test, not their joke.

'It operates all right,' George told me.

'And keeps them out in their thousands,' Shaun confirmed.

I experienced a twinge of retrospective pride. Fancy my old test still working. It was like hearing that a car one had sold twenty years ago was still on the road. I smiled to myself and sighed fondly. The great Australian phrase for expressing affection and amazement mixed rose to my lips. 'Shit eh,' I said.

They indulged my innocent nostalgia for a little while, then Bernard reminded me how we'd got on to this. 'Which is why we've dropped by to collect the answers,' he said.

'Oh, that's right,' I replied, before I realized that I was laying myself open to another imitation, 'you want the answers.'

As it happened, they misunderstood my tone, and supposed I was about to prove difficult. I could see they were coming out of Camaraderie and toying with Confrontation. In another minute or two they'd be nuzzling me into bleak submission.

I put up a placatory and reassuring hand. 'Hang on, boys,' I said. 'I'm with you on this one. I'm on your side.'

That was a pretty cruel thing to say to a Cooney. On their side? How could they be expected to know where that was?

I enjoyed compounding their confusion. And I enjoyed disappointing them, too, when I said, 'You want the answers? I'll get them for you right now. No worries.' They'd been hoping that they would have to depress the information out of me, at the very least.

Five minutes later they were sitting with their notebooks on their laps, taking down the average May mornynge temperature of the British Isles, the names of the six best youth hostels in the Maluerne Hulles, and the route numbers of the quickest roads – I thought the A44 and the B4084 – from Chipping Norton to Worcester.

I have to say that seeing them with their pens raised, their eyes screwed up, their brows clouded with concentration, each one of them intent on not missing a single item of intelligence, brought back the good old days when I first arrived in Australia and dictated my every thought to a parched and starving populace.

After we'd finished – I even gave them the answers to the supplementary paper, relating to the size of the shepe population in fourteenth-century Bretayne – they drank another beer and stood up to go. We shook hands. It's an eerie experience shaking hands with such tall men. It's like reaching up to pull a chain. When I pulled Bernard he held on to me affectionately and asked me what I thought of the motor.

'The motor?'

'The Merc.'

'Oh, the Merc. It looks pretty good to me,' I said. I had never been interested in motors or in abbreviating their brand names. 'Who does it belong to? The Croatians?'

They seemed to have forgotten who the Croatians were. They exchanged looks of extreme perplexity. 'It's ours,' George said at last.

I let out a polite whistle of surprise and admiration. 'That must have set you back,' I said.

'Well,' Bernard said, 'there *are* three of us.'

This was the first time I'd ever wished I wasn't an only child.

They walked down the corridor waving. Then Shaun came back and rubbed his head into my neck. 'Your secret's safe with us,' he said.

'What secret? I don't have any secrets.'

'We won't tell anyone that you gave us the answers yourself.'

'What do you mean you won't tell anyone?' I believe I must have sounded quite distraught. 'Tell. Tell everybody. That's what I gave them to you for. To prove I'm not the man I was. Tell 'em, Shaun. Tell 'em all.'

He stood where he was, smiling down on me.

'I'm not joking, Shaun,' I said. 'This is a serious matter. I've got stuff hidden away under my bed that's yours, or your friends', for the asking. Come again, and bring everyone you know. We can make a night of it. We can have a party.'

He ruffled my hair and bit my nose. 'You mad bastard,' he said.

'I mean every word,' I shouted, as he backed down the corridor to where his brothers were holding the lift doors open for him. The last thing he did before he disappeared was to shake his head, wink, and put his finger to his lips, thereby assuring me that my secret was safe with him, mad bastard that I was.

I collapsed into a chair once I was alone and gave in to a mood of what, even in Australia, could only be called *Weltschmerz*. An event to which I had been looking forward for weeks had been and gone and I was none the richer for it. Still no party. Still no prospect of a party.

Then I remembered the telephone and Bev Bella-donna's prat of a son who might still be hanging on the other end of it. If he'd done what I told him then Ruddles Carmody had all the proof I needed him to have of my change of heart. He couldn't refuse party membership to the man who'd flooded Australia with Asians, could he. Membership – it seemed to me I'd earned a seat on the Central Committee.

I hurried over to the phone and listened in. The line wasn't dead but the kid might as well have been. The guiltless sleep of childhood had gathered him up in her downy arms and his faint unenlightened snore reached me all the way from Melbourne. I estimated, given how long the Cooneys were with me, that the call had already cost me three thousand dollars. I was about to shout, 'Well, it looks like there'll be no personal computer for you, you little runt,' when I heard along the wires the sound of Bev and Ruddles arriving home. They were in a state of high animation.

'You beauty!' I heard Ruddles exclaiming. 'You little beauty!'

'Got it!' I heard Bev Belladonna exult. 'Got the bugger!'

They weren't referring to each other. I listened long enough to discover they were rejoicing over the approval of their projects – Ruddles's long-gestating twelve-volume introduction to the history of the Chinese in Collingwood and Bev's first Biographical Directory of Women Anarchists in Victoria – by the Australian Bicentennial Authority, the body charged with doling out the spondulicks for 1988. 'We've made it,' Bev and Ruddles called out to their sleeping children. 'We've won endorsement!'

I put the phone down. So, already the invitations were going out to Australia's two-hundredth birthday party. All over the country the scramble for front seats and freebees was afoot. It was going to be the grandest, longest, friendliest ding in history. The biggest barbie known to man. The best beano in the world.

I consulted the electronic watch bequeathed to me by my father. I calculated that I had no more than two years to come up with a compelling argument – some wholly irresistible initiative or programme – which would make it impossible for them not to request the pleasure of my company. But I feared the death-grip in which my earliest training held me. The only idea I could think of that was better than Australian Operetta: A Study of Its Roots and Origins, was Ruined Monasteries in Queensland and the Northern Territory: A Complete Listing of the Principal Sites.

It was all right for my father, flat on his little back in Botany Bay Cemetery. He could look forward to a worm's-eye view of all the fun. He was out of the running for fellowships and endorsements – at least I assumed he was – but he'd be nicely placed for the fireworks and the fly-past and the dramatic re-enactment of Cook's first landing.

But then he'd always been better at enjoying himself than I had.

I suddenly missed everybody. Not just family. Not just the obvious ones to miss. But *everybody*. If Vance Kelpie and Montserrat Tomlinson had rung me up and asked me to be godfather to the wee Maeldune, I would willingly have accepted, even though twenty years had gone by since we'd toured and bored the country towns of New South Wales together and the wee Maeldune was now a budding bard himself. If Orel Rosenfeldt had telegraphed me on any subject – maybe to ask me to love Frank Whiling – I would instantly have telegraphed him back. And maybe said that I would try. If Hartley Quibell had come around with Isadora in a matchbox I'd have begged them to renew my mandate. 'I won't say a word,' I would have promised. 'Just let me watch.' I was swollen and dangerous and past passion – I was disabused and unexpectant – but I would be nice to anyone who would be nice to me. I would join whichever spinning circle would break just long enough to take my hands and pull me in.

I went down into the street on the off-chance that I'd run into someone I knew. Perhaps the Cooney brothers hadn't driven off yet. Or perhaps Hartley was waiting to press a summons on me. I wouldn't have minded that. An injunction is an expression of friendship, of sorts. But it was quiet outside, except for the sounds of distant pleasure and the answering moan of souls in exile. I stood for a while under the impossible purple trees. It was a damp, tropical night; ideal for swooning in. Hitherto unclassified insects in hard shells – some suicidal, some merely murderous, but none as glittering as those I used to pluck from Venie's hair – dropped on to my shoulders. Tired of all the killing I left them there and began to walk towards the lights and music of the city. The stiffening of my abdomen surprised me. I didn't expect it for another day or two. Likewise the heartburn and the inconsequential jocularity. If I wasn't mistaken I thought I could also feel my tongue furring over.

The desire for the dance was upon me.

But nobody noticed. I passed on, unsuspected and deadly, a poisoned Partingtonian, a flesh-and-blood Molotov cocktail, in a street full of peaceable and unheeding Australians.

THE END